EVERY MOUNTAIN MADE LOW

ALEX WHITE

SOLARIS

To Connor, who gave me a chance.

To Mom and Dad, who gave me a fighter's spirit.

To Renee, who gave me humanity, humility and a perfect son.

CHAPTER ONE
GOOD MORNING

"Loxa-lox..."

Her eyes opened to the one room apartment, a yellow streetlight projecting her only window onto the carpet. She sighed and rolled over, pulling her blanket tighter about her body.

"Lox, Lox, Loxley... Get up, up, up," she sang hoarsely to herself. She sat up on her mattress and looked back at the indentation where her mother used to lay.

"I'm awake."

Her mother was two years dead, but the young woman announced her awakening, anyway. Loxley had been told how to wake up when she was a little girl, on account of her walks on the building's roof in the middle of the night. *You wake me up, too, baby. You always wake me up, too. Maybe I want to go with you*, her mother would say.

Several times since her mother's passing, Loxley had tried to leave the apartment in silence, but she felt her mother's invisible tug on her heart when she awoke. She'd get scared on the way to the garden and have to come back. The first days after her mother passed, Loxley never left the apartment. Eventually, hunger won out, and she learned to talk to the mattress.

She stretched, cat-like, and scrubbed the crunchy sleep from her eyes. Loxley walked to the window and opened it, looking out onto the Hole. Much of the city lay hidden behind dingy buildings, but she preferred it that way. When she was little, her mother had taken her to the top ring – to Edgewood – with its alabaster buildings. "Isn't it pretty?" her mother had asked, but Loxley didn't like looking down into the basin at all the lights. There were too many to count, and it made her anxious to think of all the ones she was missing. Then, she started thinking about how almost everyone in the city could see her if she was standing at the top edge, and she had to leave.

Loxley lived close to the bottom of the Hole, nestled into the seventh ring in the base of the terraced, crater-shaped city. The buildings in the rings above were like baffles, shielding her from the view up in Edgewood. Some folks couldn't be happy unless they were on top. She liked the bottom just fine. She didn't need much space – just a little electricity and running water.

She reeled in some clothes off the line and pulled on some skivvies before shutting the window. They were cool and damp from where she'd left them out overnight, and she shuddered at their touch. Her jeans were full of wintery dew, and she wouldn't put them on. She placed the rest of her outfit over the radiator and padded into the kitchen. She cooked an egg, and by the time she'd eaten it, her other clothes were completely dry. She went to pull on her hot garments and burned her belly on the pants button. She held her breath and shook the crackles out of her fingertips until the heat went away, then bent down to lace up her boots.

Without a sound, she slipped out her door and into the hallway. The corridors of Magic City Heights were empty, beige walls awash with clicking, fluorescent light the color of chicken fat. Loxley didn't like the halls – their lights were too random and difficult to watch. She locked her deadbolt and made for the stairs.

Birdie Hoggatt had left her trash outside her apartment for her nephew to carry down in the morning. Loxley spied some coffee grounds and a banana peel through the milky plastic. She crept to the pile and tried to undo the knot in the top of the bag, but it wouldn't budge. Frustrated, she knelt and tore a fist-sized hole into the belly of the trash bag, the cans inside complaining at her disturbance. It was a tiny sound, but infinitely louder than she'd been.

Footsteps pounded closer and Birdie's door flew open, revealing the neighbor in a fluffy, white bathrobe, her wiry legs protruding from the bottom. She sneered, her lips curled in such a rage that Loxley thought the woman might bite her.

"Well hey there, sugar. Looks like I found my little coon thief," she said softly, regarding Loxley sidelong. She looked down the hall to see if anyone else had been disturbed by the racket. "Leaving holes in the bags, throwing it all over the goddamned floor. Every day – every single day it's like this."

It wasn't every day, though. Birdie only left her trash out on Tuesday, and Loxley hadn't gone through it for three weeks. She'd only forgotten to put it back in the bag once, and that had been more than a year ago. Birdie shouldn't have been angry; It was trash, so she wasn't using it.

The older woman puffed up her chest. "You want to say something for yourself?"

"It's just trash."

"It's not *your* trash."

Loxley's heart thundered, and she couldn't keep looking Birdie in the eye. She pushed a hand inside the bag, feeling for the banana peel. Her fingers brushed against its skin, and she made to grasp it. "I just need some –"

The neighbor's slap stung Loxley's forearm, and she yanked her hand back to her side with a yelp. She let out a little hum as she swallowed tears. Everything in her body was telling her to panic and run away. She tried to stop humming, but every exhalation brought a fresh note.

"Get your filthy mongoloid paws out of there. I'm going to call Rick, you know. He's going to throw you out."

Rick wouldn't throw her out. Rick gave her the key to the roof, so he must have liked her. Loxley stood and rubbed the spreading welt on her arm. Birdie wasn't being reasonable. There had to be a cause.

"I'm sorry men don't want to sleep with you anymore," said Loxley. "I could maybe bring you some food sometime."

"Excuse me?"

"My mother told me you were a whore, but I

never see men coming to your apartment. It must be very hard to get by."

"Why did your momma tell you I was a whore?" Birdie's eyes bored into her.

"Because I heard you two yelling one time. I asked why you were yelling, and she said, 'Don't worry, Loxie. She's just a whore.'"

Birdie shook her head. She was laughing, but her face was mad – not as mad as before, though, so maybe the conversation was going well. "Maybe the world is a better place without your momma, then. What do you think of that?"

"I think it would be hard to say one way or the other, Miss Hoggatt. I liked mother a lot, but it could be she wasn't good for everyone."

Birdie looked even less mad after that. "Do retards like you even have feelings?"

"I felt it when you hit me."

"You'll feel that again if I catch you going through my trash." Again, Birdie glanced down the hallway. "I don't know what the fuck you think you're doing on that roof, but you leave us the hell alone." She punctuated this with a little twitch of her hooked nose.

Birdie slammed the door in her face. Loxley regarded the plain, red panel for a long moment, then she reached down and yanked out the banana peel and coffee grounds. She strode down the hall, leaving a trail of black specks in her wake. Her confidence faltered as she drew closer to the stairwell, and she scampered the rest of the way.

She finally reached the rooftop door, happy to see its battered steel knob. She shifted her rotting gains to one hand and checked to make sure it was locked before she fished out her precious key. Rick, the building's superintendent, had given it to her a long time ago, and she guarded it jealously. She turned the lock, savoring the sound of the tumblers clicking into place, and opened the door to the dim light of the rising sun.

Row upon row of planters stretched before her, holding her life's work – crops of berry bushes, vegetables and herbs. She grew marijuana, too, because it was easy and it sold well at the Bazaar, but she didn't like the smell. Folks complained about the way people acted when they were smoking the stuff, but Loxley rarely understood the way anyone behaved, so it scarcely bothered her.

The walls here were made from thousands of plastic bags stretched and taped over wooden framing. Her makeshift structure diffused the sunlight and kept the humidity high. Even in these winter months, it would salvage heat from the leaky rooftop weather seal and keep the plants inside nice and cozy.

Her pride and joy was her water collection system, which ran along the rim and base of nearly every planter. She'd salvaged the pipes from a nearby building's walls, though the ruined structure had been full of frightening men at the time. With the exception of the morning's compost heist, she could be sneaky when she had to be. A small electronic pump sat idle, ready to siphon her water drainage barrel back into the collection system. That pump had set her back a small fortune, but her crops had returned on the investment tenfold.

Best of all, no one could see her in her greenhouse. Some mornings, when the Foundry was operating in full tilt, she could hear the rhythmic pounding like a heartbeat all around. She took long, slow sniffs of the warm, wet plant life, and her pulse slowed. No one could come here – just her.

She locked the door behind herself and set to work.

A rhythm possessed her as she labored on her morning's tasks. She dropped the banana peel and grounds into the top of her composter, then cleaned the filter on her water collector. She started up the pump and set about pruning her plants like a gorilla searching for insects. She began to hum as she worked, an aimless, tuneless noise. She wasn't tone deaf, but she couldn't sing. She knew that fact well, though happily, there was no one around to judge.

Her makeshift wonder gave her delightful yields year round, and made her something of a celebrity in the Bazaar. The cucumbers were ready to pick, ripe and plump, their emerald skins waxy and unmarred by insects. She gathered them, along with her other staple crops, into wicker baskets and took them inside to the stairwell door. She wished Rick would have the elevator fixed, but sometimes he looked the other way on her rent, so she couldn't complain.

Rick had also given her access to the fenced in area outside, which contained breaker boxes, plumbing connections, and Loxley's beaten up farm cart. As long as she stayed out of Rick's way and kept the planters from leaking, he said she could do whatever she wanted. The aging superintendent rarely showed his face, but Loxley knew he liked her. She said so once, and he'd told her, "No. I just can't stand all the other goddamned whiners in this place. You're the least annoying."

She hauled her yield down twelve flights, two baskets at a time, over a grueling thirty minutes. She knew she looked small, but her morning chores had made her pretty strong. Once her load filled the cart, she unchained the door and set off for Vulcan's Bazaar.

The Boatman

FROM THE SKY, Loxley imagined the Bazaar looked like a giant, rusty snake. It ran down Fifth Avenue on the seventh ring, a covered aluminum breezeway filled with jabbering merchants, blaring music, burning neon and a host of strange, stinging smells. Loxley didn't like to go inside, and when she did, she had to keep her eyes on the ground or she'd feel ants marching up her legs and the crackles in her fingertips. Sometimes, people would try to talk to her, but she couldn't always tell who was talking, and she didn't know who she should listen to. She could make it quieter if she sang to herself, or covered her ears. She would often do both, and feel the vibrating hum in her chest as she tried to navigate the raging sea of lights with eyes watering.

She had a cozy alcove on the other side of the Bazaar – in a side street off the main drag – nestled between a café and a man selling old cameras. It would take her exactly twenty seconds to cross the bustling thoroughfare, and then she could wend her way back through alleyways to get to her spot. It wasn't technically legal to sell in the street outside the Bazaar, but Officer Crutchfield made an exception for her.

Loxley was early, and she wanted to get to her stall before trading bells rang – but a dead man stood in her way.

Her mother could see the recently dead. Her mother said all the women of Loxley's family could see them, but that had never been demonstrated because she'd had never met any of her other kin. Her mother always said there was nothing to fear from the deceased, but Loxley knew better. The lightest touch from a spirit would strike her like a hammer and bruise her terribly. When they could, the dead would cling to her like drowning victims. Ghosts might kill her if they were angry, and they were always angry at her for some reason.

She first spied the spirit about a block away as she neared the Bazaar. A man's silhouette, still in the open air, stood like a paper cutout in the bright winter sun. She felt his unmistakable presence the second she laid eyes on him. As she drew nearer, she could make out a pale, older face, robbed of color by death. He looked at her with scratched, dusty eyes, his jaw slack, his fingers curling and uncurling, expectantly. She edged closer, and he took extra special notice of her, raising his pleading hands for her to come to him. The dead would only range so far from the only thing they knew – their own corpses.

She didn't see his physical body, but he was blocking the way all the same. The other traders heading to the Bazaar took no notice of anything strange, so perhaps the corpse was hidden. It could have been in a building nearby, or even in the Bazaar, itself. Loxley spotted a shiny black Consortium car on the corner. She'd seen plenty of them in the past; the Consortium was everywhere. Did it have something to do with the ghost? Silhouettes of men filled the car's windows, but she couldn't tell if any of them were dead.

She couldn't go another way; this was the easiest place to cross the Bazaar. What if she got turned around? What if she got trapped in the throng as they labored to open their stalls for the day? She felt the crackles start to form in her fingers, and she shook them out. Maybe she could just run past the ghost. That would be foolish, though. He didn't have to run to catch her, and she knew it. She gritted her teeth. He wouldn't stop staring at her, longing to touch her with those furious hands of his. His palms trembled, and he began to pace back and forth, not with the gait of a man, but the awkward steps of a puppet.

"Get out of here, stupid!" she called. Several heads turned, and she felt shame in the pit of her stomach as a few people chuckled.

He leaned in her direction like a lover leaning into a kiss, but came no closer. He seemed unfazed by her words, which did not surprise Loxley. She'd met several ghosts, but none of them ever listened to her. She didn't believe they would listen to anyone. They lingered only for violence, unless they were old or died of a sickness.

She let her pullcart down onto its rests and shuffled back and forth between the handles. She couldn't bear the thought of missing a morning's sales, and what if the spirit was there tomorrow? She came to market every day. She shouldn't miss today, because she was supposed to be there. The crackles wouldn't leave her fingers, no matter how hard she shook them, and the ants started marching in her legs. She kneaded her knuckles against the sides of her hips, trying not to whimper.

"Hey, is everything okay over there?" came a familiar voice.

She couldn't run past. If she ran past, he would catch her and hurt her. The ghost cocked his head, but it didn't look like he moved his neck; it looked like one of the strings holding him had been cut. His lips locked into a silent plea. She needed to be sitting in her spot. Trading bells would ring soon and she wasn't there. If she wasn't there, she couldn't trade. Her voice began to rush between her clenched teeth without her permission.

"Loxley," came the voice again.

She wrapped her hands around the cart's handle and began to rock, feeling it grind against her hip bones. She pushed harder until it hurt. Stupid ghost. He had to move. This was the way the day was supposed to go, and if it didn't go that way she didn't know what would happen. She felt as though she were being pushed toward a cliff, unable to turn her head away from what she knew was coming.

A heavy palm came to rest on her shoulder, and she instantly batted it away with a yelp. She wheeled, wide-eyed, to see Officer Crutchfield. He smiled and took a step back, his hands up in the air.

"Why are you smiling?" she asked. "There's something bad happening."

"Just wanted you to see a friendly face, Loxie," he said. "I could tell you was upset."

She looked him over. When he smiled, crow's feet

emerged, as though his face was trying to hold up his shiny eyes. She stopped on his ginger whiskers, sprinkled through with white hairs.

"I like your mustache. It reminds me of a cat."

He stroked it. "Suppose I am a bit calico."

She imagined an old burly cop with a cat's head. Then she imagined it putting mice in jail at gunpoint and laughed aloud. After the tension of the ghost it felt good to laugh, and she drank deeply of her relief.

Officer Crutchfield folded his arms. "You do turn on a dime, don't you?"

She looked at her feet before realizing it was an expression. It didn't make sense, and it sounded dumb, so she didn't ask for an explanation. "I just like laughing."

"Why were you so tore up a minute ago?"

"I can't go to my spot, Officer Crutchfield."

"You know you can call me Burt, Loxley."

"I know."

He looked down the road ahead, but he didn't see the ghost. She knew he wouldn't. He nodded. "Okay. Why not? Someone say you can't?"

"No. Someone will hurt me if I go that way."

"Hurt you?"

"Yes. He's right over there looking at me." She pointed to the ghost, on the off chance Crutchfield would see.

He didn't. "That's just Mister Carver. Are you telling me Mister Carver threatened you?"

"No."

"Good. Carver's a good man." Crutchfield sighed, resting a forearm on his pistol grip. "Can you tell me who did, then?"

She shook her head. "Don't know his name, but he's over there, by the light pole."

The policeman looked straight at the spirit and nodded. "Okay, Loxley."

"You can see him?"

His smile returned. "No, but I believe you can, young miss, and trading bells are about to ring." He tipped his hat. "Let me know if there's something I can do."

She caught his arm as he turned to go. "Please take me around through the Bazaar. I can't go by myself."

The older man looked around, cleared his throat and leaned in closer. "You understand that it's my job to keep things fair around here, right?" She could smell the coffee in his whisper. "It's one thing when you set up outside the market, but it's another thing to ask me to take you over there and set you up myself. What am I supposed to tell people? A lot of guys get here early just to pop up a tent or a sign."

She looked over Crutchfield's expectant face, then glanced at the ghost, who hadn't moved an inch. "I could give you some broccoli or a bag of pot."

He deflated and rolled his eyes. "You're lucky you're too crazy for me to call that a real bribery attempt. Come on, girl. Get your cart and I'll take you around."

She picked up and followed him down a side street. "But I'm not crazy."

They wandered through alleyways and across busy roads for most of an hour. When they reached the north end of the Bazaar, the lights, sounds and bustle crushed Loxley under the weight of their chaos. A man shouted for fresh meat, a neon sign buzzed and blinked under the aluminum awning, twenty, no, twenty-six people shuffled back and forth through the intersection, their feet falling across the cobblestone cracks, a cowbell sounded out, a distant buzzsaw, the scent of grilling lamb, a weaver's booth blossomed with every color, two men argued, a child stood by her mother, another cart rumbled through the thoroughfare with barrels of grain *clump clump clump bumpa clump*. As she drew closer, she felt panic rising in her throat, and she was unable to take another step. She dropped her cart and cupped her hands over her ears. A thousand disparate sounds became a gentle roar, not unlike the thrum of her window air conditioner in the summer. Like the pain of a fresh burn, her fear would not diminish, and she stamped her feet and shut her eyes, willing it away.

She felt Officer Crutchfield's hand on her shoulder, and she let out a long breath. He said something, but she couldn't hear with her hands over her ears.

Her lips trembled as she spoke, in spite of her wishes. "I can't get across here, Officer. It's too much. Just too much. I can't."

She heard a muffled reply.

"Please help me. Please don't go."

He wrapped an arm around her and pressed her head to his barrel chest. He smelled like soap and cigarettes. She pulled her hands away, feeling his calloused palm slide over her ear. The policeman's heart thumped under her cheek, and she opened an eye to see him grabbing the cart handle with his free hand. He took an awkward step, moving the pair toward the maelstrom of activity ahead. She shook out her fingertips and wrapped her arms around him, squeezing him tightly as they walked.

She felt the shade of the great aluminum snake on the back of her head. They were inside the market. She tried not to look up, and counted the cobblestones as she stepped over them. She put her toes right in the middle of the round blocks, settling into a pattern. It calmed her heart with each step that she hit her target. The chaos had started to fade when she nearly tripped the both of them.

"Goddamn it, Loxley," grumbled Officer Crutchfield. "Stand up and walk straight."

She did as she was told, even though it made her uncomfortable. She could not let him abandon her here. The Bazaar did not always have a way out, as many vendors would block the roads with their stalls. Her cart surely made maneuvering difficult; the policeman would have to find a wide walkway to the outside.

BE BRAVE, BABY, her mother told her that so many times. Her mother was brave. Officer Crutchfield was brave. They could walk through the Bazaar without the crackles. The mongers could sit in the miasma of noise and light all day, and they didn't get scared. Loxley wasn't born brave; she was born with a rabbit's heart.

Sunlight spilled across her path as they found their way back outside. The wall of sound crumbled, and she felt the policeman's grip on her head relax. She looked up and saw her spot – a stucco wall in front of an old warehouse. A set of stairs ran up to the front doors, and she could nestle into the corner to protect herself from the wind. She let out a delighted chuckle to be back in such familiar surroundings, and set about grabbing her shop materials from the back of the cart.

She spread a thick quilt over the cracked sidewalk and set up a folding chair before laying out her wares. Loxley took special pride in arraying her products from largest to smallest, then by color – most intense to least.

"Uh, Loxley," said Officer Crutchfield.

"Yeah?" she asked, trying to decide which of her cucumbers was the most viridescent.

"Haven't you got something to say? I went out of my way for you."

She contemplated his meaning before snatching up a large, ripe stalk of broccoli and a small bag of marijuana. She turned to him, holding them both at eye level so he could make a good decision. "Which one?"

"Rather have a 'Thank you, Officer.'"

"Thank you, Officer," she said, and promptly got back to work.

"You're just too much, girl," he said to her back.

"Too much what?" she repeated, but when she turned to address him directly, she saw him wandering back into the Bazaar.

She shrugged and fell into her routine. Her normal customers came by, prodding through her goods. Sales were brisk, and all thoughts of Birdie and the ghost quickly faded from her mind.

Loxley fetched an old book on agriculture from the back of her cart – a Consortium manual they gave to their employees living on the Great Plains. She ran a hand over the cover; the paper had faded and crumpled along the edges, and the interior pages had turned a lovely shade of yellow. Orange block letters across the top of the cover read, *A Primer in Modern Technique*, with the Con's logo underneath. She'd gotten it from Rick almost ten years ago, and through it, she'd learned to garden. He said he hated the Consortium and was going to throw it away, but she wanted it. When she asked him why, he'd told her about being a boy before the Consortium owned everything; she'd gotten too bored to keep listening. She opened the book and read for what seemed like the millionth time. When she got to her favorite page, she stopped.

A full bleed, black and white photo of cotton rows spread over the right hand page, and the left contained a schedule of fertilization. Wispy clouds hovered in the sky, and she could almost feel the autumn wind on her face. A combine rumbled through the background, and she saw a tiny black square that she felt certain was a farmhouse. She squinted at the halftone dots, as she always did, trying to make out a window or door. She wondered if anyone lived there, if one day she might live there, too. She glanced up at the surging Bazaar. Both places were full of life, but plants were so much cleaner than people, in spite of having sprung from dirt.

She sang to herself when no one was around, keeping a beat with the distant hammering of the Foundry. She had no words, just a wandering lilt that infected her feet. She'd memorized most of the tables in the book, but she tested her memory by reciting the top ten numbers without looking. She wasn't good at the fertilizer table, but she had no idea what most of those chemicals were, anyway. They certainly hadn't been made available to her. Some of the chemicals had asterisks, marking them as combustible, so she made an effort to memorize the dangerous ones. She raised worms in a compost pile, so she had what she needed for her own garden.

"What's at the top of page thirty-three?" came a woman's voice.

"Don't know," said Loxley, turning to page thirty-three. "Oh. The end of a paragraph about rotations: '... through dissimilarity between seasons, recouping lost soil nitrogen reserves.'"

"Ain't exactly poetry."

"Not supposed to be. It's not a book of poetry." She flipped back to her table and muttered the numbers to herself. She'd missed two. "Why'd you need to know what was at the top of the page?"

"You going to say hi to me, Loxley?"

She looked up to see Nora Vickers standing over her, hands on her hips, brown hair tied into a colorful bandana. Nora was about Loxley's age, maybe a little older, and lived on her block in the seventh ring. She was a tall woman, possessed of many freckles and muscles, and nearly blotted out Loxley's sunlight where she loomed.

Loxley felt a weight lift from her chest. "Hi!"

"Give us a hug, girl," said Nora, and they embraced. "Now some sugar," she said, and Loxley kissed her cheek. "There's my green thumb. Business good?"

Loxley took her seat and put down her book. "I almost didn't make it here today. There was a ghost."

Nora frowned and cocked her head.

"He was in the way. I couldn't get past," said Loxley.

Nora nodded in the direction of the place where Loxley usually crossed the market. "What? Like over there?"

"You don't believe me, do you?"

Nora's face brightened. "We've all got to see the world somehow or another. If it's real enough for you, that's what's important."

"It's true, whether you think I'm honest or not. They like me more than anyone else. Used to be the same with my mother."

The tall woman carefully tiptoed over the produce, so as not to squish any of them. She wrapped an arm around Loxley and kissed the top of her head. "Of course they like you. You're such a sweetheart."

Loxley rested her head against Nora's neck and let out a long breath. Her friend's coat stunk of the plastics plant on the south end of town. The tall woman worked there most days from sun up to sundown.

Nora squeezed her shoulder and rubbed her arm. "I'd like you if I was a ghost."

"Why'd you come home in the middle of the night last night? I thought your shift was over at eight."

"You saw me coming home?"

"I had to pee, and I looked out and saw you coming home. It was two thirty-five."

Nora's posture reminded Loxley of a bird about to fly away. "I was having a drink with the foreman."

"Must be a slow drinker."

"He did take his time, yes. He likes to talk."

"Did he talk about plastic?"

Nora swallowed. "It wasn't interesting. Work stuff, darling." She pulled out her wallet. "I'm going to need a bag of weed."

They talked for another hour, about Birdie, about the weather and the greenhouse. Nora promised to come see it, and Loxley told her about all the repairs it needed. Several of the frames had cracked, and the weather shredded the bags over time. She was ashamed for anyone to see it. Then Nora promised she would steal a roll of plastic sheeting from the plant under the guise of taking it to the warehouse. They could replace all of the panels together. The tall woman rolled herself a joint with some of her purchase and offered a toke to Loxley, who declined.

Nora's personality was a bright fire. Loxley could stare into her, feeling her skin growing hot to the point of discomfort, knowing she would feel safer if she backed away. Every time she wanted to end the conversation and retreat, a spate of flame would bring her gaze back. The tall woman would grow loud, then whisper and giggle. She'd gossip about naughty things, then talk about music or politics in the next sentence as though they were one subject.

People's faces could be intimidating, their brows twitching this way and that – their mouths smiling even when their eyes didn't. Trying to understand them could be so infuriating, but not Nora. Loxley looked her right in her large, brown eyes and listened intently, unable to stop herself from smiling.

A black car turned onto her street, pulling across the Bazaar to the complaints of nearby pedestrians – the Consortium automotive from before. The world around seemed to dim. Whoever was driving the car, they'd brought the ghost to her.

Ice water doused Loxley's heart as she shot to her feet.

"What's wrong?"

Nora stood and took her hand, and Loxley jerked it away. Her chest felt as though it would explode as her eyes darted back and forth. The dead man was coming, but did he see her yet? She couldn't get to the cart and hope to get away. Her produce lay arrayed across the blanket, and she could think of no way to gather it all. She reached down to grab her cash box.

A cold, colorless hand seized her about the wrist, blasting her senses with searing pain. Alvin Kimball. She knew his real name with his cruel touch.

The dead man stood over her, the contours of his nude body half-eaten by shadow. He raked over her with milky eyes, face contorted with fear. Black tears streamed down his cheeks, and his mouth remained locked in a plea. The dead could only beg.

Loxley screamed, batting the ghost's hold from her even as she let go of the box. It opened upon striking the ground, releasing her hard-earned money to the breeze. Nora jumped back, shouting for her to calm down, but Loxley would not be swayed. She stumbled onto her rump, shrieking up at the shadowy man looming over her. He leaned closer to grope for her again, and she launched like a frightened cat in the other direction – toward the Bazaar with its searing lights and banging metal.

The cacophony of booths rose around her like waves in a storm, and she heard shouts as she barreled into the crowd. Neon popped across her vision like lightning, and she did everything she could to put one foot in front of the other. Her raw throat and aching wrist battered her panicked mind, and she could feel consciousness capsizing.

Static. All became noise as she fled into endless crowds of surging faces. The world was ending, and she could not stop herself from keening into the void.

CHAPTER TWO
INSIDE A PILL BOTTLE

IT'S OKAY, PRETTY baby. It's okay, Loxa-Loxie-Loxley. Come back to me.

The brightness faded. She ran her fingertips over chalky, fractured pavement as the ground scratched her knees. She recognized her own jagged voice – sharp, short intakes and long sobs. She looked to her wrist to see a burgundy welt. She could almost make out the forms of Mister Kimball's fingertips in her skin.

She remembered losing her cash and leaving her cart. That cash box had contained a week and a half's worth of sales. Her cart wasn't the best, but it was worth a good amount, and her day's stock would be gone. It was like stepping another month away from her dream of buying her own farm and moving out. It wasn't the gardening that depressed her, but her other day job.

Then she remembered her book. She'd never seen one like it, and she knew she might never see another. Its cover flashed through her mind like the face of a departed loved one. She sniffed and wiped the spittle from her chin. The winter air caught up with her, and she shivered, despite her warm clothes. She stood and shook the crackles out of her fingers.

Loxley had run a long way. The familiar brickwork of the fifth ring swelled before her, and she turned to see people staring. She heard the thunderous bells of Ely's Tower bang out the time: ten in the morning. She had to be at her next job soon. She looked at her pants; they were dusty and torn in places, and she knew her hair was crazy, but she couldn't be late. Losing her cart meant she couldn't save for her farm until she got a replacement. Losing her job at Fowler's would mean she couldn't pay for her apartment.

She trudged through the streets among the red brick terrace houses of the fifth ring. She didn't know how old this area was, but it certainly looked older than her part of town. When the original inhabitants of the Hole were carving out for the mine and foundry, folks must have put down roots here. They probably thought they couldn't sink any lower. The streets were wide, not like the claustrophobic alleyways of the rings below. She always saw a lot more cops around these parts, and a lot fewer men with caps pulled low over their eyes. People seemed proud to live here, even if weren't much better off than the folks below.

She crossed under the Hoop, a rusty loop of elevated tracks that ran around the entire Hole. No one wanted to trek down into the lower rings to get across town, and who could blame them? The Foundry and mine were far too deadly in the off hours for most. The men and women from the top rings who inspected the steelworks were carefully guided by Consortium guards to their destinations. The Con claimed to own everything on the ninth ring, but Loxley knew better. Going anywhere else on those levels could be dangerous. She knew the trick of it, though: never go down there. Seven was low enough.

She looked up the stairs into the Hoop station as she passed, and she remembered where she'd heard the name Alvin Kimball – he'd been running for mayor only a few weeks prior, and had been glad-handing in the station for votes. The blustery politician had come out of nowhere, laughing, and shook her hand vigorously as he solicited her vote. She looked down at her blistered, bruised wrist. She hadn't wanted him to grab her arm the first time.

So now he was dead, riding in a Consortium car. He hadn't died from slow illness, or else he wouldn't have made a ghost. Malevolent spirits came from those who couldn't accept death. Small children, the terminally ill and the elderly were rarely problems. She told herself to forget about Kimball; no good came of bothering the dead. Just like the youthful victims of shootings on the seventh ring, she merely needed to wait and someone would scrape them up.

The trek up to the third ring was short – just a few ramps and a pedestrian elevator once she'd crossed over the fourth ring. Once she got up high enough, the Hole below resembled a labyrinth. The far side was completely obscured by a column of steam from the Foundry. She'd always felt like that veil of mist stopped her from solving the maze of the city.

Sometimes, when the white buildings of Edgewood caught the sun right, the fog would glow, filling the streets with an otherworldly light.

She reached Fowler Brothers' Apothecary a full fifteen minutes ahead of schedule. The shop had a wooden front and curly gold letters etched across its large windows. Stained glass runners ran across the top, spilling colorful light onto the dirty sidewalk. The store sat on a crowded street in the administrative district where much of the steelworks' accounting happened. Loxley had asked for a job at the apothecary because she liked the flowers on the planters out front, but now that winter had come on, the flowers were long gone. She'd told Don Fowler she could help him build a greenhouse just like hers, but he hadn't liked the idea, saying the building had a proper appearance to maintain. She figured flowers ought to be part of that appearance, but she didn't complain.

She let herself in the front door and immediately looked down, as was her custom. Don liked to keep thousands of brown glass bottles of all shapes and sizes on the full-length shelves, and unless she made a deliberate effort, Loxley would find herself trying to mentally catalogue each one. Of course, the bottles didn't actually have anything in them. The chemicals were all in the back, each one separately packaged in a white bottle with the Consortium's orange and black logo stamped onto the side. Rank upon rank of repeating logos gave the place a kind of order Loxley could live inside. Don said the front had an old-timey feel that folks liked. She didn't understand.

Don swept around the counter the moment he caught sight of Loxley, his lab coat trailing in his wake. He was a fleshy, gnomish man with wispy hair like cotton batting.

"Sweet Jesus, Loxley. What happened to you?" He reached down to take ahold of her wrist and she recoiled. She wasn't ready to be touched again today.

"Nothing," she said, pulling her sweater sleeve lower over the bruise.

"Am I going to see track marks under that sleeve?"

She wouldn't have known what he meant, except he always talked about the junkies on the lower level. When he'd first hired her, he'd constantly warned her about the dangers of the men of the seventh ring, and eventually, he began to ask after her own habits.

She made eye contact with him for a moment, but she couldn't tell if he was angry or worried, and some of the flutter returned to her heart. She looked away.

An odd flask on the wall behind him caught her attention. It was slender and long, like a drip of water caught in a photograph. Green glass flower petals lined its sides, and a flaking cork stoppered its top. It had probably held wine or something of the like. She scanned the shelves for another, wondering if it was the only one. She found another, similar one, a little shorter... then another, a little fatter... then another, a little greener... then a brown one. Each find straightened another jangled line in her brain.

"Loxley! Can you hear me?"

"Sorry, Mister Fowler."

"You always do that." He rubbed the bridge of his nose. "This is why I can't have you working the counter."

"I know, sir. Do you have a headache?" She made for the stockroom door. "I could get you something from the back."

He looked her up and down and sighed. "You show early, looking like Hell. You don't have time to pretty yourself up, just a little? Now I know you're retarded, but surely you understand that your time could have been better spent throwing on a little makeup or rinsing the street off of you. You've seen the way other women dress, haven't you, young miss?"

"I'm not retarded." She looked down at the dull, gray carpet – nothing to distract her. "My brain works just fine."

"Just fine for the stockroom. Don't begrudge what God made you. You're taking the wrong message away from this conversation."

She wanted him to shut up, and she wished to tell him so. He would fire her if she did. She swallowed, bitterness in her mouth.

He tapped his foot a few times and slid his hands into his pockets. "I think we can both agree that I did you a charity by hiring you. A lot of folks wouldn't have done the same for a young lady from the seventh ring, no matter how sweet. And I know even fewer who'd help someone with your... condition."

"That's the message?" A knife edge entered her voice.

"No, Loxley. The message is this: next time you want to come in here looking like you washed out of a drain, you come in the back. I don't want my customers seeing a woman composed so poorly.

Now go on back and start filling those orders. And don't think I didn't notice your attitude just now, young lady. If I were you, I wouldn't speak one word to me for the rest of the morning. I hope we're clear on that."

She preferred being told to get to work, and wished he'd done that from the beginning. The stockroom was nicer for her – plain walls, boring white, beige or brown bottles, and a tiny window at her sorting counter so she could look out if she wanted. Loxley could turn on the vent on the chemical hood and drown out the rest of the world if she had to, though Don might get out of hand about the electric bill. Her first week, she'd taken to singing, but Don had told her to work quietly. She kept her out of tune singing to her garden after that.

In spite of Don's constant speeches, her job wasn't so bad. It had a lot of quiet time, and she could absorb herself in measurements. She'd gotten quite fast with her short-bladed spatula, and pills made a satisfying rattle when she shoved them into bottles. She blew through her orders in minutes, packaging the drugs Don had already compounded. She wasn't allowed to do the apothecary work, but she knew nearly everything about it. She'd watched most of her employer's formulations over the past two years, and people largely ordered the same thing every time.

The front door chimed, and Loxley looked into the shop. A middle-aged blonde strode languorously to the counter, all sighs and sadness, wrapped in a wool pencil skirt and bleached shirt. She made fleeting eye contact with Loxley before speaking in hushed tones to Don about her ill daughter. She told him she couldn't afford the bill for the drugs, to which the apothecary replied, "It's on the house, my dear. You just worry about getting her well."

Loxley watched him march into the stockroom to begin filling the capsules. He looked her squarely in the eye. "Out with it," he grunted, setting about his work.

She refocused on her task at hand, taking inventory of their various chemicals. The blonde lingered out front, inspecting the racks of pre-mixed medications on the counter.

"What?" he whispered. "I can see that brain of yours turning."

He'd instructed her not to speak, and she weighed his proscription against his current demands. "I don't understand why she doesn't have to pay."

"The greatest of all virtues is love. I wish someone like you could understand that."

"Do you feel love for me?"

He shook his head. "'Thou shalt love thy neighbor as thyself.' That's why I'm so hard on you, young miss." He filled up the bottle and rushed out front to receive the adulation of his customer.

Loxley tried not to frown, but she didn't understand. She'd seen him turn away so many needful men in their trials, but he gladly handed over a few dollars' worth of goods to a complete stranger when it was a woman. Don was a married man, and didn't treat the blonde as though he wanted sexual favors. When he'd first hired Loxley, he gave her lots of deference and patience, but that had grown thin. Perhaps she had come to bore him over time.

She crossed to the stockroom window and looked out onto the busy side street. Fowler Brothers' had an excellent view of the fourth ring ramp, and she watched people scuttling up and down the stairway. Few of them came in the direction of the shop, instead heading further into the banking district. A limousine caught her attention as it crept up the automobile ramp, chrome flashing in the sun. Its front radiator was a large silver grill with an angel on top that reminded her of a tombstone.

Much to Loxley's surprise, she spotted Nora's brown mop of hair as her friend climbed the stairs from the fourth ring. She carried the agriculture manual and another book under one arm, and wore a big smile. Loxley stifled an excited yelp and made for the front door, only to bump into Don.

"Would you please try to pay attention?"

"I'm sorry, sir. I'll be right back."

"Hold it right there. This is a constant problem. I always see your eyes drifting, and I know you're not really concentrating. We've got dangerous substances in here, and people's lives depend on our accuracy. Do you think that's worth your time?"

"I'll only be a moment." Loxley made to move past him, but he blocked her exit.

He jabbed a finger into her collarbone and she sucked in a breath. "No, ma'am. Not until you look me in the eye and tell me you're paying attention." His raised voice sent a shiver up her spine.

He folded his arms, and she looked at his gnarled hands. She hadn't wanted to be touched, and the spot where he'd poked her stung. She felt the ants in her legs again, and she tapped her foot to try to stop them from climbing higher. Her eyes flicked up to his face, but it was a contorted, nasty mess, and she looked away. A short, tuneless note issued from her throat. She took a step back.

"You're not going anywhere, young miss. Now have you got something to tell me?"

Nora should have been coming through the door any second. Loxley waited, stalling for her friend as best she could. No one opened the door. She inhaled, and forced herself to look Don in the eye. Her foot tapped harder. "I am paying attention, Mister Fowler."

"Good. So we're done having these kinds of problems?"

"Yes."

"Good," he said, stepping aside.

Loxley rushed to the door to look out, but saw no one she recognized on the sidewalk. She waited for a few moments, then ducked back inside and ran to the storeroom, past her protesting boss. She peered out the window to see Nora, chatting happily with someone inside the limousine. The tall woman had become animated, smiling and laughing as she gesticulated. Did Nora know the limo passenger? The car looked like it had come from Edgewood for sure. Loxley had seen one before, but they were a rare sight, even on the third ring. She didn't figure her friend knew anyone that rich.

Without warning, Nora nodded and stepped into the vehicle, along with Loxley's book. Her hand shot to the window as Loxley watched her most treasured possession disappear for a second time that day. Her toes itched, her legs became restless and she bounced on the balls of her feet as the limo glided away like a boat from its berth. When it was finally gone, she settled and frowned. Who was in that car? Why did Nora leave? Why couldn't she bring the book first? She turned to see Don, his hands on his hips, shaking his head.

She tried to silence her thoughts with quotidian tasks, but Nora's appearance had wrecked her concentration. No one had ever visited Loxley at work before, and she'd been hurt that it hadn't happened for the first time today. She spilled a script for cream as she went to bottle it and she cursed aloud, a rare event for her in both cases. She managed to quietly clean up the mess, but she still had to ask Don to make more, and that hadn't gone well. After that, she had to count out pills three times for a single order, and she still felt worried about the result.

The leprechaun in the lab coat wouldn't leave her alone either, taking every opportunity to remind her how to do her job. He often spoke to her as though she was stupid, but he paid extra special attention to her that day. Even her most tepid responsibilities became boiling priorities for Don after she'd spilled his order. He harangued her as she counted, as she filled, as she cleaned, as she fetched, and together, neither of them got much done.

And still Loxley could not move her thoughts from the loss of her book, of her cart and her cash. By the end of the day, she'd grown flustered and twitchy, offering up a quick, "Yes, sir," to anything Don brought to her attention. They came to a breaking point when she dropped her second bottle of the day, and capsules dashed underneath every cabinet and storage bin like frightened insects scattering under sudden light.

Don slapped a stack of papers down on the counter. "That is it, Loxley! What on earth has gotten into you today?"

Disparate thoughts of Birdie, Nora, the book and the ghost of Mister Kimball came swirling into her mind, but all that came out were sobs. She managed to say she was sorry, and wiped her nose. She didn't like Don. She didn't want to be weak in front of him. She wanted to punch him squarely in the nose. She tried to stop herself from crying, but fear of losing her job because of his lack of sympathy was too great.

"Okay, now," Don stuttered. "Maybe we just calm down a bit."

"I'm – I'm trying!"

He rubbed her shoulder, another unwelcome sensation. It did little to calm the temperature of the conversation, and it was only through mustering her courage that Loxley was able to speak. He smiled as her breathing slowed.

"Are you ready to tell me what's going on?" said Don.

A bright girl is an honest girl, Loxley. You tell me what you did, her mother used to tell her. Loxley knew a normal person would think she was crazy if she told them everything, so she replaced all instances of the word 'ghost' with 'scary man.' She told Don the whole story of her day, focusing on how much money she'd lost when she was attacked. She showed him her bruise, pointing out the subtle discolorations that indicated finger marks, and she told him about losing her precious book.

"And did anyone come to help you after you were attacked?" he asked.

"I don't think so. I had to run too fast."

"Have you got a lot of money saved up?"

She nodded, but she didn't tell him the amount.

"You can't keep living on the seventh ring, young miss. It's too dangerous down there. One of these days, you're not going to come into work, and I'll know it was one of those thugs putting the knife to you. I want you to consider taking an apartment up here."

She thought of her mother's spot on the mattress, and how she'd been raised down below. "I can't, Mister Fowler."

"When Maddie and I were your age, we moved up from the fourth ring because I felt like it wasn't safe for her. We moved into the space below the shop here, and look at me now. I'm doing well, aren't I?" He spoke deliberately, measuring out each word the way a mother might when explaining the dangers of fire to a child.

"It's too expensive to live up here."

"I'm sure you could figure it out. I don't know how you could garden up here, but you should consider leaving that to the professionals, especially after this morning's events."

She frowned. "I don't see why I should stop gardening. I'm going to own a farm one day, and I need to know how to work a farm."

"Loxley, you live in a perilous place, doing perilous things, just so you can wake up every morning and play in the mud. Isn't it time to grow up and admit how silly that is?"

"It's not silly." She had told Don about her gardening during some idle chatter some months ago, and now she regretted it. "I just need more money."

"You asked me earlier if I loved you, and I do, young lady. You can't afford to have your little farm and be safe." He brushed off his lab coat and crossed his arms. "And you know, I'm contributing to all that nonsense, too. I'm not blameless, here. A person with your condition can't always be expected to make sound decisions for herself."

"I don't have a condition."

"You only think that because you won't see a doctor. I've always suspected I was overpaying you, and here you are, all bruised and battered because of me. If I'd been paying you a sensible wage from the beginning, you might have been making sensible decisions. As it stands, I'm doing no better than giving needles to a junkie. Of course you were going to show up with a sob story one of these days."

She balled her fists. "I need every penny of my wages, Mister Fowler. I need a raise, even. I'm going to buy another cart and keep making an honest living."

Don smiled and shook his head. He worked as he talked, as though he cared little about the outcome of the conversation. "No. I'm done supporting this lunacy. I'm cutting you back to four dollars an hour."

She tapped her foot, trying to shake the ants onto the rug.

"I've got a friend from church who can let you a room up here – Sheila Handy. You won't have a whole lot of money left over for ridiculous notions, but she can keep an eye on you and help you make good decisions."

"This isn't right, Mister Fowler!"

He measured out a few milliliters of a solution, holding up the beaker to read over his glasses. "It's the only thing that's right. I don't know why I didn't think of it before. I'm sorry I didn't because I know I've caused you a lot of heartache. You could have been getting adjusted to this arrangement when you needed me most – when you asked me for a job – and it would have been easier to accept."

"You don't know what's best for me, sir." He'd enraged her to the point that she felt as though her fist might hit him on its own. She took a step back, more for his protection than hers. She wanted to flap her hands, but he would call her retarded again, so she clasped her fingers in front of her. She felt like a shaken soda bottle.

"No," he said, fetching his mortar and pestle, "but I know a lot better than you. You'd do well to listen to your elders. You could have a long career here, Loxley." He glanced up to her and cocked an eyebrow. "Or you could say what you're thinking right now, and have no career here. It's your choice. I can always find another assistant."

Little Fiddleback

LOXLEY TOOK HER key from around her neck as she climbed the green steel stairs to Harrison Hoop Station. She'd waited to ascend onto the platform until the five twenty-two had left, which gave her six minutes to get inside, get to her locker, and get tuned up. After that, the next train would arrive with deafening force and clamor. She wanted to be ready before that happened.

Reaching the platform, she found only a few people. After the day she'd had, she welcomed the sparse population. Harrison Hoop Station wasn't nearly as bad as Vulcan's Bazaar, but on crowded days, she'd have to force herself to walk inside. She hurried to the station lockers and opened hers. Inside, she had a violin case, a blanket and a glass jar. She fetched her things and put fifty cents into the locker to retrieve her key. She knew she was paying to hold onto an empty locker, but she had an affinity for that number. One hundred and five; it was hers. She picked up her stuff and rushed to her usual spot against the edge of the station.

The walls were all the same forest green as the rest of the place, solid steel and half-eaten with rust. Since the Hoop was elevated, those walls could get bitterly cold in winter, offering no comfort from the blistering winds that swept through the place. She spread her blanket over the frigid concrete floor, plunked her jar down in front of her and opened up her instrument case.

The crackled finish of her violin was a visit from an old friend – always a little new, but full of warm familiarity. It had been her mother's violin, and before that, her grandmother's. Her grandmother had been a master of its arts, traveling the world, but Loxley couldn't imagine such a thing. She'd never been outside the Hole, and she certainly didn't long to see other cities. She fetched the violin from its case, along with her bow, which had started to look a little frayed. She rosined the bow and was just about to play when she remembered the most important thing about playing in the Hoop station. She dug into her pocket and threw a dollar or so of loose change into her jar.

One minute until the next train arrived. She placed the bow to her strings, savoring the tension of the interface. A slow drag, and she brought the wild A string into line with a half-turn of the peg. She bowed across the other strings in pairs, tuning them to the perfect fifths, just like her mother had taught her. Several heads had turned her way during the few notes, not exactly friendly faces, as no one enjoyed the sound of tuning.

Once tuned, she pulled an open note across the low G, and it was like straightening a wavy line in her mind. The complicated, awful world became a single pitch as the station resonated with the sound of her instrument. Low and droning, she kept her bow traveling back and forth to keep the tone alive. Each push and pull brought a new peace to her, like laying her head against her mother's chest as she breathed in and out with restful deliberation.

She saw lights on the tracks in the distance and heard the horn. Her fingers flew across the neck, playing her first scale. She paused at the top, savoring a high E before plunging headlong into the valley of her melody. Loxley played the song in her heart, and as she became dimly-aware of the train thundering into the station, she disappeared into her music. She could not see or hear the passersby; there was only the touch of horsehair on string and the embrace of her instrument.

On the top ring, in Edgewood, they had a lot more trees, nestled amongst the alabaster houses. Squirrels liked to make their way into the city from the endless fields beyond, scurrying amongst the branches. As Loxley played, she imagined the squirrels, scampering across the ground to bound up the massive trunks, jumping between the branches, sometimes graceful, sometimes falling. In turn, her music began to patter about, dashing along nimble phrases and perching on long, thoughtful measures. Without her permission, her body began to sway, and a sleepy grin spread across her face. She wanted to tell the world about the squirrels with a voice she didn't have.

Her tune wound to a close, and she opened her eyes to see a clapping audience. The world returned. Cash poured from the crowd into her jar, and she watched the tips pile up with mounting excitement. The rush hadn't even started yet, and it would already be a banner evening for Loxley's second business.

She picked up her bow and began to play again. Through the hours, people would come and go and her jar became stuffed with bills. She'd grown used to attracting a throng, but never like this. After the hellish day she'd already had, she appreciated every shout and clap. It warmed her bones to be liked, even if she had no idea how to address the folk gathered around her. They didn't crowd her in, either. Whenever someone would stand too close, she'd simply play as loudly as she could, and they would back away.

A black fellow in the front applauded wildly, a lot louder than the others around him. She didn't like the look of him: tall and burly, a wide smile with too-white teeth. His clothes were strange, too. He sported a crisp shirt and vest under a sleek suit coat. She saw dark acne scars pockmarking his cheeks as he crouched down in front of her.

"What was that song, Pumpkin? Never heard you play it before." His voice floated to her – polished, too practiced.

"I don't know you." She squeaked as she spoke. "Doubt you've heard much of my music at all."

"That's too bad. I'm a good guy to know." He extended a calloused hand, gold cufflinks flashing from his shirt sleeve as his coat pulled back. His suit was immaculately pressed, and struck her as both stylish and restrained. There wasn't a speck of dust in evidence anywhere on his person. "Quentin Mabry."

Loxley glanced at the clock. Three minutes to the next train. She stared at his hand, willing him to retract it. She didn't have any black friends, though the lower rings were full of them. They walked in their own social circles, and she much preferred it that way. Familiar faces were scary enough. *You keep to yourself around the negroes, Loxie. They ain't all bad, but they ain't us.*

Quentin straightened up. "What seems to be the problem, Pumpkin?"

"My name isn't Pumpkin."

"And I'm giving you every opportunity to correct me." He extended a hand again. "My name is Mister Quentin Mabry."

She looked to the crowd, but they'd all dispersed. She glanced back at Quentin's hand and shook it quickly. His grip was gentle, but his skin was rough. She pulled away as fast as she could.

"Loxley."

"Is that your family name?"

When Loxley was young, she'd asked her mother what their last name was. Her mother asked her what she wanted it to be, and Loxley thought hard. There was a spider that terrified the little boys on the block. They said, if it bit you, it'd rot your flesh. They said it liked to hide, and it was ugly and strange. It wasn't mean-spirited, just scared of everyone. It just wanted to be left alone. She'd taken its name ever since for herself.

"Fiddleback," she told Quentin.

"You serious?"

"Yes." She'd told people that name for years. No one had ever questioned it before. Her cheeks felt hot.

"Then I've got a proposal, Miss Fiddleback."

"I don't want to marry you."

Quentin's rich laughter echoed off the walls of the train station, and she flinched at the volume of it. He nearly doubled over, but she didn't think it was funny at all. First Birdie, then the ghost, then Don, and now this total stranger had begun to mock her. She felt a little flare in her stomach, and she thwacked him hard across the side of his leg with the tip of her bow. He jumped back with a startled shout.

She'd had enough. She stood, the neck of her violin clutched hard in her balled fist. "Stop laughing at me!" If he came any closer, she'd strike him across the face next time.

He smiled, rubbing his leg. "That smarts. You've got some fangs, Miss Fiddleback. I meant that I had a business proposal. You understand there are several types of proposals?"

She scowled at him. Why wouldn't he just leave?

"I'm the maître d' at a nice nightclub, and I want you to come audition to play for us."

"You just made that up. No such thing."

He shook his head. "It's short for maître d'hôtel. It's French. It means I'm the host."

"You don't work at a nightclub in France."

"The club isn't in France. It's on the eighth ring."

She settled back down onto her rump and got ready to play. The next train would be here soon, and she didn't want to be caught out talking to Quentin when it arrived. "Now I know you're lying. There isn't anything nice on the eighth ring."

He slipped his hands into his pockets. "I just want you to hear me out, Miss Fiddleback. If you'll let me, I'll take you down there to play, and you can make some good money. Better bread than you make up here. A lot of folks would like to come see you saw that fiddle of yours. I can probably get you a new one, if you want."

"Don't need a new fiddle." She saw the lights of the approaching train and put her bow to the strings. "Now stop talking."

"Please listen, Miss Fiddleback. You could be making anywhere between three hundred bucks and a grand, every single night. I'm not saying you have to make a decision right –"

The station began to rattle, and Loxley shut her eyes tightly as she sliced a note from the air. She could make Quentin vanish into her music, just like the train. She searched her heart for a melody that captured him, an unctuous song, fraught with little disharmonic tones. Out of a clattering world, he emerged like a snake from rustling leaves. She wanted to walk away, but he tangled her legs. He became a phrase of minor notes that she wove into a major tapestry – always about to bite her.

She managed to keep her eyes closed the whole time, and soon she heard nothing. The serpent raced after her through the grove, and she kicked at it when it got close. His fangs passed close to her pale flesh; a single nick would prove deadly. Her song spoke of the others killed by this scaly worm, all of them innocent and gullible, and they lay sleeping in the grass until the end of days. The snake would see her on her back, too, if she didn't do something. The Loxley of her mind scurried up a tree, using the same scales as the squirrels did, until arriving above the canopy.

A sunrise stretched before her, unfettered from the walls of the Hole, and the sporty music of the squirrels dilated into a soaring ode to the silver clouds above. She grew lighter with each interval, playing away the weight of the world. Her muddy toes lifted from the branch, and she began to float upwards. She would fly away from this place, even as the snake climbed the tree behind her.

Across the expanse, there was nothing, no one. She looked down and only saw clouds. Above her was the blue haze of endless space. She could fly forever or fall forever, and neither would matter because she'd passed beyond the fearful domain of any other soul. She could be alone up here.

She opened her eyes and smiled, proud of her work. The train had left, but the crowd hadn't. She waited for them to clap for her, but no one was watching her. She saw that her overstuffed jar of money had vanished... along with Quentin Mabry. She looked up at the bystanders in panic, and saw them staring toward the station exit. She shot to her feet, fear and anger flooding her veins.

Then she spotted Quentin, straddling another man and beating the tar out of him. The prone fellow had her jar in one hand and shielded his face with the other, and he screamed with each strike. Quentin tried to take the jar, but the thief wouldn't let go. Quentin pushed the man's guard up and knocked his teeth in. Then he yanked Loxley's earnings from the thief's hand, stood up and brushed himself off.

The gathered crowd erupted into applause, and Quentin took a long bow before sauntering back toward Loxley. When he was amongst them, receiving back-slaps and congratulations, he presented the jar to each person there, soliciting their donations. "No, not me! Let's hear it for the beautiful music of Lady Fiddleback!" he laughed, and the money came in even faster than before. Folks liked music, but they seemed to like violence even more. When at long last he'd milked every last drop from the crowd, he tucked two crisp hundred dollar bills into the overflowing coffer and presented it to her.

Her eyes widened. This would more than cover the loss of her cart and cash. Why was he acting this way?

Quentin spun to address the crowd. "If you liked that, you can see more of her at the Hound's Tail, on the eighth ring! Ya'all going to come see her?" Hollers from the crowd affirmed his showmanship.

She didn't say that. When did he get that idea? Embarrassment rouged her cheeks once more. She jammed her violin into the case and snatched up her earnings and blanket, floundering with the spread as she tried to hold onto the jar. Quentin moved in like a dance partner and took the blanket from her, folding it up as she watched and fumed.

"You all done for the evening, Pumpkin?" he cooed, coming far too close for her tastes.

She went to slap him, but restrained herself. He still flinched, and that made her happy. She didn't know what he was up to, and she didn't care to know.

"My name is Loxley, Mister Mabry, and I'm not playing your game," she said, and stormed off in the direction of the lockers. She hoped to God he wouldn't follow her.

CHAPTER THREE
SHE CAME HOME

LOXLEY'S JOURNEY HOME weighed on her. The entire way, all she could think about was the roll of bills in her coat pocket. She tried not to imagine that everyone could see her loaded down with cash, but the idea kept creeping into her mind. She would not let anyone close to her on the ramps, and she scanned every single person's face for even the slightest hint of danger. The descent into the lower rings was hellish, because she had to walk through the poorer neighborhoods – her neighborhoods – if she wanted to get home. Familiar fixtures of those areas became worrisome, the streetlights dimmer, the residents more hostile. She knew if she acted suspicious, people would be more likely to hurt her, but she could not hide what she was.

She felt the ants on her legs, telling her to run home, like she did in her school days. However, that would be like running from an angry dog. It would certainly chase her down. When Magic City Heights came into view, the tightness in her chest melted away. She knew this neighborhood well, and the people knew her. She didn't stand out here. Her apartment beckoned to her from behind a fence of other buildings, promising its protection and hurrying her the final few blocks.

When she turned the last corner to the entrance, she spotted Officer Crutchfield sitting atop her cart, smoking a cigarette. He smiled and waved, and she nearly skipped as she rushed to him. He leapt down from his perch, and she threw her arms around him, squeezing him tightly. He stunk of smoke with a tinge of whiskey, but it didn't bother her; he'd brought back her cart.

She circled her property, inspecting it. She had to shake the crackles out, but only because her heart soared with pleasure. There was a new scuff on the back fender, and she felt a little like her cart was an old friend that had grown a beard: mostly the same, but a little unfamiliar. She wondered what adventures it had gotten into over the course of its day with Officer Crutchfield, and she laughed out loud.

The policeman put his hands on his hips and shook his head. "What you giggling about, Loxie?

"A cart with a beard," she replied, nearly crawling up under it to inspect the undercarriage.

"Sure. Why not?" Crutchfield grabbed the back of her coat and pulled her upright. "I can assure you it's all there. I've been waiting out here for two hours to give it to you. Question is, what do you say back to me?"

She stopped and bowed her head slightly. "Thank you, Officer Crutchfield."

"You're welcome. I've told you to call me Burt for two years now."

"But Officer Burt sounds dumb."

"No 'Officer.' Just Burt."

She frowned. "But that's not what you call a police officer. You're wearing a uniform. That's queer."

He pulled out a handkerchief from his black police parka and wiped his nose. He looked as though he'd been sitting outside in the chilly air for quite some time.

Loxley took the cart by the tongue and carried it back to the fenced area, opening the lock with Rick's key. She put the transport back where it belonged, under a rickety awning, then chained the fence and rejoined the policeman. He had sat on the front steps of the building and lit another cigarette. He offered the pack to Loxley. She shook her head no and sat down beside him.

"You got a fenced area and everything," he said. "First time I've ever seen your operation."

"My garden is up on the roof. Rick lets me use it."

"He your superintendent?"

She nodded.

"He lets you up on the roof?"

"Yeah," she said. "He's really nice to me. He hates everyone else."

"What makes you say that?"

"He tells me a lot. He gets drunk and bakes me cookies. Then he sits in my apartment and talks about his dead wife and how she liked everyone but he doesn't." She looked up at Officer Crutchfield, and she couldn't tell if he was smiling or squinting, so she stared at the ground instead. He'd always told her she should look people in the eye, but his face didn't make sense.

"Probably wouldn't like me, much," he mumbled around his cigarette. "God knows no one else does. I think the wife has had about enough of my bullshit."

"I like you pretty good." She pursed her lips. "Did you find my cashbox when you found my cart?"

"Nora found it."

"I guess I should thank her, then."

He exhaled a stream of white smoke. "I guess you should. She packed up your things, but she said she'd bring you the cashbox. I take it you didn't see her?"

"No. She got in a limo."

"What? Why did she get in a limo?"

"Because she wanted to."

"Ah, she'll turn up somewhere... Goddamn, it's cold."

Loxley jumped when he put his arm around her and patted her shoulder. He squeezed her, and she felt the flutter pass. She leaned into his armpit, enjoying the warmth of his side.

"Sorry I startled you," he said. "Just figured you could use a hug. Seemed like you were having a rough day."

"Yeah. You really think no one likes you?"

"Huh? Oh, yeah. Definitely. No one likes a cop, you know?"

She sighed. "No one likes me, either."

"Is that a fact?"

"Everyone hates me for some reason or another. They're mean to my face, and I bet they're real nasty behind my back."

"I like you plenty, Loxley."

She knew he was looking at her, but she kept her gaze solidly on the ground. "Why? I'm ugly and weird."

"No, you're not."

"Am so."

He chuckled. "Well, you're not ugly."

She swallowed. "You think I'm pretty?"

He tossed away his cigarette and turned her by the shoulders to face him. His skin was deeply tanned from his long days in the sun, dark against his salty brown moustache. He looked her over with his chestnut eyes, and leaned toward her. She moved back a little, unsure of what was happening.

His lips met hers, cold and wet, and Loxley's limbs seized up with the sudden shock of his kiss. She leaned back, but his mouth wouldn't come off hers, his tongue running across her teeth. One hand slid down to her hip, and his other hand wound up under her shirt, forcefully massaging one of her breasts and clawing at her bra. She yelped into his mouth, muffled by his skin, and he leaned against her, weighing her down.

See that man over there, Lox? That's a policeman.
Her body locked up in its revulsion, and her brain caught fire. She couldn't breathe, and she shivered violently. His mustache scraped against her face, and his hand shot down her belly, pushing against her skin, trying to worm under her belt. The words wouldn't come out. She had to scream, but it died inside her. He managed to get the tips of his calloused fingers into her pants, and she kicked out as hard as she could. He pulled at her pubic hair, trying to reach her insides.

You have to always treat them with respect and do as they say.

Loxley's hands balled into fists, her fingertips blazing with electricity. The ants boiled across her legs, biting flesh everywhere they touched. She began to sing with every exhalation, and she tore her face away from him. She pushed him away as hard as she could.

"Come on, baby. You can't tell me you don't want this," he growled, yanking her closer. His strength terrified her, and she couldn't escape his hungry grip. "It's okay. Just let me show you how. Shh, baby, just relax."

If you don't listen to them, you could get in serious trouble. Do you understand?

"Nnn!" She couldn't make her mouth say no. Her head grew light as her lungs tried to hold onto each slippery breath. "Nn! P-p –"

Loxley's arm uncoiled like a striking snake, and she brought her palm across his ear with all her might, stunning him. She scrabbled away, slapping his face and clawing at his eyes.

"What the fuck, Loxley?" he screeched. "Are you fucking crazy?"

Venom flooded her blood. Her mother was wrong about policemen. Her mother was a damned liar. The thought rolled through her mind over and over, swelling into rage. Hot tears rolled down her shaking face, and her lips curled into an aching frown. She didn't have any words, and she hugged herself, rocking to calm the storm.

He got to his feet. "Why are you looking at me like that? You seriously going to tell me you didn't want it?"

She dug under the cuffs of her pants and stabbed her bare legs with her fingernails, willing away the ants. She shivered in the winter air.

"Laying on me, hugging me and all that shit. What was that?" Some of his graying hair had fallen out of place, and he smoothed it back down. "What was I supposed to think, huh? Don't blame me for this! You're the one acting like a goddamned whore."

What if he was right? She didn't understand other people. They behaved erratically, and when she failed to grasp their intent, they'd get mad at her. What if this was her fault? Shame burned in the pit of her stomach. She blinked away some tears, trying to speak. She went to open her mouth, but she thought she might vomit, and swallowed as hard as she could.

"You got something to say for yourself, Loxie?"

She wanted to take that name back from him. That was the name her mother called her. "You're..." Her speech balanced on a tightrope, ready to tumble into uncontrollable wailing if she didn't concentrate. "You're m-married!"

"You think that's how this works?" he bellowed, blasting away what courage she'd mustered. She shrunk ever tighter, wrapping herself into a little ball. She wanted to go hide in a deep, dark hole, like her namesake. He paced back and forth. "I come home every day for twenty-seven years and don't get so much as a thank you for risking my fucking neck. Then you come along, batting your eyelashes, and it's like, finally someone appreciates me, you know. You know?"

Her muscles burned. She was doing everything she could not to disappear into the static in her brain.

He hunkered down, getting on her level. He seemed calmer, but she couldn't chance standing up. She saw tears in his eyes, too. He sniffled. "But that was just a lie, wasn't it? You wanted me to play babysitter because you're too crazy to cross a street. I'm right, aren't I? You were pretending, using me while it was convenient – never planning to give anything back."

Officer Crutchfield continued to move in on her. She might faint any second. She'd stopped breathing.

"I don't know why I didn't see this before now. You women... if it wasn't for your pussies, we'd dump you in the steelworks. I thought you could make me happy, but in the end, you're just another retarded bitch." He reached down and patted her head.

"I'll kill you." The words rushed from her at his touch, raw and primal, and she bored into his eyes with hers. "Don't touch me again."

He recoiled, considering her. His hand crept over his holstered pistol. If he pulled it, would he shoot her? Would he rape her? Loxley wondered if she was ready to die to stop him. The static rolled through her at the thought, offering to take her away from the fear, and she focused on the gun to keep her mind in place.

He took a hesitant step back, then another, never turning away from her. "You made your biggest mistake tonight, girl. You're never going to sell in my market again."

And then he turned and lumbered away, rubbing his ear and cursing. She regarded his passage for a long time after he'd left, trying to hold it together in case he darkened her vision once again. No one had ever touched her like that man, and she'd let him... How could she let him do that to her? Why didn't she hit him? Her body stung from where he'd scratched her belly.

Her arms gave out from under her, and Loxley laid down upon the frigid concrete steps. She held herself and shook, but no coat would have been able to warm her. When she was sure Officer Crutchfield was gone, she let go of her restraint. She shook the crackles from her burning fingers, kicked the ants from her legs and sang, low and hoarse, a single note. When that wore off, she wept.

Perhaps hours passed. Perhaps minutes. She had no way of knowing. It was still dark outside, and the cold had seeped into her bones. Loxley sat up and brushed her hair from her face. She wiped away the snot with the back of a quivering hand.

She wanted to see Nora. There would be a warm apartment, a nice bed and hot tea. Her friend could tell her about men, or just hold her and not say anything. Nora could tell her if she'd been a bad person, if she should have let Officer Crutchfield fuck her; Nora would want Loxley to curl up in her arms and the tears would flow freely like blood from an infected wound. Nora could make this right.

When Loxley blinked, she'd already begun to stumble down the street. She couldn't remember taking the steps. Her friend lived a block and a half away, and Loxley could see the winking yellow fluorescence of Nora's building. The earnings from Harrison Hoop Station dangled from her pocket, a stack of bills threatening to be torn away by a gust of wind. She stuffed them back inside and looked back at her path to see her friend, standing in the middle of the road a few dozen feet away.

"Please... help," said Loxley, sinking to her knees. She waited for her friend's warm arms to enfold her. "Thank you," she whispered, over and over again.

The embrace never came.

"Please," screamed Loxley, shutting her eyes tightly. "Please... Nora, please touch me."

Only the faraway pounding of the steelworks answered her. She opened her eyes and looked upon her friend.

Shadows had washed Nora's eyes – holes in her pallid skin. A single lock of tangled hair crossed her expressionless lips. Her fingers twitched hungrily at her sides, and she shuffled slowly from foot to foot.

Loxley's mouth went dry.

The ghost paced back and forth like an angry prisoner looking for an exit. The less someone expected to die, the meaner the spirit. It crawled up the nearby streetlight before vanishing and reappearing on the ground. It flickered around the scene, testing its boundaries, but every time it made for Loxley, it would turn around and go back. Ghosts didn't like to wander far from their bodies.

The static flooded into Loxley again, and she felt as though the buildings would crash down around her. Her body itched, and she still felt Officer Crutchfield's touch like a handprint on her skin. She jolted her head, throwing off some of the fugue.

Her words came out malformed. "I can't tonight, Nora. I can't... I can't... I can't."

Loxley hummed as she turned and began shuffling back to her apartment. She wrung her hands together as she walked, eying her path sidelong as she craned her head this way and that, sloshing the static from her mind.

Her brain caught on the sound of her voice, and she felt all the weight lifting from her as she repeated herself over and over again. "I can't. Hmmm.... I cann. Hmmmmmoo... Acan't. Hnnnn. Aka. Whooo... Aka-whoo... Aka-whoo..." She shambled into her building, walking past the elevator. The day began to fade away as she climbed the stairs, feeling the reverberation of her mantra as it bounced around the concrete stairwell. She padded down the hallway, drawing her keys from her pocket. Birdie emerged from her apartment, face twisted with anger, clucking about something or other, but Loxley pushed right past her.

She fumbled her keys into the lock. Her hands didn't like her anymore. She opened the door to her cozy, familiar warren and slipped inside, shutting the way behind her in Birdie's face. She shot the deadbolt. "Aka-whoo... Aka-whoo..." Loxley crossed to her window and sat down in front of it. She cracked the blinds open a tiny bit so she could look out.

Nora stood in the street, just a block away. It drifted to one side, so far it should have fallen over, but it didn't. It remained transfixed on the way Loxley had left, staring into nothing as though its eyes had followed Loxley home. Its brown hair began to boil in the still air, floating upward. Loxley hadn't seen many ghosts, but this one was different.

Loxley rested her chin on the window ledge and smacked her forehead against the frame. The cold metal felt good, and she did it again, repeating herself until she fell asleep.

Begging for Lies

"Loxa-lox..."

She awoke into a distorted world, resting against the window. It looked like her bedroom, but it wasn't. It couldn't be her bedroom, because she hadn't woken in her bed. She should have felt anxious, but she'd run out of anxiety. All that remained was despair.

"I'm awake," she mumbled, but the words felt empty. She hadn't slept outside of her bed since her mother's passing, and she felt no connection to her ritual this morning. She glanced at her bed. "Momma, I'm awake." The icy ball in her gut didn't dissolve.

Her neck stung from sleeping at the window, and when she stood, it made snapping noises like a head of celery. Her muscles were strong after years of hauling gardening supplies around, and when she slept wrong, her whole body seized. She felt like a bundle of sticks lashed into the shape of a human – some of those lashings had slipped their bonds to constrict other parts of her, and now her bones wanted to hang all willy-nilly. She stretched, trying to realign her body, but she couldn't get the tightness out.

Orange rays had started to tint her window, and she opened the blinds. Nora stood atop a streetlight, glaring at her. Fresh tears moistened Loxley's exhausted eyes, and she stepped back from the window, nearly losing her balance. The ghost had gotten used to having her nearby, and hungered for her touch. That's all any ghost wanted – to cling to her living skin for warmth.

Loxley did everything she could to reignite the engine of routine. She put her clothes on the heater as she made eggs and bacon. She tried talking to her mother's side of the mattress about her day, but her mother was dead, and that was dumb.

Her mother hadn't made a ghost when she died. Loxley had seen plenty of other folks make horrible spirits, especially people her mother's age. Her mother had died choking, and Loxley hadn't wanted to stick around. She remembered the conflicting feelings perfectly: did she stay and keep trying to help her mother, or did she run, because her mother was about to pass? Loxley had nearly lost her mind with fear as she'd watched her mother expire. In the end, she'd stayed until the woman became still, and no ghost came to trouble her.

Loxley supposed her family couldn't make spirits. When she disappeared into death, there would be no one to care about her passing, not even herself. She imagined a lot of people would have found that sad. People often got sad about dying.

She got dressed and wandered toward the garden. Birdie didn't come out to yell at her. Had the woman yelled at her last night? The hallway felt quiet. Another thing out of place. Loxley knocked on Birdie's door. No answer came, so she knocked louder.

The door whipped open to the sight of Birdie's big, white housecoat. "God damn it, little girl, if you haven't bothered me again. What on earth do you want?"

"Are you mad at me?" Loxley's voice creaked when she spoke.

"Did you darken my stoop to ask me that? The Devil himself couldn't be bothered to tempt me at this hour."

"So you're mad at me."

"Of course I'm mad at you. Jesus Christ, save me from this moron..."

Loxley nodded. "Okay... Good."

She turned to leave when Birdie grabbed her arm, sending a chill up her spine. Loxley screamed and slapped away Birdie's hand. Loxley broke into ragged breath, hand wringing and tears. She hadn't expected a touch to frighten her so.

"I'm sorry!" Loxley blustered.

Birdie's lips stretched into a long smile. "Isn't this a treat? I don't believe you've ever apologized for anything. Is this only for the stupidity I've endured this morning, or the whole kit and kaboodle?"

"I didn't mean to react that way. Touching has me on edge this morning."

"Really? So if I was to slap the fire out of you, you'd find that extra frightening?"

Loxley swallowed, turned and walked away down the hallway. She'd almost made it to the stairwell door when she heard Birdie call, "You know what? The next time you bother me, I'll slap you. The time after that, I'm going to slap you. Maybe that'll put some sense into your crazy head."

"I'm not crazy," whispered Loxley, swinging open the door and climbing to the roof. She shook out the crackles as she went, the rhythm bringing her breath back into line.

She emerged into another greenhouse. It wasn't her greenhouse – that one was back home where Officer Crutchfield was her friend and Nora was alive. She'd fallen through the mirror in her sleep and found herself in a stranger's garden. She felt the pull of an invisible tether, coaxing her to go back to bed. This place belonged to strangers, and the further she got from her apartment, the more dangerous it would become. She'd read a book about bell divers once. They had to have an air hose that connected them to the ship, and if they lost it, they would die. They lived on top of the ocean every single day, but when they jumped into those waves, they crossed into a foreign kingdom.

She imagined a fish with a crown and scepter, and that made her chuckle a bit. The mirth drained away as quickly as it came. Something else bad was coming. She knew it as well as she knew the color of the sky, but why did she feel so sure?

Feelings don't always make sense, baby. They ain't supposed to.

"Shut up, momma."

Her work in the garden did nothing to ease her mind. Every plucked vegetable was stolen, no longer hers to take. This world's Loxley would be along any moment to kill her. She worked quickly, pruning the best jewel-toned vegetables and dumping them into buckets. Her grip tightened on her pruning knife, solid in her hand. Its hooked blade flashed under the rust spots like the sun passing behind clouds. When she'd finished, she wiped the dew from her blade, folded it and stowed it in the pocket of her coveralls.

Loxley usually returned all of her tools to a large

chest near the door, but today, she wanted to keep her knife handy. After she'd lined up all the buckets by the door, she stopped and stared at the tool chest. The pruning knife belonged there, next to the oil can, not in her pocket. She wished she hadn't stopped before leaving to think about taking the blade. The memory of Officer Crutchfield's touch rushed to the surface without warning, and she stepped over the threshold without further pause. After all, her routine was already shot. She may as well be able to cut a deserving throat if it came to it.

She loaded her cart and made for Vulcan's Bazaar. It was slow going, and the further she got from her home, the more she felt bile rising in her stomach. She had to take regular breaks, and she sensed everyone's eyes upon her. They knew something was wrong with her – that she didn't belong. She kept her head down and dragged onward. She reached the thin spot in the Bazaar and crossed without incident. No ghosts harrowed her passage.

Loxley reached her usual place and spread out her blanket. She didn't have a cash box, but she could make do with her pockets. Trading bells would ring soon, and she settled into her corner, starting to feel a little familiarity return. Officer Crutchfield marching for her at full speed threw all of that to the wind.

He seemed uglier than the last time she saw him. A rosy tint had washed his face, making his white hair that much brighter.

"Ma'am, you're going to have to move that," he called when he was about fifteen paces away. Loxley had never heard him take that tone of voice before, low and authoritative, devoid of any invitation. "You can't set up here."

"Officer Crutchfield, I'm just doing what I always –"

When he reached her, he took her behind the elbow and led her to her cart where her empty baskets lay. "All right, lady, let's pack it up. Come on. Let's go."

His touch offended her senses. She tried to jerk away, but he wouldn't let go. "Officer, I –"

"I don't care, miss. You can set up on the Bazaar like everyone else, but you can't set up here."

"But I always set up here."

He let go and took a step back. "Miss, you've got thirty seconds to move that stall into the legal zone. You going to do that?"

Her stomach burned. She wanted to scream at him, to hit him or to argue with him eloquently, but the words wouldn't come. She realized her hands were flapping, and she stopped herself, folding them in front of her and locking her fingers together. Her breath hissed through her teeth, and she focused on trying to speak.

He regarded her coolly, looking down his nose. He licked the inside of his cheek, and she remembered the taste of his spit with a shudder. She saw a knife, a gun and a nightstick. He'd never seemed so well-armed before.

"Well?" he said. "How does it feel to be treated just like everyone else? Not too good, is it?" He crossed his arms. "You had a big old hoot with me on account of your condition, but I think it's high time someone taught you what real life is like."

"Y-you," she paused, ashamed of her stutter. "You're mad at me."

"I ain't mad, Loxley. I ain't anything with you. We're done."

"You just wanted to put your fingers in me!" she screeched at him, much to the surprise of the bystanders.

"That's it, woman. You're fucking insane."

"You tried to hurt me!"

Officer Crutchfield glanced around. "Bullshit, Loxley. Now you need to keep your voice down or there are going to be consequences."

"Liar!"

"Goddamn it. I told you to quiet down." He put a hand on his pistol grip. "Miss Fiddleback, I'm seizing your cart for a city ordinance violation – soliciting in prohibited areas. All of the personal effects on the cart are now property of the municipality and will be auctioned off on the first of the month."

"You can't do that. You're the one who tried to hurt me."

"I can and I did. Now one more word and I'll arrest you for disturbing the peace."

If Nora had been there, she would have said something to change his mind. She could have made him understand how wrong he'd been, but Loxley didn't know how to talk to the policeman. She was so angry, but she could not craft that anger into anything of use.

He stood stock still, looking at her with his watery eyes and slightly pudgy, red face. He sniffed and scratched his nose with his glove, his other hand never leaving his weapon. He licked his lips and shifted from side to side. "Well? Don't feel like going to jail today?"

Loxley ran her fingers across the bulge of cash in one pocket and the knife in the other. She turned and began to walk away.

"Smart girl," he called after her.

"You're a bad person," she called back, before hurrying away.

Normal people would have cried at what he'd done, but she didn't. She'd cried the first time she lost the cart, but losing it again had been somehow expected. This foreign place grated on her nerves, and it seemed only obvious that she would begin to lose things that she found precious here. Yesterday, she'd lived in a self-contained place, fragile but nourishing in the most basic ways. Today, that was all gone, and she had begun to wither.

She heard trading bells ring from the Bazaar. It was too early to go to Fowler's by a few hours. The last time she'd showed up early, Don had told her she was looking for handouts and that she should work harder during the hours she normally worked. If she went there now, he might say that, or something worse: try to make her stop gardening like he had yesterday. She remembered the pay cut. Now she'd lost her place in the Bazaar, too.

She came to the corner where she normally turned to head up to the sixth ring and stopped. Fowler's was a few miles away, but it would not take her long to get there. She couldn't go home, though. She never went home. She worked for Don every day because he worked every day, and that was the way of things. Even when she got sick, she would come to work and he would make her sit in the back.

The foreign feeling of her world intensified as

she took a step toward her house. She was doing something wrong, taking a step like that. The bell diver reeled out her hose a little further. She began to trudge home, one foot at a time.

When she got to Nora's block, there was no sign of the ghost. Loxley could see the top of Magic City Heights, and she knew her bed waited for her. She imagined stripping down and wrapping her old, fuzzy blanket around herself. When she awoke, maybe she would appear in her own bed, in her own time – or she might awaken yet another world away.

She remembered how far she'd seen the ghost travel last night; Nora's corpse must have been in her apartment. Loxley peered around for the spirit. Had they moved the body? The ghost should have been waiting for her here. After all, the dead had nothing better to do. If someone had moved the body, Loxley might never find out what happened.

A ball of anger formed in her stomach at that thought. People disappeared in the Hole all the time. Nora would be one of the uncounted: a poor woman. People scarcely gave a damn about anyone, much less some nobody from the seventh ring. If Loxley didn't go looking for the truth, no one would.

She could go home and sleep until it was time to go to Fowler's, or she could see to her friend's corpse.

"Nora," she whispered.

The endless drone of the Foundry replied, but nothing else. Loxley's eyes darted about the shadows and her legs tensed, ready to fly at the first sign of trouble. She felt a little stupid, calling out to the ghost, but she wanted to know where it was.

"Nora," she said, a little louder.

She wilted inside and knew its eyes were upon her. She blinked, and it appeared a few yards away. Its knuckles popped as it flexed its fingers, and it ground its teeth together, its dead face burning with the desire to touch her. It raised its arms like a mother waiting for a child to run to it.

"Be calm, Loxa-lox," she said, a half tuned note falling from her throat as she exhaled. She clasped her hands together. Loxley shifted from foot to foot, considering what she was about to do.

Nora sunk down, regarding her curiously. For a ghost, it seemed awfully smart. Loxley had never found one so expressive, but it made sense because Nora was better than other people. Nora, who loved her; Nora, who treated her like no one else. Loxley waited for it to speak, hoping against the odds that it might actually be different than other ghosts, but that seemed a fool idea.

"I liked it when you hugged me, you know," said Loxley, swallowing. "I wish it had been you to kiss me, instead of that dumb Officer Crutchfield. I wanted you to kiss... I – I just wanted..." She spoke without comprehending, but her voice broke when she realized what she was saying. She searched its body, looking for some of the comfort she'd once found in its living arms, but its pallid, mottled skin was foreign to her now. "I'm not supposed to be talking to you. I'm not even supposed to be walking around here. This place isn't mine."

It straightened up. Did it understand her?

Her cheeks grew wet with tears. "I'm going to come find you... and I'm going to call some different policemen and we're going to put you to rest. So..."

She stomped the crawlies off her legs, opening and closing her mouth as she tried to figure out what to say next. Her throat hurt so much from holding back the flood of sobs. "So don't kill me, okay? I loved you. Don't kill... Don – D..." She got stuck on the consonant and shook her head.

Remember, ghosts can see you breathing, baby. If you ever get caught by one, you've got to hold your breath.

Loxley took a deep breath and held it. Nora's gaze snapped about as the thing descended into a state of near panic. It scraped its hands across its filthy clothes and beat its sides with shaking fists. It crept closer to where Loxley stood, but it dared not venture too far from its body. Loxley took ten steps to the left and let out her breath. Nora looked at her straightaway.

Loxley couldn't trust the police to do this job, not without some help. She had to find the body on her own; had to see it for herself. There was no one left who loved her. The cops threw paupers into the Founder's Fire when they died. Loxley couldn't let that happen to her friend without knowing what had happened.

"Okay." She sucked in a breath and made a break for Nora's building.

Loxley raced past the ghost without so much as a scratch from its wanting fingers. Her feet slapped the ground, and her lungs began to burn. She didn't look back. She wouldn't stop until she was in the lobby of Nora's apartment complex. The corner seemed so far away, and she willed it to be closer. Ten paces... five paces... She whipped around the side of the building and through the front door before the air came blasting out of her lips.

She was a fit woman from all her gardening, but she was no athlete. She doubled over, heaving, as spittle burst from her lips. A sudden nausea overcame her, and she ripped off her coat. It wasn't the run; it was the presence of Nora's ghost. This spirit really was different. She could feel its essence like a lighthouse, warning her away. It bled into her, biting electricity on exposed bone. Loxley stumbled to a wall, her exhalations catching in her throat. Her ears rang, and the pain nearly brought her to her knees.

Static crept at the corners of her mind. She shook it off as best she could and regained her bearings. Nora lived on the tenth floor. If the ghost could feel her as acutely as she felt it, she would never make it to the body. She glanced around for the spirit.

It stood just outside, watching her through the windows. She blinked, and it vanished.

Loxley yelped, tripping over her own legs as she scampered away. She hit her face on the tile, and lights exploded behind her eyes. With no time to lose, she took a breath and held it. She rolled onto her back and saw Nora, splayed across the ceiling: motionless, frigid eyes fixed on nothing. It lay there, hair stuck to the water-stained tiles against gravity's will, demonstrating its final state. Its corpse lips rested half-open, and Loxley could see a light misting of black blood on them.

It was trying to tell her something. It had to be. She struggled to her feet and bounded to the stairwell door. She managed to make it up one flight of stairs before taking a breath. Spots shimmered in her vision. A wave of dizziness passed through her, and she caught onto the railing for support. From the next landing, a little girl laughed at her. Loxley glared, and the child retreated into the second floor, slamming the stairwell door.

Loxley didn't know if spirits could hear, but she doubted it. Nora had been slow to appear in the lobby, and it hadn't moved to block the stairwell when Loxley had dashed into it. It wasn't a matter of speed, either. Ghosts didn't need to walk; they appeared without warning. Loxley took the stairs two at a time. She made it to the next landing before she had to exhale again.

Feverish goosebumps raised across Loxley's body, and Alvin Kimball's handprint stung like a hot brand. She had to lose Nora now, before she got too high into the building. There was another stairwell on the far side of the complex. If Loxley could reach it, perhaps the spirit would haunt the more obvious path. If she fainted and the ghost found her, she was as good as dead. She took another breath and threw open the door to the second floor. She sealed herself on the other side and allowed herself to breathe normally. The kid had run back to her apartment – good.

Loxley sprinted down the long hallway to the other side, then stopped at the far door. Her pulse throbbed where she'd hit her face, and she huffed, glancing back the way she'd come. No Nora, even though Loxley still felt the sickly influence of the corpse flowing into her. Without holding her breath, however, it was easier to overcome those effects.

She stood up straight and touched her forehead.

She'd split her skin on the tile, and her hand came back with blood. She wiped it across the front of her coveralls, the useless weight of the pruning knife rippling under the denim. No amount of violence could help her here. She sighed and pushed open the door to the second set of stairs. She poked her head out, and finding no sign of her pursuer, she began to climb.

She took the stairs slowly, stopping often to check her surroundings. She could not afford to be tired if the spirit got the drop on her. With each floor, the miasma of the corpse became less bearable. Nora hadn't been much older than eighteen, in the prime of her life and beautiful. She'd laughed easily, with a luminous smile and infectious energy. Loxley had never sensed the ghost of such a vibrant person, and it made her teeth ache.

She reached the tenth floor and grasped the door handle with trembling hands. She held her breath and turned. A dim hallway stretched before her, fluorescent tubes blinking, sickly and sad, in the ceiling. No people, and no ghost. Loxley stepped inside. She crept past a dozen or so doors before coming to ten-fourteen.

The door lay partially open, a sliver of light peeking out past the frame. She placed a hand against it, trying to sense what lay on the other side. Her bruises lit up, and she grunted, unable to keep her breath. Ants raced up and down the backs of her knees as she pushed.

Loxley would only remember a few flashes from this place: a cut metal chain, dangling from the doorframe; the bright, naked bulb of a lamp laying on the floor behind a ratty sofa; the way the shadow draped across Nora's body like a black cloak. The smell of urine and excrement.

A set of curled fingertips jutted out of the gloom, and Loxley could not stop the gentle humming in her throat. She reached down and picked up the lamp, holding it aloft to better see past the couch. Nora's body lay before her, twisted in the agony of her last moments. Matted hair, flecked with blood, bone and brain, shimmered in the light. Her shirt collar was torn where someone had grabbed her.

She dropped the light. Bile and breakfast rushed into Loxley's mouth, and she emptied her stomach into a nearby trashcan. She fell to her hands and knees, unable to move without gagging harder. She wished she hadn't eaten this morning. When her guts had nothing left, she heaved over and over again. Her belly subsided, and she pushed the can away, resting her forehead on the floor.

She needed to get up, find what she wanted, and get out of there.

Loxley inched closer to the body. She'd grown used to feeling a warmth in Nora's presence. As she wrapped her fingers around the corpse's shoulder, she experienced the bitter cold of dead flesh. When Loxley's mother had died, she'd touched the body once, then never again, because people should not be that cold. In her world, people did not feel like that. She wanted to leave and forget about the whole thing. Instead, she shoved her friend's body over, its hand flopping limply to the side.

A gunshot hole graced Nora's brow, fractured and tattered around the edges. One of the dead woman's eyes had drifted lazily left, while the other had remained fixed. Its lips, once pretty, seemed waxy now, guarding a dry mouth. A nasty bruise had spread across the body's cheek, struck with burst blood vessels like tiny lightning bolts.

A tear spattered Nora's face, and Loxley blinked hard as her vision blurred. She leaned over the corpse's chest and buried her head into its cold embrace. She grabbed handfuls of the dead woman's clothing and pressed them to her eyes, fighting the oncoming rush of sobs to maintain control.

"You're not supposed to be dead," she mumbled into the folds of fabric. "It should be me. You're so bright and pretty. I'm worthless."

What had she hoped to accomplish, coming here? What had she hoped to find? She'd said she would call the cops, but who would show up? Men like Crutchfield? They couldn't be trusted, and they wouldn't help. That left her on her own. How would she ever find the person who'd killed Nora, and what would she do when she did?

She balled her fists tighter, pressing Nora's clothes to her eyes until she saw stars. "Please get up. I want to go home."

She sat back on her haunches, sighed and opened her eyes. The ghost stood over her.

"No!" she screamed, as the spirit swiped across her face. Its hand passed through her, curdling her blood and twisting her with agony. The world spun, roaring with static. Loxley tried to take a breath, but the ghost grabbed her shoulder, forcing air from her as surely as an electric shock. Her skin cracked and sprayed blood under its touch, and over the pain, she felt a warm wetness under her shirt. She turned to run, but it seized her ankle, which folded up in an excruciating seizure, sending Loxley careening headfirst into the door frame. She struck her temple against the metal and rolled to the ground, dazed.

The static grew louder. Loxley tried to cry out, but the words wouldn't come. She scrabbled forward as best she could, clawing at the short carpet, but the ghost took hold of her hair and wrenched her head backward. The ghost's palm pressed into her spine, and Loxley arched her back, unable to move. For a moment, she became weightless, lifted into the air by death's freezing hands.

Her breath came in ragged gasps, and she tried to hold onto it, but it sputtered out of her in agonized screams. Her fingers curled under and spasms locked her arms into place. Loxley's world began to dissolve around her, consumed by the rush of static. She was losing control of herself. She was going to die here.

And with a harsh silence, the touches stopped. The far wall rushed to meet Loxley like a freight train.

CHAPTER FOUR
HOW IT WAS

NORA SLICKED BACK a tendril of hair as she mounted Jack. She moaned softly as she ground him into her, savoring the feeling of their bodies against one another. He leaned up to bury his face in her breasts, pressing them into his cheeks with his hands and breathing deeply of her. She couldn't stifle her chuckle.

He fell back to the bed, smiling. "What's so funny?"

"Again with the tits," she replied, without stopping the rhythm of their lovemaking. "I can't persuade you to sit still, can I?"

He caressed her nipples. "It's a nice view."

She pressed her palm into his chest. "Then relax and enjoy it from back there."

Because you're better when you're fast. Jack Grady wasn't a terrible partner, but he wasn't all that helpful, leaving Nora to do all the work. And if she didn't do everything for him, he'd take all goddamned night. She enjoyed some of it, but he was pretty lackluster on the whole. She only climaxed during foreplay, which was a rarity. He wasn't much to look at, either, with pale skin and a lumpy body. She could only imagine how scared he must be to come down to the seventh ring without the armed guard he got at the plastic factory – he looked like an engineer, right down to the dopey shirts he wore.

Nora leaned back and pushed her cleavage together. "Was this what you were looking for, honey?"

He swelled inside her, and she let out a surprised groan. He took hold of her hips, digging into her skin with his fingernails. His arms gained a strength she hadn't felt before. She pinched her nipples and bit her lip, and he went even crazier, his eyes locked on her chest. At first, she'd only meant to flatter him with little sighs and moans, but as he continued, she found herself actually wanting more.

For the first time, they came together. She wouldn't hold her breath for that to happen again.

She slid off him and fell to the sheets, panting. When she glanced to Jack, he looked like he'd sprinted a few miles. His eyes were wide, and he gulped the air as he lay flat on his back. He certainly wasn't a typical factory boy – soft body, soft hands and all the physical prowess of a lazy dog. She took a swig from the glass of water on the nightstand and coughed. She offered him some, but he refused. She tucked a towel between her legs and sat on the edge of the bed.

Nora opened her nightstand drawer, grabbed a joint and lit up. She sat and smoked for a few minutes, wondering when Jack was going to get up and join her. His breathing came to rest in the darkness, a steady in and out. Deep relaxation spread through her body with the bittersweet smoke.

She took a huge lungful and held it before breathing out. "I heard from the other girls that there were going to be lay-offs. Is that true?"

"I don't see how it's their business," he mumbled, half-asleep.

She curled up under his arm and put the joint to his lips. "I figure their jobs are their business. A lot of those girls are my friends."

"You figured wrong. You ever managed people, baby?" He placed a hand to his brow. "It's fucking unbearable."

About a million replies coursed through Nora's head. "Yeah. I can only imagine. It must be tough to decide who stays and who goes."

"Look, if they wanted to be doing my job, maybe they should have gone to college," he said. "I mean, no offense or anything."

"It's fine, baby. I don't think I could have hacked college." *Not without rich parents or a decent upbringing. Not when there'd always been a desperate need to bring food into the house.* Luckily, both of Nora's parents had stopped being a burden on her when they'd died young. She'd sometimes imagined attending the Baptist university on the first ring, but she couldn't ever scrape up the application fee, much less tuition. She took a long drag and pressed the joint to Jack's lips again.

He sucked upon the offering. "Seriously, you'd hate it. You've got the right idea just hanging out and getting high."

"I work pretty hard."

"No doubt, darling. You're probably my best."

She ran her fingers through his sweaty chest hairs. "For a multitude of reasons."

He looked down at her. "You know what the boys upstairs would say if they knew about us?"

"They'd say, 'Good job, Grady. Let me introduce you to my mistress, Heidi. Keep that shit under wraps and you'll go far here.'"

He chortled. "Yeah. You're probably right. I know for a fact most of them are getting tail on the side."

"See? It ain't so bad to be the boss."

He reached down and rubbed her nipple. "It's got its perks." He sat up, sliding back against the headboard and leaving her head resting on his naked lap.

She wasn't sure what he was expecting, but she certainly wasn't about to entertain him for another round. He pushed her hair aside to see her lips, and Nora did everything she could not to roll her eyes. She looked at him, and his eyes darted to his groin expectantly. She wrapped her fingers around his member and sat up to kiss him, squeezing tightly. Their lips parted and she leaned into his ear.

"You've got to be kidding, Jack. You want to go again after the performance you just put on?"

"You could get him going," he cooed.

"Maybe I want him to get some rest." *Because maybe once is enough for tonight. Because I'm high as shit right now, and I don't want you trying to break my damned hips again. Because I'm sick of your high-horse attitude.* "Because I want a real fucking in the morning."

"Suit yourself, gorgeous." He took the joint from her and pulled a massive drag off it before stubbing out the remains in the ash tray. "This shit is good. Where do you get it?"

"Little girl down in Vulcan's Bazaar."

"You want to pick up some more of it for tomorrow night?"

"It ain't cheap." Nora was lying. Loxley was pretty fair.

"Yeah, yeah. I'll give you a couple of bucks in the morning." Jack got up and shambled into the bathroom to piss. Nora heard him hock up a wad of spit to deposit into the toilet before he wandered back to bed, flopping onto his stomach.

She took her towel and dabbed at the sweat covering her stomach. Without a second thought, he'd come inside her. She wondered what would happen if he made her pregnant. He'd probably want to have it aborted, but what if he didn't? Would he take care of her? As she stared at his back, any sort of life together seemed fairly unlikely. Did he have any real feelings for her at all? No. If she got pregnant, he would fire her from her job and send her away. She'd be more trouble than she was worth.

It wasn't unusual for engineers like him to maintain stables of women. Young, single fellows who managed the factory had an easy time convincing themselves they had a right to fuck anything that moved. They'd go into town to look for women willing to work the factory floor, women who were half-starved already, and they'd expect a return on that favor. In most girls' cases, they might end up streetwalking without their jobs, so it was an easy choice to make. Nora felt lucky that Jack had developed a strong sexual attachment to her.

Of course, some of the engineers didn't care about getting laid every five minutes. Those men, inevitably, hired other men, mostly white boys and muscular blacks, never women like Nora. She couldn't imagine being hired for her actual skills.

At least the factory was better than the farms. She'd heard dark rumors about those places: that they ate you up and spat you out a worthless husk; that you were never allowed to come home. The Consortium operated all transports to and from the farms, and they would send trucks out at five am to pick people up, and four pm to take people back to the city. Problem was, quitting time was at five, and the rides were expensive, too. Once they had a person staying in the on-site housing, they'd deduct all kinds of things from a paycheck. They had booze to keep people stupid and lots of stranded women to spend money on. Men would pay to have the women stay the night with them. All the girls from the farms took to the streets when they came back – it was a life they knew too well.

Loxley wanted to buy a farm, not like the big Consortium tracts, but a small patch of land to call her own. How stupid was that? The Con owned half of most cities and all the land between. Loxley would be surrounded by desperate folk who worked the nearby land, subsisting on company cash. They'd rob her blind every chance they got. And if the Con decided they wanted her land, they could just steamroll her and be done with it, because they always got what they wanted, sooner or later. No man or government could tell them no. If her house caught fire, it would burn to the ground. If God scoured it off the earth with a tornado, she'd be lost and forgotten. No help would come for little Loxley.

Maybe help was what she needed, though. There would be robbers, hucksters and all manner of people out to get her. People in the Bazaar were always trying to trick her on account of her condition, and it would only get worse the further away they got from the law.

If she asked, Nora might actually follow her out there. Sure, Loxley was strange, but she'd basically memorized that one book on farming. Nora couldn't remember the last time she'd read a book at all.

Jack's breath had settled to a whisper, and Nora looked sidelong at him – dead asleep after a roll in the hay. They'd been at it for a few months, ever since he made a pass at her on his first day. How long would he keep this up? Until he got tired of her? Until she needed something from him? Their relationship held a malignant equilibrium, a delicate tension that threatened her way of life if it ever broke. He'd never hit her or asked for anything weird, so at least she had that comfort. There were other, prettier girls who worked in the kitting area. Maybe he'd jump into bed with one of them and all his clemency would disappear.

Life with Jack was reality. Life with Loxley was a stupid, girlish fantasy. She'd have to find a way to make it last with her boss, at least through this round of layoffs.

She curled up next to him, waiting for him to fall even deeper into slumber. She'd sneak out in time, because she didn't feel like waking up to his face in the morning.

Business Opportunities

NORA SLAMMED THE blade across the spool of blanks and wiped the sweat from her brow before pulling the spent tube and throwing it into a nearby bin. Her bonnet itched terribly, as it often did when she didn't get a shower. Her building had lost power that morning, a relatively common occurrence in her neighborhood, and the water had been icy from the winter's chill. She could still smell Jack's musk on her, mingled with the solvent stench of the factory.

She went to heft another roll of blanks onto the spool rod, and her hips complained. The stupid thing had to weigh a hundred pounds, and she'd overdone it the night before. She set it down, and it thudded against the concrete.

Loxley would be setting up in the Bazaar right about now. She had the right idea, with a cozy apothecary job and her tidy gardening income. Some people had all the luck.

"Nora!" She heard Jack's voice over the droning of machines.

He stood on a catwalk above her. She waved to him. He wasn't smiling, but then again, he never smiled.

"Come see me in my office," he called, and clomped away in the direction of the corner office.

"Oh, for God's sake," she mumbled, looking around for another worker. She spotted Elizabeth walking toward her and flagged her down. "Hey, Bettie!"

Her coworker looked over the machine. "Jammed again?"

"No, no. Jack wants to have a chat with me. Can I get you to re-spool it? I'd shut it down, but I don't want to hear Starla's bitching when I get behind."

"Jack wants to chat, huh? Going to keep your pants on?"

Nora snorted. "Not like that."

"Sure thing. Just don't let him close the blinds or I'll never get you back here." Bettie winked.

"Nah. I'd be back in five minutes," she said, slapping her on the back. "Thanks, sugar."

Nora rushed upstairs and into Jack's office, shutting the door behind her. The cacophony outside drained away, leaving blank silence.

"Have a seat, if you don't mind," he said.

Jack's place wasn't nice by any stretch. It had a rolled steel desk, beige, with rusty chips in the paint, and a single bookshelf, which contained five or six textbooks. She'd never seen Jack crack one open.

"What's the scoop, baby?"

He raised a finger. "Just a second." He picked up the phone and spun the rotary a few times. "Yeah. She's here. She can wait."

As soon as he hung up, Nora spoke. "I can't wait. I've got Bettie working the spool."

"You know you're supposed to shut it down when you're not at your station."

"Yeah, but then I get behind on the kitting later."

Jack sighed. "Bettie has her own job to do."

"All right. You want me to go tell her to shut it down?"

"No. It's fine."

She leaned back and folded her arms. He did the same. A good five minutes passed between them, counted on the beats of the factory. It wasn't the steady march of the steelworks, but an allegro dance, whirring between the conveyors and knives. She watched Jack, and he watched the factory floor from his window.

"What's this about?" she asked.

He took a deep breath. "Don't make a scene, and I'll help you out afterward."

That caused a knot in her throat. She began to wonder about all of the possibilities. She'd only begun to open her mouth to speak when the office door swung open. A tall, white-haired man in a cream suit breezed into the room, a smile on his face that didn't rise to his eyes. Only rich folks wore light colors in the Hole – too tough to keep clothes clean without money. Well coifed, nice teeth... important.

"Herb," said Jack, standing and returning the business smile.

"Is this her?" asked Herb, looking Nora over.

She stood, compelled by his inspection. His eyes lingered on her breasts, and the corner of his mouth twitched ever so slightly. Whoever he was, he was only a man, after all.

"Nora Vickers," she said, extending a hand.

"I know," he said. "Herb Duncan." He pressed his palm to hers, and his smooth skin surprised her. She'd never shaken hands with such a well-heeled creep. A quick squeeze, and he withdrew. "I can see why he likes you."

She swallowed. "I'm sorry?"

"Miss Vickers, are you familiar with Duke Wallace?"

Everybody knew Duke. The man was a Consortium vice-president, and a legend in his own right. He basically ran the Hole, as well as half the businesses in town. He built schools and houses, soup kitchens, hospitals, roads and bridges. They had a big, bronze statue of him on the fifth ring, and the man wasn't even dead yet.

"Yes, sir," she said.

"He just bought our little plastics company. We're a Consortium operation now."

Just like the rest of the damned Hole. Hell, just like the rest of the country. And why wouldn't the Con buy the factory? It was big and profitable, and some of the employees looked halfway happy. At least the buyout carried one big benefit: stability. If she could work, she could eat, and if she were willing to eat Con food, that paycheck would go a long way.

"Congratulations, sir." She looked to Jack, who put his hands in his pockets.

Herb smoothed an eyebrow with his thumb. "Mister Wallace is a decent man, Miss Vickers. A godly man. He runs things differently than I do, and one of the things he does not tolerate is managers having relations with their employees. Now I'm just as culpable as anyone, having turned a blind eye to it for years, but it's a new day around here."

"Excuse me, sir?"

"I'd rather you didn't play dumb. And before you

get the urge to go making accusations, it doesn't matter how I found out." He turned to face Jack. "What matters is that you knew good and well that this was immoral, and you did it anyway."

Jack froze under Herb's icy stare like a cornered rabbit. The older man raised an eyebrow, prompting a response, but the engineer had nothing to say back to him.

"Do you understand how disappointed I am right now, Grady?" said Herb, striding to the window. "You've only just gotten on board, and already we're having these kinds of talks. That's just silly. Don't you think that's silly?"

Nora stepped forward. "Mister Duncan, perhaps it's not fair to take it out on Jack. I mean, Mister Grady. He was just –"

Herb cut her off with a look, then went back to observing the workers below. "It may not be fair, but Mister Grady needs to understand that people pay the price for his foolishness. Now that he's gone and done what he did, I can expect him to do it again, can't I?"

"I don't understand," she said.

"You're fired, Miss Vickers," he replied, sharper than a knife's edge. He turned and made for the door, his crisp movements belying self-righteous anger.

"Wait, what?" She didn't mean to shout.

"Mister Grady will take you by your locker, then show you out. Next time, keep your legs shut, ma'am."

He slammed the door behind him, and Nora heard him storming off down the catwalks. For years, the hot shots around here had been collecting girlfriends, and now it was suddenly against the rules? When she spun to face Jack, his face had turned red.

"Nora, I know you're mad."

"Too right, I am! What the fuck was that?"

"That was... regrettable."

"Regrettable? Tripping into a mud puddle is 'regrettable.' Fucking you was a goddamned tragedy!"

"Look, I'm not happy about what happened, either."

"Is that a fact?" she shouted. "Well ain't that something, because you still work here!"

"Would you calm down? I said I'd help you!"

Nora swallowed her next twenty retorts. She knew they wouldn't do her any good, even though they bubbled around inside her, ready to spill forth at any second. He'd asked her not to make a scene, and now she needed help more than ever. Her arms and legs wanted to lash out on their own, so she plopped down in her chair and crossed them, for fear of punching everything around her.

Jack took a sip of coffee with trembling hands and set his mug down. "Duke called me this morning – me, personally."

"I'm glad to hear you boys are getting on so well."

"Just shut up, Nora. You need to hear what I have to say."

She gave him the floor to speak.

"Duke is a fairly..." Jack searched for the right word, "eccentric individual. He didn't have you fired because he's mad at you. He had you fired because he's mad at me." He paused, in case she wanted to shout at him some more. "He's sympathetic to your situation, and he wants to meet with you. Called just to say that."

"Is he going to give me a job?"

"I don't know. That's certainly a possibility, if you play your cards right. He wants to meet you this afternoon at three, in Gilman Park on the fourth ring."

Nora clucked her tongue. "So until then, I'm just twisting in the wind? Your big promise of help was delivering a message that the big boss man ordered you to pass along?"

"No. I've got some advice for you that'll change the outcome."

"Out with it."

"I've heard about these kinds of meetings with Duke. Go home and get your Bible. Read it."

She sat up a little straighter. "Is that a threat?"

"No. I... Nora, I'd rather not go into too much detail, because if Duke finds out I did, I'll lose my job and you won't get a bit of sympathy from him. Can you please listen to me?"

She mulled it over. Bring a Bible? That's it? That was the life-changing advice she'd been promised? Herb and Jack, she'd spared these two idiots a bit of righteous rage so she could hear, "Go home and read the Bible." Nora climbed to her feet, brushed off her pants, and smiled.

"Fuck you, Jack. I'm ready to go get my stuff, now."

She waited for him to fire back, but he pulled on his jacket, walked to the door and ushered her through. She followed him without saying anything else.

On the factory floor, all eyes turned to the pair as he led her toward the locker room. She was a criminal on her way to the gallows. Bettie blushed, turning back to her machine. Why wouldn't she make eye contact? What did she know? Suddenly, it all made sense.

"It was you, wasn't it?" Nora blurted out, not a moment's pause between her mind and her lips.

She feigned tightening her bonnet. "What?"

"Answer me, bitch. You made that crack about Jack closing the blinds. It was you... You told them about me and Jack."

"Nora, I —"

"Ladies, let's be civil," said Jack, stepping between them. "We don't want to say anything unwise, do we?"

"Butt out, company man," said Nora. "This don't concern you." Then, to Bettie, "Ain't that right?"

Bettie drew up to her full height. "You best listen to your boyfriend, Miss Vickers."

"That's right," said Jack, putting a hand on her shoulder. "We're just going to head for the gate without another word."

"Yeah," said Bettie. "Walk away."

Anger flared in Nora's stomach, and she body-checked her former boss as hard as she could, sending him stumbling into a trio of waste bins. She took a long step forward and brought her palm across Bettie's face, turning the woman's head with the force of her slap. Nora reached out and grabbed a handful Bettie's hair through her bonnet and yanked as hard as she could. She had a dim awareness of Jack's voice, but she shut it out, smashing her fist into Bettie's nose over and over again. She saw a thin spray of red, and it stayed her hand for just a moment – long enough for Bettie to clock her and take off running across the factory floor. Nora shook the lights out of her eyes in time for Jack to wrap her in a bear hug from behind.

"You better run, you fucking cunt!" she screeched after Bettie.

"Nora!" he shouted into her ear, hoisting her from behind. He'd never shown that much energy in bed.

"Fuck you!"

"Get ahold of yourself! It wasn't Bettie, damn it!"

Nora loosed a stream of secrets about Jack she never would have told anyone. She kicked and bucked for a minute or so until the raging flames dwindled within her. She'd drawn a crowd: the fifteen other ladies from kitting, among others. She shrieked as loudly as she could, and eventually, two men from security showed up brandishing truncheons and confused expressions. When she finally fell still, she spun to find a ghost-white Jack.

"What? You said you wanted a wild girl, Mister Grady. Wild enough for you?"

He shook his head. "I am so sorry I ever got involved with you."

She chuckled. "Yeah, I'm sorry I let you touch me, too. Want to try again?"

He brushed himself off and pointed Nora out to the guards. "Get her out of here. Break her nose if she resists."

They exchanged confused glances, but inched closer, anyway. Nora showed her palms, even as she lowered her head. "No need, boys. Just show me the door."

Moments later, Nora found herself standing at the gate, unburdened by a job or a man.

The Green Thumb

NORA SHUFFLED THROUGH the streets, her feet heavier by a few hundred pounds. She tried not to think about the fact that she had recently drained her savings to pay for a bit of dental work, or that she held her last forty dollars in her pocket. If she didn't have a job before money ran out, there were only a few options for women. She'd always been so careful never to be this broke.

She didn't have to go into hooking. She could try for the steelworks or the mines, though she'd heard of bad things happening to girls in those tunnels. That all assumed anyone would hire a skinny thing like her, anyway. Maybe she could head up to the mission on the fourth ring, but that place would be full already. If you weren't in line when they opened their doors, you didn't get food. She'd tried once, when things were tight but not this bad, and starving folk crowded her out without fail. Food would have to wait until tomorrow.

As she wandered up the ramps to the eighth, and then the seventh ring, no plan of action materialized. Rent was due in a week. She'd been thrown out of the factory without a paycheck, and if she went back, they might arrest her.

She wiped her nose and sniffled. Folks were staring. She kept her eyes on the street and put one foot in front of the other. Soon, she found herself walking toward Vulcan's Bazaar. Loxley would be there. The quiet girl didn't understand Nora, or at least she didn't seem to, but she was a sweetheart. A sweetheart would be just the thing.

Nora arrived at the tin-roofed street after a half-hour, the hustle and bustle of the market in full swing. She understood why Loxley hated the place, full of clanging, banging misanthropes, hawking everything from scarves to guns. She crossed under the shade, and the neon of the place seemed to flare up, assaulting her eyes. It would be a strange person who willingly stayed in a place like this, she thought. Then again, a job was a job. Who was she to judge?

She wound down through the bazaar to the side street where Loxley set up her shop. A person could see the impromptu garden spread from the main thoroughfare, but only if they were really paying attention. Loxley sat cross-legged on her blanket, engrossed in the same book she always read, her eyes darting across the page as she mouthed the words contained therein.

Nora took a deep breath and straightened up. She didn't want Loxley to see her like this. The poor, touched girl wouldn't understand. She blinked and rubbed away her tears, then smoothed out her shirt. She tried on a smile, and though it fit poorly, she managed to wear it. She strode over to Loxley's blanket, her false confidence boiling over. Loxley didn't look up, or even notice her. She probably could have grabbed the woman's cash box if she'd wanted.

Nora leaned over her, doing her best to block out the sun. "What's at the top of page thirty-three?"

"Don't know," said Loxley, turning to page thirty-three. "Oh. The end of a paragraph about rotations: '... through dissimilarity between seasons, recouping lost soil nitrogen reserves.'"

"Ain't exactly poetry."

"Not supposed to be. It's not a book of poetry." She said, not taking her eyes from the page. "Why'd you need to know what was at the top of the page?"

Nora chuckled. Sometimes Loxley could be frightening, making her wonder how she ever got home by herself or navigated traffic or lit a stove without dying. Other times, she could be kind of cute. Burying her head in a book was an endearing trait. "You going to say hi to me, Loxley?"

Her eyes finally lifted from the page and a big grin spread across her face. "Hi!"

"Give us a hug, girl," said Nora, getting a warm, strong embrace. "Now some sugar," she said, and received a wet kiss on the cheek that sent a little shiver down her neck. "There's my little green thumb. Business good?"

Loxley took her seat and put down her book. "I almost didn't make it here today. There was a ghost."

Nora frowned. She'd heard this kind of talk before. She worried constantly about her friend's sanity, but another side of Nora feared the woman wasn't crazy. Nora believed in ghosts; The Hole was a dark, wicked place where they might do well. She'd once told Loxley that she might see spirits on account of her condition, but Loxley disagreed, saying it came from her blood, not her brain. Whatever the truth, Loxley spoke about ghosts as matter-of-factly as one might speak about spiders and snakes. Nora had gotten the sweet Loxley when she said hello, now she got the scary one.

"He was in the way. I couldn't get past."

"What? Like over there?"

"You don't believe me, do you?"

She preferred not to. The whole idea gave her the creeps. "We've all got to see the world somehow or another. If it's real enough for you, that's what's important," she said with a smile, but then worried she might have sounded patronizing.

"It's true, whether you think I'm honest or not. They like me more than anyone else. Used to be the same with my mother."

At least Loxley always spoke her mind. Nora crossed the blanket, wrapped her arm around her friend and kissed her head. Her friend's hair smelled like dirt, like the grassy patch near the house where Nora grew up.

"Of course they like you. You're such a sweetheart."

Loxley rested her head against Nora's neck, and a wisp of her hair tickled bare skin. Butterflies kicked up inside her stomach, but she forced them back down. Loxley was a good friend, but even so, Nora savored her warmth, snuggling closer.

Nora squeezed her shoulder – soft skin for such a hard woman. "I'd like you if I was a ghost."

"Why'd you come home in the middle of the night last night? I thought your shift was over at eight."

The butterflies fluttered away. Had she seen Jack? "You saw me coming home?"

"I had to pee, and I looked out and saw you coming home. It was two thirty-five," said Loxley, looking her in the eye. Nora wasn't sure what she was thinking, but it sounded a bit like an indictment.

Nora didn't want to tell her all of the awful things that had happened between her and her boss. She wouldn't understand. The tall woman had spoken a few times before with Loxley about sex, but it had mostly been as a warning about men. Now, she couldn't wrap her head around how to talk about Jack.

"I was having a drink with the foreman."

"Must be a slow drinker."

Slow other places, too, she thought. "He did take his time, yes. He likes to talk."

"Did he talk about plastic?"

If the conversation continued, she was going to end up talking about losing her job, and that was the last thing she wanted. Nora hated to cry, especially in front of others. Her heart raced, and her cheeks flushed. "It wasn't interesting. Work stuff, darling." She pulled out her wallet. "I'm going to need a bag of weed."

Nora changed the topic to Loxley's day, and they talked for another hour as Loxley recounted the tale of Birdie. Soon after, she started going on about her greenhouse as though it was part of the story. Nora loved that about Loxley: her ability to ramble from one topic to the next without so much as a hint of segue or division. Most people thought in a straight line, journeying from one topic to the next, but Loxley was a massive web of thoughts, each one interconnected to all others. She wasn't stupid or crazy; she was incredible.

Nora tightened her embrace, pulling Loxley closer. She rested her cheek against her friend's, listening to the sound of her breath as it became her mousy voice. She'd always admired the shape of Loxley's neck, hidden though it was behind a wall of strange behaviors and hangups. The tall woman closed her eyes, feeling the rise and fall of respiration. What if she kissed her?

Nora had never felt that way about a woman before, but she'd never met someone like Loxley, either. It was like the quiet woman had come from somewhere else, somewhere beyond the Hole, where people were sweet and strange. When they'd first met, Nora didn't like her; she seemed crude and unpredictable, and perhaps dangerous. Over the past few years, Nora had learned a little more about what lay inside her friend, and how to predict problems and work with her.

Nora opened her eyes. She'd been touched by many men, but never once had she felt any real love. Did she love Loxley? She imagined the feeling of her lips brushing Loxley's soft skin, and it didn't disgust her. It didn't even frighten her. She leaned in a little closer to Loxley's throat and bathed in her earthy scent.

But what if this was all just a reaction to Jack? Certainly, Nora had used other lovers in the past to satisfy her needs, be they sex or companionship. At the time, it usually seemed like the right idea, but as the relationship progressed, something always went haywire. What if she was doing it again – just using Loxley for some kind of immediate need? She couldn't do that to her friend.

Loneliness and outrage over the new twists in her life stoked the fires in Nora's heart, and her resolve began to melt. She ached to try for a more intimate touch, and as Loxley spoke, Nora inclined her head, moving in for a kiss. She just needed to feel something.

Loxley shot to her feet as though electrified, knocking Nora over as she did.

Oh, God, what have I done?

"What's wrong?" The tall woman stood, her pulse clattering in her veins. She took Loxley's hand, but her friend jerked her fingers away with surprising force. Loxley's eyes flickered about, looking anywhere but at Nora. *I've fucked up the last important thing in my life. Please don't hate me, baby. I shouldn't have tried. I'm so sorry.*

Loxley bent down and reached for her cash box. Nora stepped forward to help, but her friend screamed and scrambled back, clutching her wrist where Nora had grabbed her before. The box smashed against the ground, springing open. *Come on, Lox. Just look at me and see that I'm sorry. It's okay, baby. Calm down.*

Nora dropped down to grab the cash before it could blow away, and by the time she looked up, Loxley had gone sprinting off into the Bazaar – a place she should never be. Nora called after her, doing everything she could to gather up the loose bills, but by the time she'd sorted Loxley's affairs, the woman was long gone.

What a fool. She knew Loxley was special, but she tried to take advantage of her anyway. And for what – a moment of comfort? Her nose burned, and her eyes watered. She stuffed the bills back into the box and slammed the lid.

"God damn it all, Nora!" she shouted.

A few heads turned her way, but no one lingered. Vulcan's Bazaar contained many stranger things than an irate woman. Nora looked over the spread of the cart, the blanket and produce. It would take an hour to clean it up, and she'd probably do it all wrong, anyway. Loxley was far too meticulous for Nora to understand her system.

Nora turned and saw Burt Crutchfield headed her direction. They'd met a few times before, and she knew him to be a friend of Loxley's – the cop who let her set up outside the market. She waved him down.

"Miss Vickers," he said. "Watching the store?"

"Not exactly, Officer," she said, picking up the cucumbers and placing them into baskets. "Loxley had an episode and high-tailed it. I think I might've caused the problem."

"I'm sure you didn't mean to. Can I call you Nora?"

"Sure. You still want to be called 'Officer'?"

"Burt." He patted her on the shoulder with a rough hand. He had the build of an old factory man, his muscles covered with a blanket of fat. Underneath it all, there might have been a terrifying creature, but it lay buried beneath whiskers, kindly crow's feet and a liver-spotted head. "Now, Nora, the most important thing we can do for Loxley right now is find her. Do you know where she's going?"

"Probably to her next job. Third ring."

"All right. Thing is, I'm on patrol. If the captain found out I left..."

"I get it. I'll head up there, but I'm still not sure she's going to want to see me."

"What did you do?"

A guilty weight pressed down upon Nora's shoulders. "I don't know. Nothing. She just flipped out."

"Yeah, sometimes they can do that."

"You've seen a lot of cases like Loxley's?"

"All the time. You see them starving in the gutter every winter, no idea they need to get shelter and warmth."

"She worries me. I think she's going to hurt herself one of these days. I don't like the ghost thing."

"Tell me about it. I had to hold her hand all morning, just to get her across the damned market."

I'd give anything to be holding her hand right now. "I'm sure she appreciated your understanding and hard work."

"Could've fooled me, but I did it anyway. If I was in it for the gratitude, I wouldn't be a cop."

He looked off into the distance, almost as though he was posing, and Nora took the opportunity to roll her eyes. "I could come back later and pick up the rest of Lox's stuff this afternoon, if you want. I live near her apartment."

Burt winked. "No need. I'll take it to her, myself. Wouldn't be seemly for me to let a lady do all that hard work."

Loxley was smaller than either of them, and she pulled that cart every day. It would be heavy, made even more so by the weight of Loxley's goods, and the cash box would be a valuable thing for an unarmed woman to carry around the seventh ring. The box bulged at its edges with bills like an overstuffed sandwich. Nora had jammed them in there without much thought, but now she realized she didn't have a key to correct her mistake.

The Consortium book lay open on the pavement where Loxley had left it, and Nora reached down to pick it up.

"What's that?" asked Burt.

Nora closed it, looking at its worn cover. "Something very important to Loxley. Hopefully, she won't run away again if she sees me holding it."

CHAPTER FIVE
MY SHEPHERD

"MISTER FOWLER?" NORA held the pay phone receiver to her ear. It had been beaten up pretty badly the week prior, but it still worked. It was, in fact, the only fully operational piece of technology in her apartment building's lobby. Lights flickered overhead, and the building's elevators mainly served as outhouses for drunken vagrants.

"This is he. Can I help you, Madame?"

She clutched the handset tightly, its housing creaking. "Is Loxley Fiddleback at work today?"

"Yes. She seems a bit out of sorts." A static-riddled sigh. "I'm guessing she's gotten up to some trouble, then?"

"No. No trouble. I'm a friend of hers from the Bazaar, and I was just checking to make sure she made it to you."

"I see. So no problems with her, then?"

"No, sir."

"She's busy, but I can put her on the phone if you'd like," he said, though it was clear he didn't want to do so.

"No, thanks."

"To whom am I speaking? Should I give her a message?"

"No, sir."

"Well, all right," he said, terminating the call.

Nora hung up and trudged upstairs. It was a long, tiring walk, but one that she made every day, so she'd gotten used to it. She unlocked her apartment and took in the sweet, caramel smell of old cigarette smoke.

The room before her lay in perfect order. She'd cleaned it last Saturday, in case Jack wanted to come by. The first time he'd seen it, he'd made a crack about the rent being cheaper because she split it with all the rats. She'd felt humiliated, like some dumb slut he'd scraped off the bottom of the Hole, so she'd cleaned it up, and he never made the crack again. But now, she felt even more ashamed, because she'd changed the way she lived for that garbage.

A messy room was full of spirit: cramped, with few defined edges, like a warren. Her clean apartment had served her needs, but now it felt like someone else's place. Jack's place, to be precise.

She kicked the door closed behind her and flopped onto her couch. She absentmindedly fingered the edge of Loxley's book, feeling the cottony softness of weathered paper. She rolled onto her back and held the volume high. It looked unfriendly, and when she opened it, she found it full of ridiculous charts and data sheets. Row after row of bland numbers lined its pages, an impenetrable mass of information. She rifled through it like a flipbook, watching one esoteric topic shift to the next.

A picture flashed by, and she turned back to it. Cotton rows stretched over the earth as far as the eye could see, punctuated by a tiny farmhouse in the distance. She tried to imagine what that would look like if she spun in all directions – green earth, unobstructed by any obstacles, no other humans... just her and God under the pale blue sky. The more she dug into the thought, the more she felt the nervous heartbeat one gets looking down from a great height. She'd grown up in the Hole, always looking up, never looking out. She felt comfortable when embraced by civilization.

She shut the book and tossed it onto her coffee table. Loxley was never going to get out of the Hole, and even if she did, Nora wasn't going with her. Loxley was the kind of woman who could forget the rest of humanity at a moment's notice and disappear completely. Nora needed everyone, the pounding of the city's Foundry in her ears like a mother's heartbeat to an unborn baby. She hated herself for it.

After her parents died, she'd built a life for herself. She couldn't just leave that.

She looked over her shelves. She didn't have much, but she had a few nice pictures and a fine china teapot that had been in her family for three generations. Her Bible's leather spine caught her eye, and she sat up. Most folks in the Hole had Bibles, and unlike her, other people read them. A missionary had given it to her when she was younger, telling her God loved everyone. She'd had trouble buying that story at the time, but she kept the book because it was more beautiful than most of her possessions.

She walked over to the shelf and picked the tome

up. It wasn't real leather, and some of the gold lettering had flaked off the cover. The pages were also gold-edged, and she let it fall open in her hands. The page stock was thin, like cigarette paper, and one desperate night, she'd torn out a leaf to roll a joint. It worked exceptionally well, but the guilt had eaten her for days afterward.

Its words were arcane, and she had trouble following its meaning, but they had a soothing cadence and authority to them. Plenty of people in the Hole turned to the Good Book for guidance, but it wasn't the sort of volume a person could just pick up on their own for a bit of light reading. Then again, Darius and Geraldine down the hall couldn't read at all, and they loved their Bibles.

Prideful people turn to themselves when they should turn to God and his Word, a preacher had once told her. *When you can't carry on, you'd be a fool to seek your own help. God loves you, and he wants to be there for you.* Jack, the factory, the Hole, her dead family and all the thugs who made her life a living hell exhausted her. Could this heavy book really give her rest? If God loved her, he was most definitely alone in that.

She turned to the missing page, its ragged edge jutting out like an open wound. She ran her finger down the middle, regretting what she'd done to it. She stopped to read a verse.

5 Trust in the Lord with all thine heart; and lean not unto thine own understanding. 6 In all thy ways acknowledge him, and he shall direct thy paths.

She swallowed, and her hands fell to her sides, overcome. Numbness traveled across her skin like passing clouds. She felt so tired of being alone in a crowded city, but the preacher would have told her she wasn't alone.

"Fuck it," she said, shutting the Bible and grabbing Loxley's volume from the coffee table. "We'll try this your way, big guy."

Nora folded the two books under her arm, locked up her apartment, and headed downstairs. This Sunday she was going to go to church, and she'd ask the preacher what to do. *Go home and get your Bible. Read it.* Those were Jack's words. He was a spoiled sack of shit, but he'd been trying to help her. She'd been crazy to make such a scene on the factory floor, but she couldn't help that she had a temper. Preachers claimed to be able to help with that, too.

It was a lot easier to trek downstairs than upstairs, and she felt a little peppier on top of it all. She was going to be a better person. She was going to do things right, and in turn, she'd be rewarded for it. She'd make it to her meeting with Duke. Maybe he'd want to help her, and maybe he'd already heard about how things went down at the factory. Either way, it was out of her control. A lightness fluttered in her heart at that idea.

She burst from the lobby doors, her feet striking the ground like lightning bolts. No one was asking her to be clever, only to be good. She could do this.

The Preacher

NORA HAD JUST finished her climb up the ramp to the fourth ring, when a boxy, black limousine came rumbling up alongside her on the street. Chrome gleamed along its body lines. Polished, tinted windows perfectly reflected the sun, blotting out everything inside. Atop the front grill was a statue of an angel ascendant, her arms outstretched to embrace the infinite.

Not a speck of ash or dust rested upon the car's waxed body. That, alone, told Nora of the importance of the man inside the vehicle. It had to be Duke. Incredibly, the car came to a stop next to her. As the window rolled down, she reminded herself not to gawk, and to smile as pleasantly as she could.

To say the man on the other side of the window looked friendly would be an understatement. When people spoke about their departed grandfathers in saintly terms, whitewashing every nasty detail, they were speaking about men who looked like him. He had a bushy brow, overflowing with snowy hairs that curled upward toward a white coiffeur. His lips were made for smiling, as though he felt proud of everything he looked upon. His cheeks had inflated with weight and age, and a pinkish blush graced them.

His eyes, slate gray and clearer than glass, told her he'd once been beautiful, too.

"Are you Nora Vickers?" he asked with a tenor's voice.

She'd never spoken to a man in a limousine before. "I am."

"You're prettier than your picture." He held up an old factory photo that had been taken of her two years prior. She wasn't quite scowling in the picture, but it was clear she didn't want to be there.

"Anyone would be prettier than that, sir. Those pictures make mugshots look downright artistic."

"I see," he chuckled. "Miss Vickers, my name is Duke Wallace, and I've been informed of your situation. You seem like you could use some help."

"Mister Wallace –"

"Duke."

A vice president of the all-powerful Consortium wanted her to call him by his first name. She added that to the list of weird shit for the day. "... Duke, call me Nora, and that would be an understatement. What have you heard?"

"Not much, except that your employment was untenable in your current position."

She crossed her arms. "That's right. I was fired. They said it was in some part because you bought the factory, and that you wouldn't appreciate the kind of relationship I had with my manager."

He scratched his chin. "They're right. I don't approve, but I also don't blame you for it. Young women are prone to mistakes and all men are prone to... sin against their own bodies." He cocked an eyebrow. "I also heard you attacked one of the other workers. Is that true?"

She felt shame well inside her. "Yes, sir. I wasn't thinking straight. That job was all I had, and I knew Bettie was the one who reported me. I lost my temper."

He nodded, his smile returning. "You and Mister Grady are the reason you were fired. Not Bettie."

"I understand."

"Good." He opened the door, and she saw plush carpet and wood paneling accenting a leather interior. "Would you care to come to my house this evening to share a hot meal with me and my family? It's up in Edgewood, so we'll provide sleeping accommodations."

Nora looked up at Fowler Brothers' Apothecary in the distance. She clutched Loxley's book tightly in her hand, and she wondered if she ought to tell Duke she needed to return it. But what if Duke became annoyed? He might drive away, and she'd never get the chance to find out what he was after. She had a once-in-a-lifetime chance to dine in the richest house with the most powerful man in the Hole.

She needed time to explain to Loxley what had happened. She couldn't simply run in and hand the poor girl her book before dashing back to the car. Loxley would think her angry. Nora needed to be forgiven. Perhaps Duke would understand if she told him she needed time to explain herself. Then again, he was a busy man.

Perhaps Nora didn't deserve forgiveness yet. Maybe she needed to wait. Duke was a sign from God.

"Miss Vickers?" he prodded, scooting to the other side of the car to make way for her.

"Sure, I'll come with you," she replied, climbing inside.

She climbed out of the rotten, moist cold of a southern winter, and into another world. The interior of the limo smelled of fine whiskey and linseed oil. When she slammed the door, the sounds of the city vanished, even the rhythmic pounding of the Foundry. She rubbed the seat with her fingertips – creamy cowhide with gold stitching. A sparkling cross had been embroidered into each headrest.

Her fellow passenger wore a stark, white suit – usually a terrible decision in the Hole. Nothing beautiful could last in this place, and the smart folks wore gray, to cover up the sweat stains and occasional ash. His green cravat lay tucked into his collar, a sapphire glimmering in its folds. Rings encrusted his fingertips, and he held a cane that had been polished to a mirror shine.

"This is some car," said Nora.

"That it is. I had it specially made in Liverpool and upholstered in Milan. The thread comes from Jordan, and the acacia panels come from the Sinai Desert."

"This thing came from all those places?"

"My dear, before it even drove a mile, this car had seen more of the world than I ever will," said Duke. "I've rarely ventured out of the southeast."

"Can't you afford to go? You know, see the world?"

"Aside from the sweet hereafter, the south is the closest thing to paradise." He crossed to the other side of the cabin, sitting opposite Nora with his back to the chauffeur's window.

Nora actually snorted. She covered her mouth, trying not to laugh, but Duke seemed to take it all in stride. She smiled, trying to regain her composure. "I've never met anyone who'd call the Hole 'paradise.'"

"Then you've never been to Bellebrook."

"What's that?"

"My home." He knocked on the window behind him, and it rolled down.

His driver was a young black woman, her hair

tucked up under a cap. When she turned to ask where to, Nora noticed a hare lip in her profile.

"Marie, why didn't you get out and help Miss Vickers into the car?"

"I apologize, Mister Wallace," she replied. "It won't happen again."

He smiled and shrugged. "Don't apologize to me."

"I'm sorry, Miss Vickers."

Nora blushed and waved her off. "No, it's fine. I don't think anyone has ever held the door for me."

Duke's eyes twinkled. "Is that right? You're in for a treat this evening, then. Nora, we can go to your apartment and fetch one thing. What would you like to get?"

"One thing?"

"Yes. What kind of person are you?"

Nora thought about a change of clothes, or maybe a toothbrush, or even a condom. She'd only just met Duke, but she had no way of knowing his intentions. He might've only broken her up with Jack so he could have her for himself.

But that was nuts. With cash like his, Duke could have any woman he wanted in the Hole. He didn't need some fancy tricks to get into anyone's pants when he could just buy their pants. He watched her intently, never breaking eye contact as she contemplated her answer. She couldn't help but feel like this was a test. As she tightened her grip around her books, it came to her – the reason why Jack had told her to go get her Bible and read it.

"I have everything I need right here," she said, turning over her stack of books to reveal the Scriptures.

His smile faded, not to a look of disapproval, but one of contemplation. "You carry it with you?"

She nodded. This was the first time she'd held it in over a year, and she felt disingenuous.

"Do you read it often?"

She closed her eyes and sighed. If Duke really was sent to her by some greater power, she couldn't lie. "Almost never."

He folded his hands over his cane and rested his chin on his fingers. "And what changed your mind?"

"As you might have guessed, I lost my job today... and I hurt my only friend. I had to turn somewhere for help."

"You made the right decision, Nora. Marie, take us up to Bellebrook."

"Yes, Mister Wallace."

The Gardens of Babylon

THE GRADUATIONS TO luxury astonished Nora with each ascending ring. She'd been up to Edgewood a few times, but only as a curious party. The restaurants made her stomach ache for their fare, and the dresses in the windows of shops depressed her. Women walked the streets with a breezy, casual stride, never huddling to themselves, and folks stopped to talk on the corners. When someone from down below came to Edgewood, the locals would stare.

The car glided silently over the freshly-paved streets, smoother than a marble on a piece of glass. She stared out the window, and as they got to Duke's neighborhood, she saw something she hadn't seen before: grassy medians.

Much of it had gone blond for the winter, but she still longed to get out there and walk, barefoot, over the soft leaves. She couldn't imagine how wonderful it must be in the summer, and she decided that, when spring came, she'd come back to this place.

"Those are flowering cherries," said Duke, pointing to some unappealing, dead trees lining the road. "In April, they grow pale, pink blossoms that fall like snow, but only for a week. The pear trees about a mile up shower white blossoms for a little while longer, but I think they smell like rot, so I don't plant them on my land."

"Even though they stay pretty longer?"

"Perfect but short-lived is far better than flawed forever. Do you know why I want you to come have dinner with Esther and me?"

"No, sir. I know I'm good company, but..."

"But you were hoping to talk about your employment situation."

"Yes, sir." Had she really been so transparent?

He chuckled. "Don't you 'sir' me, girl. You don't work for me anymore."

"It's true. I don't work for anyone. Left me with more than a few frightening questions to answer, I might add. There ain't a lot of jobs for people like me."

He poured two glasses of liquor and passed one her way. "Not a lot of jobs for people... you mean women? I disagree. You just don't know where to look."

"Oh, really?"

He gestured to the tinted window behind him.

"Marie there was living down on the eighth ring when I found her. She seemed sweet enough, so I asked her if she wanted to work for me. She makes good money."

"Are you offering me a job?"

He raised his glass to her. "You know, I might be doing just that."

Nora's heart thumped. Could this actually be happening? "What would I do for you?"

"I don't know, yet. I'll pay you fair, though. More than old Jack is making, I can assure you." He took a long sip, draining about half of his glass. "I need to meet all the others before I decide who's doing what."

"The others?"

Nora was distracted by the car coming to a halt, and she turned to see where they were. A tremendous lawn stretched before them, where marble statues of angels frolicked around a gushing fountain. A colossal manor spread over the back edge of the property, its white parapets and crenellations shining in stunning contrast to an azure roof. A wide brook ran across the property, and as the car passed up the drive, it had to cross a bridge to approach the manor proper. Pairs of weeping willows stood vigil on either side of the road, their leafless branches drooping like ragged strands of hair.

"This is your house?" she breathed, straining her neck to see the rooftops through the windows as the car pulled to a halt in front of the main doors.

"This was my father's house, actually," said Duke.

Marie parked the car and ran around to Duke's side as quickly as possible, opening the door for him.

"Do you see where Miss Vickers is sitting?" asked

the man, and Marie nodded her head. "Always open the lady's door, first."

"Yes, sir, Mister Wallace."

"Well, go on, then."

Marie rushed around to the other side and opened Nora's door, ushering her out of the car.

"I'm sorry," said Nora. "I keep getting you in trouble, Marie."

"She ain't in trouble," called Duke, easing out of the other side and coming around to them. "She's just got to learn how things work. You're doing a fine job, Marie."

The chauffeur gave a demure nod. "Thank you, sir."

"Quite welcome," he replied, extending an elbow to Nora, who took it. Duke had a strong arm for an older man, especially one as rich as him.

He led her up the steps and Marie rushed to open the door for the both of them. Nora could not help but feel guilty at the doting of this woman. It was one thing to give a job to a downtrodden soul from the eighth ring, but it was another to ask her to serve another downtrodden soul from the seventh ring. Nora wanted to say she could hold her own doors, but she was afraid of offending Duke, who seemed perfectly at home in these circumstances.

As the front doors swung wide, Nora forgot all thoughts of humility. Hardwood halls over polished marble floors opened before her. Dozens of life-sized portraits adorned the walls, and chandeliers twinkled on the ceiling. Their footsteps carried through the open space, and she suddenly felt quite small. From somewhere, she heard many voices in conversation.

Duke laid his hands on her shoulders with a quick squeeze and began to remove her coat. "I want to be the first to welcome you to Bellebrook."

Nora's heart jumped at his quick, friendly touch. Was he being a gentleman, or did he have something worse in mind for her daily 'job?' She pulled her arms out of the sleeves, and he quickly passed it off to Marie, who took it and scurried away. Nora sighed as she relaxed. She couldn't stop waiting for the other shoe to drop; sooner or later, she was going to offend Duke.

The older gentleman came alongside her and offered an elbow, escorting her down the hall. The distant conversation grew to a din, and soon, she realized she could hear dozens of women's voices. As they rounded the corner, she saw a huge parlor full of ladies from all walks of life. So this was what he'd meant when he'd said, "meet all the others."

Most of them looked poor like her, their clothes a little worn, their makeup smudged. Several of them were clearly hookers; grease paint made them appealing in the streetlight, but became an oily palette in the sun. Mixed into the group were a few pale-looking folk from the higher rings, clearly unsettled by their company. These looked to be housewives and the like, and they congregated with some curiosity in one corner of the room.

"Who are all of these people?" asked Nora.

"Folks just like you, my dear. Women in trouble, women with difficulties. I've been bringing them here over the past day or so, feeding them, offering prayer where they'll have it."

Nora finally understood: she didn't have a new job;

she had a chance at a new job, competing against all of these women. She shook her head, feeling so stupid for not seeing it earlier.

"I see."

He drew up, his chest puffing with satisfaction. "And late tonight will be a feast, in honor of those who get to stay."

"And who would they be?"

Duke grinned. "You're a beacon, Nora Vickers. I do hope you've brought enough oil to keep that lamp lit. Please join the other guests. We'll be serving cucumber sandwiches in a few minutes."

She couldn't tear her gaze away as he wandered off. What had, at first, sounded like a fairy tale job was now some nutcase's idea of charity. Lamps? Feasts? She'd been a little scared when it was just her, but looking over all these other people made one thing abundantly clear: there was nothing special about her.

She stalked into the makeshift party, the stares of several women hot on her back. Some of them wore ill-fitting clothes, clearly on loan from the estate. Many of them sat quietly, unsure of what to do with themselves, while others clustered together in forced conversation. An undercurrent of desperation ran in the air, subtle but taut as a guitar string.

A man came and asked her if she wanted anything to drink, and she asked for a sweet tea. She felt like apologizing for the inconvenience, even though it was his job to serve. Within moments, she was sipping a cool, delicious drink, her nerves somewhat calmed.

She scanned the crowd again, looking for anyone she knew amongst the faces. They were folks of every color, but not one woman stood out as familiar. She spotted a man loitering near the far door, his arms crossed and a bored look upon his face. He clearly hated being there, and she took him for a minder. He lacked the formal clothes of the help, and his muscular frame was far more akin to one of the factory boys.

The group of housewives suddenly tittered with laughter, and Nora wondered what they were saying. She wouldn't get any more information standing about, and she wanted to make the best of this chance. Certainly, the ladies of the lower rings weren't talking. Nora knew their look well – stay down, never self-identify. Those who stood too tall in the bottom of the Hole became targets. Nora screwed up her courage and headed for the only active conversation in the room.

One of them was clearly the life of the party, slightly prettier and more gregarious than the others. She shot a curious glance as Nora approached.

"I'm Nora." *Remember to smile.*

The chatter halted as all eyes came to rest on her. If she'd been looking for information, she certainly had a way of stopping it.

"Emma," said the leader, offering a hand. "From three."

"Seven. Pleased to meet you. Some party, huh? More like a wake in here."

"I suppose most of y'all folks are naturally shy."

"I'm afraid I don't follow."

Emma grinned wanly. "Folks from the lowers." Her compatriots nodded and grunted their assent. "Not much for talking."

Nora thrust her hands into her pockets, trying not to scowl. "Yeah. It's tough down there."

"Tough everywhere. That's the best reason to be cheerful. Don't you agree?"

Not tough on three. Never on three. "Uh, sure. So what brings you here?"

Emma cocked an eyebrow and crossed her arms. "I'm afraid I don't understand. A car, I guess," she said, and the others giggled.

"No, I mean... do you know why you're here?"

"Do you?"

Nora's gaze swept across their faces. She was clearly the most entertaining sport to be had, and they all watched her with a mixture of condescension and unease. She'd only been speaking to them for a few seconds and already, she harbored an intense distaste.

"Lost my job," she said. "Down at the plastics plant."

Bitter smiles emerged and Nora's hackles rose. She wasn't sure what she'd said, but the others clearly disliked her for it.

"My husband passed recently," said Emma. "In fact, I think that's pretty much the case all around. All new widows." She gestured to her companions.

"All of you?"

"Yeah. Like I said, it's tough, everywhere."

"My condolences," said Nora. "Did he know Duke?"

"I think all of our husbands worked for him in one way or another." She looked to one of her group. "I forgot to ask. Did yours, Cerise?"

The woman nodded quickly.

"Yes," continued Emma. "All Consortium boys."

"How recently?" asked Nora.

"Recent enough." Emma craned her neck. Her eyes looked a bit red. "I'm not sure I want to talk about it, if it's all the same to you."

"I don't mean to be rude, but all of your husbands died close together. Isn't that a little strange?"

"Aren't you just a little detective?"

The other women chuckled

Nora swallowed. "I'm sorry. I just thought –"

"It's fine, darling. I can't expect you to understand the scope of Duke's operations. I've heard he has something like a hundred thousand people working for him. We're just the crop of widows from this past year."

"I get it."

Emma took a step closer. "Now that you do, maybe you could see fit to run on home. Some of here actually need Duke's help... Some of us didn't only lose a job."

"Excuse me?" said Nora, stepping back.

"I think I was pretty clear," she replied, with a sarcastic wink and turned her back, blocking Nora from the rest of the group.

Just that morning, Nora had about torn Bettie's head off with her bare hands; now this tiny little slip of a woman thought she could talk to her like the damned help. She wondered how Miss Glamorous would enjoy a fist into her kidney.

Still, fuck this place. Fuck these people. She'd been so stupid to come here. She wasn't going to get the job, not going up against those self-righteous bitches.

Her eyes traveled back to the man at the door. He wasn't half bad looking – maybe a little spooky. He was supposed to be watching them, but he looked less like a shepherd and more like a wolf. It was hard to blame him, though. Nora looked at one of the teaspoons on a nearby end table and thought it would go for a pretty penny at the Bazaar. Everyone else here had to be thinking the same thing.

He turned and looked right at her. Her stomach flipped. He had a pitiless, hard face, and he didn't soften in the way people normally did when they saw her. She gave him a coy smile, her hands coming to rest on her hips. After a moment, he smiled back. He gestured for her to come over, and she obliged.

"You called?" she asked as she approached.

"And so I did. What's your name, sweetness?"

"Nora Vickers. Call me Nora." She extended a hand, and he shook it, his skin surprisingly soft.

"Hiram McClintock. Head of security." He opened a tin of pastille mints and offered her one, which she declined.

They indulged in small talk for a few minutes, but Hiram was surprisingly bad at it. The weather, the goings on and politics of the Hole scarcely interested him. He'd been to the plastics factory only once, and he didn't know any of Nora's old co-workers. She could get him to talk about Duke easily enough, and Hiram didn't seem to have a taste for the man. He was happy enough to converse on his boss's proclivities, none of which were exciting, only a little annoying.

He sighed loudly. "You enjoying our party?"

"Not sure what to make of it."

"It's all bullshit. Read your Bible. Sleep overnight. Don't try to fuck him if he talks to you too long."

She flinched at his swear. It seemed out of place here, like a fart. "And then I get to work here?"

"Yeah. Though I've heard you might be a special case. Anyway, it's his 'ten virgins' thing. Did he give you the speech about lamp oil?"

"Not exactly."

He gestured to a passing maid with a plate of cucumber sandwiches. "You could be living the dream. Grand, ain't it?"

"How much do they make around here?"

"Decent. Better than factory wages, but a bunch of them have to come up together from the eighth ring every day. Probably two hours each way, all told. Leaving before sunup, home after sundown. Poor bitches live their jobs. Not to mention Duke takes an hour of everyone's morning to have a devotional." He crunched his mint. "Everyone except me, that is. Someone has to watch the homestead."

"Oh."

"Of course, you could live on the grounds in the servants' quarters. That's exactly as fun as it sounds."

"Don't you live on the grounds?"

"We got a special deal, Duke and me. He doesn't come to my house, and I watch over his. I got a cozy place on the edge of the estate, and being head of security, I've also got the only key."

Nora shook her head. "Why are you telling me all this?"

"Because you look like trouble."

Nora cocked an eyebrow and smirked. "What sort of trouble?"

"The kind of trouble I like. You want to see the rest of the house? We might end up somewhere fun."

She frowned, surprised at his offer. She looked around the room at the other women. They looked either scared or self-righteous, but not one appeared to be in control of her surroundings.

He chuckled. "Or, you know, I could go find you a serving tray. You'd probably look cute in one of those outfits."

Nora made eye contact with one of the maids. The serving girl looked anything but happy, and her professional veneer faltered for a moment. Nora nodded at her, and the girl nodded back before continuing about her tasks.

Nora leaned in to whisper in Hiram's ear. "I'm not sure I like where this is going. I just broke it off with another boy, and I think I need time." Then, she patted him on the shoulder and took a step back. "But, thank you all the same."

"Your loss. I know where Duke keeps the good booze, so come find me when you get bored."

"He got into some in the limousine on the way over. And here I thought all you Baptists were tea drinkers."

"Every church has their own rules. That's the point of being Baptist. Besides..."

"Besides?"

"Never said I was a church-going man. You have a good day, now." Hiram stuffed his hands into his suit pockets and sauntered off.

CHAPTER SIX
WHAT SHE FOUND

NORA WASN'T CUT out for society life in any way, much like the other women. As the day drifted on, they began to filter out through the front doors for one reason or another, failing to stay for dinner. Marie the driver would depart with one, only to return in time to pick up the next woman. Some of them had children to care for. Those were always the saddest, because Nora knew they needed the job, but Duke clearly required all of a person's time in order to help them.

The big fellow himself was in and out at odd moments, checking and chatting with everyone. His booming laugh carried through the halls like a marching band, as though he was deliberately raising his voice to warn others of his approach. He proved to be sweet, too, and she saw him send every woman home with three crisp hundred dollar bills and a hearty handshake.

It was a good interview process for servants, trying to see who would remain civil, who had too many obligations and who would rather have a few quick bucks than stay on for a real job. Nora knew he'd have to pay well if he wanted to keep his silverware in the drawers. He made the rounds to each woman in turn, offering many questions, always listening intently to the answers with sparkling eyes.

Nora's thoughts continually turned to Loxley. The poor girl would be distraught over what had happened that morning, and Nora wondered if she would make it home all right. She always worried about her friend's trip home, though. The seventh ring was a dangerous place, and Loxley seemed such easy prey. Nora flipped open the beaten old farming book and looked through its tables. Loxley had learned everything from this confusing book, and she worked hard in that garden of hers. She was smarter and stronger than Nora by a long stretch. Loxley had never gotten wrapped up with stupid boyfriends, and she always made her rent.

Perhaps Nora should have been more worried about herself.

"May I join you a moment?" came Duke's voice.

She put the book on the table next to her Bible. "Absolutely, sir."

He picked up the manual and rifled through it. "I haven't seen one of these in years. You know I started out on one of the Con farms?"

"I have trouble believing that."

"Because of my standing and properties?"

"Because farmers are some hard men. You don't seem like a hard man."

He laughed and leaned in. "When I was young, I believed only in myself. I did what I wanted, when I wanted, to whom I wanted. Not much better than a thug, really. A lot of us farmers were like that. Those places are more like prisons than jobs, and you cross the wrong person, you don't shovel fertilizer. You become fertilizer."

Nora folded her arms, pretending not to be surprised by his sudden candor.

"Thugs are very flexible people, my dear. They have no code but survival – no morals but to take what they can." He sniffed loudly, then steepled his fingers. "While I was working there, I met a missionary: Preacher Vernon. Vern used to sneak into the farms with about a dozen of his flock and try to make life better from the inside. He held prayer meetings, vigils and the like. The Con didn't appreciate that sort of behavior because thinking of God makes men turn away from prostitutes and alcohol: two things the company needed to keep the men in line... and in debt.

"Vern knew the Con didn't forgive trespassers, and so he kept a strict cover, working the fields with us in the mornings and praying with us in the evenings. If they caught him, that's sovereign land, so they could do whatever they wanted with him, you know. Not like anyone could stand up to the Con, their land or no." Duke picked up her Bible, running his thumb over its faux-leather cover. "Over time, Vern taught me that some things were right, and some things were wrong. 'Iron sharpeneth iron; so a man sharpeneth the countenance of his friend.' I was a flexible man, soft of character and will. I *became* a hard man, forged by the hand of God, and he made me inflexible. Do you understand my point?"

She cleared her throat. "I think so."

She had trouble imagining the old-timer working in those sorts of conditions. She saw no evidence of a difficult life on his pampered face and chubby physique. When she looked at his hands, she saw traces of the man he had been. Thick, strong fingers graced meaty palms, like a factory man's. She looked back to his slate eyes, sure that he must have been something to look at back in his day.

He set the Bible down. "It ain't that hard if an old fool like me can understand it."

"Vern... What happened to him?"

"One of my bunk mates sold him out. Said he 'didn't like Vern's uppity attitude.' I think the company gave him five hundred dollars for that information. The Con caught Preacher Vernon and strung him up, along with six of his men."

She grimaced. "I'm sorry."

"Don't be. The good pastor is with our Father now. He's a martyr and a saint in my sight."

"And what happened to the other man? Your bunk mate..."

Duke patted her on the knee. "I've had to ask forgiveness for a lot of sins, little lady."

"I, uh..."

"That's not really proper conversation, though, is it? By now, you've no doubt a better understanding of the nature of your stay here?"

"You want another maid."

"I want more than that. I want to take care of those in need. I don't want to see a good woman such as yourself turn to unsavory means of employment."

"I don't think that's likely. I'm sure I could land a job somewhere else."

He chortled. "Nora, you've already been in the oldest profession. You may have only had one client, but the things you did for Jack weren't out of love, were they?"

She flushed. She considered slapping him, but hesitated. "I did what I had to do."

"I know, sweetheart, I know... But you do understand that sort of service might be required again if you got a job somewhere else down there in the factory rings. It's a tough life, and ladies like you have to do a lot of bad things to get ahead. I can pay money like you've never seen for your time. I'll protect my investment, because I'm not just looking for maids."

Nora perked up. "That's good, because I don't dust very well."

"You didn't strike me as the type, no. Is it safe to say I've piqued your curiosity?"

"It has been piqued for a while."

"Ten virgins were supposed to greet a bridegroom with lamps lit. Five of them were wise and brought with them extra oil. Five were foolish, choosing not to bring more than what their lamps held. When the bridegroom was delayed, the foolish lost their lights, and begged for help. The wise virgins sent them to merchants, and while they were gone, the bridegroom arrived. He took the five wise ones to his wedding feast and shut the door on the others."

It took all of Nora's concentration not to roll her eyes after what Hiram had said. "The wise didn't share with the others?"

"Not at all, because you can never save a soul from foolishness. No matter how much oil you offer them, it will never be enough, and then there won't be any for you."

"Is that the point of the story?" she asked. She suddenly worried that she might have sounded a little belligerent and added, "... sir."

"We'll never be able to save everyone, no matter how hard we try." He looked over the other women in the room. "I think you'd do well to remember that, and keep your lamp filled with patience, in spite of what I've heard some of the other women say to you."

Her eyes narrowed. "Wait, you've heard them say something?"

"Patience, Miss Vickers, will always be rewarded with attrition." With that, he stood and walked over to Emma and the group of widows who'd treated her cruelly. He spoke to them in hushed tones with a polite smile, but the message became clear when he passed each of them a few hundred dollars. When Nora looked back at the door, she saw Marie waiting patiently for them, her misshapen lips curled into a smile.

The widows hadn't been trying to hide their conversation with Nora when they'd chastised her, but they'd still been reasonably private about it. No one else could have heard them over the other quiet voices in the room. Nora thought hard about who else had come near – any maids or servants, perhaps even Hiram – and she couldn't remember anyone being privy to the altercation. How did Duke know?

Nora was no stranger to gossip around the factory floor, but this was far too much. While a certain amount of intrigue could be pleasing, she began to imagine listening devices or lip readers watching cameras. Perhaps some of the women in the crowd were plants, put there to spy on the others. Perhaps that would be her job before long.

It felt good to see Emma get a bit of comeuppance, but Nora wondered what the woman would do for a job. Hopefully, the widow had some family she could ask for help. The woman's face was ashen as Marie escorted her from the premises.

Duke winked at Nora as he strode past. "Do stay for supper," he said, patting her shoulder.

That was the last straw. She was going to keep hanging around until she got a free meal and a few bucks, but that was it. She wasn't going to play these games. Duke seemed to have some idea about her that simply wouldn't do.

She saw Hiram out of the corner of her eye and looked back to find him grinning. He pushed off the corner and languidly made his way to her. "Everything you expected?" he drawled, clucking his tongue at the end.

"How did he know?"

"We'd better take a walk if you want to talk about that, sugarpop." He offered her his arm.

So much misery and disappointment lay bottled in a single parlor. The others around her were truly wretched, and whatever job Duke wanted to offer, she wanted no part in it. They'd been there for hours, with women afraid to speak too much or ask to take a piss – a flock in need of leading.

She stood and took Hiram's arm. Maybe he could show her the way out after they were finished talking.

A Conclusive Interview

HIRAM LED THEM through the colossal hallways of the house, each corner a new wonder. She saw statuary and paintings. Ornate carvings of angels and demons danced along each panel of wood through clusters of ivy leaves. She couldn't imagine living somewhere like Bellebrook. It had an uncomfortable magnitude, much in the same way staring at the night sky came with a fear of falling upward. Her ferryman silently plodded forward, not looking once at her.

They strolled through an empty ballroom and out of doors onto a veranda. Nora looked out over the backyard and gasped.

Just two or three trees stood between her and uninterrupted fields that ran on for miles and miles. The earth swelled and rolled with patches of fence before becoming obscured by the blue haze of a cool winter's day. The clouds in the Bellebrook sky were not like those anywhere else in the Hole – not a rising column of steam from the Foundry, soaking in the sun that reflected off the alabaster houses of Edgewood. Rather, soft white giants rolled across the horizon, unfettered by the rows and rows of buildings that usually ringed Nora's sight.

The scale of the house paled in comparison to the scale of the world beyond. At the edge of the grounds, she saw Hiram's place: a small stone cottage with wavy glass windows and an electric line running out to it. He probably had the best view of all.

"Close your mouth, Nora. You're letting flies in."

She glanced in his direction to scowl, but returned her gaze to the beauty beyond. "He wakes up to this every morning?"

"You can see why he doesn't want to go into the Hole too often. All that petty shit down there drives him crazy."

She felt a deep relaxation spreading through her. "Yeah."

This was the farmer's sky, Loxley's sky. Out there, for miles around, there were men who were little better than slaves, but they still awoke to glory above them every single day. She'd seen the world outside once or twice when she'd ventured up to Edgewood in the past, but she'd never considered owning the sight of it for herself.

"There are listening devices in every room of the house," said Hiram.

"I'm sorry?"

"You asked how he'd heard you. That's how he did it. There are microphones planted everywhere, disguised as lamps, statues, plants... you name it. Hidden cameras, too. We host a lot of parties at Bellebrook."

"Why?"

"Why the cameras and such? Or the parties?"

"Why listen in on everything?" she asked.

"Because the richer you get, the more dangerous things are. Duke didn't get to the top by just making friends."

The rush of the view faded, and her heart sank back into place. This all seemed too much for her. She didn't need to be a maid somewhere like this... but Duke had said he wasn't looking for that.

"Duke told me he wasn't interviewing me to be a servant," she said. "What did he mean?"

"Why don't you ask him, yourself?" he replied, pointing behind her.

The big fellow strode across the veranda, lacking a bit of the showmanship he'd carried through the parlor – more businesslike. "I see you've decided to take a walk. I believe I told you to be patient."

A little anger flashed inside her. "I've been sitting around all morning. Maybe I was tired of playing that game."

"Even if it might cost you the job?"

"I'm a smart girl. I can find another."

Duke smiled and turned to Hiram. "Miss Vickers and I have to discuss her future here. Stay close in case she decides to leave."

Hiram nodded and slunk away.

"What did you mean by that? You going to try to stop me from walking out the front door?" asked Nora.

"Not at all." He pointed to one of the rocking chairs arrayed across the veranda. "What's going to happen is this: I'm going to go sit in one of those chairs. My offer is sixty thousand dollars annually, with a cash bonus for any good performance. I expect that you will make over a hundred thousand on a bad year. I am not asking you to work as a maid. I am not asking you to take off your clothes."

"And what are you asking?"

"It's God's work. I'm sorry, but secrecy is still of utmost importance. If you agree to the job, I want you to come sit down next to me and we'll begin our discussions. It's good money, and it's an important job where you can make a real difference in your life and the lives of those around you. Don't take the offer if you're uncertain, though – I take dereliction of duty very seriously. If you don't want to come sit with me, go talk to Hiram over there and he'll sort you out. I'll give you a meal and two thousand dollars just for visiting me today."

Two thousand dollars. Nora could eat for half a year on that if she planned it right. She started to ask another question, but Duke turned and walked to a chair, sat down and pulled a fat cigar from his pocket. She watched, still reeling from his offer, as he clipped the tip and lit up. Her eyes darted to Hiram, who shrugged.

What the hell was wrong with these people? The offer was incredible: five times what she was making at the plastics factory. The base pay alone was way higher than Jack's, and who knew how many of those cash bonuses she could get? She could move up from seven, make a life for herself somewhere cozy and happy, and maybe find someone exciting with whom she could settle down. Then again, maybe the job would provide the excitement, and she'd long for someone boring.

The strange interview process, the bargain and its secrecy still frightened her. She couldn't imagine what the hell Duke was going to ask of her, but she knew the Ten Commandments well enough. They'd been the only part of the Bible her father drilled into her before his death. Duke wasn't going to call it "God's work" and then have her go around murdering and stealing. It would be all right.

Hiram gave her a self-satisfied smile. He certainly approved of the situation, not that he struck her as a shining example of the Lord's way.

Her heart thundered in her ears. She stood at the edge of tumultuous waters, and here was Duke, beckoning her forward. She lifted one foot off the ground, its sole electrified. Duke might ask her to do anything, but he was a Christian, right? His whole day had been spent showing her the practice of his faith, to show her he was a good man.

She put her foot down in front of her. Then she took another step forward, and another. By the time she reached Duke, she'd built up such an anxiety that she needed to sit. She plopped down in the rocker next to him and sighed, her eyes wide.

"You made the right decision, girl."

She looked at him. "I'm going to take some convincing."

"Let's start with a history lesson."

"Con ain't sent me to school."

"I know it, because the first question any child would ask of the Consortium would be... what?"

The thought about it. "I guess I'd ask why they run everything."

"Of course you would. Everyone would. And the answer is anything but pleasant. I didn't learn it until college, and even then, I failed to grasp its realities until I'd been working for the Consortium for a good, long time."

She waited for him to continue, partially out of

deference, partially out of nerves. Her heart had yet to slow.

"In the late 1800s, ours was a country of opportunity for the right men. We'd torn ourselves in half over just war, and the North strove to repair ties with the South. And you know what the South was? A glistening jewel in the American crown with no facets to capture her beauty. She had no factories, no good labor force and none of the political realities of the burgeoning labor unions."

"Labor unions?"

"Yes, my dear. Thanks to Allan Pinkerton, we needn't worry about those anymore. Now, three men: Andrew Carnegie, Thomas Edison and John Rockefeller decided that they had a direction for the country—a vision of a free-marketeer's utopia. They merged their efforts, and together with a few nudges of Congress, they were able to establish monopolies in most sectors of our economy. In 1910, they chartered the Consortium, which spun tendrils into every aspect of mundane life. And seventy years hence, the Consortium still stands as a testament to the power and greed of individual men."

"You're talking like you don't like the Con."

"That's because I don't. Good business and godliness don't often overlap." He smiled. "You ever been to Atlanta?"

"Never been out of the Hole."

"You're going to be getting out a lot more, dear heart. Atlanta is a city of troubles, and I need you to open some doors for me over there."

"What do you mean?"

"Just like here... just like *everywhere*, it's controlled

by the Consortium, but I sense an ill wind coming for any company folks." He took a few short puffs to kindle a long one. "I have a few operators in the city's labor movements, trying to pull them in the right direction, but I feel like things are going astray. I need you to get in there, work amongst them as one of their own, and report back with critical bits of information: people's whereabouts, their intentions, et cetera. I need to know which way the winds are blowing, so that when I act, I don't look the fool, you see?"

"You want me to snitch for you?"

"That's one way to look at it. If you don't understand the scope of what I'm doing, I can see how you'd think that, but make no mistake, I'm here to bring the glory of God to all the cities of the South."

"I'm not sure how I'd be helping you do that."

He glanced at Hiram. "You may as well know the whole story. Bright girl would figure it out after awhile. You know the Con owns the land we're built on, right?"

"Of course. Sort of. You own this house."

"But I pay taxes on the land, so I don't own it. Nashville, Atlanta, Jackson and Mobile – they ain't any different. But, you know, I've seen what the Con can do to a place. I know the kind of soul suffering that goes on around here, and I can assure you, it's worse in Atlanta. I've seen children kill one another and I've seen starvation take a lot more bodies than that." He stared out over the distant fields. "I want to take all these flocks and lead them back into righteousness. I want to make a new nation in the glory of the Word, and we'll show the whole world what the light of Truth can do. You understand me, sister?"

Her stomach turned ice cold. She thought of Preacher Vernon and his men, strung up and buried in some godforsaken unmarked grave. "You're crazy. That's just... just crazy. The Con owns everything, you, me, the government... You aren't the mayor, but everyone knows you run this damned – dang – place... and you want to kick them out? Aren't you a VP or something?"

"That's just it, Nora. I know everything about them. All their emergency protocols, all their weapons locations, all their food storage, their critical infrastructure, power, hospitals and such – I'm an expert. I might be the only man who could pull off something like this. That's why I need you."

She regarded him, searching for a joke, for some kind of play in his face. Instead, she found only zealous determination. He wanted her to spy for him? She could barely keep a set of friends in the Hole. And what if she were found out by the Consortium? She had about as much chance against them as a rabbit against a coyote – better just to keep her head down and hope no one has noticed her.

This had to be a test. Sure. She'd heard of such things: the Con setting one person up to take all their friends down, too. Duke must have thought she was part of some kind of labor movement or something – maybe a union – because if he was actually plotting, he was a dead man. All the Consortium needed was one sniff of conspiracy, and they'd send their armies down here to raze Bellebrook to the ground.

"Duke... sir, can I make a phone call? I haven't told anyone where I am."

"You're not going to tell anyone about your new job, are you?" he asked, producing a roll of bills and placing it in her palm. She'd never held so much money in her life.

She gave him the smile she'd used on Jack a thousand times. "Of course not. I just want to tell my friend that I won't be home tonight."

"That's fine, dear. Hiram? Take Nora to my office and let her use the phone." He closed her fingers around the cash. "I trust you understand that discretion is of utmost importance."

"Yes, sir." *Goddamn right it is.* The Con was going to rip him to pieces when they figured out his game, and she wasn't going to be collateral damage when they did.

Hiram gestured for her to follow him, and the pair made their way back into the house. She noticed far less of the extravagant works of art as she passed through the halls, and Hiram kept grinning at her.

Finally, she stopped, and he turned to look at her.

"What?" he asked, not taking his smile off for a second.

"Did you know he was going to offer me this?"

He moved in close to her. He smelled of fine tobacco. "Of course. I helped pick you myself."

"So that's what today was about? Hiring a spy?"

"Nah. We're still going to hire some maids, too."

She folded her arms. "I still don't get it. Why me? Why not you?"

"You're nobody, no offense. You come from nowhere. People die down there every single day, and people cry for exactly that long – a single day. Your lives barely matter to anyone, which means a bright girl like you, with a little training, can go anywhere we need her to. No one has ever heard of you."

"And no one will care if something happens to me."

"That's about the long and short of it."

She looked at the door and motioned him away. "Can I be alone?"

"You're not taking this as well as I'd expected."

She stared at him until eventually, he chuckled and left. She sat down in one of Duke's cushy chairs and ran her fingers over the top of her roll of bills. She thought about carrying it down to her apartment on the seventh ring, and how some of the men that stalked about there already gave her predatory looks. Just existing made her a target for them, and now she had a boatload of cash.

Duke wanted to send her into the lions' den. Wasn't there a Bible story about that too? She couldn't remember. People in Atlanta would be looking for her when things went wrong – Consortium thugs with their black cars and shiny pistols. They'd want to know who'd been meddling in their affairs. What if Duke got caught out in the open and needed a bargaining chip or a scapegoat? The whole reason for her to be there was because he was afraid of doing it himself. He wanted her to set working folks in Atlanta up for a fall, and she couldn't shake her discomfort.

The overbearing, posh decorations of Duke's office weighed down upon her. She'd never seen anywhere so fancy in her whole life. The big man could change hundreds of lives with a snap of his fingers, and she couldn't even keep a lousy job. This was like a fight between gods, and if she stuck her nose into it, she'd wind up dead for sure. She knew who would win in the end, too. The Con *always* got their way.

The ivory telephone sat, gilded and beautiful, on Duke's polished hardwood desk. She didn't have to use the telephone. She didn't have anyone to call. Loxley didn't own a phone and Jack couldn't see her anymore. Perhaps she'd only wanted Hiram and Duke to think she wasn't as small of a presence as they seemed to believe.

She thumbed the rubber band on the bank roll. She'd have to give it back if she reneged on the agreement – years of pay just wasted. She sighed, stood and walked to the door, swinging it open to find Hiram patiently waiting on the other side. He made no attempt to disguise the fact that he'd been listening in.

"Take me back to Duke," she said.

"As you wish, princess."

They wandered back through the halls, and she finally started to understand the house's layout – not that it mattered, since she'd never be coming back here again. They found Duke as they'd left him, reclining on the back porch in spite of the cold.

"You get things squared away with your friend?" he asked, his breath fogging the air.

"With all due respect, sir, there's no way I'm doing this," she said.

"You can't mean that." What was that look he gave her? Disappointment?

"You know I appreciate the things you've given me today, sir. You've been really hospitable, and you've made me feel a sense of pride in myself again. However, spying on the Consortium for someone who works there is about the scariest thing I can think of."

"I don't work for the Con anymore, dear. They just don't know it yet."

"That means you're due for a fall, Duke. I don't care how big you are, they're bigger."

He banged his palm on the armrest. "I could change these people's lives! We could feed the hungry and heal the sick!"

She recoiled from his sudden outburst. His cheeks flushed, and he tensed his grip on his rocker. A stray, snowy lock fell across his eyes. He must not have been used to hearing "no." Perhaps no one had said it to him since he'd been a farmer. No matter. She was about to say it to him right then.

She spoke slowly, to be clear on every word. "You're going to have to do it without me."

His eyes widened; his brow furrowed in anger. When she'd first met him, she couldn't have imagined him furious. Now, she couldn't remember his smile.

She stepped back. "And, uh... you're not going to change my mind on that. I have friends here, and I'm not going to Atlanta."

He nodded once. "No, I'm sure you're right, Nora. You're not."

Cold steel crashed against the base of her skull, and the ground tumbled up to meet her.

*   *   *

A Birth

WHEN HER VISION returned, the world spun lazily, throbbing in time with her head. She swallowed, gagged on her dry tongue and groaned as she searched for her bearings.

A single, naked bulb on a wire illuminated bare, brick walls. Black, plastic sheets covered the floor underneath her, the same kind she made at the factory. Her hands had been taped to a folding chair, as had her legs.

"Help," she slurred, and the weakness of her voice terrified her.

"'Think not that I am come to send peace on Earth,'" said Duke, stepping out of the shadows. "'I did not come to bring peace, but a sword.'"

As the large man slid into focus, she noticed Hiram standing behind his boss, a pistol in his hand.

"Please," she said. "Please let me go. This ain't right."

He came and knelt in front of her. "That's true. It's not..." He put a hand over hers. "It's not right when innocents have to suffer for the wars of their betters. We have to run the Consortium out of this town, though, no matter the cost."

"I'll help you, then. I'll do whatever you want."

He squeezed her wrist through the tape. "I want you to pray with me."

Tears rolled down her cheeks. Cold fear gripped her stomach. "I... Okay, but –"

"Nora, look at me," he commanded.

She obeyed, meeting his gaze.

"If you pray, you will be spared."

"Why are you doing this?"

"Because of the things you know about me. You're right that the Con is a dangerous group of folks. I told you not to work for me unless you were sure, didn't I? Now pray and be free."

She felt so scared she could barely move her lips. "Wh-what do you want me to say?"

He placed a warm hand on her wrist, and her skin crawled at his touch. "Our Father, who art in Heaven..."

She swallowed, choking on her spit. She spluttered. "Our Father, who art in Heaven..."

"Hallowed be thy name. Thy kingdom come. Thy will be done, on Earth as it is in Heaven."

She repeated each word as spoken, and her eyes drifted to Hiram. He yanked back the slide on his pistol, and the room rang with an awful, metal snap. Her heart thudded, and she screamed.

Duke seized her chin and pulled her face back to his, so close she could smell his breath. "Look at me, child. Look at me. It's going to be all right. You're going to say a prayer, and we're going to take you back to your friends."

"Yeah... Okay..." *Just say the words and get back to Loxley. Whatever he fucking wants, just do it.*

"Give us this day our daily bread. And forgive us our debts, as we forgive our debtors. And lead us not into temptation, but deliver us from evil. For thine is the kingdom..."

She repeated as she was told, stammering half the words. Hiram took a step closer, and it was like the room chilled by fifty degrees. He was an ice cube on her spine.

"Look at me, Nora. And the power, and the glory."

Hiram took another step closer. She was so cold.

"And the p-power and glory. What is he doing? Get him away from me!"

Duke led her as though spoon feeding a child. "Forever. Amen."

"Please don't let him near me. Please," she sobbed. "I'll do whatever you want!"

"Say it, Nora. Be saved. All you have to do is ask."

With quivering lips, she said, "Forever. Amen. Now please let me go. You said you'd let me live. You promised. Please, you promised."

Duke patted her arm and stood. "You're going to live forever in the embrace of our heavenly Father, Nora Vickers. You're one of the lucky ones."

Hiram put the gun to her head, and she screamed a final plea.

CHAPTER SEVEN
SLEEPYHEAD

LOXLEY STARTLED AWAKE with a cry so loud the walls rang. Her fingers curled under, hard as marble, like the rest of her stiff body. Spasm after spasm rocked her, each one taking her higher than the rest, until releasing her with a sudden calm. She lay very still, infused with pain into every muscle and joint. She took whistling breaths between clenched teeth and focused on the dark ceiling.

She rolled to one side, the convulsions not fully subsided, and slapped a palm to the ground. She pressed down, pushing up onto her hands and knees, and very nearly fainted. Loxley looked down to her forearm to see a bright bruise peeking out from under her sleeve. She pulled it back to see Alvin Kimball's handprint, throbbing fresh and red. Her throat burned, and she reached up to touch her sensitive skin, feeling another bruise around her neck. She needed to get to a mirror.

Her eyes darted over to Nora's body. It lay in peace: a cold hunk of meat. The blood around the bullet wound was completely congealed, and the corpse had lost much of the shock it held before. It still hurt to look at her, but there was no suddenness in it. When she looked at Nora's loose arrangement of limbs, posed in no particular fashion, she understood that the body had been dumped here.

Loxley had borne witness to the last day of Nora's life. She knew it like she knew up from down. So many people's eyes passed through her mind – Nora was always watching eyes. So many things had been left unsaid, too. Nora had never spoken of how she felt about things, and in the end, it got her killed. Loxley couldn't understand why her friend had kept so much to herself.

She wished Nora had told her everything, especially that day at the market. Loxley would have kissed her.

She allowed herself a moment to be with her friend, to try and remember everything about the body. Then, it was time to get up and get away. She'd come here for answers, and she'd gotten more than she ever expected.

She staggered to her feet, her knees knocking as she did.

"Loxa-lox... Time to get up, up, up."

Her strength returned to her in waves. She brushed the hair out of her eyes and let out a long breath. Why was she still alive? Where was Nora's ghost? A ghost would kill her if it could, right? Was it still there? Would it torture her? Would she have to feel its touch again? She felt her overalls for her hooked pruning knife and let herself relax a bit, as foolish as that might be. What would she do? Stab the spirit?

She shambled to the door and shoved it open. Only an empty hallway lay on the other side, its sickly lights buzzing and flickering. Three flickers and a buzz, then four, then two – no pattern. She was too far from her house and needed to get home, to sleep in her bed and forget the prickly world that lay beyond her walls. She could dive back in tomorrow, but for now, this wasn't her world. This was a land where the ghosts showed her bizarre stories and Birdie didn't hate her.

Time to get home, time to get home.

She scuttled out the door, closing it behind her. She pulled it to, looking both ways down the hallway – no one. Her eyes darted nervously about, searching for the ghost, but she no longer felt the miasma of its presence. The air seemed freer, cleaner. She traveled downstairs and into the lobby, which had struck her as a dimly-lit, terrifying place the last time she'd been there. It had been morning then, but now the last rays of the sun bounced across the dirty tiles like a mud puddle. How long had she been in Nora's apartment? Was it still the same day?

She stepped onto the street and saw Hiram McClintock standing at the corner, leaning against a light pole.

Goosebumps crawled across her skin, and the blood drained from her face. Nora may have noticed his eyes, but the first thing Loxley saw were his long legs, sure-footed and strong. He had broad shoulders and big hands, too, and though he looked on the skinny side, Loxley knew better – he was built to kill.

He hadn't seen her, yet.

You don't look strangers in the eye, Loxie. Makes people bother you. You go about your business when you're out there, you hear me? If she kept her head down, maybe Hiram wouldn't see her. *Just do what momma says. Don't look at him. Keep walking.* What did momma know, though? She'd been wrong about Officer Crutchfield; maybe she didn't know about Hiram, either. Maybe her mother couldn't tell her a thing about bad people.

Nora knew so much from looking at a person's eyes – whether or not they were angry, or lying, or sad. Loxley had to figure out other ways to know a person's intent, and she was usually wrong. What was he here for? Was he mad? Maybe she could try to be like Nora and look him in the eye. She glanced up at him.

He was staring straight at her.

Loxley saw nothing in his expression, and she quickly looked away. Her hands balled into tight fists without her permission, and she forced herself to relax. He stood between her and home, so she changed course and started walking west. She could circle back around. She didn't have to go near him.

Why was he still here? He'd dumped Nora's body a day before. It didn't make sense to come back and hang around. Nora had once told her that people from the lowers didn't matter at all, that they could just disappear. If that was true, why risk revealing himself? She looked again.

He was following her.

Blood rushed through her veins, and she felt her thumping pulse in her neck. She skipped a step, not really meaning to. *Don't look back again. Just keep walking. Hiram will go away.* She placed each footfall away from the cracks in the pavement, just as she had in the Bazaar, and she fell into a rhythm that becalmed her nerves. When she looked back, the killer was just a stone's throw behind her.

She bolted.

Loxley's legs had grown stronger from years of hauling produce up and down flights of stairs, but she wasn't built for speed. She had to duck and weave, vaulting over piles of trash. The world became electric beneath her feet.

The winter wind roared in her ears, deafening her and drowning out the surprised shouts of bystanders. Ahead of her was Rockford Mills, the abandoned building where she'd gotten her piping for the garden. She rounded the base of a fire escape and scampered up the ladder, not daring to look down. Once atop the first platform, she kicked in the window and clambered through, avoiding the jagged edges.

Rockford was very dangerous, with falling debris, collapsing floors and the dozens of vagrants who called the place home. If she did not tread carefully, she could be killed by the building instead of Hiram. With her heart in her throat, she pressed on into the innards of the abandoned mill.

She whipped open the door to the colossal sewing room and saw two dozen iron girders standing silently as they waited for her to pass through. This place had once been full of workers, but now only spiders and homeless folks remained. Not even the slightest scrap of value had been preserved. So many details surged forward as she made her way across the room, the cobwebbed fixtures, the dozens of rivets lining the wooden floor in a speckled pattern, the hundreds of parallel cracks that ran from the boards underfoot. Hiram cursed somewhere in the hallway behind her.

Loxley stepped on a particularly spongy board and felt it give beneath her foot. If she placed her full weight upon it, she would certainly fall. She padded around, looking for the size of the rotten area so she could jump across. It had been a stupid idea to come in here, and her fingers sizzled with crackles as ants swarmed her legs. She was taking too long. Hiram would catch her.

She managed to step over the weak patch as she heard the click of metal.

"Stop," called Hiram, lacking any of the charms he'd used on Nora. When she turned to face him, he was holding the gun he'd used to kill her best friend.

Loxley stopped, though she shook out her fingers. The gun seemed to radiate in Hiram's hand as he pointed it at her face. Her surroundings dimmed, while the chrome pistol only glinted more brightly. Light danced over it like fireflies, and she could see the floorboards reflected along its sides. Hiram said something to her, but she only craned her head, trying to make the lines of the floorboards align with the side of the gun.

"What the fuck is wrong with you?" he laughed. "Never seen a gun before?"

"I've seen one," she whispered back.

He licked his lips. "Do you know who I am?"

"No."

He tightened his grip on the gun. "You're a bad

liar. You looked right at me on the street like you knew me."

His pistol flashed again, reminding Loxley it was the only important object in the room. She stared into its barrel, wondering if she would see the muzzle flash before she died. She wanted to take a step closer, to look inside it and see if she could spot a bullet. She forced herself to look at Hiram's face – he smiled.

"Tell me what you know about me."

Loxley thought of the lusty looks he gave her friend, of his cynicism and of the cold finality of his murderous glare. Nora was always looking into his eyes. She tried to gaze directly into him to see what he held there for her. She couldn't make it out.

"I know you're going to die for what you did," she said. "You killed my best friend."

"Now, we're getting somewhere. How do you know that?"

Loxley shrugged.

"And who's going to kill me?"

"I am," she said.

"Then I guess I'd better shoot you now, huh?"

Her stomach turned inside out. "You can try. Get closer so you don't miss."

As he stepped forward, pushing the gun toward her face, his foot plunged through the rotten floor. He sank into the structure like quicksand, and the pistol erupted next to her head, deafening her in one ear. Hiram shouted, and she spun to flee, not caring to see what became of him. She needed to put distance between her and the killer – long, desperate strides that carried her toward the opposite door as fast as her legs could go. She couldn't worry about rotten spots any longer; she had to barrel forward and let fate do what it would.

She threw her shoulder into the door and the far hallway opened to her. Two vagrants peered out at her from their hiding places behind stacked crates, their bodies stinking of sweat and rot. A million details swarmed her mind like insects: flaking paint, the long rows of shattered glass panes that ran along the hall, a pile of chicken bones stacked next to a barrel, the scent of urine. She dug her nails into her palms and listened to the ringing in her right ear. She sang along with it as quietly as she could.

The men made no motion to emerge from their safe spots. She dashed between them toward the smoky windows on the north wall. Once there, she shoved open one of the louvers and clambered out the opening. The bruises covering her body lit up like fire as she squeezed onto the ledge, but fresh air greeted her nostrils along with the sight of the setting sun. She could see Magic City Heights a block and a half away, and she'd already lost Hiram.

The ground was at least twenty feet below her, but she spied a catwalk only a few feet away. She leapt down onto it, and it detached from the wall with a crack. Steel and brick screamed against one another. The ground rushed up to meet her. She was thrown free, skidding across the asphalt and ripping the arm from her shirt as she rolled.

Deafness and pain drowned out all other distractions. She raised a hand to her right ear and felt blood. Static pressed upon her thoughts as she arose, staggering toward her apartment building.

She'd had too much, and concentration slipped from her grasp. She couldn't hang on any longer. Hiram might find her like this. She wouldn't be in her own mind when he did. Humming emerged from her throat, mixed with giggles. Nothing was funny, but everything was.

Let Hiram come and kill her.

Let the world end.

Baby

BEADS OF SWEAT ran down Loxley's hot back. The air was close inside her bedclothes cocoon – a sharp contrast to the chill of her apartment. The stagnant taste of her breath smothered her, and she heard her own blood rushing through her ears. She didn't remember coming into her building, nor did she remember wrapping herself up in her mother's thick comforter. She was naked; she often used to wake up this way as a child.

You can stay in there as long as you like, Loxie. I'm going to go to work now, okay? You don't leave here.

"Okay, momma," she said, her words loud and muffled. She clutched her knees tighter to her chest. Her throat hurt, and she said it a little louder, just to be heard.

A syrupy trail of blood ran from her right ear, and she couldn't hear anything out of it. She began to rock herself, and all of her aches and pains came rushing to the surface. She continued in spite of her body's complaints, and the soothing sway calmed her. Her stomach churned in the oppressive heat. How long had it been? Minutes? Hours?

There came the sound of footsteps, and a key sliding into her deadbolt. The noise pressed on her like the tip of an icepick.

Loxley's lips trembled, and her breath quickened. She covered her mouth to stop the hum, and her knees knocked together as she shivered. Maybe she misheard, and it was her neighbor's lock. She became as still as possible as she listened for any more noises beyond.

A sharp bang pierced the air, and Loxley gave a short shriek. It hadn't been a gunshot, more like a mallet. She heard men's laughter and several muffled voices outside. She hugged herself as tightly as she could, willing her rabbit heart to stop throbbing.

Another bang, and her lock jiggled. Then another bang, and she heard the deadbolt unlock. The doorknob turned, grinding against the striking plate before the door creaked open.

"This is definitely the place," came Hiram's voice. "See what I mean?"

"You want to just do her here?"

"Nah. He said he wanted to talk to her."

Silence settled over the room, leaving Loxley to quiver in her comforter. She felt faint.

"Do you seriously think I can't see you?" asked Hiram. "Now get out of there, or you're going to get the everliving shit beaten out of you, Loxley Fiddleback."

She peeled away the top of her covering, cold air rushing inside to make her shiver. Three men stood in her apartment, each carrying a shiny, silver pistol.

She looked the guns straight down the barrels, as though she was looking into their eyes. Maybe the guns were holding their owners. She imagined the guns trying to load themselves, and she chuckled.

"That's freaky, man," said one of the men, and she snapped back to reality. He had stern lips, all gathered at the center in a pucker.

"How did you find me?" she asked Hiram.

"You think there are a lot of retards around here? I just had to ask around for your name."

She pulled the comforter tighter. "I'm not retarded."

He stepped closer. "Do I look like I care? Get the fuck out here."

She pushed the comforter from her body and stepped, legs shaking, onto the cold, cement floor. She wrapped her arms around herself to hold in the heat, and her teeth chattered. Her legs itched, and she shuffled from one foot to the other, scratching herself with her toes. When she looked back upon the bed, she saw dozens of scarlet strokes lining the bedclothes – blood, from her many cuts.

Loxley's comforter was supposed to be white, but this one was speckled, like a cuckoo's egg deposited in her bed. She leaned over to see that her mother's place upon the mattress still lay untouched. The alien anxiety that had plagued her since she'd woken up swept over her again. The strange reality had begun to mutate her bedroom, as well. Soon, it would reach her garden.

Hiram slapped her hard enough to turn her head. "Pay attention! Jesus Christ, I've been talking to you for five minutes!"

She rubbed her cheek. "Sorry, Mister Hiram."

"First, you're going to get some clothes on. Then, you're going to tell me why you know my name."

She hadn't thought before speaking his name. She'd been so distracted by the bed. "No. You're just going to kill me."

"Is that a good reason to annoy the piss out of me?" he asked, pressing the gun to her scalp. "Now, either you get dressed, or I let these boys do their favorite thing in the world to you."

She looked up at Hiram, meeting his gaze. "What's their favorite thing in the world?"

"They like to stick it in girls like you. Just get your goddamned clothes on."

Loxley did as he bade her and pulled on her ruined garments. They felt crusty with sweat, and they were cold. The men with Hiram raised their weapons after she had covered herself.

"I'm guessing you ain't got anything better," said Hiram.

"No. These are my best coveralls."

The other men snickered, and Hiram shook his head. "You need a dress or something."

"Coveralls are better than dresses. Can't work in a dress."

"Whatever, creepy." He gestured to the door. "We got a car to catch, so let's go."

He took her hair and shoved her in the direction of the hallway. She resisted, stumbling back toward him, only to be rewarded with a painful blow to the back of her neck. She cried out and fell to the ground, clutching her head. The ants were all over her now, and her fingers were on fire.

"You're just going to kill me if I come with you!" she screamed, her head throbbing.

Hiram locked back the hammer. "I'm going to kill you if you don't. Now let me ask you what's better: living some or living none?"

Loxley focused on the question over the roaring static trying to flood her brain. Reluctantly, she rose to her feet.

"Good girl. As long as you're alive, you've always got something, right?"

She didn't answer. He shoved her out into the hallway and holstered his weapon; Pucker-lips and the other man followed suit. Hiram grabbed her by the arm, his grip rough and angry, and began to lead her toward the stairs. Neighbors peered out through the cracks in their doors, curious about all the screaming. It was the most attention Loxley had ever received. Birdie stepped out into the hallway, her arms folded, a cigarette hanging out of her mouth.

"Excuse me, ma'am, but please stay back," called Hiram. "This one is dangerous."

"Where are you taking her?" asked Birdie, pulling the cigarette away.

"Gardendale, miss, where she'll be comfortable and safe." He let go of Loxley's arm to approach Birdie, and Pucker-lips took his place.

Gardendale was a sanitarium on the third ring. For much of her life, people had talked about sending Loxley there so she could "be with her own kind." Birdie often threatened to check her into the institution, which was one of the few government buildings in the Hole. Loxley wondered if they really would take her there and lock her up.

Birdie folded her arms. "Bullshit. You got some kind of identification?"

"Don't need any. Step aside. This girl is dangerous, and I don't want you getting too close."

"That sweet girl ain't ever hurt a fly. Take another step and I'm calling the cops."

Hot tears welled in Loxley's eyes. "They're going to kill me," she said, her voice catching.

The round woman shook her head. "No they're not, dear. They're not going to leave this building, or there's going to be trouble."

Hiram gestured to Loxley. "Do you see all that blood on her, ma'am? Not all of that's hers. She's been up to Edgewood, and she hurt a man pretty bad. Now can you honestly say that you didn't see that coming? We get this in Gardendale all the time – orderlies get too comfortable with our patients, and then they get hurt or killed for it. Do you want to take that chance for yourself? For your community?"

Birdie seemed less angry when he said that, but Loxley noticed something else: the men flanking her rested their hands on their holstered pistols. Hiram had a polite smile on his face, but his fingers also hovered inches from his weapon. Birdie was trying to look into Hiram's eyes, but she should have been looking at his hands; she would have seen the truth there.

"I think she's a perfectly good kid," stammered Birdie, cutting a glance to Loxley.

"You think, but you don't know? Listen, lady, you may not be sure, but I am. I've seen a thousand cases just like hers; one minute, they're fine, and the next, they're wild dogs. Have you ever seen her exhibit repetitive, nonsense behaviors?"

Loxley started to talk, and Pucker-lips squeezed her shoulder so hard she gasped.

"Have you ever seen her act against her own best interests? Have you ever found her to be inaccessible or vacant? I'm sure I already know the answers." Hiram gestured to Loxley. "I don't think Loxley wants anyone to get hurt. I think she's really smart, and she understands that she could drag you into her problems if she stays here. What do you say, Loxley? Don't you care about your neighbors?"

She looked between him and Birdie, eyes wide and burning. Her neighbor appeared confused, as though she couldn't see through Hiram's ruse. Perhaps she couldn't. Hiram had made the choice clear, though: either leave voluntarily, or he would harm Birdie.

We don't hit people. It's wrong to hurt others, Loxie. It's only okay to hurt someone if they are hurting you.

"Just let them take her!" called one of the other tenants from his door down the hall. "Those guys are trying to help her!"

"Go fuck yourself, Norman!" Birdie shouted back before jabbing Hiram in the chest with her finger. "You leave her here and bring back some goddamned identification. I don't want to see your face unless there's an ambulance waiting outside to pick her up."

"That's not an option, ma'am. We're going to take her today whether you believe us or not."

"Over my dead body you are!"

The third kidnapper turned to face down the

hallway. They were going to shoot their way out. The round woman would be the first.

"I care about my neighbors," whispered Loxley.

"What was that, honey?" asked Birdie.

Loxley straightened up and sniffled. "I care about my neighbors. I want them to be happy. They won't be happy while I'm here."

A wide grin spread across Hiram's face, and he pulled out a tin of mints before popping one into his mouth and crunching it. "There you have it, ma'am."

Birdie reached out and touched her face. "Honey, are you sure?"

Loxley's fingers and feet burned. Her heart thundered, and her breath felt short. She couldn't have felt less sure about anything. Still, she was worthless, disliked and weak. Officer Crutchfield had proven that to her. Everyone would be mad if something happened to Birdie, but no one would miss Loxley. "I care about my neighbors," she repeated.

The big woman gave her a warm, smothering hug, and Loxley wanted to shove her away – too much touching. She couldn't breathe, wrapped up in those arms. She stamped her feet and flapped her fingers, and her neighbor released her. With the sudden ease of her burden, clarity and calm returned momentarily to Loxley.

"Oh, God," said Birdie. "I hope they can help you."

"They're not here to help me," said Loxley. "They're here to take me away. You're never going to see me again, and you can be happy about that because you don't much like me."

Her neighbor wiped her nose. "Don't say that, now."

"It's the truth. Thanks for the stuff I took out of your trash. Especially the banana peels."

Without another word, the men led her downstairs and to the front drive, where a waiting limousine idled. They shoved her inside, banging her head against the door frame. She sat down on the rear bench and found the ever-smiling Duke Wallace at the far end. The others piled in after – Hiram across from her and his two men on either side.

Most places in Loxley's life had been touched by rust and ruin, but the inside of Duke's limousine was clean as a whistle. It had many gaudy details, such as the embroidered crosses, but she felt considerably more level atop its smooth leather seats. Duke's suit was an extension of the limousine, blending into it like they'd been cut from the same animal.

"Fiddleback is a strange name," said Duke. Everyone always said that to her.

"I chose it for myself. It's a spider that likes to be alone."

"And a dangerous one, too. One of them bit my maid last year. Lost a melon-sized chunk of her leg. Do you bite, Miss Fiddleback?"

"I bite my food."

Duke snickered. "I don't doubt it. Hiram has told me a lot of interesting things about you." He knocked on the window to the driver's cabin, and it cracked a bit. "Bellebrook, Marie." The window snapped shut. "He told me you said you were going to kill him for the death of your best friend."

She must have been bundled up in her bed for hours, giving them the chance to track her down.

Loxley nodded. No reason to lie; she wasn't any good at it. "I am."

The car lurched forward and they sped down the serpentine streets of the seventh ring. It disoriented Loxley to be in a car, and she tried to remember how Nora had gotten over it. She took deep breaths and always kept the windows in her sight; the rushing scenery helped her to stay oriented. Duke folded his fingers over his gut and smiled. He reminded her of the pot-belly stove that Rick kept in his apartment. She shook her head, trying to focus, but her mind kept racing to take her anywhere but here.

"Did you know that your friend did something wrong?"

She sensed something rare to her – the bitter taste of anger, settling in the back of her mind. "No."

He shook his head. "It's the truth, I'm afraid. Your friend –"

"No, she didn't do anything wrong," Loxley interrupted.

"Now how can you know that?"

"Because she told me. She told me lots of things – everything she knows about you," she said, forcing herself to look him in the eye like Nora would. Duke's facial muscles moved, but Loxley couldn't divine how she'd made him feel. She wanted him to get scared – as scared as she was – but he didn't seem different to her.

"Did she now?"

"Yeah. You had Hiram kill her, so you're a murderer and I'm going to kill you, too. Either me or the Consortium."

A blush crept over Duke's face, and he looked to

his men in turn. She watched each of their faces, trying to make out what they really thought. Hiram's lips went taut and his irises contracted. Duke's face remained impassive, but he took a big, long breath. The men on either side of her tensed, their muscles bulging beneath their coats. That remark had upset them, but she didn't think it had made them scared.

"Murder is a sin. I served justice in the name of the greater good. Miss Vickers lied to me, and she was going to get a lot of innocent people killed if she told them what she knew."

Loxley cocked her head. "You're not a cop. You can't do that – just kill people like that."

"I'm the highest authority in the Hole. I helped build this place. That makes me a righteous revenger to execute wrath upon him that doeth evil."

Her pulse quickened. She wanted to hit him, to slam her arms against him until there was nothing left of his face. "That's not a law."

"It's from the Bible."

"That's just some book. It's not the law. The law says murder is wrong."

Hiram snorted and Duke frowned at him. "But God gives man the authority to carry out executions."

"There is no God. Not your God, anyway."

Improbably, Duke began to laugh. The car slowed; closing bells must have just rang at Vulcan's Bazaar, and the streetwalkers would be coming out soon. Loxley spotted the steel snake writhing past the car, and she squinted, searching the faces in the crowd. The limousine slowed even more, surrounded by the throng of shopkeeps headed home alongside their customers. Marie honked the horn.

Marie – she must have known what was happening to Loxley. Nora thought of her as a plain, hare-lipped woman, put upon by the oaf in the ice cream suit, but Loxley knew the driver must be complicit in these affairs. Loxley wondered if Marie had helped deliver Nora's body to her apartment, but she already knew the answer would be yes.

"Loxley, I want you to pray with me," said Duke. "We're going to pray for your soul."

"No. Then you'll just kill me. That's what you do."

Duke began to laugh harder. He slapped Hiram's leg, and for some reason, the killer didn't take offense to the gesture. Loxley hoped that one man hitting the other would be construed as an assault, but not at all – Hiram laughed, too. The fat man looked at the killer and shrugged.

"Don't you want to be saved?" asked Duke.

Loxley held her fingers in a crushing grip to keep from shaking them out. "Yes. From you."

The car was at a crawl. She looked past Duke, observing a dozen faces in the crowd: the meat man, the blacksmith, the mechanic, the pornography salesman, the chicken vendor, the man who sold stolen purses, the watchmaker, the wig lady, and on and on. Then she saw the policeman, and he turned to face the car – it was Officer Crutchfield. He looked right past them, unable to see through the tinted glass.

But he hated her. Would he help her?

"OFFICER CRUTCHFIELD!" she screamed over and over, even as Pucker-lips tackled her to the footwell. She continued to scream as he ground her face into the clean, cream-colored carpet. He tried to get his fingers over her mouth, and she bit him. She kicked out, and her leg solidly struck the door panel with a loud thud. She did it as fast as possible, hoping the muffled sounds would get through to Officer Crutchfield.

"Shut up!" shouted Pucker-lips, and her vision flashed as he plowed a fist into the back of her neck.

Her words became slippery, and she lost control of them in favor of aimless shouting and stilted humming. He drove a knee into her back, crushing her chest against the floor. She felt something hard in her front coveralls pocket – her curved pruning knife. She refocused to grab hold of her voice. She had to make contact with Officer Crutchfield. She pushed back against her assailant, sending him off-balance, sat up and screeched as loudly as she could.

Outside, Crutchfield turned to face the car and placed a hand on his gun. He stepped in front of the vehicle, out of sight, and Loxley could hear him shouting at Marie.

Loxley was pummeled to the ground for her trouble. The man on top of her drew his pistol and placed it to her cheek as he crouched over her head. "You keep your mouth shut," he rumbled.

Hiram had his gun out in a flash. "You ready to shoot a cop if this goes wrong?" he whispered with a grin. The third man unholstered his weapon as well, making Loxley and Duke the only unarmed people in the car.

"Look what you've done, Miss Fiddleback," said Duke. "If we have to hurt that man, it's on your head."

Tense seconds ticked by. Loxley heard the driver's side door open. Then Officer Crutchfield was in view, coming around the car toward the door nearest Duke, his gun at the ready. There was no way the policeman could see them through the tinted windows. All eyes were diverted from Loxley, and she sneaked a hand to her breast to slowly unzip her coveralls pocket.

"Wait until he opens the door," breathed Hiram. He scooted away from Duke on his seat to aim better. "Get a clear shot."

She slipped her fingers inside her pocket and grabbed hold of the pruning knife's wooden handle. Outside, Officer Crutchfield took aim at the window next to Duke and stepped backwards out of view.

"Come out with your hands up!" he shouted.

"I've got a shot," said the third gunman.

Pucker-lips kept his gun to her cheek.

"Wait for it," said Hiram. "Come open the door, you motherfucker."

Officer Crutchfield didn't come any closer, though. Loxley pulled her knife partway out of her coveralls and got a solid grip on the handle. Still, no one looked at her.

"His backup is going to be here any minute," said Pucker-lips.

"Yeah," said Hiram. "Take him on my signal. Three... Two... One..."

Loxley spun around and jammed her hooked pruning knife deep into Pucker-lips's inner thigh. She yanked, opening up his leg, hot blood spraying her face. Pure red sloshed over creamy white carpet, and the cabin filled with a chilling howl. Pucker-lips brought the gun to her face and she shoved his arm up. His pistol blasted twice, and she kneed him in the groin as hard as she could. For a heartbeat, she made eye contact with the man as they wrestled, his face turning pale, his blood still gushing over her.

Other hands clawed at her hair, and sunlight flooded the cabin as the passenger side door whipped open. The hands let go. Shots cracked through the car and shouts filled her ears. She shoved Pucker-lips off of her; he gave no resistance. She didn't look around to see what else was happening; she scrambled to her feet and grabbed the driver's side door handle. Her slick fingers lost their grip, and it took her two tries to get the door open.

She heard Officer Crutchfield shout her name as she rolled out onto the street. When she looked up, it seemed as though a million eyes were upon her – a sea of frightened faces keeping their distance. All those eyes; her chest tightened and she clawed her way across the ground, trying to focus on the asphalt. She painted the pavement red with each movement, like a brush on canvas, and her hands lay empty; she'd left her blade in Pucker-lips.

Someone from the crowd helped her up, and she screamed, shoving the person away. She dared not look them in the face – too many strangers. She hazarded a glance back at the limousine and saw Officer Crutchfield shooting into it, trying to get behind a light pole as he did.

He made eye contact with her right before a bullet tore into his face.

She did not stop to scream his name. She did not wait to see if he was dead. She turned and shoved her way into the throng, smashing through them full-force. Behind her, doors slammed and tires screeched. A dozen different shouts filled the air, and she covered her ears. Static loomed in her brain, and she swallowed it in sandy gulps.

Loxley wove through the forest of legs, watching the ground rush by as she ran further and further away.

CHAPTER EIGHT
THE RIVER JORDAN

LOXLEY WOUND THROUGH back streets, down alleyways and under bridges. She sought water and shelter. Her vision shrunk to only what lay before her, and she did not allow herself to waver from her task. Sunset came quickly in the bottom of the Hole, and soon she was able to flit from dark corner to dark corner, hidden from the sight of all the normal people.

Pucker-lips's blood caked on her as it dried. He was surely dead. She hadn't expected him to bleed that much when she'd stabbed him, certainly not the torrential outpouring that happened. With a single slice, she'd carved his body from his ghost.

Some people were scared of corpses. Loxley was, too, in a way; corpses were the heralds of spirits, like dark clouds that brought tornadoes. Some feared the dead body, itself, but a corpse was no different than something one might find at a butcher's. Butchers sold all kinds of meat, and she never saw where it came from. She giggled at the idea that they might sell off their own dead, but then stopped short, realizing that might actually happen from time to time in the Hole.

What was lost when a person died? A ghost wasn't a person, nor was a corpse. At least, she hoped a ghost wasn't a person, all cruelty and violence. In the transaction between life and death, choice was removed from a person, and all that remained was anger. Her body dragged from the wounds Nora's spirit had given her, and she shuddered when the wind kicked up.

She couldn't go back home. Those men would be there. The police might be there, too, and by now they would be working for Duke. He could pay them to do bad things to her, or bring her to him. And what were Duke's men doing now? Would they be in her garden, shoving her stuff around and looking under planters for a way to find her? After she'd stabbed one with a pruning knife, they might take all of her tools – things that had taken her years to collect.

She stopped walking and leaned against a wall. Her garden would die in her absence, her cart was gone, Officer Crutchfield would no longer protect her in the Bazaar and the Consortium manual was lost. Nora had left it at Duke's before she died. It was all finished: all of her dreams and her future were forever changed. There was no way forward, no plan. She wanted to kill Duke and Hiram, but that was never going to happen now. She was nothing.

She reared back and thunked her head against the bricks, the clay rough on her forehead. She thought she should cry, but the noise felt empty. She didn't have any more tears. She'd cried so hard the night

Officer Crutchfield had tried to fuck her, but that seemed distant now. Hope made her cry, and now she had absolutely none.

She sunk to her knees, resting her knuckles on the frigid concrete. Up close to the bricks, she could see tiny grains of sand in the clay, and they had a little sparkle to them. She rolled her face from side to side, watching them scintillate under her gaze. Freezing to death made a lot of sense now. She should just die. The old and the sickly never made ghosts. She wondered if it would be the same for suicides.

"You all right?" came a man's voice from a few feet behind her.

"N-n-no," she stuttered. "Are you going to hurt me?"

"Wasn't planning on it. You're going to freeze to death out here."

Her body felt like lead in spite of her shivering. "Good."

"I think we need to get you washed up. Is that your blood?"

"A little of it. Most of it is someone else's. Please don't try to fuck me or kill me."

For a moment, she heard nothing. Then, "Ain't crazy enough to make for a woman covered in someone else's blood. What happened to you, sister?"

She tried to wrap her mind around all the things that had brought her here. "E-everything."

A heavy hand came to rest on her shoulder, and she screeched, knocking it away. Another hand joined the first and they seized her shoulders. She couldn't break free of their grasp, and she sang as she tried to pry them off. After a moment, she realized the hands were attached to arms, which were in turn, attached to the rest of a man.

His dark skin alarmed her, and she couldn't look at his face for fear of what she might find. *They ain't all bad, but they ain't us. Just keep to yourself.*

Her fingers were electrified, but she hadn't the energy to shake them out. "My mother said you ain't all bad."

"Do I know your momma?" He tried to get in front of her eyes, and she looked away.

She couldn't meet someone's gaze right now. Faces were too frightening – too difficult.

"That's true," he said. "Not sure anyone is all bad. You going to look me in the eyes?"

"No. I don't want to look at you."

"All right, then." He let go and held a hand in front of her sight line. "Take my hand and we'll get you cleaned up."

He pulled her to her feet and led her deeper into the Hole, through passages she'd never seen before. As they traveled, their surroundings became more and more industrialized, and she heard the incessant clang of the Foundry, long and melodic. Down they went, descending a rusted ladder onto the eighth ring, ducking from alley to alley, then climbing down further, into nine. She'd never been down here before, and she'd heard stories of a lot of folk disappearing on this level.

She found the courage to look at the back of his head. He had short, curly black hair with a mix of white and gray. His shoulders were broad, and his clothes were ruined by greasy patches and threadbare spots. She couldn't smell anything with her nose so stopped up, but she knew a homeless man by his look. Her mother had warned her about men like him, but her mother's warnings had already been wrong too many times. There was no plan; no routine anymore.

Further into the tangle of pipes and machinery they went. Workers toiled in the distance, and the homeless fellow cautioned her about being seen. They slipped through holes she never would have spotted and climbed across many yards of conduit into the heart of the steelworks itself. She saw the massive smelter far below her, its orange glow like the sun on a summer day. It radiated a sweltering heat, and Loxley welcomed it into her bones with a sigh. She laid down on the pipes, ignoring how much the hot metal almost hurt to touch.

"Can't stay here. You'll get a bit cooked. Know that from experience," said the man.

Her guide jumped down onto a catwalk, then helped her to follow. They stood before a huge structure that continuously belched white clouds into the sky. She'd seen it many times from all over the city, and wondered at its purpose. It filled the Hole with so much steam that the streets glowed every sunset on the eastern side. The man heaved open a great steel door and waved for her to follow him.

It was dim inside, and she could barely see anything. Running water echoed through the chamber, so loud that it drowned out all other sound with a wall of white noise. Her tightened muscles began to unwind as her heartbeat slowed. She inhaled deeply, savoring the hot, moist air as it wet her parched throat. She stood, rejuvenating, for a long minute before her guide came to her and motioned her forward to the middle of the catwalk. He pointed below, and she could not see anything through the steam.

"Follow me," he shouted over the roar of the room. He climbed over the edge of the catwalk and leaned out, holding onto the railing. "And be sure and clinch up your butt."

He let go, disappearing into the clouds. His fall didn't frighten Loxley. The hot, rushing water did so much to calm her nerves that she felt a deep and abiding sense of well-being. Without a second's pause, she scrambled over the railing and leaned back. What waited for her below? Why had he brought her here? Would she die? Did it matter?

She let go, allowing gravity to take her. All became weightless, then she plunged into warm water. She didn't know how to swim, but she felt bubbles tickling her entire body, and the current pushed her upward. She broke the surface, and as she opened her mouth to breathe, she tasted clean water in which she swam. It was unlike anything else in the Hole, sweet and pure. It fizzed and wasn't much hotter than her skin.

The light was better down here, and she could see that she was in a massive pool, as wide as a street and almost as long as her block. The metal walls surrounding them were lined with vents at regular intervals. The black man swam back and forth in it, lazily tumbling about under the surface. All along the edges of the room, Loxley spotted huge patches of moss, like plush green carpet.

After all she'd been through, it felt divine. The warmth, the caress of the bubbles, the taste and the smell rolled through her mind, along with the noise of a dozen waterfalls, to smooth out the ragged edges inside her. She held her breath and dipped her head under, listening to the way the chamber became a muted rumble like distant thunder.

"It's a cooling station," came the guide's voice as she resurfaced.

"What?" She spun to face him, struggling a bit to control her orientation. She found it difficult to stay upright, but whenever she relaxed, bubbles pushed her to the surface.

"This building. It's where they cool the runoff for the big pumps that heat the foundry over there. I'm Floyd, by the way."

"Okay, Floyd," she said, but it was hard to stay high enough above the water to talk.

He took her hand and led her to a shallower part where her feet easily touched the bottom. The current tried to pull her back toward the center of the room, and she stood strong, letting it wash away Pucker-lips's murky blood. She ducked down under and ran her fingers through her hair, feeling it untangle in the weightlessness, then popped up with a sigh. It was a little quieter on this side of the room.

"There's a smile on you," said Floyd. "You got a name?"

"Loxley."

He repeated it to himself. "That's really pretty. Why are you covered in blood?"

"I killed a man."

"I see. It's a might weird, you looking so happy about it."

She searched her heart, but she felt no sadness in what she'd done, only shock. Pucker-lips and his friends had been going to hurt her, and now they couldn't. If she killed enough of them, they'd never be able to harm her again. "He was going to kill me, and his friend killed my best friend."

"How'd you do it?"

In this peaceful place her mind felt sharper than it had been in days. Memories of the terrible event came streaming back in perfect clarity. "Split his leg open with a knife. He bled out on top of me."

Floyd nodded. "Okay, then."

"He was really surprised."

"I'll bet he was. You don't seem like the dangerous type."

She thought about it. He was right, she didn't look like someone who killed people. "That made it easy to get my knife in him."

He took a few steps back. "You're making me a little nervous."

She shrugged. "You asked."

"That I did."

"I like you okay, Floyd, but I'm glad you're nervous around me."

He nodded. "So I won't try to do anything bad to you?"

"No," she said. "Because it's only fair. I'm always nervous around people. Someone else should be nervous around me."

He laughed, and she scowled. He grinned and swam away a few feet before turning back to say, "Don't worry. You still make me nervous."

They continued to float around the pool for another hour, and she found it easy as long as she didn't fight the current. Floyd told her how sometimes he came there with other men to go swimming. He said he was glad his friends weren't there today, because he didn't trust them to be nice to her. She didn't ask what he meant. Her fingers began to wrinkle. Floyd said he had to go get something and scrambled up onto a mossy bank before exiting from a door she hadn't noticed before.

All alone, Loxley stood on her big toes and closed her eyes. She hovered, letting as little of her body touch the ground as possible. She focused: on the scent of wetness, on the thousands of bubbles popping under her chin and spraying her neck, on the fizz winding through her pants legs to tickle her inner thighs, on the constant crash of water. In this place, she could become nothing. She never wanted to leave, but she knew she couldn't stay.

Floyd came back and she saw a pile of clothes in his arms.

"Where did you get those?" she called to him.

He began to strip on the bank, tossing his soaking clothes aside. "The lockers are near here. Lots of clothes in there, and the locks don't work for shit. I got you some, too. Hope you don't mind a work suit." Floyd's body was hideous, but she didn't look away. He was the second naked man she'd seen, and she wasn't much impressed; men were flabby, weird creatures, and the penis had an unpleasant appearance. She thought back to Nora's experience with Jack, and didn't think much of him, either.

"A work suit?"

"Yeah. Foundry boys wear them. Figured it was fine for you, since you showed up in coveralls. Not exactly high fashion."

"I like my coveralls."

"Yeah, but they're wet, and bloodstained... and it's freezing outside. You go out there in those, you're going to die."

"I don't want to go out there at all."

Floyd stopped lacing up his stolen boots and looked at her. "You can't stay here. People come around to check this place every morning, and I don't know what those people might do if they found you."

She loped through the water to the mossy concrete and pulled herself out of the pool. The carpet of plant life felt cool and refreshing on her palms after the hot water. She unlatched the straps of her coveralls and yanked them down past her panties. Floyd turned away.

"I'll wait outside," he mumbled.

"Why? Cold out there."

"Wouldn't be appropriate for me to watch you dress."

She stripped out of her skivvies and stood up to grab the gray foundry worksuit from Floyd's pile. "I watched you get dressed. We're not going to fuck."

"Yeah, all right."

She slipped into the suit and zippered the front. He helped her into the Consortium-issue boots, which had to be the least comfortable shoes she'd ever worn. They looked old, and her feet bounced around in the empty space inside. When she stood, she felt like a different person – no longer a farmer, but a company girl. She hated it, and the clothes stunk of someone else's sweat.

Her old clothes sat in a sopping wet pile, patiently waiting for her to pick them up. Pucker-lips's bloodstains were all over them, even though the water had faded them. Loxley didn't need them anymore; they were corrupted, useless. Her old self never would have left them behind, but her old self wouldn't have knifed someone, either. Her new thoughts exhilarated her as much as they frightened her.

"I don't need you, anymore," she said.

"What was that?" asked Floyd, wringing out his clothes.

"My clothes. I don't need them anymore."

"Oh. Okay, then. You really are a strange one."

Strange. Not crazy. Not retarded. She forced her eyes to lock with his. She would have hugged him if he'd been closer. "Thank you, Floyd."

"Let's get you back upstairs before someone sees us."

The Summoning Bell

FLOYD AND LOXLEY parted ways on the seventh, a few miles from her house. True to his word, the man had never once tried to touch her inappropriately, and when he held out his hand for her to shake it, she took it. He disappeared with the coming sunrise, leaving her with no idea how to find him if she needed him again.

She ached to return to her apartment, if only for a little while, to see her garden. Someone would be waiting there to kill her, though, and her real garden was in another world. Maybe the other Loxley had stayed behind to work on it with Nora. Maybe that's why she wasn't herself anymore, because her real self was at home, across the stars, where life was good.

She hugged her jumpsuit tightly; it didn't shield her from the wind much, and she walked closer to the walls to avoid the chill of the open streets. She only had one place to go – Don Fowler's. He owned the whole building, and he would have somewhere she could stay for a little while. Once safe, she'd start formulating how she would murder Hiram and Duke. Maybe she could hike up to Edgewood once a day to watch the house, and if she got a gun, she could shoot into Duke's car when it left Bellebrook. She imagined Duke and Hiram in the back seat of his already-bloody limousine, oozing gunshot wounds dotting their skin. She considered killing Marie, too, but if she tried to kill everyone who helped Duke, she'd never finish.

Officer Crutchfield had died trying to shoot everyone in the car. It wasn't a good plan.

These thoughts occupied her mind all the way up to the third ring, where the apothecary shop stood unlit in the murky morning light. She'd never been here so early in the day before, and she intensely disliked the look of the place. There was a sliminess to the way the shadows clung to its frosted windows. Sometimes, things offended her senses in a way that didn't seem to disgust other people.

She slipped around back, to the alleyway that led to the door to Don's home. He often went upstairs during the day because she gave him headaches. He would always tell her the same thing, "You're killing me here. Call me if you see someone come in. Don't try to help them yourself or you'll scare them off."

She reached out and banged on the wood as loudly as she could.

No response came. Between the clangs of the steelworks far below, she could hear snoring through an upstairs window. His bedroom must be above his door. She banged again, and she heard a man and woman's hushed voices; one was Don, the other must have been his wife. Loxley had never met her.

She knocked again for good measure, and she very clearly made out the word, "Jesus."

After two minutes of rustling from inside, the peephole on the door lit up, then winked at her as someone moved between it and the light. Don swung the door open. He wore a threadbare housecoat and a tuft of fluffy white hair sat upon his chest like a boll of cotton. It made her feel badly to look at him in his state, like he was naked. Don wore a lab coat and his hair was always slicked back; he did not wear these clothes. This man had wild white hair, greasy from sleep. He frowned.

"Why are you sad?" she asked him.

"I'm not sad," he replied, his voice growling with congestion. He hacked up some phlegm and spat it out. "You're fired because you didn't show up for work yesterday, and you're not helping your case by waking me up. What are you wearing?"

"I borrowed a jumpsuit because we went swimming at the Foundry."

"Is that why you missed work? To run around with your little friends?"

"I was going to come to work, but then someone hurt me a whole bunch," she said, pulling back her sleeve so he could see the bruises. "Then some men tried to kill me."

He leaned against the door frame, his eyes locked

on her arm. "Loxley, I have tried to help you time and again, and for what? You never take my advice, and I don't know if you can even understand it. I've been praying for you, child."

"Okay. Can I come in?"

"No."

Loxley shivered, and she felt a twisting in her guts. The cold ring of the steelworks counted out the seconds for her. *Clang... clang... clang...*

Don shook his head and held up his hands. "Mrs. Fowler and I have both talked for a long time, and this... this whole thing just isn't going to work. I can't stay involved with you and watch you plunge to whatever dark fate awaits you."

"I need to come in, Don."

He looked her over. "No. It's going to be the same thing every time. Good luck, Loxley. I really do hope you find the peace you're looking for."

At the edge of perception, she sensed something about Don she'd never felt before – something about his reasons for being who he was. He always liked to be a respected caretaker, if a harsh one. Her observations struck her as odd, because she normally didn't notice those sorts of things. He reached up to close the door, and she made herself look him in the eyes. He stopped dead and stared right back at her. She concentrated on the feeling, using the heart of the steelworks to steady her mind.

Clang...

She held his gaze, even though her heart hammered her for it. The ants and crackles harried her limbs, but she held still, as one might hold one's hand to a flame. There were a billion miles of circuitous thoughts inside her head, but she felt as though she could straighten a single section. She tugged at herself and images of Nora erupted into life all around her. How was it that Nora could see the animal aspects of other people? What secrets did she have? What would she say to Don?

Clang... Louder. *Clang...* Louder. The steelworks became static and she unwound from infinite tangled pathways. The crackles reached a crescendo before dropping off entirely, leaving relief in their wake. The banging faded, too. Only the misty morning of the third ring remained.

Don started to close the door.

"Don, wait!" she shouted, slapping her palm against it and blocking the way. "I know you. I understand that you've only ever wanted to help people, and I respect you for it."

His eyes narrowed in confusion. She noticed it that time. The man definitely felt confused.

"But I can't help you, Loxley."

"Yes, you can, but I'm not like everyone who comes in here to buy medicine. You can't just give me a prescription and send me on my way. I can't take a pill and magically be someone else. I know you care, and I am genuinely trying to accept the things you tell me. You want to be a hero to everyone you meet – to the rich man trying to save his child, to the poor woman who can't afford the medicine she needs – but I'm different. If you want to be a hero to me, it takes time and patience."

The words spilled from her lips with startling precision, appealing to aspects of her employer that she'd never cared about before. She left out the parts where he was a bossy, arrogant piece of shit, but the fact that she thought that at all was somehow remarkable. She'd never considered the possibility that her friends might tell her one thing when they felt another.

"You've been a good boss to me, even though I couldn't always see that, and I'm sorry. I wish I could recognize the gifts I'm given, but it's part of my condition, and for once, I have the clarity to admit that. I'm not asking you to change your whole life for me. Hell, I'm not even asking you to feed me. I just need a warm place to stay today or I'm going to die out here."

She straightened her back and shoulders. She stepped closer, into his personal space, astonished that she could muster such a feat under stress. His jaw dropped, and his hand slid down the door. She took the opportunity to push it open a little further.

"Just do me this one last favor... This one last thing. After that, you can say you did everything you could, and I was beyond saving, but if you turn me away today, you're giving up on the reason you got into this business in the first place. You just want to help people, but it always turns into you giving them advice they won't take. Well, I'm here right now, asking you not for advice, but to help me. I'll be gone with the evening, but please, give me somewhere to sleep. Just today, okay?" She rested her head against the doorframe. "Just today..."

She sounded just like Nora. She wasn't Nora, but she could conjure all the turns of phrase and speech of the dead woman. She could hold her body in such a way as to make it more appealing. It wasn't as though she could draw forth the ghost's memories, but she could sense its subtle influence on her mind. She could look at Don's face without trying to puzzle through the multitude of muscles that created his expression.

"Loxley, I don't know what you expect me to say here."

"I expect you to say, 'For your years of service, I'm going to let you sleep on my couch for one day,' because you're a good man, and because I'm going to die if you don't. I can't go home. I don't have anywhere else."

The steelworks fell silent, and fatigue bit into Loxley's joints. Her knees buckled, and she was glad she'd been leaning on the door.

"Just today, girl?"

"When have I ever lied?"

His shoulders fell and he stepped aside. She shuffled past him, into the sickening potpourri warmth of his house. Cross-stitched platitudes hung on the wood panel walls. Plush carpet sunk underfoot. In the dim gloom of the back room, she saw an older woman glaring out at her, thin as a skeleton, with taut lips and sunken eyes. Loxley had never been to Don's house, nor had she ever seen his wife. Judging from the hatred evident on the woman's face, she'd heard stories from Don.

Loxley spotted the couch at the edge of the den and walked toward it.

Don stepped in front of her. "Not before you get a shower. Maddie and I already agreed that I'm done making special exceptions for you. I'm not having you ruin my couch."

The world started to spin. Without the Foundry hammering in her ear, her breath became short and her legs itched. "Yeah," said Loxley.

"Maddie, would you take her to the shower?"

The woman stepped into the light. "Don't you ask me for anything, Donald Fowler. We talked about this! You said you were done helping her!"

Things got blurry. Loxley swooned, placing a hand on the couch arm to steady herself.

"I am, honey. Just today, and Loxley will be on her way."

"And what happens when today turns into tomorrow?"

"It won't, honey."

"You don't know that. She looks hurt. She needs a hospital, not a couch."

Her eyes swam in and out of focus.

"We're better stocked than the hospital."

"So you're giving her free medicine, too?"

"It's the right thing to do, Maddie. Am I supposed to let her die?"

"You're supposed to be looking out for us!"

"We'll have this discussion later. For now, Loxley... Loxley, are you all right?"

Her knees gave way, and the ground beneath her feet flipped sideways to strike her face.

Home

"LOXA-LOX..." HER mouth moved on its own as she opened her eyes to see the cold winter's light spilling into her room. Her room. Her apartment, back in her world.

"Lox, Lox, Loxley... Get up, up, up," she sang.

She lay flat in her bed, her arms and legs so heavy

they felt as though they were melting down onto the mattress. Who had taken off all of her clothes? Was it her? She couldn't remember. She smacked her lips, expecting the rotten taste of sleep to linger, but she tasted nothing. She watched the pockmarked ceiling, wondering if she could ever count all the nodules.

"I'm awake," she said, her fingers traveling across the mattress to the divot where her mother once laid. They met with warm flesh.

Her eyes slid down Nora's slender back, just barely covered by the blanket, her dark, brown hair curling across the sheets like ivy. Loxley rolled onto her side and placed her hand on Nora's hip, feeling the heat of her body. Her friend's shoulders rose and fell with each breath.

Loxley remembered the bullet hole and the cold weight of a corpse, and her lip trembled. "Nora... Stop being dead..."

Her friend turned over to face her, healed and whole, bright eyes shining with a sleepy smile. Her hands snaked around Loxley's body and she pulled her close with a sigh, pressing Loxley's cheek to her breast. Every detail of Nora's naked form electrified Loxley's skin, and she breathed in deeply of the scent. Loxley wrapped her arms around her friend's waist and squeezed, pressing together every inch of flesh she could.

"Please. I love you."

No words came in reply, but a kiss fell upon her forehead. Loxley craned her neck and her lips met Nora's – soft, wet and wonderful. In spite of Crutchfield's forced first kiss, she knew what a real kiss should be. She took to it naturally, following

Nora's passionate lead. Tears welled in her eyes, and she broke the connection with a sob, pressing her face between Nora's breasts and holding her tighter. Nora stroked her hair as Loxley's composure crumbled: all of her strength and the weight of all the pain she felt.

This was the world that should have been.

The Promised Land

LOXLEY BLINKED, HER head spinning, and the cloying scent of potpourri invaded her nose once again. When she tried to turn her head, hot dizziness rushed her, and she sat up to retch. Footsteps pattered closer as her guts bucked again. Before she could vomit, someone thrust a bedpan in front of her. Her reflected breath in her face made her puke even harder. She made to grip the pan herself, but something stung on her right hand.

"Careful, now, girl! I've got you," came Don's voice. "Don't tear it out."

After she finished, the bedpan was taken away, and she looked over to see Don standing next to her. She tried to focus on him, but her eyes didn't want to stay in one place. She became aware of the sweaty jumpsuit on her body.

"Sir, what's –" she began as she looked down at her right hand to investigate the sting. A tube ran into a vein on her arm, a plastic bottle dangling from a shelf over her. She'd seen intravenous drips before, but she'd never had one. She pulled at it with her left hand.

"Don't play with it, Loxley," grumbled Don. "Took me forever to get it in there."

He'd taped it to her. The tape was bad. It made her

feel ants on her arms instead of her legs, which was worse because it was different. People shouldn't put things like that on their skin. It made her itch to know it was there, adhered to her. She scratched at the edge of the tape, trying to peel it away, but it held fast to her like it had a million tiny hooks looped through the surface of her skin. Don placed his hands over hers.

"Loxley, stop it. You need that. You're dehydrated and you need antibiotics."

He grabbed her left wrist and yanked it away. She kept her hands close together, humming and picking at the plastic as quickly as she could. She had to get that tape off. No one should tape stuff to themselves, because now, instead of skin, she had tape there. She had to get her skin back. She wanted to explain, but all that came out were jumbled noises, probably because of the tape. If she could rip it off, she could probably speak normally.

Don's grip intensified, and she shoved him backwards without a second thought. He let go, and she heard a loud crash, but that stupid tape was on her. Shouting happened, but she'd managed to get a fingernail under one side, so she'd have to deal with it in a minute. She yanked, and it came halfway up, leaving behind a bright red welt and a fresh slice of pain. Stupid tape wouldn't come off without some kind of fight. She peeled it the rest of the way, and the needle tore away with it, allowing some of her blood to leak from her hand.

She threw the tubing to the ground and held the back of her hand to her face to inspect the damage. A crimson drop oozed down her skin and she smeared it, enjoying the color across her pale flesh. More yelling and loud noises. She wiped her finger on the couch without thinking about it, and the blood came away with no trouble.

"I hate sticky stuff. I didn't want you to put that on me."

She looked up to see Maddie standing over her. The older woman blistered her cheek with a hard slap.

"Goddamned ingrate!" screamed Maddie.

Loxley turned to see Don sprawled out on the floor, holding the back of his head and groaning. He lay next to a toppled end table, and broken glass littered the floor. He must have fallen and hit his head when she'd shoved him.

"For four years," Maddie began. "Four years I've listened to Don tell me all the stupid things you've done! I told him not to hire a retard, and look what it got him."

"I'm not retarded."

"Yes, you are, you little freak! It's obvious to everyone else!" Her voice's pitch grew even higher, and Loxley clapped her hands to her ears.

"Don't call me that," said Loxley, rising to her feet. "I want you to shut up."

"And you always get what you want, don't you? You know what our friends say about you? They say, 'Look! There goes Don's little spaz. Isn't he just a saint for hiring her?'"

She started to get angry again like she had in Duke's car. "If you say anything else, I'm going to hit you a lot harder than you hit me."

"The police are looking for you, and you know why, don't you?"

"Yeah."

Maddie took a step back, her hand over her mouth. "Oh, my God. You did do it, didn't you? What they're saying? You killed that guy in the Bazaar, didn't you? Oh God, you're a criminal!"

"I'm not a criminal. That man was a bad person."

"Get out! Get out, before I tell the police you're here!"

"Stop shouting at me."

"Get out!"

Loxley marched into the kitchen and grabbed a small serrated knife before whirling around to find Maddie standing in her path.

"Don't you come any closer!" screamed the woman.

"Get out of my way."

"What are you going to do? Stay away from Don!"

Loxley sighed. "I'm leaving just like you asked me to."

She walked straight at the woman and hoped Maddie would move. She didn't want to touch her. At the last second, Maddie swept out of the way, as though Loxley were a moving train. In the living room, Don sat upright, shaking his head.

"You have no idea how much you disappoint me," he said.

"It doesn't matter, because your opinion isn't important anymore. I don't work for you," she replied. Loxley thought back to Officer Crutchfield in the Bazaar, standing around waiting for gratitude. "Thanks for letting me sleep here."

"I shouldn't have done it. You killed someone."

"Wasn't planning to kill either of you, even though you're making me very angry. If Maddie tries to stop me, I might hurt her though."

Both Fowlers stopped talking and watched her with wide-eyed expressions. Don's gaze flickered between her face and the knife as he sat, belly hanging out, on his floor. He looked like a frog, or maybe a dog dragging its ass. Then she imagined what it might look like if a frog dragged its ass, and she began to laugh. The more she thought about it, the funnier it got, and she wondered what the frog might look like in a lab coat, serving out prescriptions. She thought about it hopping up onto the counter to hand off a pill bottle, and then she remembered all the different glass lining the walls of the apothecary next door – too much to remember correctly – and it made her nervous. She suppressed a hum and blinked herself back into the moment.

"Maddie, get upstairs and call the police," said Don, making no move to stand.

Loxley looked him over. "Thanks again for letting me sleep here."

She took off through the front door, bursting onto the streets. She felt well-rested, and the sun told her it was late afternoon, which was usually her quitting time. She began walking and pocketed her knife, hoping she wouldn't have to use it on anyone soon. She would, though, if it came to it. The more she thought about what she'd done to Pucker-lips, the more she felt like he deserved to die.

A chill wind whipped through her clothes, and she shuddered. She needed shelter. Loxley jammed her hands into her armpits and trudged in the direction of Harrison Hoop Station, and the last person who'd offered her help.

She couldn't trust him, but at least she had a knife.

CHAPTER NINE
HANDSHAKE

WHEN LOXLEY FINALLY entered Harrison Hoop Station, her nerves were shot. There seemed to be an abundance of police officers out and about today, and she no longer felt comfort in seeing their uniforms. They all had searching eyes, scouring for her, and rotten hands, ready to grope her. They carried guns because no one wanted to listen to them; that way they could kill resisters. In spite of their omnipresence, she'd managed to avoid notice, and she made her way across the station toward the lockers.

It was the wrong time of day, but if she could play, maybe she could make Quentin Mabry appear. He'd certainly materialized out of thin air to her playing before, but she usually didn't play for another hour. What if he didn't take the train today? He wouldn't be in the station, but she didn't want to contemplate that. What brought him up to the fifth to take the Hoop, anyway? Where did some low-born black from the eighth ring go every day? All of the whores and bars were on the sixth ring and lower. Her mother told her the negroes liked whores and bars quite a bit. Her mother had also said they could be thieves, though, and Quentin Mabry wasn't one of those.

Her mother told her to trust policemen, too.

When Loxley arrived at her locker, she patted her pockets for the key, but her pockets were empty. She didn't have the key. It would be on her dresser, or worse, in the blood-soaked clothes that lay at the bottom of the Foundry. Crackles shot straight up through the floor into her fingertips, and she shook her hands as hard as she could.

"No, no," she sang, over and over as she scrabbled at the locker, looking for a way into it. The words transformed over a dozen repetitions into "no-nee," but she paid little attention to herself. The rolled steel plate door offered little purchase for her fingernails, and she couldn't figure out how to get at the spring latch that lay tantalizingly on the other side of the metal.

The incessant screech of metal grew in the air, but Loxley didn't recognize it until it was too late. A train thundered into the station, and Loxley fell to her knees, covering her ears and shouting over the din. Trains made a jagged clang, like a saw blade being dragged across her brain, and she usually played her violin to stop them from existing. She could've played outside, but she never made as much money in the streets. Trains had a hurtful noise, and like the sliminess of Don's house, she couldn't explain to normal people how she knew that. Music was a good noise, and harmonics could protect her from the rusty jangle of train tracks.

"Stupid, stupid!" she screamed through clenched teeth, knowing it was her fault for neglecting the schedule.

Brakes squealed, and the cars rattled to a halt after an eternity. Loxley wiped the cold spittle from her chin and stood, coated in a fresh patina of sweat. She stamped her feet, shaking the ants from her legs. Folks waiting for the train were looking at her, but as soon as the doors opened, they went about their day, paying her no mind.

The train would depart soon, and she couldn't be here when it did. Trains arriving were far worse than trains leaving, but that didn't change her distaste for their noises in general. She spun on her heel and walked out of the station. She only faintly heard the departure from the bottom of the stairs, and she turned to look over the crowd of arrivals making their way out of the station. Several blacks, but no Quentin.

She wanted to wait at the base of the stairs, never entering the station. After all, the platform was only a good place to make money if she had her violin, which she didn't. It would work best to wait until a train arrived, then dash into the station to see who got off. Satisfied of Quentin's presence or absence, she could return to the relative safety of her hiding spot. She tried this several times, and though people took notice of her, no one ever questioned her, because most folks only move through a train station, never dawdling.

She repeated this procedure at least ten times before spotting Quentin as he disembarked the train. Clad in a perfectly-pressed suit, he looked far wealthier than his fellow passengers. Loxley thought back to what she'd seen of Edgewood fashion during Nora's last day of life. Quentin would have fit right in up there, save for his skin color. He smiled at her, but the train was about to leave, so Loxley turned and ran down the stairs without getting to talk to him.

Once outside, she patiently waited for him to appear, and he rewarded her in decent time. "Miss Fiddleback!" he called to her.

She closed the gap between them. "Please don't call my name. The police are looking for me."

"No shit?"

"My friend Nora used to say 'no shit' and I think it's dumb because it doesn't mean anything."

Quentin folded his arms. "So you made her stop saying it?"

"No. Someone shot her, so she can't talk anymore."

"Does that have anything to do with the cops?"

"No. The cops didn't shoot her. One of them tried to fuck me, but I don't think it's related."

"Jesus, Loxley." He held out his hand. "You need some help?"

That was the reason she'd come, wasn't it? Going with Quentin seemed like severing the connection on her diving suit and growing a pair of gills. It was a decision to stay in this strange place, instead of trying to reclaim her home. She looked down at his hand, at the difference in color between his sleek, black leather glove and his skin. "I think my mother was wrong about blacks."

"A lot of people are. Is that why you don't trust me?"

"You're more brown. Not a very good name."

He stuck his hand back in his pocket. "Oh, uh, okay."

"There are some people who really want to kill me, Mister Mabry."

"Why are you telling me this?"

"I was just at Don's house and his wife hit me even though I was just trying to stay there. They put tape on me and I didn't like it, but then I had to leave." She hugged herself against the chill. "Maddie was helping me because she had to, and Don was helping me because he thinks it's good to help people, even though he doesn't help people for very long. I didn't even get to spend the night. Floyd was nice to me, too, but he said he lived with bad people, and I thought I knew what he meant, but now I don't. I don't know who the bad people are anymore."

He removed his coat and placed it around her shoulders. It was warm from his body, and she didn't know how she felt about him putting his heat on her. She couldn't put her finger on why, but she thought of Nora and Jack, and how good that felt when they fucked. The coat smelled sweet, like machine oil or hot sugar, and it weighed on her like a hug.

"I believe that's the most you've ever said to me." Quentin shivered, left only with his gloves, vest and collared shirt. "Listen here, chatterbox. You can come stay at the club, but eventually you've got to play for us if you do. We'll dress you up so they don't know who you are."

"Is that honestly the deal?"

"Yes. Everybody has got to sing for their supper."

"I can't sing."

"It's a metaphor."

"Oh. So you don't sing, either... And I don't have to be a good girl and I don't have to fuck anyone?" A square deal, on her terms. Not charity, and no ulterior motive.

"No, you don't have to be anything but yourself," he said. He reached out and lifted her chin to look into her eyes. "A lot of people treated you bad, haven't they?"

She didn't understand the tears that trickled from her eyes, but her lip enjoined them by quivering. "I can't get into my locker. My violin is in my locker. Please don't leave."

He wrapped an arm around her shoulder. She smelled cologne on him and something like warm bread. "It's okay, baby. We don't have to worry about that just yet."

She sobbed a little harder. "I just wanted to go home. You're going to let me stay at your home? You're not lying to me?"

"We've got a place for you."

"They said the same thing to Nora before they shot her."

"I'm going to level with you, so you know there's no funny business" said Quentin. "I want to make money off your talents. I heard you play. I know I can cash in. And yeah, if you can't play, you can't stay. You get me?"

She wrung her hands until it hurt.

Quentin smiled. "And if this works out, I'm going to treat you like a queen."

"I'm... I just..." she stammered, but she couldn't get all the words out. She was happy, but something he'd said or done made her drop her guard for a brief second. It was like she'd let out the breath she hadn't realized she was holding.

"Come on, now," he said, gently nudging her forward. "No point crying in the street."

The Hound's Tail

THEY WALKED FOR an hour and a half, until Loxley's feet ached. Quentin took many paths Loxley's mother had warned her never to take, and soon they were in the middle of the eighth ring, sifting through a murky winter's fog. A pink haze permeated the labyrinth of decrepit structures, and it soon coalesced into a neon sign. It depicted a pair of dogs dancing in two frames of rudimentary animation. The female dog had her hindquarters toward the viewer, her tail high in presentation.

Loxley had always feared the neon of the Bazaar, but this lone sign scarcely bothered her. When she was a child, her mother had once bought her a head of cotton candy, and though Loxley could not bring herself to eat it, she sensed its nature: sticky, fluffy, a little scratchy if it were crushed. This sign was cotton candy in the air, and she tasted its syrupy sweet nature. Perhaps Quentin would also be just like cotton candy – flamboyant and exciting, yet almost entirely devoid of substance.

"There she is," said Quentin. "The Hound's Tail."

When they got closer, she could make out features of the building over the blaze of pink. The club was a three-story building, capped on each floor with a ring of elegant stonework. The bottom floor had no windows, only a mildewed concrete relief depicting the sun rising on a field of farm workers. The top two floors had rows of tall windows, scrollwork snaking around each one. This building had been built in the old style, with a large amount of money, and seemed out of place here – the one good tooth in a rotten mouth. It was nowhere near the beauty of Duke's house, but Loxley didn't imagine there were a lot of places in the world like Bellebrook.

Shapes loomed in the darkness around it, swaying and chattering: a few dozen people, waiting to get into the club. The brass façade on the doors flashed like a knife blade as people shuffled inside. Loxley reached out and grabbed Quentin's arm, stopping in her tracks.

"I can't go in that way," she said.

"Not a problem, sugar. I wasn't taking you in that door."

"You weren't?"

He laughed. "Hell, no. We got standards here, and you don't meet a damned one of them until you have a bath and some new clothes. Maybe a little lipstick to help out that cute face."

Nora had tried to put makeup on her once. It was a lot like tape – greasy, smeared tape.

"No makeup," said Loxley.

"Suit yourself. Lipstick would look good on you, though."

She wondered why anyone would want to make lipstick look good, but she dropped the subject. They circled the building and went into the back door, directly into the kitchen. The smells of fresh bread and sizzling meat assaulted her, along with the clang of dishes. A million tiles on the tiled walls. Clusters of six pots here on a rack, eight pots there. Five plumes of steam. Twelve cooks of every color, their uniforms bespeckled with grease stains. Flickering fluorescent lights. Four ovens. Three butcher blocks with ten knives apiece. At least a hundred jars of spices. So many shouts. So much motion.

Loxley whimpered and spun to bury her head in Quentin's chest, trying to shut out the tempestuous kitchen. Up close, the man was solid as a rock. She'd surprised herself by acting so familiar with him, and remembered Officer Crutchfield. Maybe he'd tried to fuck her because she'd asked him to take her across the Bazaar. Maybe, if she'd just gone home, instead of forcing him to help her, nothing would have changed. She wouldn't be in the weird world. He wouldn't have touched her in that way. Was it all her fault?

"Are you scared?" he said, stroking her hair. She could hear his heartbeat and the thunder of his voice through his skin.

She nodded. "Sort of. There's too much. I don't know if we can go in this way."

"How do you manage to handle the train station?"

"Every time a train comes, I start playing my violin. Music straightens out the tangles."

"Hey, boys!" he shouted as he gently pushed her aside. "Stop doing your shit for a minute!"

Everyone turned to look at him, but the sounds, sights and smells continued to ravage her senses. "Are you going to sing? That would make me feel better, and momma says negroes like to sing."

"Your mother was kind of a racist, wasn't she?"

Quentin took a few steps into the kitchen, looking back at her expectantly.

Loxley bit her lip and followed him, her shaking fists balled at her sides.

The cooks grinned at her, staring in her direction. Did they think this was funny? She forced herself to return the smile of the nearest fellow, but judging from his reaction, she had no idea what face she'd made. The kitchen had to be as long as her apartment hallway, and by the time she got to the end of it, she'd counted fifteen men, cooking everything from deserts to ducks. It all smelled incredible, and she grabbed her tummy as it rumbled.

Quentin stood by the door on the other side, holding it open for her. "Come on, baby. Let's go."

She stopped and pointed to some hanging spices. "That sage looks bad. I don't think that parsley is good, either. You could do better."

"You a cook?"

"No, I'm a –" A what? An apothecary's assistant? Not likely. Her time with Don was over. A farmer? Her garden probably didn't exist anymore, and by the time it was safe to go back home, it would be long gone. A merchant? No produce, no cart, no merchant. "... nothing. I'm nothing."

The clatter of the kitchen spun up like a rickety engine. She scooted through the door after Quentin and into a wood-paneled hallway. She saw glasses stacked along shelves and a dark, velvet curtain at one end. Stairs led away in the other direction, and her guide climbed ahead of her.

"Where are we going?" she asked.

"We got to meet your new boss, honey."

Then she remembered the answer to his question from moments before. She was a woman, and a killer. No matter what else, that would always be true.

Tails or Heads

WHEN THEY GOT to the third story of the Hound's Tail, Quentin stopped and waited for her on the landing. She climbed up and found it to be entirely unlike the other two floors. It was wealth, but not like the loud opulence of Bellebrook. Polished cherry boards covered the floor, offset by emerald paisley wallpaper. Flickering gas lamps in ornate brass fixtures fought a losing battle against the shadows. Loxley smelled dust and peered into the depths of the building, seeing little beyond tiny flames.

Festivities had already started below, and she could hear muffled music and laughter.

Quentin placed a hand on her shoulder and squeezed. "Now I want to ask you one thing before we go talk to him."

Loxley brushed him off. "Please don't touch me right now."

"Fine, but I want you to take my question seriously, all right?"

She nodded.

"Do you mean any harm to anyone here?" he asked. "Have you taken any sides, ever in your life?"

She thought of Nora and her fists balled again as her heart thumped. It made her want to hit something. "I've taken a side against Duke Wallace.

Are you with Duke?"

"Is he the one that shot your friend?"

"Might as well have. I'm going to kill him and Hiram McClintock."

Quentin took a long, whistling breath through his nose. "You'd better tell all that to the boss." He gave her a push on the small of her back. "Now, come on. Let's get you two acquainted."

The paisleys crawled along their walls as Loxley walked. Her shadow danced in the gaslight, the figure just as nervous as she was inside. Even before Quentin pointed out his boss's door, she knew which one it was. Its edges were clearer than the others, its molding more polished. A blink later, it didn't appear physically different from the other doors. The air here felt crisper, almost electric, compared to the stale hallway. She glanced up at Quentin, his brown eyes glimmering in the shadows. She didn't understand his expression, but it was the first time he hadn't returned her gaze when she looked at him.

He rapped on the wood three times, the sound sharp in the muted hallway. "Boss."

"Send her in," came a low reply, almost inhuman. Loxley drew her arms up to her chest on instinct, and her breath quickened. What kind of man lay in wait on the other side?

"Don't you lie to him," said Quentin. "You'll just piss him off, and you don't want that."

He gestured to the crystal doorknob, whose complex facets twinkled as though filled with stars. Loxley felt like a bug on a spider's web. First, Nora had walked into the house of a rich man, now Loxley. She was an idiot for coming here. She probably could've scraped together the money for a train ticket and left for Atlanta or something. She could still go work the coal mines. They never asked questions in the coal mines, and they kept the lady miners separate, so they wouldn't get raped; didn't pay them as much on account of it, though.

If she wanted to leave for Atlanta now, she could make it after two weeks in the mines. She might not be beyond Duke's reach, though. She thought of sinking the knife into Pucker-lips's leg. It had felt good. If she left, she'd never be able to do that to Duke. She wrapped her fingers around the knob and twisted the door open.

The first thing she noticed was a crackling fire in the tremendous fireplace. Above that was the severed head of an elephant, gray ears unfurled like flags, mouth frozen in mid-roar. A dozen barn owls, hawks, eagles and other huge birds perched around the ceiling, all posed in various states of attack, as though her entry would trigger a feeding frenzy. Loxley had never seen a stuffed corpse before, and the effect unsettled her. Atop a mahogany buffet, a surprised red fox carried a dead squirrel. A pair of snowy wolves padded nearby, their lips curled into snarls. Three hedgehogs lounged in a fruit bowl on the ornate desk. Mice scampered along the edge in various states of play, some of them apparently dancing with one another.

She then noticed the twisting columns lining the walls, their bark-patterned stone untangling into branches with silver leaves. A moon had been painted across the ceiling, along with hundreds of lines and numbers sweeping out like some kind of map. The wallpaper was a deeper shade of green than the paisley in the hall, and depicted trees receding into a murky mist.

Loxley felt like she'd walked into a teeming forest, and all the animals had stopped to look at her. In a moment, they'd thaw from their surprise to come tear her to pieces.

Quentin's boss stood at the desk, hands clasped behind his back, his body covered with a red silk housecoat which rippled in the firelight like flowing blood. He had a stern face, with a wide jaw and thick brow, and the kind of eyes she dared not meet. He had huge, imposing shoulders, but thinner arms and legs – a pie wedge standing on its tip. She spied hard muscles lining his abdomen through the open front of his robe, and felt confident the rest of his body was similarly strong. He leaned forward, uncurling his long fingers to place his palms on his desk.

"Come on in, sugar," he said, his voice a rumbling growl.

Quentin stayed out, and shut the door behind her as she walked in, wringing her hands to keep the crackles out.

The boss sniffed, perhaps because he wanted to catch her scent. "What's your name?"

"Loxley Fiddleback."

"Your family name is Fiddleback?"

"No. I don't know my family name, so I got to pick one. What's your name?"

He crossed his arms. "Tailypo. That's what people call me. A pleasure, Loxley."

"Why do people call you that?"

He grinned widely, flashing his teeth. They struck

Loxley as a little sharper than they should have been, but it was hard to tell. "Because I used to have a tail, but now I don't."

She imagined him with a furry cat's tail, bright orange with blotchy stripes, and giggled aloud. "No, you didn't."

"People don't usually laugh when I tell them that."

"But it's funny because cats are funny."

Tailypo put his hands on his hips. "Ain't a cat, Loxley."

She shook her head, still laughing. "I didn't say you were. Tails are funny because cats are funny, and cats have tails."

"Well, I still ain't a cat. I'm a ghost."

Loxley stopped laughing. She shook her hands out, even though he was definitely lying. "I know some of those, and you're not one, Mister Tailypo."

The fellow drew closer to her, his olive skin radiant with flickering light. "You know ghosts, do you? What's the difference between me and them?"

"Ghosts aren't people."

"Ain't a person," he said as he circled her, looking up and down her body. He was crazy or lying.

She swallowed. "Ghosts are mean for no reason."

Tailypo ran his fingers along her shoulder and she shuddered. "Oh, everything has got a reason, no matter what it is."

She stamped her feet as he walked behind her, running his hand up the nape of her neck. "And, ghosts... they aren't alive."

He leaned in to whisper in her ear. "Neither am I."

She yelped and danced away from him, anxiously shifting from foot to foot when she'd put some distance between them. She wasn't about to let him touch her anymore – not for a hug, not for a handshake. He took a step toward her, but she wasn't having it, and backed further into the room.

"You want to know about the tail," he said.

She nodded.

"Let's start the story at the end, first. You know they're always chasing iron down below, don't you, Loxley?"

"Not chasing. Mining."

"Call it what you want, but they'll move the whole earth to get it. They dug so deep that they about tapped this whole place out of the ore. They carved mountains into dust, made them low just to pull it out of the dirt. And when they mined out one layer, they carved another, leaving behind the first like a carcass with all the good meat stripped away. The new folks who came for the iron moved into the new ring, building houses and shops, and the folks on the higher rings fucked them over with taxes and land rights. That why the people from Edgewood are always on top, no matter where they're at in the Hole."

He licked his lips. "I was here before this place was the Hole, before it was ever a mine, back when it was just a couple of hills with endless coal and iron tucked underneath. Used to be all kinds of trees back then. We ain't got any here on the eighth ring. You like trees?"

"I plant things."

"Used to be a forest here, as far as the eye could see. Big one, too. They start knocking it down. So one of the farmers goes to plant crops where the trees used to be, and those crops don't do so well – all ash and dust after a couple of weeks. And this farmer, he gets hungry; so hungry, in fact, that he ignores the warnings of the foresters and takes his three dogs to come hunting what's left of the woods. That place was my home."

She already didn't believe him. "How did you live in the trees?"

"How does anyone live anywhere? I had a house, but nothing as fancy as this. That house stood in our exact location, a couple of hundred feet up, sticks and mud. I looked a little different back then, too. Maybe a bit more hunched. Maybe a bit more hairy. Maybe with a tail, and far fewer human bits. And the dogs, they pick up on my scent, and they go crazy. They decide they've got to have a piece of me."

Tucked into a shadowy corner of the room, Loxley spotted three hounds, their bodies stiffly pointing.

"They chase me for hours, and so does the farmer. He's a hungry son of a bitch, so I understood. I was hungry, too, and if the situation was reversed, maybe I'd have taken a snap at him. Then he finally thinks he has a good shot and takes it, blowing my tail clean off. Musket ball tears the goddamned tree in two behind me. I let out this howl, and the farmer lowers his gun, knowing he done something stupid. The dogs catch the smell of blood and it whips them up even more. So that time, I ran. I don't like dogs. What do you think of my story so far?"

"It's just a story."

"You know what? Let me ask you again in a minute," he said, waving her statement away like a bad smell. "I go back for my tail. Just find a bloody patch and a bit where those bitches had licked up some scraps of meat. I figure that farmer took it. It was a good tail, strong like a monkey's and full of muscles like an ox's. That night, when the stars come out to play, I make like a thief out to the edge of the woods, and you know what I smell?"

It wasn't hard to guess. "Cooking?"

Tailypo crossed to his desk and plopped down in the chair. "People will eat anything, and I don't mind telling you: in a time of hunger, with all the game scared away and all the crops dead... I want to go get a bite of my tail, myself. But I can't. He would have killed me quicker than a heart attack. So I perch in a tree, bleeding and crying, the pain of my empty stomach cutting me as I smell my own cooking meat. Eventually, the fires die, along with the candle lights in the house, and my moon, she hangs at the top of the sky, looking down at all creation. I get to thinking of scraps, and I'm seeing red.

"I sidle up to the farmhouse porch, and hear them snoring. I can see those hounds through the window, fat and happy from eating part of me. I get up real close to the glass, and without thinking, I mutter something in the tongue of the humans. I say, 'Who's got my tail?' And wouldn't you know, the old farmer startles awake, screaming for his hounds. Fear takes me and I bolt for the woods, and all three of those mongrels give chase, in spite of the farmer shouting for them to come back.

"I get down into the deep dark and scrabble up a tree, and I go leaping through the branches in a mad dash to get away. Two of them dogs is too stupid to find me, but one stays hot on the trail, and he keeps me good and treed for a long time. So I wait until his back is turned, and I drop down onto him like a hawk. I dig my claws into his sides and I open up his throat with my teeth."

Loxley sniffled and wiped her nose on her sleeve. "You ate a dog?"

"You like puppies, do you?"

"I don't know. I've never eaten one. Did it taste good?"

Tailypo licked his lips and gave a shivering sigh. "Baby, it was the sweetest taste I have yet had. I will never drink something so rich and warm as to fill up my soul like the blood of that mutt. And that's when I see it: something I never realized before that day. It's something the first Americans knew, and something I'm going to tell you right now – a home ain't a home until you lay the bodies of your enemies down on your hearth. Any folk may come and go on your land, but a home stays bought and paid when you've washed its stones in the blood of rivals."

"No," said Loxley. "Homes have deeds and cost money. I know because I'm trying to buy a farm from the Con –"

"Would you shut the fuck up and let me finish?" barked Tailypo, his voice sharp against her ears.

Loxley's fingers itched, and she balled her toes in her shoes. She looked from the fox to the wolves, to the hawks, anywhere but at the big boss. She didn't want his eyes on her.

"Jesus," he grunted. "So let me cut the next part down for you, since you're so eager to tell me about your real estate ventures: the next two nights, I lure the other two dogs away. Every bite of their sweetmeats revives me that much more. Then, finally, it's just the farmer, alone in his house, and all I can think about is how good he's going to taste. I get on top of his roof, and I start stalking around, clacking my claws on the shingles. I can hear him breathing in there, loading his musket. I can smell his sweat – almost like I'm cooking him, boiling him in his own juices. At this point, my human tongue is crude, but I start mumbling, 'Who's got my tail?' I hear him lock back the flint. I dash to one side of the roof and call again. I dash to the other, and he fires up through the boards, screaming at me like a madman. 'Who's got my tail?' I yelled back."

Tailypo leapt up from his chair and stalked around his desk toward Loxley. "Then he gets a lucky shot on me, and it goes straight up through my head, spraying out my brains like a fountain."

"You're lying. Your brains are in your head just fine," she said. "Stop trying to scare me, or I'm just going to leave."

"Don't leave, baby," he said, getting close and pointing to a patch of lighter skin on the base of his jaw. "See that scar? That's where the bullet hit."

"Then you'd be dead. Someone just shot two of my friends... someone shot my friend Nora in the head and she died. I saw it." Loxley didn't want to think he might be telling the truth. She backed away.

"I thought I was dead, too, and everything kind of twisted to the right. It never did untwist, either. But I stayed standing. I could taste that farmer down below, and when I blinked, I was standing right behind him. 'Who's got my tail?' Oh, God, Loxley he smelled so good, and my mouth hung open, and I felt drool or blood pouring down my chin like a warm waterfall. The farmer turns around, eyes wide, and I whisper into his ear..."

Tailypo's body heat winked out in front of her. Loxley knew in that moment that he wasn't lying. They weren't in his office; they were in the dark forest, and all of these animals had come to bear witness to her final moments at the hands of this creature. The stuffed animals turned to watch her with their glittering eyes, and the full moon blazed up above. Loxley's skin raged with millions of electric prickles, and she fell backward before him, screaming.

"I said, 'You've got it!'" he growled with milk-white eyes.

The room became a rush of beating wings, teeth, claws and eyes. Wolves howled for meat and rabbits screamed under the whistling trees. Blood and disease whirled in a death spiral above her head.

The static took her.

CHAPTER TEN
ANOTHER GOOD MORNING

TAILYPO SAT BEHIND his desk, working in a ledger. He wore glasses low on his nose, his imposing presence somehow disarmed by the dainty appliance. He sighed, licked the tip of his fountain pen and continued writing. The animals did nothing to react to his placid nature.

Loxley found her arms resting on the arms of a chair and she sat up, her heart pounding. "You're a ghost!"

Tailypo didn't look up. "Quentin came by a few minutes ago, looking to make sure you were all right. I told him you got scared and clammed up. He didn't want to go when he heard that." He looked up at her and smiled before returning to his work. "Do you think he's sweet on you?"

"I want to leave!"

"No one is stopping you."

"Good." She jumped to her feet and made for the door.

"You'll die, you know. Duke and his boys are

going to slaughter you like a lamb," he called after her.

She stopped and turned, half-expecting the animals to wake from their slumber again. "Maybe I won't try to kill him. I could run away."

He put down his pen and took off his glasses. "Not far enough. Never far enough. I could help you."

Tailypo sickened her. He was too open, too forward. Being in the same room as him felt like they were rubbing their spirits together. The boards slipped underfoot as though they'd soaked up buckets of blood, but she crept back to her seat.

"How?" she said, sitting down.

"You could give yourself to me. I always get back what's mine."

"No. Goodbye." And once more, she turned to leave.

"Quentin says you can play the violin pretty well. Is that true?"

She wiped her hands on her clothes to stop them from flapping. "Don't have a violin. It's locked up in Harrison Hoop Station."

"We'll sort that out when it becomes a problem, sugar," he said, steepling his fingers. "Do you want to play? You can live here while you do, and we'll feed you."

She scowled. "You're stupid."

"So you won't do it?"

"I came here to play violin for you. You're the one that scared me. Why did you do that?"

"It's hard to control myself around you, Loxley Fiddleback. I see the way you shrink, and it just makes me grow."

"If I stay," she began, "I don't want to see you around. I don't trust you."

He capped his pen and tapped it against the table. He beat a steady rhythm, and she couldn't help imagining the things she might play along to it. "You're not exactly in any position to dictate terms to me. You're standing here in stolen clothes, and my guess is that we were the last place on your list to come for help. Now you're going to come into my club and try to tell me what to do just because of what I am? Let me put this as clearly as I can." He dropped the pen. "Fuck you. I'll do whatever I please."

"I don't trust you to control yourself."

"Yeah, you probably shouldn't. Now do you want some clothes, food and a violin or not?"

She considered his offer. She'd come here to play for Quentin, and playing for Tailypo wouldn't be all that different. He wasn't like the other ghosts, and she briefly entertained the notion of learning more about the dead from him. She wouldn't, though; it would require her to be close to him, and the thought of sharing a building was unsettling enough.

"Why do ghosts want to hurt me?"

He chuckled. "I once knew this dog that'd had the ever-living shit beaten out of it as a puppy. It had a clipped ear and a broken tail, and walked with the worst hump in his back you've ever seen. He was the sweetest thing on four legs, though, and whenever he came around the kitchen, we'd feed him scraps. The cooks named him Brutus, in spite of the fact that I told them not to get attached. See, I knew something they didn't – Old Brutus was destined to die."

"Because he was beaten?"

"Not at all. Because of the way he carried himself. Something about that hump in his back or the sad face he was always making compelled the other dogs to try to rip him to shreds. They couldn't help but pick on him, you see. I could sense that in a way the humans couldn't. And one day, they found Brutus lying cold in the gutter, guts strewn everywhere. I'd seen it coming, but everyone else was stunned. You're like Brutus, Loxley."

"I don't have a hump in my back or a clipped ear. Not a dog, either."

He stood and walked around his desk. Each step that brought him closer made the bile rise in Loxley's throat. "No, but you have a way about you that makes us want to tear you to pieces. You have a weakness about you, and we can all sense it. Even now, I look at you and some part of me asks, 'What could she possibly do to hurt me?'"

He raised the back of his hand to brush her hair, and she flinched away. He laughed as she did. She didn't need him getting any ideas. She stood up and scowled at him.

"The last person who tried to hurt me got his leg opened up with a pruning knife. The last ghost who touched me..." Loxley began, but stopped short. She'd never considered it before. "The last ghost who touched me, my friend Nora, she lives inside of me now. She's not stalking around, haunting. She's just a part of me. Do you think that could happen to you if you were stupid?"

He smiled. "Now I just like you more."

She retreated to the other side of the chair, ready to shove it into him if he made any sudden moves.

"Then you have to buy me the best violin you can find. I don't want my old one anymore. I want good clothes, too."

"Anything for you. Not keeping your old violin?"

"Why would I do that?"

He shrugged. "I figured it had some sentimental value to you."

She thought about it. "No... Not really. My mom might have wanted it, but she died." She crossed her arms. "And I want another knife. I don't like the one I stole from Don."

"All in time, then." He pointed to a wardrobe, half-hidden behind a lounging jaguar. "I might have something in there for you to wear."

She went to the wardrobe and opened it up. Inside, a dozen silk dresses danced in the firelight, their lines teeming with brocade patterns like spun silver. She ran her hand down the side of one, and it gave her the distinct caress of flesh, soft and warm. Her other senses dulled as her arms coursed with prickly hairs. She rolled up her sleeves and put her arms into the closet, feeling the dresses on her bare skin, and hummed with hot breath. An orange glow chased over the fabric like sunlight on rippling water, and the threads tickled her like fingernails running gently over her arms. She reached in deeper, closed her eyes and pushed her face into one of the dresses. Her palms found the rough wood at the back of the cabinet and she startled, the illusion broken.

She pulled her arms back. She now understood why the rich always wanted silk, in spite of the fact that it was flimsy, expensive fabric. Silk brought memories of Nora's last night with Jack rushing to the surface. She blinked Jack away and recalled her dream: just her and Nora alone in her house. She tried to imagine the pleasures of silk sheets.

She turned to find Tailypo leering at her.

"I take it you've found something you like," he said, his voice smooth. "You could wear those onstage if you want."

"Why do you have these?"

"A lot of women have come and gone over the years, Loxley. I always get back what's mine." With that last word, he rubbed his fingers together as though handling cash. "I protected them from the forest outside, and they repaid me by leaving, though one or two died of old age."

The heat of the fireplace became unbearable on her cheeks. She walked toward the door. "You said people were coming to watch me play violin."

"Folks want a meal and a show, yes."

She wouldn't be able to handle wearing silk in public. It would make her feel too exposed – naked. Two weeks ago, she would have thought nothing of being so adorned in front of an audience of strangers. People were nothing more than animals; some of them she liked, others wandered away without consequence. Officer Crutchfield had tried to dominate her because he saw something he could fuck. Duke's men had stared at her body when they broke into her apartment.

The thought of Officer Crutchfield drained all of the heat from her skin. Tailypo wanted her to make a feast of herself. Silk was bad. Dangerous. She wasn't going to have it.

"I want a pair of denim work pants and a shirt," she said. "I like plaid. It has nice lines in it."

He snorted. "I run a classy place. You can't wear jeans and plaid."

"And give me good food. I like vegetables, but I don't like tomatoes because they're too sour. Turnip greens and bacon. I'll cook it myself because your cooks aren't me or my momma."

He laughed. "I got the best chefs anywhere, honey."

"No. My mom cooked better than them because she knows what I like. They don't know what I like, so they're bad cooks."

"Anything else?"

"No dresses. No silk," she said. He kept smiling at her and she stomped her foot to drive it home and shouted, "No silk!"

He flinched. She liked that.

She'd gone as far as the door when he said, "Be careful you don't walk around acting like the cock of the walk. You ain't the only special one. Got no idea who else lives down here, honey."

Tailypo was a ghost, but he wasn't. He could control how much of his true self she saw. He didn't have to hurt her like other ghosts. "Is Quentin also like you?"

"Only one special thing about Quentin: he belongs to me. He took the deal you chickened out on. Also, don't you get any weird ideas about him, because remember: I always get back what's mine."

She left, quietly closing the door behind her. The paisley walls had slowed their meanderings, now calm like a puddle after a storm. The gas lamps had grown brighter, and the hallway held no mystery as she walked toward the stairs. Someone called her,

227

and Loxley looked downstairs to see a smiling black woman in a stained chef's robe waving up at her.

The lady was plump like perfectly-ripe fruit: not too large, but not without curves. She beckoned, and Loxley descended.

"You must be Loxley." She had a musical lilt to her voice, and her short hair had been shaved flat across the top and covered by a hairnet. She'd painted her lips the color of an apple, and bore a bit of green across her eyelids. Loxley had never seen a woman wearing makeup like that so deep in the Hole. "My name is Jayla. I'm a cook. Tee said you were hungry?"

"Who is Tee?"

"The big guy upstairs."

Loxley didn't step any closer. "You're not a cook. I saw all the cooks when I came through the kitchens before. I would have remembered your eyelids because your face looks like an apple tree."

"I see." Jayla smirked. "And when was that?"

"This evening."

"It's morning. Let's get you some breakfast."

It couldn't have been morning, though, because that would mean she'd been in Tailypo's office all night. Then again, Nora's ghost had kept her out for a few hours.

Jayla took her hand without warning, and Loxley shouted in surprise. The whole episode with Tailypo had left her twitchy, and she jerked her hand back, rubbing the fingers as through they'd been burned. Jayla's palms were rough – coarser than Nora's – and Loxley didn't appreciate the suddenness of the cook's actions.

She hadn't meant to scream, and she wasn't angry, but now she felt scared to say anything else. Jayla looked her up and down with the sort of surprise that usually ended with a statement like, "Suit yourself." In a second, the cook would probably walk off and not want to talk to her anymore.

"You've got problems," Jayla chuckled.

"I'm not crazy."

"Didn't say you were. You've just got some nerves, and we can sort those out with hot biscuits and a little sweet coffee. You want me to make you some?"

She didn't want a stranger handling her food, and she knew Jayla would mess it up. "I don't like coffee. I'll cook for myself. You're not as good at cooking as my mom."

Jayla sighed. "That's the problem with being a cook. You wouldn't believe how many of the boys around here say that. They always come to my way of thinking in the end, though."

"And what is your way of thinking?"

"That I make the best goddamned biscuits around here, now let's get a move on, girl. Other hungry folks here, too."

Jayla took a rag from her waistband and circled Loxley, swatting her hip lightly. Loxley whimpered a bit, but allowed herself to be corralled to the kitchen. When she turned the corner, she'd expected the cacophony of the night before, but found a peaceful arrangement of cooks eating breakfast around one of the large steel tables. Some of the serving staff also joined them, all of them bleary, and Loxley wondered if they worked through the night.

The scent of frying bacon hit her nose and wormed

down into her stomach. Loxley became painfully-aware of how hungry she felt, and her gut refused to stop rumbling. She clasped her hands to her abdomen and squeezed, not wanting to draw any attention.

Jayla pulled out a stool for Loxley and she sat down. The table wasn't as cold as she expected, warmed by the arms and plates of a dozen hungry men and women. Loxley tilted her head, watching the silver feathering of the brushed metal finish undulate with the light. She imagined that there had been many silver ducks, and their feathers had been plucked and lacquered together into this metal table. The butcher would have to wear gloves to pluck them, because they would be so sharp and dangerous. He'd probably wear goggles, too – the kind that made people look like raccoons. What if the butcher was a raccoon? Then, when he took off his goggles, everyone would be surprised, but they'd know that's how raccoons were supposed to look. That would be pretty funny, and so Loxley laughed.

She craned her neck this way and that, counting several hundred different formations on her end of the table. When she looked up, the rest of the staff were staring at her. She made eye contact with each of them in turn, then went back to watching her patterns.

"Do you want gravy on your biscuits, Loxley?" called Jayla.

"No," she replied.

"She wants gravy," said an enormous cook with a lazy eye. He had a voice like a snore. "She just don't know it."

Loxley ran a finger down one of the brushings. "How can I want it? I've never had it."

There was a mass clatter at the table as silverware struck en masse. Then came a flood of questions. *You never had brown gravy? What about sawmill? Are you from around here? Do you eat meat? Why don't you put gravy on it? Do you know how to make it? Did your momma love you?*

Loxley clasped her hands to her ears, turning the dozen voices into a noisy rush like running water through a pipe. She closed her eyes so she didn't have to see their faces, and they stopped talking altogether. She felt sure they were staring again. Someone called out to Jayla, so Loxley let her hands down.

"What's wrong with this one?" asked the cook. "She's covering her ears."

"You're talking to her, that's what's wrong," said Jayla, returning with a heaping plate and shoving it in front of Loxley. "I'd cover my ears every time you started yapping if I could get away with it."

Loxley inspected her plate. White sauce with brown bits smothered two golden biscuits. Thick slices of bacon lay next to the biscuits, touching the sauce. She picked up her fork and pushed some of the gravy off the top of the nearest biscuit. People began to laugh and talk amongst themselves.

"What do you think?" asked Jayla. "Be honest."

"We used to have this mad dog in our neighborhood," said Loxley. "One summer, I saw him eating a bunch of milkweed that was growing up through the pavement, and I think he was sick because he was panting real hard. He kept wandering back and forth outside of our building, and I wanted to go outside, but I couldn't because he was out there, and I was scared of him. He bit me one time and I thought he might bite me again. Just before the sun went down, the dog came up to the door, threw up and died."

Silence descended over the table once more.

Loxley pointed to her gravy. "This kind of looks like that."

When the shouting and laughing resumed, she realized she'd said something wrong. Some people sounded angry, and others sounded amused. She didn't eat foods together – at home, her biscuits didn't ever touch her vegetables; she didn't like the look of the gravy, but she'd embarrassed herself once again. Loxley pushed her fork into one of the biscuits and took a big bite. Butter, salt and the cake texture of the biscuits flooded her mouth, balanced against the sausage and fat of the gravy. With so many different flavors, it was impossible for her to answer the most important question of all: did Jayla make better biscuits than her mother?

"It's good," said Loxley.

It's good? You like dog vomit, girl? She's crazy! Jayla who is this? Her hands went to her ears, but this time, they murmured to one another without paying her any mind. Loxley stood, pushing back from the table and Jayla took hold of her shoulders. With a few unintelligible parting words, Jayla pushed her back out the kitchen door and to the stairs.

"Why are we leaving?" asked Loxley.

"They're rowdy as fuck for a morning crew. Sorry if they bothered you."

"I'm hungry."

"I know, sugar, I know. I'll bring up your biscuits in a moment," said Jayla, following her upstairs. "First, I've got to show you your room. You can take your breakfast up there."

They crossed onto the second floor landing and into the hallway. Loxley pointed up the next flight. "Who lives up there, besides Tailypo?"

"Each one of those apartments belonged to one of Tee's wives before she left him. We've been told never to go up there, not even for cleaning." Jayla held up a hand to interrupt Loxley before she could talk. "And yes, I know what that sounds like, and no, Tee didn't murder his wives. Some of us have personally seen them run out on him."

"You shouldn't go up there, ever. Tailypo isn't good."

"He gave me a job when no one else would, and he didn't ask me for hooking money," said Jayla. "Maybe it would be better if you didn't talk about him like that, because a lot of folks depend on him."

"Yeah, but he's not good. He's a ghost."

"What? I don't give a fuck what he is. He keeps me and my friends off the streets, and he's buying your clothes. If you want this conversation to get ugly, keep this up and we can get ugly." Her voice sounded tense, but she was smiling. Why would she smile if she was mad?

"It's the truth."

The smile disappeared. "Last warning, Loxley. You shut your mouth about our boss."

Loxley's gaze fell to the ground, and she didn't speak again as they roamed around the eastern wing.

Her stomach tensed, and she flexed her fingers. "I'm sorry," she said, her voice barely a whisper.

"It's already forgotten," said Jayla, never looking back.

"I have... trouble with faces. You smiled when I made you mad."

"Just listen to what I'm saying next time."

"Yeah, but you said you'd cover your ears every time that fat guy talked to you, and you don't do that. If I only listened to what you were saying, I might think you did."

Jayla glanced back at her. "You retarded or something?"

"No. Don't call me that."

"All right. I'm sorry I confused you." They stopped outside a door. "It's just, Tee has done a lot for everybody here. We all owe him a lot, so I'd be careful going around saying bad shit about him. Most of us won't take too kindly to that."

Jayla pushed open the door. It opened onto a plain enough space, with two twin beds on chipped steel frames. Scuffed, wooden floors were hidden by a rug that had seen better days. Striped beige and blueberry wallpaper bore old water stains, and exposed beams formed the ceiling. A fan buzzed overhead, preventing the air from growing stale, but with a nagging, off-kilter pattern that grated on Loxley's nerves.

In addition to the two beds, there were two nightstands, two vanities and two tallboys. One set of furniture already had occupants, like makeup, clothing and an empty vase.

"Why is there two of everything in here?" asked Loxley, walking to the vanity and picking up a tube of lipstick. The rows of makeup were arranged perfectly, according to color, and she appreciated the layout.

"That's because I'm your roommate, Loxley."

Loxley dropped the tube to the table, where it bounced onto the floor. Whereas before, Jayla had been a minor curiosity, she now became a much more imminent threat. Loxley had only ever lived with her mother, and that hadn't always gone well. Now, here was this black woman who thought they could share a room. Loxley would have preferred a white roommate, but more than anything, she wanted to be alone. Why hadn't Tailypo told her of these arrangements? Why hadn't he told her of any arrangements?

She still had no replacement clothes, no food and no instrument. Even if she played onstage, she couldn't use her real name because Duke's men were looking for her. And when she made money with Tailypo, what then? How was she going to kill the man from Edgewood? And one floor up, a ghost lurked, waiting for her.

"I've made a mistake," said Loxley, marching for the door.

Jayla moved to block her. "Okay, no ma'am. We are not doing that."

She weaved, trying to pass. "Please move."

"No."

But Loxley refused to give up. She pressed forward, surprised when the larger woman's hands fell on her to hold her back. Still, Loxley tried to circle around.

"No!" Jayla gave her a big shove and shouted, "Sit down!" as Loxley stumbled back onto the bed. In a flash, the black woman was standing over her, jabbing a finger down at her. "Now you listen here, touched or not, you are going to accept our hospitality, sister! You smell like a sewer, you look like hell, and Quentin stuck his neck out for you to get you a spot here. You should have heard the way he begged Tee for a job for you! I'm not going to let you walk out of here until you have eaten, dressed and played at least one show for our troubles. And no, I am not going to let you walk around like you own the place just because Quentin thinks you're some big deal."

Loxley glared up at her. "I don't like you."

"Ain't that something special? I tell you what, Miss Thing: I'm going to go get you your breakfast so you've got something to eat, and then I'm going to serve it to you in here so you don't get too scared of people talking or whatever. Then I'm going to go get you some clothes to wear while you're eating the food I made for you. Is that going to suit you okay?"

"Yes. Where's Quentin?"

Jayla sighed and shook her head. "He's in town, buying you a brand-new violin. Because of that, maybe you could be nice when you see him."

"Okay." Loxley crossed her hands in her lap. "What you made for breakfast today, can I have it so that the biscuits don't touch the gravy and I can just dip them?" Loxley was worried about another outburst, but she needed to get her breakfast. She'd told Tailypo to let her cook and no one would listen to her.

"I've got more biscuits and gravy, but why can't you eat the ones I gave you before?"

"Because, to me, biscuits aren't supposed to be covered in anything. I like to put things on biscuits, like jelly, but they aren't supposed to come that way. I don't like to have my foods touching."

"What if you think of it all as a single food, like you would with a sandwich?"

"I could call it something else, like Jaylabiscuits, because it's not really biscuits."

"If that works for you."

Loxley watched her turn to go. "I like Jaylabiscuits a lot."

Her new roommate smiled. "Oh, yeah? More than regular biscuits?"

That was like asking whether someone liked frogs more than rocks. They were two completely different things. However, Loxley had messed up so much already, and she was a little afraid of Jayla, so she nodded.

"All right, then."

"One more thing: can I get some more bacon that didn't touch the gravy?"

The smile disappeared. "'Jaylabacon.'"

"That's weird," said Loxley.

Jayla left the room without saying another word. The artifacts of someone else's life, little trinkets and everyday objects, unsettled Loxley like the steel worker's uniform she wore. It was one thing to wear someone else's things for a little while; it was another to live in them.

But all of her old clothes were gone, along with her book and greenhouse, all her tools. She surveyed her new surroundings with the sinking feeling that this truly was her new home.

The Gift

THAT NIGHT, LOXLEY slept naked under the covers, happy that she wasn't at Don's house, on the street – or lying on her belly with a bullet in her head. When she awoke, her Foundry uniform had been taken from the floor and replaced with a stack of fresh clothes – a white, cotton button-up shirt and black slacks with a shiny stripe that ran down the sides. Her shoes had been replaced, too, with a pair of gleaming black leather loafers. She found a note in her pants pocket

No dresses, no silk.
–T.

After she'd slipped into her clothes, she pulled back her hair and tucked in her shirt. She looked funny: rich, but not Edgewood-rich. Jayla later told her she was very dashing in her new clothes, but that she needed makeup. Loxley thought of the way tape felt against her skin and said no thanks.

It would be two days before Loxley saw Quentin again. She asked after him at every opportunity, but he was always "out" or "making deals" or "way too busy for whatever the fuck you could want." This last one had come from the fat cook, who identified as Cap.

Whenever Cap spotted her in the halls or the kitchen, he'd pepper her with questions, chuckling at every response. The less funny they seemed, the more he would laugh. He wanted to know when people were too loud, what sorts of things made her angry, what scared her, who she liked (Quentin), who she didn't like (Cap). When she'd told him she liked Quentin, he wanted to know everything about why, and kept telling the other staffers that she was "sweet on Quentin."

Cap liked to laugh at her, that much was clear. Loxley had a difficult time with subtleties of expression, but she knew when people were laughing at her. Loads of people thought she was funny, even when she had panic attacks. She'd been trained to recognize that expression of amusement her whole life; she knew exactly what people like Cap were thinking.

Loxley learned something important over those two days: Jayla didn't think Cap was funny at all. She didn't like his face, how he smelled or looked. She'd say mean things behind his back, and when he appeared, she'd say mean things to his face. So whenever Cap started to bother Loxley, she'd make her way toward Jayla with all speed. The strategy worked, and Loxley had much more free time to wander the grounds and learn about the Hound's Tail.

No one asked anything of her. Aside from Cap and Jayla, they maintained a comfortable distance that Loxley enjoyed. She was allowed to come and go as she pleased, and Jayla took special care to ask her what she wanted to eat before cooking. Sometimes, Loxley's requests were even heeded.

The building had more than twenty rooms, some more lavish than others. Loxley found many a broom closet, languishing with nothing but spiders and dust for company, but found just as many places like the green room – a gorgeous whirlwind of finely – crafted furniture and glass. It was not, contrary to the name, green. Jayla told her that was where actors normally waited before going onstage, leading Loxley to wonder whether or not actors had an affinity for green, and whether or not they found the green room of the Hound's Tail disappointing.

The stage was in a great hall filled with dining tables. The dining area was stepped, like the Hole itself, and upholstered walls ran around the edge of each level. Atop these walls were blooming flowers of blue and white. Loxley had never seen them before, but admired the way they glowed in the soft incandescence of their lit planters. She was told Tailypo personally tended the flowers and employees were not to touch them. If customers wanted to ruin the plants, that was their business. Loxley would have protested that she was a farmer, but she had no training in these flowers, which grew in almost complete shadow.

Long, rectangular panes of glass twinkled in the chandelier above, fitted into brass rings. The prisms provided a sense of purpose and guidance to the room, creating a lit halo in the center of the floor. Loxley stood in the middle of the halo and looked straight up, imagining the panes drooping down to create a golden forest of warm glass.

The actual stage was a circular affair made of polished maple and rimed with limelights. From the stage, it was easier to see the various can lights dangling from the rafters. When she spoke, it bounced back at her as though she was standing behind herself. She couldn't imagine a fully-packed room, bristling with starbursts of stage light. Just the thought of all of those shadowy faces made her heart race.

When she finally saw Quentin again, she was standing in the middle of the stage, looking out on the dining room. He wore the same sharp suit she had seen him in before, his shoulders dappled with mist from the rain outside. He held a brown paper package at his side and wore a wide smile.

"Taking a liking to the stage, Pumpkin?" he called.

"A little scared."

"That's normal, but pointless. I've seen you play. I know you can do a good job."

"I'm not scared of that. I don't want all of those people looking at me."

"Imagine how I feel. I have to greet all of those motherfuckers at the door," he laughed. He brushed his shoulders off with a gloved hand.

"What's that?" She pointed to the package.

"This is your violin. You want to see it?"

She nodded, and he brought it to her. Together, they sat down on the stage and tore the paper and packing twine away. The case underneath shocked her with its newness. She'd become accustomed to her old case with its myriad dents and scuffs, but the black faux leather covering this case was like Nora's Bible – untouched and perfectly preserved. She ran her fingers over the bumpy surface, coming to rest at the first brass latch, still cold from the chilly air outside. She looked to Quentin, who nodded it was okay.

She barely recognized the instrument inside as a violin. It was an ashen brown, almost gray, with a satin sheen across its surface that seemed to glow at the edges. The ebony fingerboard and tailpiece felt as smooth as Tailypo's silks, with no nicks from decades of hammering fingers. The tuning pegs, string nut and saddle were solid silver, and flashed as the lights traveled across them. She flipped the instrument over and found the maker's mark, along with a tiny emblem of a spider's web notched into the wood.

It would have been something beautiful to see in a shop window on Edgewood, or perhaps in a far-off city across the ocean. She didn't own anything even remotely so fine as that violin, and now that Duke's men knew where she lived, she didn't truly own anything at all. Holding an object that elegant felt like a dream, like Nora's day at Bellebrook – something that could never happen to Loxley.

"This is mine?" she asked, her voice breaking.

"That's what I said. Yours."

In a split-second, she'd gone from being worthless to holding something worth more than her entire old life. She felt an unexplainable fullness of being, and she began to rock back and forth on her knees, the dizzy world spinning past. Her voice came out in happy sighs with each back-and-forth motion, and she clutched the instrument to her chest. Static nipped at her brain, but she rode the crackles and ants, her knuckles white against the poplar housing. Quentin was talking, but his words dissipated like smoke in the thunderstorm of her mind.

Warmth fell across her shoulders as Quentin wrapped an arm around her and squeezed. "It's okay," he said, his voice soothing as a cat's purr.

"Let's calm down, Loxley. I'm worried you're going to break it, you're squeezing so tight."

Her jaw relaxed; she'd been clenching her teeth. She loosened her grip and swallowed. "I'm so happy right now."

"I can see that. You're something else, and I wanted you to have an instrument that showed the crowd just how special you are. Had to personally go all the way to a luthier in Nashville to get it."

"What's a luthier?"

"Person who makes violins. This one was a strange woman – a little bit like you, but I guess you have to be strange to make violins."

She turned it over to look at the maker's mark once again: Kate Batts. It was a scrawled signature embossed into the wood, almost clumsy, compared to the rest of the instrument. The luthier was meticulous in her craft, yet sloppy in her identity. Black ink had been painted into the notches of the spider's web before applying the finish, and looking closer, Loxley spied hairline strands of dyed wood poking out from each line.

"Can I play it?"

"I'd hoped you would," said Quentin.

She picked up the bow from the case and examined it. Also made from the same gray poplar, the bow had a band of polished silver running down the back that would no doubt sparkle under the spotlights. She took it by the frog and wound the strings tight before rosining them from a small tub in the case.

Resting her chin upon it, the violin was a stranger to her. All of the notches and dings of her old companion were absent, replaced by a smoothness that did not quite fit her. Normally, the unfamiliarity would have bothered her, but this time it was exciting, like pushing a garden trowel into undisturbed earth. The precipice of expectation and discovery thrilled her.

When she drew the bow across the strings, she found the instrument more tuned than she'd expected. With a minor adjustment, she found her notes and drew once again. The violin sang with such a clear harmonic that the whole room seemed to shrink to be filled with her sound. The note bounced off the far walls, feeding back into itself to become twice the power it was. It was a pane of glass, more flawless and warmer than those prisms dangling from the chandelier above her. She'd been able to make sounds on her old violin, but now they seemed like hoarse imitations of real music.

She walked up and down the A scale until she found a curve in the midmorning light – the supple sculpt of Nora's hip as she lay in bed – an image from the dream at Don's house. Loxley's fingers lightly traveled over the strings, gently teasing out more details of Nora's shoulders, her breasts, her long neck. She played her friend's sleepy smile into the composition, swaying in time as the music streamed from her.

She played of Nora's eyes: green, sure and aglow with a confidence Loxley could never possess. So much of Loxley's music had been long, straight lines conjoined by harmony alone, but this tune flowed through an ocean of itself, its boundaries continually challenged by each expedition across the fingerboard. She played to recall water, and a dewdrop hanging in the summer light of a dawning day.

The Nora of her song didn't belong to anyone else, didn't exist in any shared space. She wasn't the same person who failed to share her feelings outside the Bazaar. She didn't bother with men like Jack or Hiram. This Nora lay naked in bed, warm and wonderful, driving out any thoughts of awakening. She had no flaws, only beauty, because the real Nora wasn't food for the public ear. The woman of Loxley's song was a bent half-truth, idealized for Loxley's ease as much as the music.

A hint of uncertainty crept into the tune – a tiny amount of discord curling some of the notes. A trickle of blood spilled across the little hairs of Nora's brow. Just a tiny cut at first, a thin halo of burned flesh faded into the skin around it. A bone-cracking rip sounded as Loxley slapped the bow across the strings. Hair matted to the back of Nora's head, slick but not smooth. Loxley's old apartment became Nora's living room, and Loxley brought her discord to a tiny tremble as she rediscovered her friend's corpse. She arpeggiated in tense, minor steps, coming closer to the body with each drawing of the bow.

Loxley looked over the body, the light of the green eyes replaced with the sheen of old meat. She plucked the string and let it hum – a teardrop.

Sadness and fear intermingled as the thought of ghosts surfaced. She'd never imagined what one might sound like in musical form, but she sawed across the low G string, and it groaned hoarsely. The instrument had a character Loxley hadn't predicted in that note, as though it sensed what she wanted and gave her more than she'd hoped. Nora arose from her place at Loxley's side to hover in august malevolence before the violinist. Cold hands clutched the air aimlessly; pale lips uttered meaningless words.

Loxley squeezed her eyes shut, and the harder she squeezed, the more she could see Nora – and feel her presence. Loxley breathed in the cool, slightly damp air of the stage, and she heard something she hadn't heard in days: the rhythmic clang of the steelworks below. She stomped a foot in counterpoint, a bass drum to its cymbal. Her hands itched to follow the beat, but terror gripped her heart. Unnatural ripples stirred around her, and she grit her teeth. The song was almost over – two more bars. She couldn't stop early; she would be done soon. But what would happen when she finished?

She stopped without finishing. She lowered the bow.

A wave of applause crashed into her, and Loxley screamed, covering her ears as she fell to her knees. Silence followed just as quickly. She looked out and saw Quentin standing at the vanguard of a dozen or so surprised cooks, cleaners and serving staff. How long had she been playing? Why hadn't she noticed them?

Quentin looked her in the eyes and nodded before spinning to face the others. "All right, ya'all: you know you've got work to do! What the fuck are you wasting time out here for? We open in six hours, now get to it!"

Loxley winced as he clapped his hands, shooing off the other staffers. Her gaze drifted downward to the violin laying on the stage. She'd dropped her precious poplar beauty. Her eyes burned with embarrassment.

"It's okay, Loxley. I guess you weren't ready for all that," came Quentin, climbing onto the stage to sit next to her.

She fingered the edge of the upper bout and found a chip in the satin finish. "I'm sorry," she stuttered. A sob fell from her lips, but she caught the next one. "I don't know what happened. I chipped the violin." She held it up so he could see.

"No need to apologize to me. It's yours, you know." He gently pushed it away. "Now, Loxley, I have seen you play a half-dozen times at Harrison Hoop. They clap every time. What happened this time?"

"You're going to kick me out, aren't you?"

"Are you going to scream every time you play?"

She picked up the bow. "No. I swear I won't. I'm so sorry."

"Are you going to play something happier next time?"

She thought about it. There wasn't much to be happy about. "I don't know what to play. I like to think of stories when I play. My stories are all stupid now."

"I could have Jayla bring you a piece of chocolate cake. She could bring you a lot of cakes, actually, and you'll have a story about the time you ate yourself silly."

"I don't eat sweets."

He raised an eyebrow. "Jayla!" he called to the kitchen.

Loxley's stomach knotted up and she folded her arms around the instrument. Quentin had offered too much, gone out of his way too many times, spent too much money. Now, he wanted to feed her a cake just because she felt bad. She wasn't that special. A lot of folks could play the violin, and no one gave them shiny new toys from Nashville. What if Quentin was just like Officer Crutchfield, pretending to like her because he wanted her body?

She ran a finger across the F holes and sniffled. She wanted him to be telling the truth. She wanted him to be her friend. Was she sure he was lying? Did she know anything about him at all?

"Stop," she said, pulling his hand down. "I don't want anything more."

"It ain't a big deal. I'll just –"

"I said no, Mister Mabry," she said, standing up. She set the instrument down on its case. "You've done too much already. Everyone told me so."

He sat up straight. "Who's been saying that to you? Was it Cap?"

Her cheeks pricked with heat. "He says... He, well..."

"What did he say?"

"He says I'm sweet on you, but I'm not. I'm never going to have sex with you. Not ever."

Quentin nodded and stroked his chin. "I believe we already agreed to that."

"You're buying me expensive stuff, and you keep making people serve me and some people don't like me because of you. I don't know why you're being so nice, because when we first met I didn't like you."

He also stood. "I'm doing this for you because

you're going to make me and Tee money. You're the talent, and you're going to keep these tables full... I want to be your friend because I feel bad for you."

She looked away. Staring him in the eyes bothered her too much. "Everyone thinks they're better than me. You're just going to call me crazy, too, aren't you?"

"No, I'm not."

"But that's probably what you think."

"Why would you say that?"

She didn't know why she was being so forceful with him. What if he had always been nice because he simply liked her as a person? Loxley liked Nora the first time she'd met her. Then again, Loxley couldn't get Nora's nude figure out of her head. Did she want to fuck Nora? Was anybody ever honest about how they felt? She'd trusted everyone in the past – everyone her mother had told her to trust – and that was wrong because of Officer Crutchfield. Her mother had told her not to trust blacks; was that wrong, too?

The world didn't work right anymore. Alvin Kimball had changed it the day he touched her in the Bazaar.

"If you care about me as a friend," she said, "stop being so nice to me."

"Loxley, honey, that doesn't make sense."

She shook the crackles out of her fingers and her breathing sped up. "I'm sorry. I'm confused. Please go away."

He jammed his hands in his pockets and sighed. "Okay... Okay. Look, just keep the violin. When are you going to be ready to go onstage?"

"Tonight, but I want to practice."

"All right. We'll give it a try tonight. You can stay in here and get to know your new toy until then." He sauntered to the edge of the stage and hopped off, headed up the steps to the entrance. "Oh, and be in makeup in four hours."

"I don't wear makeup."

"It's part of the job, so you'd better learn."

For some reason, her mind had gotten stuck on the morning she saw Alvin Kimball's ghost. She thought of Officer Crutchfield, and how he'd wanted her gratitude. As Quentin reached the door, she spoke up once more, calling his name. When he turned, she said, "Thank you."

He chuckled. "At least your momma taught you some manners."

"Wasn't my mother."

"Whoever it was, they were a good influence on you," he said, pushing through the swinging doors to disappear around a corner.

Loxley's limbs felt heavy as she reached down to pick up her new violin with trembling fingers. Officer Crutchfield was a bad person, even if they'd shot him when he tried to rescue her.

He was a bad person. It wasn't fair to feel otherwise.

CHAPTER ELEVEN
A HILL OF BEANS

PRACTICE WAS GOING poorly, and every interlude brought back Nora's ghost.

She held the most wonderful thing she'd ever seen, her poplar beauty, but where was the music inside it? Inside her? Disgusted, she placed the instrument into its case, checking to make sure it was carefully seated, then slammed the lid. The explosive clap felt good, like she'd chipped away at a binding around her heart, so she opened the case and slammed it again, humming happily. *Clap! Hum. Clap! Hum. Clap! Hum.*

She eased into it and closed her eyes, making a drumbeat. *Clap. Breathe in. Clap. Breathe out. Clap. Breathe in. Clap. Breathe out.*

"Hey, stop that!"

Another voice. Go away. Clap!

Rough, warm hands grabbed hers, and she looked up to find Jayla scowling at her. "You're going to break it! Calm down."

Loxley ran her fingers along the open edge of

the case and found that she'd dinged it up pretty badly. Exposed wood poked out from under the faux leather, and one of the brass latches had gotten roughed up. First, she'd chipped the violin, and now the case. Could she take care of this precious thing? The heat rose in her cheeks, and her fingers wouldn't listen to her, so she shook them out.

"It's mine," she spat.

"Well ain't you just the most spoiled thing on two legs? You think that gives you a right to break it?"

"Yes."

Jayla scowled. "You want to rethink that?"

"You don't know me."

"Idle hands. I know you just fine. You finished your practice and you didn't have anything to do next, so you let your hands do whatever they wanted."

She wanted to tell Jayla that her mind needed to be flattened out, that she was pounding out the bumps, but the words wouldn't come. "Ain't my hands."

"It's that brain of yours, right? It needs to feel like it's doing something."

"Go away. I'm practicing."

"Come with me. I've got something to show you."

Loxley frowned, but she stood and followed Jayla. It was for the best that she get away from the violin for awhile. It beckoned to her, but she knew she'd only get angry if she picked it up again. She stomped her feet a few times before she left the stage, savoring the warm, bass boom of the planks through the main hall.

Jayla led her to the kitchen, which lay empty, save for a big apple crate, lined with plastic, stacked on the steel tables. The lid had been pried off and inside

Loxley spotted a huge pile of red lentils almost bursting from the top.

"I heard you playing out there," said Jayla.

"Okay."

"I heard you when you stopped, too, banging around like a wet cat. You need something to do with your hands."

"Okay."

Jayla's eyebrows did something, and Loxley was pretty sure she was making a nasty face. "I want you to try something." She crossed to the open crate. "You know what these are?"

"Lentils. I don't grow them because –" *Because I don't have a garden.*

"Wrong, baby. These are heaven on earth. I want you to do what I do." Jayla sank her hands into the pile, all the way up to the elbows and took a deep breath.

Loxley scratched her nose and watched as the other woman pushed her hands through the pile, letting the lentils slip between her fingers. "Why?"

"Just do it. You'll like it."

Her chest felt tight, and she shook her head no, but Jayla wasn't looking. Loxley flapped her fingers, balling and opening her fists. She stepped closer to the open crate, looking over its endless array of tiny red pulses.

Jayla withdrew her hands and splayed her fingers, positioning them over the hill. "Like this."

Loxley stretched her hands until the skin of her palms burned and pushed them partway into the lentils. "Okay."

Cool shells effervesced her skin as her hands

sank into the crate. A sudden sigh escaped her lips and a sharpness seized her mind, focusing her surroundings. She looked around the kitchen, at the rows of hanging pots and pans, at the dozen butcher blocks bristling with knives, and felt no need to take inventory. She didn't hear the endless voices of other workers throughout the club as they prepped for their day. She spread her fingers and pushed them around, the weight of dry pulses tickling and compressing simultaneously.

"I heard you in there practicing. Sounded good," said Jayla. "Except at the end."

"I was mad." Her voice sounded clearer somehow, like her lips didn't want to trip over each other. "I kept thinking of someone I don't want to think of."

"We've all got those, sweetheart."

Loxley started to correct her, to tell her that Nora was different than some jilted lover, but then she remembered that in the Hole, everyone knew someone who'd been murdered. It was just the way of things. Jayla probably had some sob stories, too.

Jayla raised her hands from the pile, and let lentils trickle from them. They made a pleasant patter. Then, she plunged them back into the beans. "Don't worry about it. You're going to be fine."

"Everyone keeps thinking I'm going to be something, but I'm not," she said. "I'm not anything, and I'm not going to be."

Jayla's hands wrapped around Loxley's wrists, deep under the grains, and squeezed. They were strong and sure, warm, but far from soft. Loxley looked into the other woman's eyes and blinked. Another quick squeeze, and Jayla broke contact. She felt a sudden emptiness on her wrists, and the lentils felt colder than they had before.

"Hush. Your bad practicing was better that most girls on that stage ever get."

They stood in silence for a few minutes, enjoying the dry lentils. Loxley rained them onto the pile, passing them just in front of her eyes like a red storm.

"Do you do this all the time? With the lentils?" she asked.

Jayla smiled and looked away. "Only when we get a new shipment. These will tide us over for a few weeks, and once they're in the pantry, I don't mess with them much."

"You should. This is nice." Loxley swallowed. "You have really strong hands, like a man's."

"You're one to talk! I've seen your arms, girl."

Loxley's cheeks prickled, and she looked away. Her hands brushed up against the other woman's. She looked up.

Jayla beamed at her. "You feel better?"

"I do."

She drew out her hands and shook them free. "Go on, then. Get back out there and play something pretty."

A New Face

WHEN LOXLEY GOT back to her room for makeup, she found a clean tuxedo awaiting her. She'd begun to sweat during practice, and as she passed Jayla's vanity mirror, she saw that her hair had become disheveled and greasy. She stripped down, donned a housecoat and padded down the hall to the communal bathroom.

Several employees lived onsite at the Hound's Tail: Jayla, Quentin, Charisse the maid, Marcus the bookkeeper, and two of the repairmen, Leandro and Alphonso (who confused Loxley because they were identical twins). Almost all of them lived on the second floor, and they all shared a bathroom, which meant that no one was allowed to leave their things in there. The pristine ceramic tiles comforted her, a blank slate.

As she washed up in the claw-footed tub, she tried to imagine what makeup would feel like on her skin. She took her bar of soap, which had become soft from soaking in the tub, and smeared a streak across her cheek; nothing but calmness followed because she knew it was only soap. She'd been taking baths her whole life, and as much as she tried to imagine it was makeup, she couldn't. Makeup was weird: it changed the color of your skin and it sometimes didn't come off when you rubbed it.

Her mother had tried to put lipstick on her once as a child, so she could attend the funeral of a family friend. The second the grease had gone on, Loxley wiped it across her sleeve, leaving a huge red streak across the white cotton of her Sunday dress. *Baby, what the hell?* her mother had screamed. She'd roughly grabbed Loxley by the shoulder and tried to put on another coat, and Loxley had resisted, falling into a state of screaming panic that had lasted the better part of a night. They'd missed the funeral.

Loxley tried to imagine a mask of colors coating her face, beautiful and exciting like Jayla's. Jayla's lips were especially fascinating, because they were actually three shades of red, meticulously blended into a luscious tone. There was a wetness to them, as though they were always recently licked, and Loxley wondered if they tasted good. She shook the thought out of her head. No one would like her if she tried to kiss a girl – that much she knew.

Loxley washed up and dried off, returning to her quarters. When she arrived, she donned the tuxedo, and had barely tied her laces when Jayla breezed in to take her to the dressing room.

"I'm going to be doing your makeup today, Loxley!" she said, dragging her out the door and down the hall. "Isn't that exciting?"

After her thoughts in the bathtub, Jayla's hot hand felt strange on Loxley's skin. "No. I thought you were a cook."

"If it wasn't for me, everything would fall apart around here."

"I thought that's what people said about Quentin."

"Sure... Him, too, but he ain't as smart as me."

The hallways came alive around five in the afternoon, and for the past two days, Loxley had retreated into her room at that time. She hated the motion and noise; they reminded her of Vulcan's Bazaar with its boisterous crowds and barking vendors. Now the Hound's Tail filled with clinking glass and hissing steam, bustling colors and so much shouting. *Warm up the lights! Did you get the sign? I need those veggies over here! Thirty more of those! Get on it! They're lining up! Get out of the way! Soup is on! Get the butcher on the horn! Twenty minutes!*

She focused on the feeling of Jayla's hand as they wound through the chaos and down several hallways. Loxley's heart thumped, but she could take it as long as she held on. She stared at the place where their skin touched, for fear that looking up would send her into a panicked fit. Her jaw clenched, and she squeezed Jayla's fingers even more tightly.

"What are you singing back there?" asked the cook.

Loxley hadn't realized she was humming again. "N-nothing. Just scared. Too many people."

"It's okay. Dressing room is right here."

They passed through a doorway to find a row of mirrors, each surrounded by a dozen naked bulbs. Underneath each mirror was a table containing many of bottles of makeup, hair supplies, combs, scissors, tape and more. Each station also had a large leather chair that had been worn in a few spots. Between the incandescent wall of mirrors and the creamy paint scheme, the dressing room exuded a pleasant warmth.

That changed when Jayla sat Loxley before one of the mirrors. The myriad of makeup bottles seemed to multiply before her eyes, their colors and eccentricities compounding into a wall of chaos. She wanted to straighten them or sort them by color and shadow to make sense of the mess. She could fragment the complexity by only looking at individual bottles, but each time she tried, another would pull her gaze.

She shut her eyes, staring into the dark pink of her lids. She should've fought back when Quentin told her she'd have to wear makeup, should've stood up for herself. The thought of greasy film being rubbed onto her face was too much for her, and she feared what she might do when Jayla started.

"You okay, gorgeous?" came Jayla's voice.

"No. I don't want to do this."

"Why not?"

"Because it's like tape, and when you have tape on your skin, you have to take it off."

"Five minutes of wearing it, and you won't even know it's there," said Jayla. Tiny glass bottles clinked, and a plastic cap was unscrewed.

"Do you promise?"

"I promise, but you can't touch your face, okay? Not even to rub your eyes."

Loxley thought about it. This all sounded awful. She wasn't pretty, anyway; she didn't know why anyone bothered to try to fix her. "Okay."

"Good," said Jayla. "Just keep those eyes closed then."

Something soft and wet dotted Loxley's cheeks and chin, leaving behind a residue. It was almost impossible for her to keep her hands down when she felt that, but she managed to grip the chair. A foam sponge worked the residue in, spreading it over her face. She found that sensation more pleasant, as well as the scent of Jayla's breath mixed together with the heathery smells of the makeup.

She looked up to find the other woman mere inches from her face, Jayla's large, chestnut eyes aglow in the shadow of the mirror's lights. Up close, Jayla's lips were even more stunning – full and slick, promising a burst of juice like the waxy skin of a red apple. Loxley's breath grew hotter and her stomach twisted into a knot.

"What are you doing?" asked Loxley.

"Just putting on a base to get you all smoothed out.

We'll build on top of that."

Jayla finally pulled away so Loxley could look in the mirror, and her withdrawal seemed to suck away all the heat. She met her own gaze and a different woman stared back at her. All of her blemishes had been covered, and her skin had a sheen like the body of her poplar violin. It wasn't reflective, but seemed to drink in the light. It felt greasy, yet looked clean.

Jayla unscrewed the cap on a fat container of rouge and grabbed a brush from the table. "Okay, now hold still. I don't want to get this in your eyes." She leaned back in and began to smear Loxley's cheeks with the red powder. When she breathed out through her nose, warm air tickled Loxley's bare neck.

She kept her eyes fixed on those wonderful lips. "Are you going to do my mouth like yours?"

"You like my lipstick, honey?" A curling, glistening smile.

"Yeah... I think it's really pretty."

"I tell you what, I'm not sure you need this blush. You're pretty flushed right now."

"Just scared. I don't like things on my skin."

But that was a lie. She wanted to kiss Jayla the way she'd never kissed Nora, in a way that would wipe the stink of Officer Crutchfield off her face; the man who'd died saving her from Duke. The pleasant twist in her stomach became a cold ache, and she felt the makeup on her face more keenly than before. It had replaced her skin. She had to wipe it off now.

"Whoa, girl," said Jayla, catching her hand as it went to her face. "Hey, now, it's okay. Just chill, honey."

"I don't like this!" said Loxley. "It's stupid! Let go of me!"

She easily wrested her arm from Jayla with muscles she'd trained to carry hundred pound bags of soil up thirteen stories to her rooftop garden. She brought her sleeve across her face, leaving a beige streak along the tuxedo, but there was more – so much more on her, like she'd never get it all off. The fractal web of makeup bottles loomed before her in their chaotic pile. Too many bottles, no rows – they needed to be thrown down. She lunged forward and scrambled at them with her clawing fingers, trying to knock them from the table. Jayla snatched her right hand and placed it against her own cheek, and the warmth of Jayla's skin flowed into Loxley's body.

"It's okay. I want you to look at me. *Look at me,* Loxley."

Loxley looked into her eyes, her ragged breath calming.

"What are you thinking?"

She dug fingernails into the arms of the chair and looked away. "I like your lips."

"And that was a good reason to fuck up my makeup?" asked Jayla. Her words were angry, but her voice wasn't. Touching the woman's skin made Loxley feel like she could hear her better.

"Last week, Officer Crutchfield kissed me," said Loxley, startling as her voice creaked.

"I don't know Officer Crutchfield. Is he sweet on you?" Jayla reached out and stroked her hair, the gentle caress holding the tears at bay.

"Yes," said Loxley. She swallowed and shook her head. "I hate him."

"Oh?" The stroking stopped, stumbling momentarily. "Oh. What are you saying? Did he do something bad?"

"H-he pushed me and then he tried to put his fingers in me and it hurt, and it's my fault."

"Oh, Jesus. No, it isn't. Don't say that."

"It is my fault!" she screamed, her whole body tensing – static and ants, crackles and fire on her skin. She beat her fists into her eyebrows a dozen times, lights exploding behind her eyes with each strike. "I should have known he was going to try to fuck me! I should have told him to stop! I w-would have, too, if I could've, if I wasn't so –"

"Let's be calm. You need to calm down, honey."

Despair washed into her head, pouring down her eyes. She slumped forward, her brain spinning, and whispered. "... if I wasn't so retarded."

The room shrank around her, filled with the sounds of her sniffling breaths. They sat in silence, and Loxley counted the squares in the carpet pattern to keep the ants at bay. She imagined cars driving along the lines as though they were city blocks.

"Everyone is right about me. They all know I'm crazy because they're not."

Jayla pulled Loxley to her breast, the woman's heart pounding in her ear. Softness enfolded Loxley, and she felt like she might faint in those kind arms. It was as though she'd pulled the blanket up over her head on a cold morning, and even if it would suffocate her, she stayed under, savoring the texture. She wrapped her arms around Jayla and held her in turn.

"Loxley, baby, you got to listen to me. The things

men do... they ain't ever our fault. You understand me?"

Nora's face flashed through her mind, the bruised hole on her brow. Loxley didn't answer, but squeezed more tightly.

"You want to hate him... you go on and hate him," said Jayla.

"He's dead. He got shot trying to save me from Duke."

"I see." Jayla patted the back of her head. "He may have done something right, but that doesn't mean you have to love him. You ain't his property."

She considered that for a moment. Folks were always on about how people owed each other for the things they did. If someone owed money, that person paid it back. If someone saved a person's life, that person was forever in debt. "It's not fair. I should be allowed to hate him."

"It's okay to hate him. He was going to do bad things to you, and you know that."

"He was the only person who ever kissed me. Only person who ever wanted to."

Jayla pushed her back to arm's length and looked into her eyes. "You're a beautiful girl. I'm sure a lot of people have thought about kissing you."

"Have you?" Some of the tension returned to her fingers. She mouthed the words twice before they came out. "Would you?"

Jayla's arms fell to her sides, and a look of surprise crossed her face. For once, it was Loxley keeping eye contact while another person looked anywhere but at her. The vein in Jayla's neck throbbed, but Loxley couldn't tell if she was blushing.

It almost hurt her to talk. "I j-just want to kiss... someone other than Officer Crutchfield. Someone I think is pretty... I like your lips. That's what I was talking about before."

The crackles weren't just in her fingertips; They spread into the air, tickling her entire body. Her skin grew hot, like she was running a fever, and her being stretched toward Jayla, even though she was sitting still. She couldn't un-say what she'd said, and now she'd have to suffer consequences. People hated girls who kissed girls.

Loxley's sadness returned. She'd ruined this, too. "I... I'm sorry. I never meant –"

The distance between them suddenly collapsed as Jayla leaned in, closing her eyes, and their lips met. Loxley felt sticky lipstick and breath as she snaked her arms around the other woman, pulling her closer. Her body scintillated like it had in the cooling tower – a million little bubbles rushing over her skin, tickling every sensitive area.

After a too-brief moment of tenderness, they parted.

"There," said Jayla, her voice barely a whisper. "Now you been kissed by someone else."

A smile pulled so hard at Loxley's mouth that her cheeks hurt. "Yeah."

"I was just filling in. I know you'd probably rather get a kiss from Quentin."

"No."

Loxley waited for her to say something else, but Jayla fiddled with the makeup bottles instead. She laughed for no apparent reason. "You going to let me do your makeup, girl?"

"If I don't, they're going to throw me out, aren't they?"

"Tee might not let you play. I'm already going to have to swap out your jacket. Those sleeves are coated." Jayla strode to the closet, where Loxley spotted an array of tuxedos. She began to dig around inside, and soon reemerged with a jacket, and a lacquered, white half-mask – the kind that went around the eyes. "Look what I found."

"A mask?"

"This would be perfect. Then we don't have to do anything up top of your face – just the lips. Besides, didn't you say Duke knows what you look like?"

"Yeah, he does..." Loxley far preferred the idea of the mask. It had been tough enough wearing the base. She could only imagine how bad it would be close to her eyes.

"This is going to be so cute with the violin and tux; so classy," she giggled. She picked up six of the containers and arrayed them upon the table.

"I thought lipstick came from a stick."

"Not if you want lips like mine, honey."

Jayla laid down a foundation of powder over Loxley's lips, still swollen from the exhilaration of her kiss. Then, she smeared a brilliant crimson over the skin: a liquid that looked like fresh paint. Jayla alternated layers of color and powder over and over, surprising Loxley with the complexity of the task. She traced Loxley's lips with a dark pencil before grabbing a tiny brush to work in the edges. When the woman finally moved out of the way of the mirror, Loxley gasped.

Gone were the long, thin lips she'd seen her whole

life. These were plump and perfect, kissable, wonderful things the color of blood. She turned her head from side to side, her mouth slightly open, watching as the light danced across the paint and marveled at how different she'd become under Jayla's hand. Even if she didn't wear the mask, Duke would never recognize her.

Jayla had her stand, then helped her replace her smudged jacket. She slipped the mask over Loxley's face, completing the stranger in the mirror. The violinist on the other side of the glass was beautiful and confident. Mysterious. Strong. A little wild. Her dull hair poked out around the mask at odd angles; she hadn't tamed it after her bath.

Jayla seemed to notice the unkempt hair at the same time. She stroked it once. "We've still got a lot of work to do."

"I like my hair like this."

"I could make it even better."

Loxley shook her head, along with the violinist across from her. She thrilled to see this side of herself, and her voice came out easily and clearly. "No. This is perfect. This is the real me."

A Song and a Game, Played

LOXLEY STRODE THE back hallways toward the stage, the customary thunder of her heart displaced by a swell of delighted anticipation. The mask had superseded her skin, creating a safe house from which she could look out at the world. No one could see her, but she could perceive every detail with the clarity of a meticulous voyeur.

The other staffers looked upon her as a stranger and stepped out of the way as she passed. They stared and apologized, an action Loxley had never inspired in her life. She reveled in their acquiescence, their confusion, and, she hoped, their admiration.

"Whoa! That you, Loxley? You going to wear a dude's suit onstage?" called Cap as she passed the kitchen.

In previous days, she'd have shied away. "Yes," she said, and stared at him.

"I was looking forward to seeing you in a dress."

"I ain't for you."

"Okay. Well, uh... good luck, sweetie." He wilted, and she moved onward toward the backstage entrance.

The lipstick was a badge, commemorating Jayla's mark upon her body. Loxley wanted to touch it, to warmly fondle the paint in the hopes of rekindling her moment with the woman, but Jayla had made her promise she'd do no such thing. She lightly licked her lips, imagining soft skin upon them, and was rewarded with a deep, tingling ache in her belly. As she moved into the darkness behind the curtains backstage, she felt an abiding sense of one-ness with her surroundings, like sliding into her bed after a long day. The shadows that surrounded her were not frightful places of uncertainty, but close and comfortable.

Music drifted back to her from the other side of the curtains – acoustic guitar and a trumpet playing a song she'd never heard before. It was cheerful, but repetitive, only evolving over the course of a refrain. It didn't tell a story, or if it did, she certainly couldn't figure it out. At long last, the trumpet belted a series of phrases that took her somewhere, though really, the song only seemed to meander about the Hole on a sunny day.

She knelt down and removed her poplar treasure from its case. She couldn't make out its features in the shadows, but ran her fingers along its back until she found the engraved spider's web. Now that she was alone, with no one to reflect her newfound identity, cold nervousness settled into the pit of her stomach.

She nearly leapt out of her skin when a heavy hand fell on her from behind. A dim flashlight clicked on, illuminating a gaunt face. The gentleman to whom it belonged was a stage hand named Felix, whom she'd met once before when she'd arrived. She found him agreeable enough, if only because he almost never spoke.

Felix placed a finger to his lips, silencing her, then motioned to his watch. "You go on after this song. Are you ready?" he whispered.

Another piece of her bravado chipped away as the moment drew closer. "Will I be able to see all those faces in the audience?"

"Not a chance. The lights are too bright. You afraid of crowds?"

"I don't want all of those people looking at me."

"You're wearing a mask and a tux. I don't think they can see much of you. You ought to see the things the other girls wear onstage."

Loxley gulped. "Silk?"

"What clothes they manage to wear are made of silk, yeah." He fell silent for a moment as the song ended and applause roared. "Okay, go up there after he introduces you and do your thing."

Loxley peeked out from behind the curtain to see a man standing out on the stage in a black satin jacket and white gloves. He put his arm around the singer, a woman in a blue sequined dress like sparkling water, and waved to the crowd. She held a trumpet, and Loxley surmised she was the one playing earlier. They stood before the darkened audience, receiving their applause like torrential rainfall.

The man glanced back at her – it was Tailypo – and winked before speaking into the chrome-capped microphone. "Let's hear it for Veronica! Our very own angel in the deep!

Loxley's stomach sank as she watched the host pat Veronica's behind, signaling her offstage. If he did that to Loxley, it might hurt, leaving a mark just like all the other ghosts who'd touched her. The roar of applause scattered into a few sharp claps popping across the room, and Tailypo folded his hands behind his back.

"Tonight," the rumbling host began, "we have a rare treat – a diamond of the roughest origins. She will spin you a song unlike any other, chaotic in its attachments, yet astonishingly beautiful in its order: a spider's web," he placed a gloved finger to his temple, "glimmering in our minds; somewhere forbidden, yet somewhere we must all be caught, inexorably to struggle until stillness settles our hearts. She could so ensnare our thoughts that even the spirits of the dead must heed the siren call of her strings." He turned to glance at her with a smirk before continuing.

He unclipped the microphone and prowled across the stage, his heels quietly clicking against the breaths of the rapt audience. "We discovered her: squirreled away in some dark alcove of the Hole, a genius of the bow, lonely and afraid, and we brought her here, tonight, to show you all the wonders her deft fingers can weave." With this, he waggled his fingers in a way completely unlike a violinist. He straightened. "I humbly invite you, on behalf of all of us at the Hound's Tail, to enjoy the musical styling... of the Spider."

Polite applause greeted Loxley as she took the stage. Her skin prickled, but thankfully, Felix had been right; She couldn't see a thing aside from Tailypo's black coat. She tried on a smile, but it fit like a too-tight glove. She focused instead on making it to the stand where her host was re-seating the microphone.

She gasped as Tailypo took her arm and whispered in her ear. "If you can make it through just one of those songs, you'll still have a job in the morning. If you embarrass me, though, I might just sell you to Duke."

It didn't hurt. His touch hadn't wracked her with pain like the others. Had the things in his office only been an illusion? The deadly whirlwind of teeth and claws of the old woods came screaming back into her brain, and she decided to trust what she'd seen. Just because Tailypo was different, that didn't make him alive.

"I don't think Duke would speak to you," she said. Tailypo chuckled, but she hadn't meant it as a joke.

As he backed away, she turned to speak into the

microphone. She froze. This close, she could make out the shapes of dozens of faces looming in the shadows. She let her eyes unfocus until all that remained was the bright haze of the spotlights.

"Hi," she said to no one in particular. Her voice bounced off the walls, and her hackles rose when it sounded as though she was speaking from behind herself. "You're, uh... supposed to wait until after I play something. Then you can clap."

A few audience members tittered with laughter. Of course they were laughing at her. She raised the violin to her chin, then lowered it again with a sigh. More giggles and chuckles. She couldn't do this. She never could. *The world works better when everybody knows their place, Lox,* her mother had once said. It's better to fit in and be safe.

Then Loxley remembered seeing herself masked in the mirror, fascinating and happy. That was the woman the audience saw, not the retard, the madwoman, the fool. She put that reflection of herself between the microphone and the audience, a guardian angel to save her from humiliation. She squared up her shoulders, raised her instrument and placed the bow to its strings where it bounced slightly, a spring waiting to be unleashed. The audience grew quiet.

She exploded across the fingerboard with a set of ecstatic trills like a red bird fluttering across a spring sky. The world opened up with all of the possibilities of flight, rising and falling, ducking and weaving through the currents of air. She looped through the musical staves, high to low and back out again before shifting key one step up to rise in altitude.

Higher and higher she went. In her mind's eye, the Hole fell away to the vast expanse of farmland around it, leaving only the cut rings visible to the naked eye. No more ignorant humans could be seen dotting the streets, only the geometric perfection of the crater's steps. The ever-present pillar of steam from the foundry rose into the sky, and she circled its rotund, lazy folds.

Her fingers slowed to a crawl as she coasted on the wind, interrupted by the occasional note as a feather ruffled. Floating along a stream of augmented fifths, she could stay here forever, watching the clouds drift by, far away from the rest of the world. She sawed back and forth, maintaining a steady altitude for a number of bars before looking back down to see the Hole again, still waiting for her. She rolled and dove toward the ground.

A strange key set in as she crashed through the industrial jungle, wheeling between buildings and darting through alleys. The houses became blacker the further down she spiraled, and her instrument's discord became an incessant rhythm of angry notes. Then, with a burst of flames from the foundry, she hit the very bottom, and the piece became a long tangle of minor chords. Molten steel splashed perilously close to her as the pounding machines rang out in the choking dust. Narrowly, she escaped to the eighth ring, where she found the Hound's Tail awaiting her.

The building may have been straight, but everyone inside was a bunch of curvy lines, and so Loxley switched to a syncopated beat. She played through the chaos of the kitchen and the thrill of the stage, and she'd almost hit her stride when something drew her out of her trance.

The audience had begun to clap in time with her music. For the second time that night, her spine tingled with pleasant electricity.

She began to sway back and forth, feeling her hair brush against her neck with each motion. Her music danced around each slap of their palms, swinging from it before catapulting to the next one. She'd never had a beat prescribed to her before, but she felt rapturous joy at the synchronicity. She knew she was humming, so she backed away from the microphone in the hopes it wouldn't hear her. Her voice wouldn't be controlled; she needed to calm down, or the world would hear her terrible, off-key singing. Time to change the subject.

She started the first minor strains of a movement about the forest in Tailypo's office, her legs suddenly crawling with ants. The bells of the foundry surged in her mind and her fingertips stung. She nearly threw the bow for wanting to shake them out. Bad choice. She shouldn't play about ghosts.

She dragged out a long, major third, then halted, quiet flooding into the theater like syrup, impenetrable and viscous in her ears.

She had to play something, somehow, to appease them. Her mind went blank, and all she could think about was Tailypo and the screeching of claws. She still smelled the blood in his office, of thousands of dead animals locked in an eternal cycle of carnivorous fury. She thought of the way his eyes bored into her as he told the story of his death and sudden rebirth – of his lustful overtures to her and heavy breath.

A silhouette emerged in that wicked place: Jayla's hips, swaying as she walked down the hall ahead of Loxley. Back and forth, it became the foundation of her next musical journey as she drew her bow across the strings. She allowed herself to fall into a rhythm before punctuating each musical phrase with two plucked high notes – the soft patter of Jayla's powder puff on her face. The puff moved from her forehead, to her cheeks, to her chin, to her neck, and then came the eyebrow pencil – a sharp draw of the bow from the center to the edge. She injected her anxiety into the fluttering half-steps of her song, the fear of her skin being replaced by the makeup, counterbalanced against the calm she found in Jayla's deep, brown eyes.

The chrome microphone gleamed more brightly before her, as if responding to her presence, and she moved closer. Her chest heaved, and she felt a tingle on her cheeks. She remembered the touch of paint on her lips and paused, leaving the note to hover in the minds of the audience.

She drew back, then dove into the kiss with deep, passionate phrases, whirling around a jubilant melody. Sticky, sweet plucks danced across long sighs of the strings, and Loxley felt a great release like a fist relaxing after years of tension. Pride flowed through her fingertips, spilling across the fingerboard and out of the poplar body to echo across the audience. Someone wanted her. Someone liked her. She soared inside.

A half-toned photograph of a cotton field under endless sky – that was what Jayla had made her feel. The farming manual was gone now, left somewhere in Duke's house, but Loxley had memorized it. Under the weight of the Hole, of all the smoke and rot, of Duke's plotting and Tailypo's advances, Jayla had made her feel free, if only for the briefest amount of time. Perhaps that's what a kiss was supposed to do.

Loxley drew the last note and lowered her instrument, closing her eyes and sighing as the crowd exploded into mad applause, blasting like hail on the tin roof of Vulcan's Bazaar. She'd done it – played in front of all of those people, in spite of the fact that Duke had taken everything from her. A voice cut through the din, Tailypo's, shouting, "The Spider, ladies and gentlemen! Isn't she something?"

Tailypo took her arm and whispered in her ear, "See me after the show in my office."

When Loxley re-opened her eyes she could see the dozens of faces of the crowd, all beaming with delight. Before the show, she wouldn't have managed to look at the audience, but something had changed in her, untangled somehow. Each and every person in that room loved her.

Except for the hare-lipped woman sitting close to the front row.

Except for Marie.

Entrapment

LOXLEY COULD SCARCELY breathe as Tailypo gently ushered her offstage. Like the snap of a rat trap, all of her false freedom had crumbled at the sight of Marie. What was the chauffeur doing there? Was she there to spy for Duke? Did she recognize Loxley for who she really was?

Backstage was a maelstrom of clapping and patting hands, rough congratulations and unknowable smiles. Loxley curled her arms inward against the onslaught, the joy fading from her face. She stomped her feet and flapped her hands, but the crackles wouldn't come off.

"Don't you all have jobs to do?" she hissed, and the felicitations faded.

"That's no way to treat these people," came Jayla's voice, and Loxley spun to face her. "They came to hear you after they saw your practice. You going to be nice to them?"

"There was a woman in the audience."

"That happens sometimes," said Jayla.

"She helped kill my friend!"

Loxley ripped off the mask and threw it into the darkness, her fingers seizing, almost refusing to let it go. It had become too tight, replacing her skin. She made to wipe the lipstick onto her sleeve, but Jayla caught her hands and held them tightly. Jayla's brown eyes centered Loxley enough to calm her down, though she still itched to wipe her lips on her shoulder.

"Which one is she?" asked Jayla.

"The one with the weird lip."

"Marie..."

Loxley twisted her hands free. "You know her?"

"Only by reputation. She's got money. Go look out and see if she's still there. I'm going to get Quentin." Jayla hustled off, out the backstage door.

She crept to the curtain and looked out, only to find Marie preparing to leave. Loxley glanced back to tell someone, but found only Felix. This was her chance to attack Marie outside of Edgewood and find out how to get to Duke, or perhaps just kill her. The ants had become unbearable, and she felt static encroaching on her brain. Fear and fury twisted into a ball in her stomach, threatening to overwhelm her. Marie gathered her things and tossed a small stack of bills onto the table before turning to go.

Loxley strode to the backstage door and flung it open. If she waited for Quentin, it would be too late. She had to move right then. She rushed down the hallway and to the coat check, where she saw the front door swinging closed. She bolted forward, barreling through the door and into the cold night.

Her usual attire, denim and a heavy coat, always protected her against the wind, but the tux did little to ameliorate that. The frigid air whipped right through her, and she flashed back to several days before, when she'd been blood-soaked and alone, wandering the streets of the Hole.

She looked up and down the street before spotting her target, sprinting up one of the cracked sidewalks. Marie knew she'd been made, that much was clear. Loxley gave chase, her shiny loafers clapping the ground. They wound around the block and through an alley, and before long, Loxley's lungs burned. Sill farther they ran, past wrecked shops and abandoned, stripped cars, around deserted buildings, across a decaying bridge before racing down the embankment into a culvert.

Marie might have had terror fueling her feet, but Loxley was faster. Years of hauling supplies and produce up many flights of stairs to her rooftop garden had served to make her legs strong, and with each stride Loxley gained on her prey. She focused on Marie's silhouette, keeping it in the center of her vision at all times.

They reached a tunnel, almost pitch black in the moonlight, and the two women dashed inside. Before Loxley's eyes could adjust, Marie's fist crashed into her jaw, sending her flopping to the ground. Broken concrete and jagged rubble cut her hands as she caught herself, and she tasted blood. Static roared in her ears, and she feared she might lose control of herself, like she might disappear. If she fell apart now, there was no telling what Marie might do to her.

She snatched a rock off the pile and swung it, striking the woman's ankle. Marie screamed and fell, and Loxley scrambled forward to hit her again. They tangled and rolled across the toothy ground, each movement bringing Loxley fresh pain. Marie scratched her, pulled her hair and bit, but Loxley was stronger. She grabbed a handful of Marie's hair and slammed her head against the concrete. She slammed over and over again, until Marie's grip loosened, and Loxley was able to straddle her chest.

She grabbed the largest rock she could find and hoisted it over her head.

She focused her mind on the bells of the foundry, barely audible over the ringing in her ears. She wanted to feel Nora's spirit inside her again, to be present for this moment. *Clang.* Her senses grew sharper, snapping new details into the world. *Clang.* Her mind opened up and her breathing steadied. *Clang.* She felt the cold rock cut into her hand, and her mind shifted, becoming more than just her own.

Marie groaned and opened her eyes, barely visible in the dark. The expression on her face shifted from dazed recognition to abject terror – a subtle twist, but one Loxley could now sense. Looking on her, she could feel what the woman felt – fear and confusion – and it caused a twinge in her heart.

"Do you know who I am?" growled Loxley.

Marie nodded.

"Do you understand that I could kill you right now, and no one would try to stop me? I could break your fucking skull and leave you here, and no one would be any wiser. Do you get that?" Her voice sounded like her own, but her words flowed smoothly. She instinctively knew what she could say to frighten her victim.

Again, Marie nodded.

"And how would you feel about the person who helped me dump your body?"

"Please don't kill me," Marie whispered, her mouth distorting the words. As Loxley's eyes adjusted to the light, she saw dust caked on the woman's face where tears would have been. "Please, I got a kid. Please."

She reared back to strike, shouting, "Did anyone listen to me when I begged? Huh? Did you? Go ahead and trot out your kid when it's your turn to be judged!"

"I just drive the car."

"Since you're okay with letting others die in Duke's fights, I guess you don't mind me killing you on my way up the chain. How does that sound?"

Marie whimpered.

"Fucking answer me, bitch! Explain your worthless

fucking existence! Do you want to die? Duke wants to kill me and all you can do is cry. You had better get useful real goddamned fast."

Loxley wrapped her free hand around Marie's throat, but the beaten woman didn't struggle. She made no attempt to do anything except pant and stare at the rock poised over her head. Blood ran down the side of her temple, and she shook uncontrollably. Spittle flecked through her exposed teeth.

Something alien crept into Loxley's mind. She'd never noticed it before, but this woman was hideous to her. The hare lip, it repulsed her in a way she didn't expect. Marie was a freak – and a sheep to boot. She was someone for bigger people to step over on their way to important things. Normally, such a lowly person wouldn't be worth noticing, but now that Marie had made the mistake of helping Duke with a despicable act, well... she was downright repugnant. Was Nora disgusted?

"Nora Vickers hates you," said Loxley. "She hates that lip of yours.

Marie mouthed the words before she managed to say them. "She's dead."

"Look into my eyes and tell me I'm not her." She looked out from behind Nora's smile like the mask she'd worn onstage. Loxley and Nora tangled up inside her, becoming one, like playing her violin to the rhythmic clapping of the audience. The clanging of the foundry grew deafening.

Marie's eyes met hers and her mortified expression betrayed her belief. "Oh, sweet Jesus, save me."

The more in-step Loxley became with Nora, the

more she had a gnawing feeling in her gut that what she was doing was wrong. The raw fear radiating from her would-be victim infected her, and her rage and disgust transformed to a morbid pity. As much as she tried to shut it out, she thought of the child, no doubt alone and waiting for Marie to return home.

"What were you doing at the Hound's Tail?"

"Buying coke for Hiram. I heard you playing, and I stayed to watch." The woman was miserable, frightened and meek. She had to have been just as abused as Loxley, maybe more so.

"Do you like your job?"

She sobbed. "Not anymore. Oh, God, not anymore."

Dizziness washed over Loxley, and she reeled. Her time was almost up. Nora's tenuous hold on her body had begun to dissipate. "Why not?"

"They're murdering folks. They make me drive them places and... They didn't use to. It started after they shot that Alvin Kimball. I saw them, and Duke... he just looked at me and said, 'I own the police.'" Her voice cracked, barely audible through her lisp. "I can't leave. My son has to eat."

Loxley swooned. The ground swelled under her knees. "I can find you another job. I... I need to kill Duke and Hiram. They... they need killing. You... I'm going to let you live."

Marie's expression changed to dark resolution – still afraid, but she clearly sensed a new path. "I can help you."

"Do you believe it? Do you know I can wipe these men off the earth?"

The hare-lipped woman nodded in response, not

a single gesture, but an ongoing convulsion. Again, disgust surged in her, but the emotion was not her own. Loxley knew her gaze was still Nora's.

The rock tumbled backward from Loxley's fingers, clattering onto the rubble. Her viewpoint spun lazily to one side before her cheek struck cold stone. Marie crawled out from underneath her as all strength fled Loxley's limbs. Blackness tugged at the periphery of her vision. As the spirit of her friend fled her body, Loxley collapsed the same exhaustion she'd felt the night she'd knocked on Don Fowler's door. Summoning spirits taxed her to helplessness, and she had no choice but to trust Marie.

"You don't have to be bad anymore. I need you to take me back... to the Hound's Tail."

CHAPTER TWELVE
CHILDISH THINGS

LOXLEY HELD A book in her hands as she sat at her dining table in Magic City Heights. She shifted her weight, feeling the splintery, rickety wood of her old dining chair. With the events of days past, the familiar had become alien – like returning to places she'd seen as a child, only to find them smaller now. She looked up to find Nora luxuriating across from her, clothed only in one of Loxley's work shirts. She smiled widely.

Unable to translate Nora's expression, and a little nervous, Loxley looked down at her book. Orange block letters across the top said something, but what? She squinted at them, and they wandered across the page in rebellion. Was this her farming manual? She opened it, flipping through the pages, unable to read a single letter or number. When she found the half-tone picture of the farm, she stopped, seeing it with pristine clarity – perhaps clearer than she'd ever seen it.

The little black square in the background came into

focus. She'd always wondered if it was a farmhouse, and it was. Microscopic men streamed from its door, their shoulders hunched and beaten with the day's coming work. She pulled the book closer to her eye to see the sweat drenching their bodies even before they'd accomplished their first tasks. One of them turned to her, his slate gray eyes boring into hers. It was a young Duke Wallace.

She yelped and dropped the book, its pages flapping closed. Her eyes burned with tears, and she glared at the cover with its slippery letters. How dare he go there, to her special place?

She looked back to Nora, still wearing that unnerving smile. Loxley touched her own lips and remembered: she'd been smiling like that as she'd mounted Marie. She remembered what she'd been thinking, too, as she sized up Marie's hare-lip. She'd been disgusted. She thought the woman was a freak. She'd nearly said it out loud, but had managed to stay in control of herself. As Nora's emotions had filtered into her, Loxley had begun to feel compassion and empathy, but that hadn't changed her first reaction.

"Did you think I was a freak when you first met me?"

Nora said nothing, but stood from her place at the table, the chair scooting out with a loud squawk. She sauntered around, slowly taking each step as though caressing the floor with her bare feet. She wouldn't stop smiling, unbuttoning her shirt as she walked, to reveal more of her freckled flesh. When Nora was still inches away, Loxley caught herself humming nervously, recoiling in her chair from the approaching figure.

"P-please. I want to know if you thought I was stupid, or crazy."

Nora stopped, and looked away.

"You can't talk, can you?"

The other woman's shirt was fully-unbuttoned, and Loxley's eyes trailed from her slender neck to her vagina. Nora held out her hand without making eye contact, and Loxley let it hang in the air. She couldn't forget that nasty thought that had rumbled through her head: that Marie was pathetic, not worth stepping over in the street. Ugly.

"You've got parts I don't understand," Loxley said.

She turned from Nora and grabbed the agriculture manual from the table. She willed the pages to make sense, to give her brain some perch to land on so it could pick apart the text, but they wouldn't unscramble. Letters slid crossways, distorting under her gaze, twisting and writhing to decouple themselves from the constraints of meaning.

She didn't comprehend the letters, but the truths. These things she wanted – a farm, Nora – they were so far from her grasp. Nora wasn't simply a doting friend and potential lover; she had hatred just like everyone else. The feelings that Loxley had channeled, the things she said and noticed, unsettled her. They'd been friends so long that Loxley couldn't remember, but Nora might have patronized her when they first met. Loxley had gotten better at reading faces since then, sensing when people made fun of her.

The farm was a place for men like Duke – killers and thieves. He was strong, influential and well-spoken, but even he wasn't the leader of a farm out there. Farms belonged to the Consortium, and he was just a cog in their machine. He still hadn't escaped it, and so he would kill to try. Loxley would be nothing out there in the farmlands: just another dead body joining the thousands of others.

Her apartment seemed unfocused, frosted like glass. Who was she, if not a farmer? Nora's hand remained outstretched. Loxley batted it away. She didn't want to be soothed.

She wanted to be powerful.

Warmth

"Lox, Lox, Loxley... Get up, up, up."

Loxley's eyes opened to her dim room at the Hound's Tail. A shard of yellow light cut across the floor where the door had been left slightly open. Her eyes drifted upward, and she counted the boards between ceiling joists.

"I'm awake," she said.

She didn't know what time it was. There weren't any windows in the staff area. She still felt exhausted. Her bra and panties scratched uncomfortably at her, and she slipped them off under the covers, dumping them onto the floor. She didn't sleep in clothes, no matter what. It was something she'd told Jayla to get used to. She huddled under the covers, pulling them tightly around her like an embrace.

Voices drifted into the room from the hallway: Jayla's voice, against Tailypo's low grumble.

"Not right now, you can't, Tee," said Jayla, her voice quiet but forceful.

"This is my building, and I've got business."

"And she's got to rest."

"You backtalking me, woman?"

"Yes, I am. You pay me to get shit done, and that's just what I'm doing right now."

Tailypo chuckled. "How is this 'getting shit done?'"

"That girl is going to pack the house tomorrow night, Tee. You let her get her strength."

Loxley heard the rustle of Tailypo's silk suit. "Fine, but you tell that girl I ain't giving a goddamned job to that straggler who brought her in. Freaky bitch can stay one night and that's it."

Footsteps sounded down the hallway, then paused. "Unless," said Tailypo, "Loxley wants to take my deal."

"Like Quentin?"

"I take care of him, don't I?"

"That you do, Tee. That you do."

Loxley listened as footsteps receded down the hall. The door creaked open, and Jayla poked her head inside. "You *are* awake. Thought I heard you creeping around in here. How you feeling?"

Loxley pulled down the comforter to uncover her mouth. "I'm hungry. What time is it?"

"Four in the a.m."

Her joints ached, and she remembered passing out in the tunnel after beating Marie. "Did Marie bring me back here?"

"She came and got us. Said you'd passed out. I think Quentin was about ready to bust her nose when he saw you." Jayla leaned against the door frame. "You were bleeding and bruised, half frozen on a pile of rocks. I thought you might've been dead."

"No, but I saw a ghost."

She chuckled. "Other than Tee?"

"Yeah. I saw the ghost of my friend Nora. She was happy to see me, but I don't feel like I know her anymore."

Jayla shook her head. "I'm fairly sure Tee isn't dead, honey."

It dawned on Loxley that her friend had been sarcastic moments before. She kicked herself for not recognizing that. "You don't think I can see ghosts."

Jayla put her hands on her hips. "When did I say that? Touched people can see a lot of things the rest of us can't. I think some of those things are real. I believe in ghosts, too."

"Touched?"

"Different in the mind."

Loxley sank back into the covers, half-muffling her words. "Crazy, you mean."

Jayla came and sat on the edge of Loxley's bed, patting her leg through the covers. "No. Just different."

Loxley sat up and the covers slid from her shoulders. "I can see ghosts because my mother could see them, and she wasn't different like me. And she could see ghosts because of my grandma. Neither of them were touched. Ain't crazy to see ghosts. It's crazy *not to*."

"Okay, but honey, the Hole is a dangerous place. Why don't you see ghosts all the time?"

"Most people burn the bodies around here. I can only scc a ghost when the body has some juice in it. That, and sometimes the ghosts just give up and go away." She pulled her knees up to her chest. "Did you know you're the first person to ask me how it works, being dead? Nora never asked."

"I'm pretty sure Nora knows by now," said Jayla, making a strange face that Loxley didn't recognize, sort of like she was going to laugh but sort of like she'd just sat on a tack.

"Yeah." Loxley smoothed down the ripples of her sheets. "Can I ask you something about Quentin?"

Another chuckle. "You still sweet on him?"

"No. I don't like men. Not like that."

"Oh, uh... Okay. Well, uh, what was your question?"

"Is he Tailypo's boyfriend?"

Jayla's braying laughter startled Loxley enough that she had to cover her ears. The woman doubled over, slapping one of Loxley's knees as she struggled to overcome the fit and draw a normal breath.

"Boyfriend!" Jayla wheezed.

"What?"

"More like bitch, if you ask me."

Loxley was never sure what someone meant when they said that. "Okay, but they're fucking, right?"

"No!" Jayla giggled, wiping a tear from her eye. "Who told you that?"

"When I first got here," Loxley began, hugging herself, "Tailypo asked me if I would give myself to him. When I said no, he told me Quentin took the deal."

"Aw, baby, no. He's just nuts like that. He says shit all the time. Tee and Quentin have a partnership, and Quentin does anything he can to keep this place going."

"Don't call people nuts."

Jayla laughed again. "Why not? They all are. We act normal, but there ain't a normal one among us. You ought to learn to like the way you are."

"Why? Everyone else hates it." Loxley's voice sharpened as she spoke, a little anger flashing inside. She gripped her legs tighter. She made eye contact with Jayla for a moment, annoyed to see the woman staring at her, and diverted her gaze back up to the ceiling. She slid her gaze up and down the parallel lines, almost wiping away the discussion before her.

Jayla caught her chin, forcing Loxley to face her, even if she wouldn't make eye contact. "Loxley, honey, I think you're great – so does everyone who heard you play tonight. Even after you beat the shit out of that lady down the hall, she still tried to bring you back here."

"Marie is down the hall?"

"She's resting three rooms down... and you're going to let her."

"I told her I could get her a job."

"You're just going to have to think about that later," said Jayla, standing up.

"Okay." Loxley itched her nose. "You said Tailypo and Quentin weren't fucking."

"Yeah."

"What about you and Quentin?"

Jayla snorted. "What are you, the love police?"

Loxley shook her head. "You don't have to love someone to fuck them. I know because Nora –"

"*Pshaw.* Every woman knows that."

"Okay, so are you? Have you? With Quentin?" Loxley imagined she was. After all, he was tall and scary, but kind, and a lot of girls probably wanted that. Loxley couldn't pick men, but she was willing to bet Nora would have wanted him because he was better than Jack. Jayla would want him, too, because no one good could want Loxley. Never had happened. Never would.

Jayla came and sat on the edge of the bed and patted her knee. "I give you one kiss and you think you own the whole damned world."

Loxley's heart fluttered and she sat up straight, pulling on the sheets. Her hands didn't want to cooperate, and she gripped even harder.

The woman's soft chortle stung. She wasn't taking Loxley seriously. "I ain't got to tell you who I have and haven't laid with."

"No... Yeah, but you do!" She hadn't meant to shout, but her voice gave way like a rusty faucet – squeaky at first but pouring forth once started. Now, the reverberations of her outburst drained away through the cracks in the floor, leaving only surprise. *Always shouting, Loxa-lox! You keep it down; Gonna embarrass your momma!*

Jayla's eyebrow cocked, and she tongued the inside of her cheek. Loxley swallowed hard – she knew that face: the face of disappointment. It was one of the only expressions she had consistent training with.

"Why?" asked the woman. "Why do you need to know?"

"Because you kissed me and n-now I want to..." She couldn't explain it better, because her mouth didn't want to help. It locked around the word 'know'. She wanted to understand Jayla, to see where her tastes lay – to find out if it was a kiss or pity.

"All right, then," Jayla began, "yeah. I've been with a lot of boys around here. Had my first when I was twelve. Sweet little boy named Shaun, and I stole the sweetness right off him. So many others after that I lost count. Tried to get with Quentin, too, couple of years ago, but he wouldn't have me. Been with a couple of girls, wouldn't you know? And out of the whole lot, men and women, ain't a damn one of them worth anything."

"Why do you say that?" It was all going wrong, just like it always did. Jayla didn't understand, and now she would hate her.

"You see a ring on this finger, sugar?" She stood, looking down on Loxley. "So how about that answer? How do you like that kiss now? You happy, knowing you licked the same piece of candy as everyone else?"

Loxley had to stop her, had to show her she cared. "No!"

"I thought not. Everyone wants something until they got it. Never should've given you that kiss."

"No! I... I – I – I mean, I don't mind."

"You don't *mind*? What does that mean?"

Loxley's eyelids flickered as she blinked away her nerves. Her fingers burned, and she white-knuckled the blanket. "A piece of candy... is always sweet."

One hand rose to the curvy woman's hip to rest there. "Is it now?"

"And I haven't licked you yet, so I don't know, uh, what you taste like."

Jayla suddenly went wide-eyed and looked away. She coughed loudly, clearing her throat. "You hungry? You want me to make you something?"

"Jaylabiscuits."

"You ever going to ask me to make you something else?"

"And fried okra. Don't put gravy on it."

She paused at the door, looking back. "You're a weird one, sugar... maybe I like that."

Loxley smiled feebly as Jayla exited, then laid back down, hoping to nap until the biscuits were done. No matter how hard she tried, she didn't feel remotely tired, and soon she padded out of bed to don some clothes. She slipped into a pair of canvas pants and a thermal cotton top, then crept out of her room.

She'd been in the Hound's Tail long enough to know which rooms were occupied and which weren't. She'd pretty much been introduced to everyone over the course of her time there, and had seen inside each of their little worlds. Even though she despised Cap, she was often drawn to his room, which was filled with dozens of brightly-painted, handmade toys. They lined a couple shelves that Cap had erected, covering the stained, chipping walls. Apparently, he had a wood shop somewhere around the back – a gift from Tailypo – but Loxley hadn't been out to see it. Cap particularly favored horses, and the big man had carved his share of them. He did a lot of the detail work in his room, and so had a wide array of razor-sharp knives, too.

The solid grip of a knife gave Loxley a comfort she hadn't had before, and Cap owned the best ones she'd ever touched. She'd expected the kitchen to be well-stocked, and it was, but there was something about the alder wood handles of Cap's blades, and the swirl of the steel. He'd told her his very favorite knife was made by a local blacksmith, eight layers folded ten times, and it had cost him nearly a month's pay. He showed her how it sliced through the wood, shaving off slivers as though they were butter. When she'd asked to hold the tool, he'd flatly refused, handing her one of his cheaper ones. She'd pocketed it without a second thought when his eyes were turned.

She realized as she'd passed his door that the only time he didn't act like an asshole was when he talked about woodworking. What if she was like that about farming or music? She hadn't considered the possibility before.

She passed Cap's door, then Felix's, then stopped in front of the next one. The room on the other side belonged to nobody, and that thought unsettled Loxley. It was a blank slate, worse than a stranger's house. Humans left a warm tread wherever they went, like footprints in snow; they would eventually be gone, but not for awhile.

What if Marie wasn't inside? What would greet her then?

She pushed open the door and peered in, her eyes following the light spilling onto the bed. Bare floors, bare walls, the lump of a woman buried under the covers, her chest slowly rising and falling. Her soft breaths whistled through her teeth, and she turned over, snuggling into her pillow.

A scuffed, wooden chair sat in the corner of the room. Loxley sneaked inside and shut the door, enclosing the room in darkness, then made her way to the seat. She sat down and it creaked. Marie's breath started.

"I'm not here to hurt you," Loxley whispered.

"Thank you," came Marie's lisping voice.

"I don't know what to think about you."

The sheets rustled.

"I want to think you're bad, and I should kill you," Loxley said. "That seems really easy, and you did some bad things. But I know people just want to use you because your face is weird. They do that to me, too, because I can't think like everyone else."

"I... I guess I appreciate that."

"You have to help me, though – tell me things about Duke and Hiram – or I'll probably hurt you. Might change my mind about what I just said."

"Are you trying to threaten me?"

"No. If you don't tell me what I want to know... then you're helping your old boss, and people who help him need to die."

Marie swallowed loudly. "I heard the boys say that your name was Loxley. How did you know that I drove Nora on the day she died?"

"I used to work at Fowler's Apothecary up on the third ring. I saw you pick her up from the window."

"Oh."

"And also I have her spirit inside me. I know everything about the day Hiram murdered her."

No response came. Loxley wondered what sort of face Marie was making. It was a little easier to talk to her in the dark, where Loxley could focus on the sound of her voice. Voices told more truths than faces, but it was hard to un-jumble them when she had to deal with both at once. The hare-lipped woman was doubly-difficult, because her voice and face weren't like anyone else's. Loxley couldn't use the lessons she'd learned about everyday people with her.

Eventually, Marie whispered, "That's crazy."

"We all act normal, but nobody is normal," she replied, paraphrasing Jayla. "I can make myself like Nora because her ghost did something to me. What happened to your lip?"

"I was born like this."

She didn't know much about men, but she knew they didn't like strange women. "And you have a kid? Did your boyfriend like your lip or something?"

"The father is out of the picture. We're not talking about my son."

"Why not?"

"Because you're trying to decide whether or not you want me dead. Jesus Christ, do you think I'd tell you anything about my family?"

Loxley scratched an itch on her nose. Her eyes had begun to adjust to the tiny amount of light seeping around the door, and she could make out a little of Marie's shape under the covers. "Why did you help bring me back here?"

"You said you could get me a job. I don't want to work for Duke anymore. He and Hiram been killing a lot more than just Nora."

"Alvin Kimball."

"Yeah. Had to drive him around, too, down to the furnace at the Foundry."

"You weren't driving your limo that day."

"How did you know?"

"I saw you. Why didn't you just dump him somewhere, like Nora?"

Marie laughed. "You can't just throw a man like

Alvin Kimball on the street. He could've been mayor. Some slut from the seventh ring gets dumped off in her apartment, ain't nobody going to ask questions. She's a never-was – nobody to anybody. Cops are going to say she did something to provoke a man, maybe even someone hiring her for a lay, and he shot her. No one is going to spend time on that."

"Nora wasn't a slut."

"You think that matters to anyone but you? Cops are busy. They want to shut a case down."

"No, they don't. Officer Crutchfield always helps find people who steal stuff."

It was true. On more than one occasion, the man had chased down a thief in front of Loxley, settled a dispute and generally kept the order. He was a bad man, but he wasn't lazy. She shook her head as if to slough off the memories. She didn't like remembering the good parts. He was a bad man and a dead man, and that was that.

"Oh yeah? There's a going theory about what happened to Nora among the locals, and I think the police share the view. Turns out some retard broke into the place and killed Miss Vickers. No one knows why she did it, but who knows why retards do anything?"

The words had barely escaped Marie's lips when Loxley slapped the fire out of her. Loxley brought her hand back, electrified, yet cool with spittle. That had felt far better than shaking out the crackles.

"I'm not retarded."

Marie slowly brought her hand to her cheek. "Who gives a fuck? Nobody gives two shits about you, little girl, except that you stay dead. You get that? They ain't here to ask questions about your life and make sure they get all the facts straight. They're just here to take what they can get, same as me... same as you."

As the woman lisped the words, Loxley sat in silence, stunned by the sudden outpouring.

"You want me to feel sorry for you because I misjudged you or something? Try to find a job with a face like mine – when everybody's looking at you, trying not to throw up. Duke's the first man to ever to give me half a chance, and I'm quitting because, one of these days, he's going to decide I know too much. I want a job when this is all over. I want food for my little boy who's sitting at home right now, wondering where his momma is."

Loxley swallowed. "I need to know about –"

"No, what you need to do is let me go home."

"We could bring your son here."

"Are you crazy? You think I want him running around a place like this?"

"What are you going to do, then?"

Marie shrugged. "I'm going to tell Hiram I saw you, and you want to meet him at the Foundry to turn yourself over in two days' time. And after that, I'm going home."

"That's it?"

"Yeah, and you're going to make sure he don't come home from that trip, or I'm going to tell Duke where you been hiding, and he's going to take care of everybody here."

Loxley imagined Hiram's leer, and her guts lurched. Her wish was coming to fruition: she would get to face Nora's killer. She imagined his face in the hot steel glow of the furnaces and smelters. She thought about him traipsing around the catwalks, pistol drawn, ready for blood. Involuntarily, she pictured him swimming through the cooling tower pool, and she fumed.

"No, that's my place," Loxley growled.

"Well, then you better put Hiram in the ground."

"What? I wasn't talking to you."

The door swung wide, flooding the room with light. Marie raised a hand to shield her vision, and Loxley did the same. When her eyes adjusted, she saw Jayla standing in the doorway with a plate of fresh biscuits and steaming gravy in one hand, and the other hand on her hip.

"Loxley what the hell do you think you're doing?" shouted Jayla. "Get your ass out here right now! Right now. The fuck I tell you about bothering her?"

Loxley inched toward the door, glancing back at Marie. She couldn't read the hare-lipped woman's expression.

"Don't you look at her," snapped Jayla. "You look at me. Get out here right now. She ain't going to talk to you anymore."

"Two days, at midnight," said Marie, as if to prove her wrong.

"By the furnaces," said Loxley.

With her free hand, Jayla wrenched Loxley out the door by her collar. Loxley flinched as her friend slammed the door shut and shoved her toward her room.

"The fuck I tell you, girl?" grumbled Jayla.

"You told me to let her rest."

"And you didn't!"

"I just wanted to look at her... to be sure I still wanted to let her live."

Jayla rolled her eyes. "Oh, is that all? What did you decide?"

When they reached their room, Loxley pushed open the door. "I think I should let her go. She said she didn't want to work for Duke."

They entered, Jayla slinging the hot plate down onto the dresser top. "Do you know where you are right now?"

"Yes. Why wouldn't I?" She sat down on her bed and folded her hands into her lap.

"And who is in charge around here?"

"Tailypo?"

"That's right. Who do you think gets to decide what happens to Marie?"

"I do. I could have slit her throat in there. Cap let me borrow one of his knives." Loxley said it without rancor.

Jayla crossed her arms and leaned on the door frame. "You know, it's hard to see who you really are, girl. One minute, you're this cute little thing, talking about farming, scurrying around humming to yourself."

"I only hum when I'm scared."

"It's adorable. And the next minute, you're talking about slitting a woman's throat while she sleeps with the same tone you'd use to describe cracking an egg. Don't you see how that's what makes you look crazy?"

Loxley thought about what it would be like if murder was that simple. She imagined the police storming into someone's house, only to find a fried egg buried in the basement and a ruthless, skillet-wielding murderer. The idea made her chuckle.

Jayla scowled. "See, now that scares me when you laugh like that."

"What?"

"Out of nowhere, at odd moments. I've seen you do it a couple of times since you got here. Loxley, I like you, girl, but –"

"You like me?"

Silence enfolded them. Loxley watched her fumble for words, but the door to change her mind rapidly closed. Now the phrase hung in the air between them like a bright balloon, neither woman being able to avoid looking at it. Jayla had said "but." "But" what? But Loxley was crazy? But she was stupid? But she was ugly? She'd never considered herself pretty or ugly, but if she had to evaluate herself on a scale with Nora, she'd lose. Her mouth felt dry, and she itched her calf muscles to forestall the ants. She hummed without thinking.

Jayla sighed. "But I don't get you."

She hung her head. Her skin felt leaden. "If *I* don't get people, they think I'm retarded. If they don't get *me*, they think I'm retarded."

"I didn't say that."

"You just told me that we're all crazy. Just ten minutes ago. Now you're telling me it's my fault – my fault you don't understand me."

"That's not what I said."

"You should try harder before just giving up on me, because –"

"Loxley, that's not what I said!" shouted Jayla.

Loxley stopped talking. A door opened down the

hall, and Loxley heard Cap call for them to keep it down. Jayla leaned out and shot him a 'fuck you' look that Loxley had no trouble deciphering. The door shut in the distance.

"Wh –" Loxley tried to speak, but the words didn't want to come. Her light humming filled the room, along with a creaking rhythm as she bounced her knees. Her ears rang from Jayla's shout, and her skin crawled. She didn't like shouting for the same reason she didn't like guns: too loud, too sudden.

Jayla shook her head and snorted. "I said I liked you." She pushed away from the door with her back, unfolding her arms as she did. "And no, I don't know what that means." She gestured to Loxley's thermal top. "Now put a different shirt on. Tee was asking for you."

The Wolf at the Door

LOXLEY'S STOMACH QUIVERED. Her fight with Jayla had left her jangled, and she hadn't touched the plate of breakfast before leaving to see Tailypo. The early hours of the morning transformed the building from a popular, exciting club to a cold, dank crypt. Twitches of exhaustion jolted her as she walked. She moved down creaky hallways and up a flight of stairs, and before long, she stood in Tailypo's paisley hallway. The convulsing patterns of the wallpaper were only worsened by dingy light and severe anxiety.

She hadn't been able to stop humming the whole way. Her grip on her mind seemed tenuous, as though any second the static would sweep her up and she'd wander away. She kept walking toward Tailypo's office, pulled by invisible chains.

She didn't want to see him again. Not now, not ever. Her favorite part about the club was the fact that Tailypo spent most of his time up in his office, barely interacting with the staff. He could stay that way for all she cared. His ravenous gaze and handsy mannerisms were jarring, as if he couldn't resist touching her. He was quick to put his bare skin against hers, to touch her hand or neck as he passed, and it gave her jitters thinking about it.

She stopped outside his door, lowering her head as she raised her hand to knock. A couple of odd sounds escaped her lips; "Speaking to nonsense," her mother had always called it. It happened when the static got too close. It had happened when she saw Nora's ghost for the first time. And now, on the edge of unconsciousness, Loxley was supposed to go and parley with this monster? She wanted Jayla to be there with her – angry Jayla. She'd stood up to Tailypo in the hall. Could she do that again? Then she remembered Quentin's understanding manners, quick laugh and kind smile, and wished for him instead.

"Quit muttering out there and get in here!" came Tailypo's voice from inside.

She very nearly turned around and marched back the way she'd come. Instead, she pushed open the door. She wrapped her arms around herself, in spite of the roaring fire across the room. Tailypo stood at his desk, grinning widely with his arms spread over its surface. Those damned animals still littered the room, and she felt a fresh wave of nerves at seeing the forest-patterned walls.

"Come on in, kiddo!" His voice boomed with joviality, and Loxley hummed even louder, trying to even out the ragged edges in her brain.

She ventured further into the room, and he crossed around the desk to meet her. He wore a red silk bathrobe and flannel pants, and he'd left the coat open in front, exposing taut skin and rippling muscle.

"You did great, baby. Really great," he said, clasping her hands in his, hanging on too long.

"Thanks," she mumbled, yanking her hand back. "I'm going to go now."

"Oh, don't do that. I got a lot to chat about. Pull up a chair," he said, gesturing to an empty seat by his desk. "Can I make you a drink?" He stepped over to a hidden bar, opening up a cabinet and removing two glasses.

Her stomach was a ball of acid. "Yeah. I'd like some milk."

"Sweetheart, let me make you something that a person would drink for fun."

"You can put sugar in the milk. My mother used to do that for me."

He laughed and returned to his task. "You made a big splash. A big splash. I bet they're going to send people in from Nashville and Atlanta to see you play."

She watched him carefully as he poured two glasses, one from a bottle of whiskey, and another from a bottle of schnapps. "That's not milk."

"It's got plenty of sugar. Keep you nice and warm, too."

"No."

He considered her, his eyes twinkling in the firelight. His index finger tapped the rim of the glass meant for Loxley. "Well, all right then, baby. I'm just going to have to drink it myself," he said, setting both glasses down on his desk. "Quentin tells me that you near beat a woman to death in the streets after the show. I'm not one to tell the talent how to celebrate, but..."

She folded her hands across her lap and began to rub her thumb over the dry skin. Tailypo's face was too strange to decipher, so she chose to look at her knees. "Yeah, but I didn't kill her because I don't think she's all bad."

"I don't give a shit about that."

"You don't?" She glanced up at him.

"Do you remember what I said to you right before you left the stage?"

She thought back. She remembered her disgust at his sudden grip on her arm, the thrill of the audience's rhythmic claps and the blaring stage lights. She recalled the warm wood of her poplar beauty and the spider's web pattern on the back. She tried to figure the number of apertures in it, and concentrated hard on the memory of its form.

"I told you to see me in my office after the show," said Tailypo.

"Okay."

"And you didn't do that, did you?"

"No. I saw something more important, so I did that instead."

He swept up the whiskey glass, its amber contents sloshing with satisfying arcs of refracted light.

"Why would you think that there's anything more important than what I told you to do?"

She shrugged. "You're not very important to me."

She'd meant to offend him, but he laughed. She couldn't tell if it was a genuine laugh, or the sort of chuckling someone does before they start yelling.

"It's up to me whether or not you get to sleep inside. It's up to me whether you get to play your violin again. It's up to *me*," his voice rose to a crescendo with that word, "whether or not I sell your whereabouts to Duke for a few bucks."

"Yeah, but you don't control me, and I didn't take your deal. I don't have to do what you say. I could walk out of here and you won't stop me."

"You don't look that strong to me."

"That doesn't matter. I think you like me. I think you might love me. You're not going to hurt me." She glared at him. "You want me to like you, too."

He swallowed loudly, but kept that smile of his.

Keep on mouthing off to me, Loxley had once heard her mother say before a swift slap. Her mother had been leering the same way. If he hit her in anger, would his ghost side emerge? If it did, she would draw him into her – just like Nora – and solve that problem right there.

Tailypo scratched his nose. "So you got this woman downstairs who knows who you are: Marie. You know why I'm okay with your big fight with Duke?"

"No."

"That's because he's Consortium, and them company fucks are what took away my goddamned forest. So when I hear you want to kill the most important shill in the Hole, I think it's a good thing. Bat shit crazy, but good. I can see you're about to say something; just keep it to yourself." He ran a finger around the lip of the glass. "When I got my tail back, I hid it away. Buried it in the woods and got myself a good old rest for a couple dozen years. But then these fucking miners... I don't even know where those bones are anymore. Crushed to powder I guess."

She made herself stop tapping her feet and rubbed her sweaty palms against her pants. "You don't like Duke either?"

"Hell, no. I want to turn this whole place into a ghost town — just feed it to the kudzu. But that takes time, and you think you can just shortcut it with Marie."

"She says she'll tell Hiram to meet me in the foundry so I can turn myself over. If we don't show up, she's going to tell him where I've been hiding."

"Too much risk. Let's just put a bullet in her and be done with it. I can have some of the boys dump her body off into the smelting furnace."

"The smelting furnace?"

"Sure. More bones in the steel around here than you might think. I got a bunch of friends that work in there."

"That's what Duke did to Alvin Kimball, and I don't like it. Marie doesn't need to die." She shook her head. "Her plan is good."

"You just don't give an inch, do you?"

"If you don't do what I want, I'm going to leave, or Duke will eventually kill me. I won't be around anymore."

He opened his mouth to speak, then closed it. He laughed, and tried to say something else, but trailed off. He snatched up his glass and took a long pull of his whiskey. When he set it back down, his hand tensed, and a few drops slurped over the sides. He muttered something and strode to a stuffed deer, inspecting its black eyes. "Do you know what this is?"

"It's a deer. I saw one in a book."

"And you don't think that's impressive that I have one?"

She didn't follow. She had grown used to people taking conversations in random directions, but this one seemed even stranger than normal. What was he trying to tell her? "Other people are going to figure out who I am," said Loxley. "I got the crowd to clap with me, so I bet more people will come see. You said that people would come from all around to hear. Duke will know about me."

"I bet you've never been out of the Hole, have you?"

"No."

He stroked the deer's head, running his fingers along its ear. "Never seen a forest... I've got one here, though, enough for both of us. You can have it, if you just give yourself to me."

"This is just a room full of dead animals."

"Don't you have an imagination?"

"Yeah, but I also have eyes."

He roared and shoved the deer. It slid across the marble floor into a murder of crows, which toppled like bowling pins. "You are so infuriating sometimes. Why don't you just do as I say?"

"Help me kill Hiram."

He wheeled. "Shut up about Hiram!" He swept

across the room toward her, his red silk coat billowing like fire, his skin growing sallow. He planted a boot on the seat between her legs and loomed over her, furious. The temperature plummeted, and Loxley saw the stuffed deer in the corner kick its legs momentarily. Black wings fluttered.

A nervous, atonal hum erupted from her and she cringed. When she glanced about the room, all eyes were upon her. Every head had turned to see.

"I've never wanted anything like I want you. There's something about you. I need every part of you," he rumbled. "Are you scared?"

She flapped her hands. "Yes."

"Why? What happened to all that strength from before?" he asked, his voice suddenly smoothing like a singer's.

"I'm scared that you're weak and stupid."

He arched an eyebrow.

Loxley wiped her eyes, and her hand came away slightly damp. "You can't seem to control yourself. You might hurt me or worse, and then you won't have me around at all. You don't understand that there is only one way to do things around here." She struggled to control her breathing as she let her eyes fall closed. She couldn't look at his face anymore – not so closely, with its twitching muscles. "My way or nothing."

"You don't have to take my deal, then, if you want Hiram dead." He leaned closer, and she felt his cold breath on her neck as he whispered into her ear. "Maybe if you sweet talked me a little. Maybe with a kiss," he cooed.

Her eyes shot open and she struck him solidly

across the cheek. Her palm arced with pain as though she'd broken a bone, and she screeched in agony. He bolted upright before stumbling backward, clutching his face in shock.

The room's warmth returned. A blink, and the stuffed animals had returned to normal. She rose, her chest heaving in time with the throbbing of her hand.

"I don't need your fucking permission," she snapped. "For anything."

She made for the door. Tailypo didn't stop her.

CHAPTER THIRTEEN
JUST A TASTE

THE STAGE LAY empty, the theater lights long since extinguished, save for one of the table lamps Loxley had switched on. It bathed her immediate surroundings in its incandescence, but stopped after a few feet – a tiny sphere submerged in a darkened sea. She traced the patterns of the lacquered maple wood tabletop, unable to count the striations because of the way that they faded into one another like cirrus clouds.

She hadn't grown the gills she'd hoped for; she'd carried her own air down into the depths, and she had the distinct sense that it was running out. Loxley imagined the lamp dimming, the light shrinking, until it flickered out like a candle, leaving her to drown. She rubbed her eyes, crushing away a tear with her palm.

Her hand throbbed where she'd slapped Tailypo. A nasty pink bruise spread over her palm. Tomorrow, it would be yellow and purple, the same as Nora's touch, and Alvin Kimball's before it. Loxley's theory had proven out: when Tailypo lost control of himself, he became a ghost.

What if he'd entered her the same way Nora had? What would it be like, to channel a creature like Tailypo? What sorts of unwelcome thoughts would consume her? She considered how betrayed she'd felt when she gathered Nora's feelings on Marie, then settled on the idea that Tailypo would be profoundly disturbing.

Before she'd come to the theater for peace and quiet, she'd stopped by Marie's room. Jayla told her they'd sent Marie home, and the hare-lipped woman had left a note. It read:

Stacker. Thursday. Midnight.

Everyone knew the stacker – the enormous, filthy machine on the southwest side of the foundry spraying coal from the rail lines into mountainous piles with its boom. The cloud of coal dust often swept across the southern side of the eighth ring, staining every house black in its wake. Loxley hadn't been up close to it, but she often watched it at night from the roof of Magic City Heights, vibrating with its yellow sodium vapor lights and low thrum.

So that was where Hiram would be. She was clever and quick. She could hide and stick Cap's knife into him, then get away before he made a ghost. Would he be ready for her? After she'd killed his friend in the limousine, almost certainly. He might even have new friends. Would her bruised hand be better by then? Hiram might prove more difficult if it wasn't. Still, Duke would be a lot easier to murder if he was out of the way, and she needed to take it one ghost at a time.

"You pissed Tee off pretty good, Loxley," came Quentin's voice. He sauntered around the table and pulled up a chair, scooting into the light.

"I hate him."

"So I gathered."

"He won't stop trying to," she thought about it for a second, "do things to me. I think he's trying to fuck me."

Quentin removed a long, silver tube from the jacket pocket of his silk suit. He opened it and pulled out a cigar. Three o'clock in the morning, and he was still dressed like he was working the restaurant. "I've met most of his ex-wives. You don't seem like his type."

"You don't believe me?" she asked with a scowl.

He clipped the stogie, depositing the tip into an ash tray. "You and I both know Tee wants more from you than sex. You know he's not like the rest of us."

The flash of his lighter was blinding in comparison to the darkness around it. Leaves flared red to black like the coloring of some poisonous insect, and a torch flame ejected from the end of the cigar with each puff.

Curling smoke, billowing and clouding. Rapid flashes. Lips. Puff. Lips. Puff. Eyebrows rising. Nostrils flaring. The lamp and the lighter both bright. A hundred chairs in the shadows.

She scrunched up her eyes, but the leathery smoke drilled through her nose and into her brain. It threatened to overwhelm her. She'd never been close to a cigar before, and she hated all of it. Humming loudly, she slapped at where Quentin sat, and a prickly burn slashed her palm as she hit the cigar. She batted at it again, the tips of her fingers just brushing Quentin's stubbly face. She wanted to tell him to stop, but the word wouldn't form in her mind.

"Jesus, girl!"

She didn't stop slapping the air until she was sure he'd retreated.

When she opened her eyes, she saw that Quentin had jumped to his feet and was frantically brushing the front of his silk suit. The stogie lay shattered on the table, a thin wisp of smoke trailing from it before snaking wildly through some unseen turbulence. She reached out and thumped the stick onto the floor.

"For fuck's sake, Loxley!"

With a yelp, she noticed the black burn mark on her already-bruised hand. The pain of it roiled around the thought of the ash on her skin. Now she had ash there instead of skin, and that was bad. Get the skin back. She rubbed the mark to no avail. She brought it to her lips and licked; an acrid tasted filled her palate. The room tilted, and she struggled to orient herself. She retched, but managed to keep her lunch as she scrubbed her hand across her pant leg. Searing pain jangled her spine from the bruise and the burn.

Then, she pressed her thumb into the burn so she couldn't see the mark. The fluctuating pain became a constant stab, and stability returned. Up was up again. Words came back.

"Jesus Christ, haven't you ever seen someone smoke before?" Quentin boomed, stooping to pick up the cigar. He dropped it into an ashtray a few tables away.

"Nora smokes pot," croaked Loxley, and she got the distinct impression of a toad in the summertime. What would a toad think of so much smoke? Would it ribbit out a smoke ring? Would the other toads jump through it? That seemed like something they'd like. She chuckled.

"What's so funny?"

"Toads."

"Are you always like this?"

"Yeah."

Quentin swore under his breath as he picked at a piece of ash on his sleeve. She hadn't meant to hurt him or scare him, or even ruin his clothes, yet there he was, angry and burned. Her hand stung so much that her eyes watered, but she could still see how much she'd upset him through the pain. She didn't know how to make him feel better.

"I'm sorry," she said, but he shook his head.

"Why is it okay for Nora to smoke pot, but I can't light up a cigar without getting slapped?"

She'd never considered that question. She thought on it for a moment. "Because pot is small. It doesn't make a big flame and lots of smoke like cigars do. The smell is weird, but it's Nora's smell and I love her."

"You're something else, girl."

"Why did you take Tailypo's deal?"

"Can I make myself a gin?" he asked.

"Sure."

"You're not going to slap it out of my hands or anything? Gin smells weird."

Shame burned in her cheeks. "Don't make fun of me."

"All right, all right," he grunted, rising.

She watched him saunter over to the bar – a long, polished counter that curved around the whole back wall. It sparkled with hundreds of different bottles and glassware, and Loxley averted her eyes, not wanting to be taken in by its details. After a minute or so, Quentin returned with a large glass of clear liquid. She could detect its Christmastime scent from across the table.

"When I was growing up on the eighth ring, there wasn't nothing here worth a damn," he said plopping down. "It wasn't the kind of place you could walk around, day or night, unless you wanted to get all your valuables boosted, or worse. My momma worked in the mines – not a place for someone as pretty and nice as she was. Every day, me and Elsie, my sister, went up to my Gran's house on the fourth ring, and momma went to work. Every day, you feel me? Not just the weekdays, but weekends and holidays, too. One day, we came home, and there was a Con-man waiting for us. That's what we used to call the Consortium administrators.

"Told us momma had been killed in a collapse. Gave us a check for three hundred dollars. We didn't have to buy a casket, because they said they couldn't dig the bodies out. So we started living with Gran, but she wasn't the same after mom's death. Gran started drinking, and she went downhill fast. She didn't live more than another year. That put me and Elsie on the street."

Loxley remembered the police carrying away her

mother's corpse. She'd screamed and banged her head until Birdie came and told her to stop. She didn't know how long she'd been at it, but it had left her forehead bloody, along with a dark, red streak on the wall. She swallowed her tears and shook her head as hard as she could, pulling herself back into the moment with Quentin.

"You should have taken up farming," she said.

His voice laughed, but his face didn't. "I'll be fucked if I ever go out to those farms, girl. That ain't no kind of life for anyone. And I wasn't going to let Elsie go out there, either. The kind of men that choose that life are either desperate, vicious or both. I was going to take care of us, no matter what, but a farm ain't the place for taking care of anything. I enrolled myself at the mines, just like momma, working for her old boss. I brought home a paycheck. I reconnected with some lost family. I was on track to become a foreman one day.

"But, you know, in the end, it didn't matter. One day, Elsie disappeared. I searched for weeks. I even paid a guy everything I had to investigate. He took my money and moved to Atlanta. My cousins couldn't help me. No one could find Elsie. I don't think she's alive. I started drinking and making a pest of myself. I robbed a few places. I hurt some people. I may not look it now, but I got pretty mean back then."

"You beat up that guy in Harrison Hoop Station," said Loxley, remembering the clobbering Quentin had administered the thief who'd stolen her money.

"Aw, Hell. That was just a little love tap. You should see me when I actually mean someone harm."

She tried to imagine it. "No. That sounds scary."

"So I spent my whole check every week on partying. I couldn't pay my rent, but I could always find an excuse to go drink on the second ring. The bars up there were top-notch. Unbelievable furniture, decorations, the works. Loved it up there. Only reason I didn't drink in Edgewood was that none of them would've let me in."

"Why not?"

He snickered. "Shit. Don't worry about it. They just didn't like the look of me, is all."

"But you're nice now."

"I'm getting to that part. I'd ruffled more than a few feathers all over the Hole, and everyone was just about done with me, I think. Some kids jacked me on the eighth ring, not far from here. When things went wrong, I wound up with a knife in my ribs, bleeding like a stuck pig. I crawled maybe thirty feet before hitting the pavement face first." He pulled up his shirt, showing a light, jagged scar sliced under his ribs. "See that right there? Had to be at least a seven inch blade. Straight on in."

She imagined something larger than her pruning knife sliding into his skin. She'd opened up a man's leg with little trouble, but Quentin had survived far worse, or so it seemed.

He pulled his shirt back down. "I wanted to see the sun one last time, so I rolled over onto my back, and there he was... Tailypo... looming over me like some kind of tombstone. He said, 'You want to die, boy?' I didn't like him calling me that, but I wasn't in a position to argue. He offered to save my life if I'd swear myself to him. I didn't know why he chose me. I still don't. I said 'let me die'."

"You said no?"

"That wasn't a life worth saving, Loxley. No purpose or good to anyone, you know? He asked me what I wanted instead... what would help me live. I told him I wanted to run the best club in the Hole. A real classy place – I guess that was because of where I'd been spending all my time. I told him if he could give me that, I would do whatever he wanted. Then, I laughed at him and passed out. When I woke up, I was here. That was ten years ago." He leaned in, the lamplight washing under his face. "I've been all over the eighth ring in my days, Loxley. This place wasn't here before the day I made that deal with Tailypo."

Her eyes widened. Maybe Tailypo was a more dangerous ghost than she'd previously thought. She could scarcely believe she'd slapped him. "Did you ever try to leave?"

"Why would I leave?"

"Because he's got you! Tailypo is bad and you're trapped!" she said, raising her voice without meaning to.

Quentin placed a hand over hers and shushed her as quietly as he could. "But I'm happy."

"But you made a deal with the Devil!" As she said it, she still wasn't sure if the Devil was real. She never much liked religion because it made almost no mention of ghosts.

"Then I got some pretty good things out of it. I have the best club, the best people and the best life of anyone I know. I'm pretty happy with the Devil. I can come and go as I please, provided I show up to work every night on time. Hell, some folks can't keep a job at all."

"But he's bad. What if he hurts you?"

"Then I probably deserved it."

"What if he hurts me?"

He leaned back. "I guess we'll just cross that bridge when we come to it, won't we? I'd never let him do that."

But he wouldn't have a choice. She knew that, even if he didn't. She pushed back from the table, her stomach curling in on itself. Shaking the crackles out, she got to her feet. "Stupid," she spat. "Stupid stupid stupid."

"Don't be silly, Loxley."

"Don't be silly, Loxley," she echoed back. Her mouth had become fixed upon his words, and she silently whispered them once more.

"Don't be mad. I'm your friend. I've helped you when no one else could."

"Mm – I'm not mad. I just can't trust you because you belong to Tailypo."

"It ain't exactly like that."

She shook her head. "It is, Quentin. Even if you don't know. Tailypo always gets back what's his."

He regarded her without a hint of animosity. She felt sure he'd be angry with her. "I guess we'll see, child. No sense in trying to change it now."

Covers

BY THE TIME Loxley could return to her room, the sun had begun to rise. She saw it in the crack between the front doors, an orange slash cutting into the cloistered club. She hadn't slept in almost twenty-four hours, and exhaustion tickled her muscles. Each tiny jolt elicited a jump from Loxley's voice, and she grunted melodically as she shambled down her hall.

She pushed open the door and slipped inside, the pie wedge of light shrinking in the windowless room. Carefully, she made her way to the edge of her bed, where she stripped out of her dirty clothes and dropped them on the floor. Nude, she stared at nothing and focused on the way the air prickled her skin with goose bumps. She ran her fingers over her bare arms, enjoying the puckered surface.

Jayla's breath whistled through her teeth, the only sound in the stillness of the room. Loxley allowed her own breathing to fall in time.

She would sleep late. She could do that now – nothing to sell at the Bazaar. Loxley's sheets felt frigid beneath her legs, and she imagined how unpleasant it would be to immerse herself in them – nothing like the mild, effervescing waters of the cooling tower. She smiled, thinking of how the bubbles had tickled her entire body. How different things had become since that night.

So many times, the world had felt as though it would end over the years. Each change that threw her whole life into disarray was unforgiveable and terrifying. Her mother's death had been the worst, and yet Loxley had survived, even finding the strength to care for herself. After Nora's death, though, nothing had made sense.

Her eyes adjusted to the thin light leaking under the door, and she watched Jayla's back rise and fall. Their kiss had been too perfect. Loxley touched her own lips, trying to call the moment to mind, but all the sticky lipstick had worn away. She placed the back of her hand against her mouth, but her skin had grown cold in the chilly air. Frustrated, she let her arm flop to her side.

She wanted another kiss. Her heart hammered, each beat multiplying the little jolts of sleep deprivation. She felt so tired, and so desperately alone. Her icy bed had grown unbearable. The line of light under the door wavered as someone passed in the hall. Her fingers burned with electricity, and she shook them, trying to get them to loosen up. She could get up, walk over there, climb into bed with Jayla and have that kiss. A throaty hum erupted from her chest, and she flapped harder, trying to restrain her voice so as not to wake her roommate.

Just stand up. Stand up and go kiss her.

Her feet stung, but she couldn't stomp them for fear of making noise. She rubbed them together, trying to scrape away the crawling nervousness. She grabbed balls of her bedding and squeezed as hard as she could, clenching her teeth. She pulled until her arms burned, her whole body starting to shake from the effort and the cold.

Go on, then. Go kiss her.

She sat up and swung her legs over the edge of the bed. The cold wooden floor was like a thunderbolt on her bare feet as she padded toward Jayla's sleeping form. The woman faced away, and she didn't stir at Loxley's approach. Without allowing herself to reconsider, she pulled aside Jayla's covers and slipped into bed with her. She wrapped her arms around Jayla, pulling her roommate back into her.

"Oh, Jesus – Loxley, what?" she mumbled, startling awake.

Loxley buried her head between Jayla's shoulder blades, not daring to see what face her roommate was making. Jayla was clad in bra and panties, and Loxley enjoyed the heat of her exposed flesh. She squeezed as tightly as she could, inhaling her scent.

"What's wrong, baby?" asked Jayla.

"I wan..." she began, but stopped. "I wan..." The phrase felt good, and she said it a few more times to calm her racing heart.

Jayla turned over and Loxley found herself face to face with deep, brown eyes, glittering in the thin light. She smiled, her lips still so succulent, even without makeup. She put a finger to Loxley's mouth. "Shh, calm down. It's okay. Take your time." She took her finger away.

The words snapped together with a well-polished precision, as though they were always meant to be said together.

"I want to kiss you again."

Jayla's hot hand snaked under Loxley's jaw and to the nape of her neck before pulling them together with surprising firmness. Their lips fused into a wet jolt of pleasure, and Loxley's knees trembled. She would have fallen, had she been standing. A muted moan escaped her throat, not at all like a hum, but some other delightful sound entirely.

She broke contact, breathless. Her chest tightened, and she felt an aching between her legs, radiating into her belly. "That was even better than before," she murmured.

Jayla giggled like someone else, not the firm woman

who guided Loxley through crowded corridors by her wrist, but playful, like a bird. "You know how to French kiss?"

She shook her head. "I've never been to France."

"When we kiss, open your mouth and let my tongue touch yours."

Their lips met another time, and Jayla's tongue darted into Loxley's mouth. It startled her at first, tasting another person's saliva, feeling another person's teeth. She was about to stop and say she didn't like it when Jayla's other hand slid over Loxley's right breast and gently squeezed. It filled her with a heat she hadn't known she'd been craving. Her vision flashed, and the room pitched to one side as her roommate pinched a nipple and slowly rolled it. She'd wanted this so badly, but what was it? What was supposed to happen? She pulled away to take a trembling gasp, but Jayla's hand didn't retreat. Her roommate wrapped a leg around Loxley's thigh and began to caress both breasts as she nibbled Loxley's neck.

The two women lay entangled for long minutes, Jayla's soft palms exploring every inch of Loxley's chest and back. She gave up control over her body as her partner's lips brushed her ear. She reverberated with Jayla's low groans – relaxing, in spite of the crackles that begged to be shaken from fingers. And most of all, she enjoyed the hot friction of skin against skin, moving her heart in ways she never could have predicted. They began to sweat, the bedclothes steaming like a greenhouse.

Jayla pushed her flat against the bed by her shoulder, then straddled Loxley's hips. Cool air tickled her now moist skin as the comforter fell away, and she noticed the trickle of wetness between her thighs. Her partner unbuttoned her bra, exposing two large breasts, silhouetted in the dim light. She took Loxley's hands and cupped them to her chest, where Loxley began to mimic what her partner had done.

"You've got something special, you know that?" Jayla sighed, grinding her hips across Loxley's pubis. Her panties had been soaked through.

"You're really pretty."

Jayla giggled again. "I didn't see this coming when you got here. I thought you didn't like me."

"I didn't, but I do now."

"Well, I am just so glad."

Her partner leaned down to slide her tongue into Loxley's mouth once again. Jayla's hand brushed up and down Loxley's stomach, lightly caressing her ticklish spots. The deep ache had become almost painful. She bucked her hips, trying to press her most sensitive skin into Jayla's.

Hot water streaked across her cheek, instantly growing frigid – a teardrop. Loxley blinked, and two more followed. It was as though her body was trying to remember something horrid, but her mind wouldn't let her – rough hands, a gray mustache and calloused fingers. The memory threatened to pour into her exposed mind like molten candlewax. Her moans became humming, and her fingers jolted.

"Shh, baby," Jayla whispered, wiping away a tear. "Just be here with me. Forget everything else that's happened."

"I want you to f... Can you fuck me?" Her voice

broke and more tears wet her cheeks. "I don't know how – just... just make me feel something else."

"I think I can arrange that."

Loxley squeezed her eyes shut and felt soft lips on her neck. Her partner's weight lifted away as she climbed off, but her touch grew firmer on Loxley's torso. Hands roved further down, and fingers ran through her pubic hair, tugging gently before retreating. One at a time, two fingers traversed the length of her opening before slipping inside.

Her body was a cascade of sparks and stars, a web of tangled lights aglow in Jayla's electric touch. It would be hours before she found sleep –

– Blissful, deep and safe.

Lockpick

THE NEXT TWO days were a knot of legs and tongues, fingers and sighs, sidelong glances and whispers. Jayla had many obligations, but Loxley only needed await her moment onstage. Other than calling her to shows, folks generally left her alone. She ventured out of the room on occasion to take lunch or dinner, but she spent many of her hours resting comfortably in her nest of sheets and blankets. Her roommate returned with every stolen spare minute, depositing them in the room like bars of gold.

It was as though a dam had burst inside Loxley, and what flooded through was a burning need to have her skin against Jayla's at every opportunity: holding hands, little kisses, fingers through hair. She quickly learned to reciprocate her partner's actions, closing her eyes and focusing on Jayla's voice and quivers. Without the distraction of her sight, Loxley felt she could understand her partner in a way she hadn't before.

The only snake in paradise was the clock, ticking ever closer to midnight, Thursday. Jayla had to leave so often to handle the trash, coordinate the kitchen, settle a dispute or take food to Tailypo; it was in those lonely minutes that Loxley's eyes wandered over to the battered chrome alarm clock. She'd do the math in her head.

Thirty-two hours. Twenty-six hours. Sleep. *Eighteen hours.* She'd slept away eight of what might be her last hours. The clock injected churning venom into her veins, and she'd lay, near paralyzed, waiting for Jayla to draw it from her with a kiss.

They didn't speak of what Loxley was going to do at midnight. Jayla knew. Quentin and Tailypo knew, too. When five o'clock Thursday afternoon rolled around, a knock came at her door. Jayla didn't knock. A guttural yelp burst from Loxley's throat, else she'd have pretended she wasn't there.

She pulled on pajamas and padded to the door. "Who is it?"

"Quentin. Do you have a moment to talk about the show tonight?"

She opened the door.

She found Quentin leaning against the frame, hands in the pockets of his dapper suit. He glanced down the hallway and sniffled. "Tee said to tell you that you've got the last spot this evening. You go on at eleven-thirty, so you'll need to be in makeup by –"

Don't flap your fingers. Look him in the eye.

"No."

"Loxley, I –"

"No."

She tried to shut the door, but he wedged it with his foot. "Just listen to reason, damn it. Tee thinks you're going to get killed down there. I'm inclined to agree."

"You said you were my friend."

"I am. And a friend wouldn't let you do something so crazy."

She opened the door and tried it again, but his foot wouldn't budge. The opening to the hallway had become a maw, and she needed to close it as soon as possible. "I'm not crazy. Go away."

"What the hell are you planning? You don't stand a chance against this guy."

"I'm smart. I'll kill him."

He put a shoulder into the door and knocked it open, shoving her backward. She lost her balance and landed hard on her rump. The person who entered the room may have had Quentin's body and voice, but he wasn't anything like the kind man she'd seen before. He towered over her, his fists balled and steady, his suit taut with muscle, his eyes dreadful and cold. This was the person who'd beaten the thief in Harrison Hoop Station – the Quentin of the bad old days.

"You think you can take a man who means to kill you?" he bellowed, shaking a meaty fist in front of her face. "You think you know what it's like to be in a fight for your life?"

Quentin's mass seemed to grow before her eyes, as if to wrap around her entire field of view. He hadn't actually changed, and yet he loomed like a bear before her, his footing as sure as if he'd been nailed to the ground. The tide of static began to rise around her. What if he punched her? What if he did something worse?

Her voice burst from her chest, no matter how hard she tried to stop it, and so she shouted at him. She summoned up all the rage inside and pounded her fists against the wood so she wouldn't have to shake the crackles out. Her voice filled up the room, rippling from the boards, multiplying upon itself. She wasn't Quentin's to command. She wasn't Tailypo's. She wasn't weak. She wasn't crazy. She was powerful, and nothing would come between her and fate.

She meant to say those things, but her mouth was too full of fury to hold the words, and so she only screamed.

Quentin took a step back. Faces gathered in the doorway, peeking in at the pair: Cap among them. Loxley rose to her feet, tears bursting the light in her eyes like exploding stars – too sharp. She softened it, passing her spread fingers before her face like a fan. Her lips locked around a hoot, and she repeated the noise until the static went away. When she finally lowered her hands, she found Quentin standing with arms crossed.

He straightened his tie. "I think you get my point, pumpkin. There's no way you could handle a fellow like –"

She stepped forward and kneed him in the balls as hard as she could – with the legs that had climbed thirteen stories to her rooftop garden every day for the past five years – legs that had dragged a fully-loaded vegetable cart to the market from Magic City Heights – legs that had outrun Hiram and Duke.

When Quentin doubled over, she wrenched open her nightstand and snatched the knife she'd borrowed from Cap. Without another word, she pressed the point of it to her opponent's neck. His eyes went even wider, and his torso froze mid-breath.

She wanted to threaten him. *You don't know me. I could open you up like that man in Duke's car. Just a push would do it.* Instead she hummed long and low, half a growl, half a song.

Quentin didn't speak. He kept his palms flat against the ground, his brown skin slick with fresh sweat.

"Fuck off," she finally managed, and made for the door. She pushed past Cap and into the hallway.

"Wait," said Cap. "That knife..."

"I'm going to borrow it," she said.

"I know. Let me get you a sharper one. You're going to want a jacket, too."

The Old Path

THE CITY CAME out to watch her passing like mourners at a funeral procession. Above her, on the terraced steps of the Hole, city lights shimmered in a great bowl. The omnipresent column of steam that rose from the Foundry caught the light, glowing and churning like a summer thundercloud. It suffused the sky with a sick, sodium vapor pallor. Loxley imagined what it would be like to fly through its swirling mist; would it be warm? Would it carry her up into the heavens?

She imagined other souls hitching a ride on the mist to travel far away from their corpses. After a while, all ghosts vanished, and perhaps this was how. Perhaps the steam carried them up to God, and they were so happy that they never returned. Perhaps that's all the steam really was – the ghosts of the dead. Part of her wanted to laugh at the thought, and the other part of her had suffered too much abuse at dead hands to make light of it.

The path to the ninth ring was, in some ways, the oldest part of the city, and in others, the newest. The ever-sinking nature of the Hole meant that it was constantly being changed and lowered as they dug deeper, hungry for more ore. But at the same time, people had been walking this path since the first shovel turned Alabama soil. It was well-worn by the boots of hundreds of thousands of men and women – many of whom would never leave it. So many people had been buried down here by accidents, people whose lives had all held meaning to someone or another. Their passage had warmed the hard-packed earth, wearing it to a dull sheen.

She kept her eyes peeled for ghosts. She usually didn't venture down so far because of the dead. Accidents, as well as rapists and murderers, ensured a high degree of danger the closer she got to the bottom. Armed policemen supervised the changing of the shifts, but at this time of the evening, she was on her own. No one would help if she got into trouble. An undiscovered body could spell disaster.

And yet she passed, unmolested, through the

eighth ring as she made for the ramp into the works. No one emerged from the silent, dark row houses that lined the filthy avenue. No voices beckoned to her from dim alleyways. The landscape lay empty, almost like a stage, waiting for her and Hiram to take their places in the light. Would she see him on the way? Would he already be there? Would he be alone?

She shivered in the frosty air. The temperature must have dropped twenty degrees in the past day or two... not that she'd been outside her room much. She regretted not wearing more layers, and crossed her arms tightly as she marched onward. It wasn't a windy sort of cold, but the kind that seeped into her bones no matter how fast she walked.

Quentin had been right: she was going to die, even if she'd never admit it. She was cold and alone, armed only with a knife against a professional murderer. She'd accepted what would happen to her with the same sort of detachment one might have for the death of a distant relative. However, she had to try, and she had to do it her way. She'd wanted to ask for Quentin's help, and perhaps even Tailypo, but she'd been unwilling to pay the prices such help would cost.

What would she feel when she sunk the knife into Hiram's chest? Would she be swept up by an ocean of his blood? What noises would he make? These questions occupied her during her descent, until she reached the lowest level of the Hole – the Foundry.

The Foundry had a filthy coal storage facility, endlessly belching clouds of black soot over the rest of the ninth ring. She could see the stacker boom looming over her approach, a colossal machine for vomiting heaps of coal onto mountains, but silenced at this time. Yellow light sprayed from its length, illuminating everything around in a nasty wash. A fence separated her from the rest of the facility – a sad, rusted thing, fraught with breaches. She pulled away the chain link and slipped inside with nary a sound.

The dirt on the other side was black and chalky, suffused with coal dust. It edged onto her shoes, staining them as if to mark her as someone who belonged to the Hole. Much open ground lay between her and the stacker, and she could see it perfectly from her vantage point.

The backdrop of city lights sloped upward, flashing neon and hazy sparkles, spinning around Loxley's vision. Her stomach turned as she realized that this was the second place where anyone in the city could look down and see her, provided they were on the right side of the Foundry's plume. She'd disliked Edgewood as a child for the same reason, looking out over all of those people, and now, they were all looking down on her. It was an arena, just like the boxing hall near Vulcan's Bazaar, but on the grandest scale. Would others watch with casual disinterest as she and Hiram carved each other up?

She clambered over the stacker's tracks, a pair of heavy silver rails that shined unlike anything else around them. Had this machine always been so big? She'd never seen it up close, but when her eyes followed the boom's length, she realized the assembly was larger than most buildings, maybe as large as Bellebrook.

Dirty white and yellow paint flaked from its surface, and a massive Consortium logo adorned one of the larger panels. A random patchwork of details threatened to overwhelm her senses, but the form of its boom calmed her – a long series of interlocking triangles wrapped around a wide conveyor belt.

Upon reaching the stacker, she looked around and found some scaffolding with stairs. Five and a half hours early, she would take shelter and await her prey. She couldn't hide on the ground level; she might never see Hiram's approach. A high vantage point would be required to spot him first. Taking hold of a railing, she grunted and began the long ascent.

The metal was icy under her palms, and her hands began to go numb. She wished she could have crawled back into bed with Jayla and warmed them up. Loxley had wanted to tell Jayla she was leaving, that she was sorry, but it would have been too painful. She'd never say all the right things to calm her lover's mind – she could barely calm herself. Loxley didn't know how to make people feel better, only to hurt them, and in turn they would hurt her. Better to face Hiram alone with a worried friend back home, than to face him with no one waiting for her at all.

She climbed higher, and the wind whipped her hair into her eyes as she reached the end of the path. To her left lay a door to the interior chambers, locked, and ahead of her, there were a few tenuous footholds. She could see better hiding spaces further up the boom, but no railings and paths. She hoisted herself over the side and continued onward, trying not to look down. She was already at least fifty feet above the ground, and though it looked soft and ashen from up high, she knew better.

After a few harrowing minutes of climbing, she'd reached the end of the boom. The machine was turned off, except for the lights. She eased onto the conveyor belt and laid down on her belly to survey the coal yards.

Empty and quiet, save for the distant thrum and clang of the steelworks.

She rolled onto her back. The column of steam climbed away from her, gargantuan in its proportion this close to the Foundry. The rings of the Hole were like a belt of stars, a halo surrounding the great blackness of night beyond. Every human was only a brief flare, sliding into this pit to be reborn in steam.

She drew Cap's carving knife from its sheath and ran her thumb across its worn handle. The other side of life's veil, Heaven, Hell or otherwise, was close at hand now. Soon, she would be a ghost, just like all of the others... or would she? Did crazy people even make ghosts? She wasn't like anyone else she'd ever met, so perhaps not. Maybe she'd stop existing and no one would ever care that she'd been there in the first place. It might be better than hurting everyone through the simple act of dying.

She lay perched on the thin place between the living and the dead. Surrounding her, the lights of all things familiar and warm, but above, the ragged edge of the cold, open sky. It was a bubble, and the stacker's boom was a needle, lifting her, pushing her through. The longer she lay, the closer the infinite night drew, and the colder it got. She shivered and held herself tightly. She wasn't imagining it – the temperature had dropped as the hours wore on.

Something tiny and white fluttered in front of her face. She blinked, looking around, but couldn't see what it had been. Then, another movement and another, and her eyes focused upon snow. She recognized twisting wisps of it extending from the column in long tendrils. Had it really grown so cold?

The first time she'd seen snow as a little girl, she'd screamed. She'd looked out her window, and the world was all wrong, white and cold, framed by an icy haze. Someone had come in the night and kidnapped her and her mother both, wrenching them away from the familiar.

No, no, it's okay Lox. Hey, no, it's okay. Everything is still the same as it was, just with a little extra on top, is all. We're still at home. You're safe. It's okay.

She had no idea how long it took to calm her down; time was slippery. When her mother took her up to the roof, Loxley found she loved snow. It fogged the world around, obscuring the distant buildings, and it muted all noises as if there was no one for miles. She could draw in it. She could count every footstep she took. When she got too cold, the snow made her mother's embrace feel that much warmer.

And now, as she watched the tiny flakes flit and dance around her, absorbing the city's incandescence, her heart was at ease. It was one last gift to her from the Hole, before she went to join those in the steam. Tomorrow, they'd find her body shot through by Hiram, lying helpless in the fresh white powder.

She curled up and willed time to wait, to give her a little longer.

CHAPTER FOURTEEN
TALONS

A LOUD CLICK, the throw of a massive switch.

A buzz, the grinding of a gearbox.

Loxley startled as surely as if the air had caught fire. How long had she been alone with the snow? How long had she been staring up at the sky? Slippery, stupid time. Why couldn't she pay attention, just this once? She'd planned to find a good place to ambush Hiram once he arrived, but now she was isolated on the most dangerous part of the machine.

She rolled over to look down the conveyor belt and see if she could spot the person in the driver's seat. Lights all along the boom erupted, and she shouted in surprise, covering her ears and shutting her eyes. Vibrations rattled the bucking metal, and she screamed louder. Coal dust shot down her throat as she inhaled, leaving her coughing and sputtering. The crackles popped in her fingertips like gunshots and she kicked her legs against the conveyor as hard as she could, trying to shake off the ants. Static rose in her brain like the tide.

She sheathed Cap's knife with shaking hands; she had to, in case the static got her. She might drop it if she lost control. Her body didn't want to listen to her, but she forced her feet under her and stood, grabbing onto the conveyor's cage for support. Her hands were black – covered in coal dust where the skin was supposed to be. She spat on them and rubbed them on her pant legs, but the streaks wouldn't come off. She tried not to imagine that it covered most of her body, but she knew it did.

With a deafening roar, the stacker pivoted hard to one side, threatening to rip her from her perch and fling her into the open night air. Loxley caught the boom cage just in time, clinging on for dear life. She had to find some way down, but the stacker continued its merciless spin, taxing her every action. Knees quaking and fingers straining, she hefted her weight forward, carefully stepping around shivering piles of coal. With a few more steps, she'd be able to see the driver's cabin. She knew she'd find Hiram behind its windows. The conveyor belt whined to life, taking her feet out from under her. Her fall wrenched her hands from their holds, and her face slammed into the gritty rubber belt with a bright flash. The cage rushed past her as she scrabbled for another hold, anything to stop the forty foot drop that was coming. Then she saw the end of the boom, and the open air.

All became weightless.

Air fled her lungs as her back struck a jagged coal pile. Searing pain flooded her. She couldn't scream; she couldn't breathe. She tumbled end over end through the flying rocks and dust, the coal slicing any exposed skin. Her limbs tried to bend in ways they shouldn't have, and up became meaningless. The stacker's running lights flashed through her vision.

She came to rest with an agony she'd never known, not even from the touch of a ghost. She couldn't take a breath, her mouth agape in a silent scream. She tasted blood. Her fingers curled into jittery, aching talons. Her left knee blazed like a torch. Her cheek rested against coal gravel. She could not lift her face from the choking soot. Rocks showered onto her from the still-running stacker.

She thought the static would take her – make her not care about any of this until Hiram came and put a bullet in her. Instead, it waited at the edge of her mind, rendered all too distant by the pain that suffused her every fiber. The only time she'd ever wanted to forget herself, her mind had failed. Coal sands sifted over her, weighing down upon her body, covering nearly every inch of her. The stacker above ground to a halt.

"Miss Fiddleback?" she heard Hiram call with a chuckle.

Every exhalation brought another tuneless note from her throat. What would Nora do? Nothing. She'd die just like she did before. She heard the chunk of his heavy footsteps, the crunching of coal.

Her heart thundered as he came into view, every bit as terrifying as she remembered. He looked like a man composed: one who could kill a human as easily as wringing a chicken's neck. His clothing was stained with soot and he held a shining chrome pistol. He looked right at her. His smirk told her there was no time to hide or run.

With great pain, she reached down to her rubble-covered leg, to Cap's knife, and drew it partway. She focused on Hiram's exposed neck. Maybe she'd get one chance to put the blade into him before he shot her if he did something stupid. Let him come closer. Let him underestimate her just like Quentin, just like the men in Duke's limousine.

"Is that you, sugarpop?" he said, his voice lilting. "You know, I was wondering, because I thought, to myself, *Only a retard would choose to hide at the end of the stacker boom.* And there you were! Can you believe it?"

"I'm not retarded," she said, surprised that she could still speak.

Hiram was still too far away. She'd never be able to get to him before he blew her head off. She needed him closer. He stopped a few feet away and leveled his pistol.

"What'cha got there? Like a knife or something? Baby, please. I'm a professional."

He locked back the hammer.

"I would like to know what's going through your head. You know, before a bullet, I mean. Call it fucking morbid, but I ain't never shot a mongoloid before."

"Why?"

His self-righteous smirk faltered. "It's just, like... I just want to know. You thinking of your daddy or something?"

She released the knife, put her palms against the ground and pushed. Fifty pounds of coal fell from her body as she excavated herself, and she got her legs under her. Her hips strained, and her back felt wretched, but still she rose. She forced herself to meet his eyes. She found no insight in them, not like Nora would have, but she stared as long as she could.

"I'm thinking of dots," she said. "I don't live in a line like you do, but dots."

"Do tell."

"I was so scared in that limousine when I opened up your friend's leg. He was screaming and red, but do you know, I think of it now, and I only think of cutting meat. Like trimming the gristle off a pork chop."

"Girlie girl, I think that's the best description I've ever been offered of what I do." He took a step closer, but he was still too far. "I think you really get me. I wish we could have gotten to know each other a little better."

"You don't have to shoot me."

He shook his head. "No, but I want to."

A pair of distant pops echoed across the coal stacks, and Hiram screamed obscenities. He clutched his arm and stomach, nearly dropping his gun, and Loxley saw blood oozing between his fingers.

"Loxley, run!" It was Quentin's voice. He crouched behind the stairs of the stacker, his gun smoking.

Hiram turned his gun on Quentin and returned fire, making long strides toward cover. She flinched with each pop, and the muzzle flashes struck her eyes like a slap. She wanted to run straight to her friend but feared getting shot in the exchange. She hobbled toward Quentin, trying to steer clear of the line of fire. When she looked to see if Hiram was about to shoot at her, she saw him running off into the darkness.

The words to tell Quentin what was happening on the other side of the stacker eluded her grasp. She flapped her fingers and gestured in the direction of the fleeing killer. Quentin came charging out of cover only to grab her hand and drag her back behind the stacker. She tried to wrench free; his grip was ironclad.

"Tailypo said he'd have my skin if you went and got yourself killed," he panted, checking around the corner for Hiram. "Are you hurt?"

She grabbed hold of her sentence and forced it out of her mouth. "He's getting away!"

"I know. I fucked up his motorcycle, and he's twice wounded. We can take our time and do this right. Now are you hurt?" He hugged her, and even though she ached all over, she buried her face in his chest.

"Yes," she mumbled. "Everything hurts. I have to kill him. We're doing that, right?"

"I can handle him on my own. You don't have to come along."

"Yes I do!" she shouted, and Quentin flinched.

"All right, pumpkin." He nodded once, twice. "I understand. Stick close to me."

He took her to where the shots had struck Hiram and looked around in the dust. He found footprints and spots of blood. Loxley reached down and touched the drops, squishing them between her fingers. She didn't mind his blood on her skin. Quentin took a few more steps, searching out the trail, and she followed after him.

They made their way in silence, Quentin's eyes constantly darting this way and that, ever alert.

They found Hiram's motorcycle kicked over, ignition wires ripped from their housing. Quentin chuckled. Loxley pulled her knife from its sheath and clutched it tightly. The buildings of the Foundry rose around them as they followed the path, and soon they departed the dirt for concrete, which made Hiram that much easier to track.

"He's lost a lot of blood. Going to be weak when we find him," said Quentin.

The longer they walked, the weaker Hiram would be, and the more strength Loxley would regain. Her whole body ached, but movement worked out some of the pain. She hadn't fallen as hard as she'd thought, and soon she'd be able to run if she had to.

Hiram's blood spatters became crimson skids dragged across the concrete. His feet weren't rising and falling the way they should have been. He was dying. Loxley felt a pang of disappointment that she hadn't made the killing blow herself. What if he died before they got to him? How long would he take to make a ghost? Would he be like Nora's ghost? She'd have to run the second he drew his last breath, or he would ravage her with dead hands.

The trail led them into the furnace building, which rumbled like an endless peal of thunder. Blood was harder to spot on steel gratings, but there was so much of it now. They passed a fleeing worker, who took one look at Quentin's pistol and darted away. Had Hiram scared the man before they arrived?

The blood drops scattered through an open steel bulkhead, which glowed with reflected fire. Just being close to it was like the sun beating down on her back on a hot summer's day. The heat surrounded her, pressed against her, and it took all her conviction not to stop and savor its embrace on her aching bones. The static rushed forward at her small comfort, and she blinked and flapped it away. Quentin stopped and looked her over and she gestured down the corridor with her knife.

"He's getting away," she said.

They wound through the dense forest of pipes and tanks inside the furnace building, Hiram's trail far harder to follow across the metal grates. Twice, they nearly took wrong turns. They climbed a set of stairs and found a long catwalk, several offshoots leading away through the almost-impenetrable pipes to the right, to the left, the hellish fires of the steel furnace. Loxley peered over the side and saw viscous, bubbling fluid, bright white and orange, at least sixty feet below. Its heat stung her face and exposed hands, and she had to look away. It was like laying down on asphalt in the summer. Even her knife felt overly hot in her palm.

Quentin reached back and patted her arm, then gestured to the end of the catwalk. She followed his line of sight to a doorway, past the thick maze of ducts and pipes, and spied the tip of Hiram's bloody boot. A pool of crimson had spread under it, and its toe was up, as if Hiram lay just around the corner on his back. Quentin glanced back at her and she nodded. They began to move up, weapons at the ready. She only hoped he was not yet dead, so she would have time to escape before his ghost emerged. They could rush him, stick him with Cap's knife and be done.

One hundred paces and they'd be on him. The

furnace's blaze seeped into her, becoming less bearable by the second. Sixty paces. Quentin locked back his hammer. Forty paces. The boot hadn't moved. Quentin craned his neck for a better look.

When he took his next step, a hail of gunfire erupted from the blind alcove to his right, and he shouted in surprise: five shots in all. Each pop jolted Loxley, and she instinctively jumped backward. Quentin went stumbling toward the railing before sinking down against it, a look of horror covering his face. Red poured from his neck, and several dots appeared upon his shirt.

The click that came at the end of those five shots was deafening.

Her mouth full of rage and terror, she dashed around the corner to find the grinning Hiram lying on his back, clicking his empty pistol at the air. His own shirt and jacket were soaked with his life, and his skin was ashen even in the scorching light. He was wearing only one shoe.

"Oh, fuck," he chuckled. "I didn't think you'd come with –"

The knife hot in her palm, she lunged at him. He raised his arm to stop her, and the blade sank into his forearm, glancing off bone. He screeched, clawing at her with his free hand as she straddled his hips. She stabbed again, still blocked by his feeble defense. She ripped aside his arm, now as weak as a child's, and plunged the knife sidelong into his chest. Hiram's ribs guided it into his softest parts, and she yanked it free before stabbing him again. His cries became gurgles, and his smile transformed into terror. A dozen more times she pierced his chest, face, neck and stomach.

By the time she'd finished, he wore no expression at all.

Once his screams had faded and fury subsided, she became aware that she was crying. Her shuddering breaths burst from her in long, mournful sobs, and she released the knife, still buried in Hiram's heart. She hadn't seen the dying man in the limousine, but she'd felt his blood. This time, she'd been able to touch the whole thing – to see him as he changed from a person into nothing more than meat. She'd ripped him into a tattered husk.

Her first thought was to run. He'd be coming back soon.

When she turned around, she saw Quentin, his convulsing hand held to his blood-slickened neck. His eyes rolled back in his head, and his hand fell to the ground, allowing his life to pour from him like water from a tap.

"No!" She scrambled over to him. "No, you can't!" She pressed a palm to his neck, but the wounds covering his chest were myriad and catastrophic. His sticky blood coated her arm, mixing with Hiram's. He was going to die. The world was ending again.

The din of the furnace mingled with Quentin's gurgling, and her hands shot up to her ears to cover them. Quentin's eyes had become unfocused. He wasn't looking at anything anymore. She reached out and touched his face, but he didn't react.

You can't leave me. You can't die right now. I'm sorry. Please, I'm so sorry. I just want you to get up.

His wounds were no bigger than coins, but they'd downed the large man. His whole body shuddered, then his breath ceased to flow. His chest wound no longer sucked at the air. Behind him, the furnace roared, drowning out Loxley's cries.

Two men lay mortally wounded at her feet. It was time to leave.

She forced herself to stumble down the catwalk. Duke would die for this – for Nora and Quentin. She'd go to his house this very night and gut him in his bed. She'd spill his blood across his rich floors and sheets and walls and curtains and anything else she could find.

But she'd never get that far. Quentin had died helping her because he'd been right about her. She couldn't kill on her own. Hiram would have murdered her with little trouble if it wasn't for Quentin. Her body ached; her mind was fried. Duke would have a far easier time with her.

Below her feet, the diamond grating seemed to undulate with each step. It made a pleasing pattern in her vision, offering her a way to calm down. She could pick out diagonal lines in two directions, but also straight, fat, horizontal lines and long, thin, vertical ones. She liked the way threads interlaced when she lined up the diamonds in her mind.

She shook her head. Hold off the static. Just get out before the ghosts come. Otherwise, they'll...

She stopped and turned to look back at Hiram. When she'd been invaded by Nora's ghost, she'd found herself able to emulate her friend's behaviors. What if she let Hiram touch her? Her eyes drifted to the empty gun at his feet – something she could never hold. Every shot terrified her, but if she was more like Hiram...

Her feet refused to carry her back to the corpses.

Her instincts begged her to run. She began to sense a distortion, a sour note in her surroundings. The furnace became deafening, though its orange light dimmed before her. She heard the clang of the Foundry, closer than ever, keeping time underneath the chaos. The dead stirred.

One foot plunged forward, then the other. Loxley fought her dread, pushing against the flow of a river as each footfall carried her closer to Quentin's body. The crackles jolted through her hands and into her arms, swirling around her spine. She stopped and kicked her toes against the grating. She came to rest in front of her friend and knelt down.

Two spirits might kill her outright. No, there couldn't be two ghosts – Hiram, not Quentin. Her friend had been strong, but she needed the man who killed him, the man who knew everything about Bellebrook and murder. She grabbed his shirt and pulled him onto his side. He was heavy, but she had carried many heavy burdens. She ran a hand over his sweat-slickened cheek, his stubble scratchy over his soft skin. His deep, brown eyes regarded some distant sight, and she covered them so she wouldn't have to look.

"I'm sorry. I'm just..."

The dead only stayed with their bodies when they were juicy. She didn't want Quentin to be one of those horrifying things. She wanted to put him in the column, to rise into the steam. The heat of the furnace below intensified, hungry, as she positioned her friend's body at a gap in the bottom of the railing. She pushed his torso through so that his weight would drag him off the moment she let go.

She could almost see the flames below, reaching up for them.

And then, the only thing that held Quentin's corpse in this world were Loxley's slender hands. She opened her fingers and let him fall. His legs slid from the grating and he was gone with a fiery hiss and an arc of bright, orange flame. She regarded her splayed, bloody fingers for a long time, tears streaming from her eyes. Gone forever in an instant, like so many others before him.

She felt a presence over her shoulder, like someone staring at the nape of her neck. She sucked in a breath and held it. She turned to see Hiram's ghost, his eyes hollow, his skin ashen, groping for her. She ducked under its clutches; its nearness to her felt like an infected wound – feverish and aching. She couldn't let him take her here.

The ghost's face distorted, desirous of her life. Loxley sobbed as its empty sockets bored into her. It swiped, its arms blinding fast, but she had already jumped back. She stumbled to the ground and it got ahold of her ankle.

Crushing pain rushed through her unlike any ghost's touch she'd felt before. Her leg went numb, but she kept her breath and jerked her foot away. She clambered back, and as she rose, she broke into a loping, wounded sprint.

Hiram's ghost was so much more than she'd prepared herself for, but she needed what he knew. She made it to the blast door and rounded it without looking back. What if it killed her? She banged down a flight of stairs, out of the heat. What would be left of Loxley if that happened? Her hip felt like she'd torn a muscle inside it, and the more she ran, the more feeling returned to her leg. But how could she kill Duke without Hiram? Was this the price of her revenge?

With that thought, she stopped, and a tide of bleak horror rose around her. She waited for the spirit's touch, and it did not disappoint.

CHAPTER FIFTEEN
WHEELBARROW

WAR OF THE *Worlds* – the pages felt good in Hiram's hands, browning though they were. He took a long drag on his cigarette before starting the next paragraph. The alien tripods had just emerged with their heat rays and began frying the populace of Earth. His eyes flicked to the cherry on the end of his smoke, trying to imagine what the heat rays did to a person's skin. An old Duke Ellington record hissed on the player as if to imitate the noise.

Hiram's stone cottage at Bellebrook may have looked like a servant's quarters on the outside, but the interior boasted a posh elegance. It held thousands of books and records, collected anywhere he could find them. The high fidelity system could really bang around, too. Back in the day, the cottage was used as a kitchen for the main house, in case of fire, and it still had the wine cellar, which Duke kept stocked. His house was positively sedate when compared with the mansion across the green; Hiram preferred it that way. He filled the space to the brim with loud music, smoke, booze, drugs and pussy as often as he could, and the ostentatious Southern royal bullshit tended to get in the way of that.

Duke was less than understanding of Hiram's predilections when he gave him the place, as though that was supposed to stop him from indulging. Constant admonitions, invitations to church, meals and other lunacy were extended to Hiram, but he couldn't stand Duke or his people. The dumb bastard could stay inside and pray the day away; the night belonged to the smart folk.

The Bell family hadn't bitched about Hiram's activities when he'd been working out of Nashville ten years prior. They couldn't give two shits what he did in his off-time, provided the right people got what was coming to them in a prompt and professional manner. It was a fun start to his career, running jobs against the Con, blood in the streets every night. The Bells were righteous warriors, just like Duke. The big difference was that they were union boys, not Bible thumpers. All good things came to an end, though, and Hiram had sold out the Bells for a better gig at their hated enemy. Once at the Con, he'd ended up assigned to Duke, another asshole working a coup. Sometimes things were just too easy.

They didn't have to like each other to do business. Being Duke's favorite pet killer was worth a lot of money, and it was about to be worth a lot more. The old fucker was losing his grip, coming unhinged over this Loxley bitch. Hiram supposed he could understand the man's frustration: the limousine would never be the same after the freak had torn open Ray's leg in there – plenty of blood for a perfectly-white leather interior.

Loxley was decently creepy, too; she knew things she shouldn't have known. She'd laughed when they had her naked at gunpoint. She'd split Ray open when they hadn't searched her for a knife. No part of her sat well with Hiram.

And then there were the things Marie said: chilling things about supernatural feelings or some such. He shook his head and took another drag. And to think he read *books* for their crazy stories.

Duke was falling to pieces, and a lot of guys would have followed him to the end of that tunnel, but not Hiram. He knew everything about the forming coup, the locations of resources, the names of most of the players in Nashville and Atlanta, potential targets and strategies. He'd carefully documented it as it unfolded, just in case things started to slip, and to his delight, they had. A great trader can make money in any market, and Hiram thrived on change. The Consortium would pay him handsomely for his information, and he'd already started working the back channels to broker the exchange. Duke would pay him for his current services, then die. The Consortium wasn't a group to fuck with.

And screw Duke's glorious revolution, too. Sure, he needed hitters when he wanted power, but as soon as everyone was holy-rolling there wouldn't be any room for men who got their hands dirty. Hiram would have his turn against the wall first. Get paid, don't get betrayed. It was a matter of playing chicken until the time was right. Wait too long, and Duke would ice him. Take action too soon, and there'd be no money in it.

Loxley was a sign of the times, and Duke was

done. Time to sell the old fucker out. He glanced over at his bookshelf where he'd hidden his notes inside an old copy of *Dracula*. He could take them to the Consortium's man on the fifth ring, get paid and get out.

There was a knock on the door. He stood, switched off the record player, strode to the door and opened it. Marie stood on the other side with the mildly disinterested look she always had around him. When she'd been hired, he'd given her Hell about her lip, hoping to get a rise out of her. She only responded by becoming more polite and withdrawn. Once, he'd asked her how she sucked a dick, and Duke had jumped all over him after, but Marie never said a thing. She didn't usually look him in the eye, either. At least, not until she'd helped them move Nora Vickers's body out of the cellar.

"Shiner's still looking as nasty as ever, Marie."

"You called for me?"

"What'd she hit you with, anyway? Like a bottle or something?"

"A rock," she looked him over. "What do you want?"

He snickered. "Rude as ever. I need your help moving another body. Cellar. Same place as before."

Her eyes met his, and he felt a jolt. She was a rebellious little freak, that Marie. He enjoyed watching this new side of her awaken. If it wasn't for her lip, she might be a looker, and Hiram liked a girl with attitude. Nora had been pretty sparky; he hadn't enjoyed executing her. If she'd started spying for Duke, maybe they could've hooked up. It seemed as though she liked him at the time.

He stepped aside so Marie could enter, then followed her to the stairs. In the spacious wine cellar, racks upon racks of dimly-lit bottles stretched before them; some open holes where a bottle had been removed. He'd made more than a few of those holes, particularly in the dry reds.

They rounded the corner to where he'd shot Nora and Marie stopped short. No corpse awaited them, only a blank stone wall. She bowed her head, and Hiram figured she knew the score.

"Why?"

"The usual reasons. You know too much, and you've been talking to that Loxley girl. Can't afford for the Con to get wise."

"Is Duke going to take care of my son?" she whispered.

He untucked the gun from its hiding place in back of his pants. It had been uncomfortable waiting for her to arrive with it stowed like that. "Yeah. Said he was going to put your kid up in a fancy school in England. You know this is nothing personal, right?"

"Then he'll be better off with me dead. May I pray?"

Hiram shrugged. "Why not?"

Marie sank down onto her knees in front of the wall and clasped her shaking hands together. She closed her eyes. "Dear heavenly Father," she began, but Hiram's gunshot stopped the rest of her sentence.

The woman's body crumpled forward, and he put a second shot into the back of her head. He waited for the twitching to stop, which didn't take long. He glanced over at the wall, which had been painted a sticky red, flecked with bone.

"Just being nice," said Hiram. "Thought I'd spare you all the suspense. I'm sure Our Lord and Savior got the message."

He stuffed the gun into his belt and spun on his heel to head back upstairs. Duke was going to tell him to clean all of this up, he was sure of it. Fuck that. He'd be long gone by tomorrow, after he took care of Loxley. Hopefully, the Consortium would let him come back and get his books after they raided Bellebrook.

Hiram stopped at the foot of the stairs and chuckled. "Thanks for helping me move your body down here."

Misdirective

HIRAM ROLLED OUT of bed to the sound of his alarm clock hammering his skull. He silenced it, ambled over to the sink and spat a wad of yellow, smoked phlegm into the drain. He then took a big pull of gold mouthwash and swallowed it, feeling it burn its way into his stomach. It slammed into his guts a bit harder than he was used to, and he swore loudly. His stomach had been heinously irritated recently, and he knew why: today was the day to make his move. After he met Loxley at the stacker, he'd disappear. Better to quit this job before he was shitting blood.

He strode to the gun cabinet and armed himself with his favorite pistol. It wasn't much, but he certainly wasn't going to talk to Duke without being strapped.

After throwing on the cleanest clothes he had,

he faced the daylight to stalk across the lawn to Bellebrook proper. The temperature had plummeted over the past two days with the storm front. He shivered in his wrinkled suit, thinking briefly on his attire for tonight. Too many layers meant less mobility. Then again, the last time he'd seen that bitch she'd ripped someone up with a knife. Maybe layers weren't such a bad thing.

He found Duke in the study, a technical manual spread across his lap. Hiram couldn't see the title, but he saw several circuit diagrams.

"I heard Marie didn't come home last night. Her son came here looking for her," Duke said, shutting his book.

Applied Concepts for Radio Relays the cover read. It was a Consortium technical manual. Duke stood and shelved it next to his other manuals, including the one Nora had been carrying about farming. What kind of woman went to the farms, anyway?

"What did you tell him?" asked Hiram. "Obviously not the truth, or there'd be at least one bloodstain over here."

"I told him that the police had come around asking the same question, then I had some orderlies put him up for the night in Gardendale."

"The sanitarium? That's cold-blooded."

Duke smiled. "Not at all. They bedded him down in the warden's estate. He'll be on a boat within the week after he finds out about Marie... that's done, right?"

"All sewn up, chief. Mind if I smoke?" He shook out a cig from a pack of Silver Coins.

"I do."

"Fine." He put his smoke away. "She's still on the property, though. Ain't got time for that today."

"Had to be done. A pity, really. I'll call some of the boys to clean it up in the morning. You'll be supervising."

Hiram jammed his hands in his pockets and rested against the arm of a leather chair. "Sounds like a plan, Stan. You getting into the radio business?"

"And television. We're going to broadcast our ministry to anyone who can afford to listen – anyone with a set top. Pastor Barber is already on board."

"Sounds like the signal will stop somewhere around the fourth ring."

Duke cocked his head to one side and smirked. "Until we secede. Then we'll be installing televisions on all levels and in the common areas, too."

Never going to happen, fat man. "Don't be sad when the folks down there rip them up for the copper wiring."

"I think you'll be surprised what the word of God can do. I take it you have a plan for dealing with Miss Fiddleback this evening?"

"She's soft in the head, big guy. Don't need a plan."

Duke turned his back to peruse the bookshelf, but Hiram knew what face he was making. It was the same face he always made when Hiram did something he hated – a strong dose of boredom with a pinch of derision. "I still haven't gotten all of the stains out of my limo. I think it's about time I call it a loss."

"It ain't going to be a problem. She won't have a chance to get close to me. But you know, maybe we could've shot her instead of trying to bring her in for an interview like we did."

"Or maybe you could have done your job and searched her properly, Mister McClintock." Smugness dripped from every chortling word.

Laugh it up, you self-righteous shitbag. Tomorrow is fucking payday for me. "Too right. I won't make the same mistake again."

Duke turned to him. "Do you think she's likely to bring friends?"

"Doubt she has any, but maybe. Marie said the girl knew a few folks, but I don't think anyone would follow her to meet me."

The older man's gray eyes locked onto Hiram's. "If she has anyone with her, that person has to die, too. I don't care who it is, just take care of them."

There was an authority and confidence in Duke's voice that hadn't been there when he'd ordered the death of Alvin Kimball. Over time, the bastard had gotten used to his role of cueing up killings, and Hiram knew Duke would relish the bullshit state trials that would come after the fall of the Consortium. It was all too easy to imagine the man sitting on a panel, sentencing people to death for dancing or fucking or anything else fun.

"Sure, boss. Anything you want," he said, and turned to go.

"Hiram," Duke called.

"Yeah?"

"We're doing what's right. We're going to feed these people. We're going to give them shelter. And in those provisions, they're going to find the light of Christ. I won't abide a few sinners ruining all that for the rest. The Consortium has to go, so the rest of us can live."

Hiram's eyes flicked across paintings and statues, as well as a dozen mahogany bookshelves with etched panes of glass protecting the older tomes. He might could bargain with the Con-men for a few of those books, too.

Yeah. Just living. That's what you're doing, right, old timer?

Hiram tapped his ear and pointed back do Duke as he turned to leave. "I hear you loud and clear, big guy. Look, I've got shit to take care of. I'll be home late, so don't wait up."

"You take care."

That's It

WHY THE FUCK had he just stood there like that? What could he have possibly been thinking, letting that black bastard get the drop on him? Hiram clutched his stomach and limped toward the furnace complex. The moment that motherfucker's bullets had dug in, there hadn't been much pain – just a sharp blow – but now... Each step was a new exercise in self-control not to cry out. It felt like his muscles were ripping away from his hips. Glancing down, he realized how much blood he was losing. If he didn't get out of there soon, he'd pass out. At least the ground was covered with coal dust, so he'd be hard to track.

He looked closer. His blood trail stood out to the naked eye, congealing as it struck soot into dusty black spheres.

"Fuck," he gasped with each single step, occasionally swapping it for, "that... crazy... cunt..."

His head spun as he reached the door to the furnace building. He wrenched it open to find a couple of workers in reflective suits playing cards. They jumped up when they saw him, and Hiram's gun snapped up to level with the nearest man's head.

"No alarms, prick," Hiram wheezed. "Get the fuck out of here."

The men left him gasping in the antechamber. He couldn't get enough air. Why not? Breathe too shallow, and things start to darken; breathe too deeply, and the whole world pitches. He staggered to the stairs.

Hiram needed a buttonhook – a trick his uncle had taught him in Cambodia. He was too wounded to dare try it outside; The paths around individual buildings were too large, and he'd be visible all around. The furnace was claustrophobic, however, teeming with blind corners and poor vantage points.

His feet didn't want to listen. They drunkenly clopped around, scarcely cleaving to a straight line. "Just follow the blood, you dumb bastards."

Upon reaching the blast chamber, he was greeted with the sight he desired most – a jungle of pipes with a wide open catwalk to one side. His eyes sluggishly scanned the room. Goddamn, he was so tired. He hobbled as quickly as he could down the catwalk, and reaching the corner, bent over to take off his shoe. He neither screamed, nor did he faint, but his guts felt all twisted and shredded as he reached down. *You're not going to die here.*

Once removed, he propped the shoe toe-up, so its sole was just barely visible around the corner. Blood had pooled at his feet, slurping toward the open grating of the catwalk. He felt morbidly pleased with the addition of his blood. The puddle gave his distraction all the authenticity it needed. The first part of the buttonhook in place, he slunk down the hallway looking for another path back to the pipe jungle.

He wound through the machinery until he could see the catwalk ahead of him and stopped. His right hand didn't want to rise, as though the weight of his gun had grown twentyfold. Was this what it would be like to die? Just take a few bullets and bleed out alone? He sunk down and rested his gun on his knee. He had a good vantage point, and the catwalk was less than ten feet away. He wouldn't miss from this distance. He checked his clip. Five bullets left.

The black man entered his sights, and Hiram shook the bleariness out of his eyes. The man looked to be alone, and Hiram raised the tip of his barrel ever so slightly. If he didn't shoot now, he didn't think he'd get another chance before he passed out.

One. Two. Three. Four. Five. Click.

His target, flopped back against the railing, shaking and covered in blood. *There you go, Duke. I killed anybody helping her. Now do your own job, you fat fuck.*

The mousy little bitch poked her head around the corner. Hiram didn't bother to pull the trigger again. He knew how many bullets he had left. It was over.

"Oh, fuck," he chuckled. "I didn't think you'd come with –"

She charged. The blade sunk into his palm, into his arm, into his chest. He went to scream, but nothing would come out of his throat. It sliced into his neck. It cut into his eye, pressing down through his head.

Colors. A bitter smell. Jolts.

*　　*　　*

Resolve

LOXLEY AWOKE TO rough, gloved hands grabbing her bruised arms and hoisting her to her feet. Hiram's last moments still ricocheted inside her head. All of her muscles felt strained, and she groaned as the hands moved her. Men's voices jabbered, and still she heard the roar of the furnace from the chambers behind. Somebody was repeating something, and he had to say it a few times before the syllables aligned in her brain.

"You're okay, honey. You're going to be all right."

She struggled free, staggering a few steps, her legs refusing to work together. "Get away from me!"

Three men in reflective suits gathered around her. Millions of details pushed forward, jockeying to be noticed – rows of bolts along iron girders, valves and switches, lights, warnings, sprinklers, the way the exposed pipes ran parallel along the walls, the forests in Tailypo's office. The animals were probably still screaming there. The eagle would be eating the mice. She shook her head. Focus on the men.

One of them had stepped toward her, his palms open. "We're not here to hurt you. Are you all right? What happened?"

She shifted on her legs. She couldn't run yet. Should she run? What if they wanted to help her? No, she didn't need help – didn't want it. No one else needed to die helping her. She didn't ask for it. She didn't have her knife. Must've left it in Hiram.

The men were talking, their suits rippling with

the lights of their surroundings – gray and black, yellow sodium lamps and green fluorescents, orange cautions and red... What was red? A little box on the wall with a lever. Too many voices; a disagreement arose between the men. What was the little red box? She stumbled for it and saw that it controlled the sprinklers. She closed her fingers around the lever and one of the workers shouted at her. She yanked the valve open.

Icy water showered upon her, drowning the sounds of the room with its hiss. All of the disparate sensations across her skin became the single, random pattern of rain. White noise across her hearing and body washed away her confusion, and she focused on the startled workers, shielding their eyes. The jittering reflections disappeared from their heat suits, dissolved by the mist.

She spun and ran. She saw no reason why they ought to follow.

Her thighs burned with the exertion, but with each passing step, the stiffness faded. She stumbled down a stairwell, caught the railing and whirled down another flight. By the time she burst loose into the wintery air, her body once again belonged to her. Her wet skin chilled instantly and, though she shivered, she continued her breakneck sprint for the far edge of the Foundry, where the cooling towers lay.

Alarm bells sounded from the buildings behind her and several lights went on in various structures, but no one seemed to be chasing her. Maybe they'd seen what she did to Hiram and no one wanted to risk confronting her. After all, they might toil the

day away in the steelworks, but they didn't own it –
so it wasn't up to them to police it.

Icy fingers of wind dug into her as she tore across
the open staging area before reaching the towers.
She tried the door, but it was locked. A quick scan
revealed a loose ventilation duct a little way up.
She scaled some pipes that ran up the sides of the
building, locking her fingers around the mounting
brackets with each push upward. Fifteen feet off the
ground, she drew level with the vent and kicked it
open. She scrambled inside, slicing the heel of her
palm on sharp metal. The heated ductwork was an
instant balm on her skin.

Climbing in a little way, she found another vent
and kicked it out, dropping into a hallway. She
recognized it from before, when she'd been here with
Floyd. There were clothes nearby. A quick search of
all the doors along the hall located a washroom and
a set of wooden lockers. The collection pool of the
cooling tower had to be somewhere near here. She
longed to feel its burbling depths and fizzing water
against her tortured skin, but there was no time. If
the workers decided to fan out into search parties,
they might find her.

She opened one of the lockers and found a
Consortium uniform, a musty towel, a can of
shaving cream and a straight razor. The towel stunk
of old sweat, but she dried off anyway. She slipped
on the warm jumpsuit, which smelled very similar
to the towel. A few months ago, Loxley wouldn't
have touched someone else's clothes, much less worn
them. Now, she grit her teeth and did what she could
to live. When this was all over, she would peel them

away and wash the scent from her skin, assuming she wasn't dead. She took the straight razor and pocketed it.

The shivering slowed, then stopped. She took a deep breath, closed the locker and set out, this time for Bellebrook.

CHAPTER SIXTEEN
GRAVEROBBER

BUSHES DAMPENED THE wind that rattled the tree limbs overhead. The air in Edgewood came blowing off the farmlands beyond, untainted by the acrid industrial smell of the Hole. Unfamiliar freshness set things askew in Loxley's mind, and unease gathered in the pit of her stomach. She wrapped her arms around her shoulders and rubbed for warmth. It didn't help much.

She parted the foliage and looked upon Hiram's stone cottage. Bellebrook lay warm and inviting behind it. Even though it had to be three o'clock in the morning, many lights were still on inside the house. She thought of its myriad opulent rooms, pictured through the eyes of Nora and Hiram. Would they really be the same as all the other things she'd seen in her visions? Would she be able to find Duke?

She spied men smoking on the back porch of the distant manor, but in their thick jackets there was no way to tell whether or not they were armed. Loxley needed to get across to Hiram's house, get inside and help herself to a loaded gun before anyone got wise to her plans. She took a cautious step from the bushes into the shadows of a sycamore tree.

Then she saw Marie in the window of Hiram's stone cottage, looking straight at her with inky eyes. Loxley blinked, and the spirit stood directly in front of her, arms outstretched. She did what she could not to shout, but a quiet hum escaped her mouth as she scrambled backward. The ghost took a reluctant step forward and glanced back to the cottage. It reached for Loxley, uselessly clutching the air.

Then, it covered its face as though weeping. Ghosts didn't cry; at least, Loxley had never seen that happen before.

She got her legs back under her and took a step closer. It didn't react. A glance to Bellebrook's back porch told Loxley to hurry. The men might come to the cottage, and she wasn't here to hurt anyone but Duke if she could help it. She hadn't intended to kill Pucker-Lips. Loxley held her breath and stole past the ghost, her heart thumping in her ears.

When she reached the rear door of the cottage, her eyes flicked back to the spirit, which remained in place. The familiar nausea roiled inside her, and the chill of the dead filled her bones. Was it letting her pass? She exhaled, and the ghost jerked its head like it had been yanked with a rope, but it didn't turn to face her.

Loxley ducked through the kitchen. Filthy dishes littered the sink, and trash lined countertops. She shook her head and tilted it, trying to keep her gaze on the open pathway through the clutter and lock out all other details. A glint of silver caught her eye – the blade of a butcher's knife as it dangled from a rack. She seized the handle and yanked it free. It looked nice, and she needed to replace Cap's blade. The straight razor wasn't good for stabbing.

Her foot grazed a beer bottle that had been left on the floor next to the table. It toppled with a clink and dumped its amber contents over the dirty tiles. Loxley jerked back and clenched her teeth, her limbs overcome with electricity. *Clumsy!* She could hear her mother's voice saying. *Why can't you pay attention?* Loxley pounded her forehead with the palm of her hand before shaking the crackles out.

The puddle spread, running up to the sole of her shoe and dampening her foot. This was Hiram's beer. She needed to get it off of her. She glanced around for a towel and saw Marie's ghost, just inside the door, its back turned to her. Its hands still covered its face, its arms taut with effort.

Then Loxley knew: the spirit couldn't help wanting to touch her. All ghosts wanted to touch her. But this one also knew why she was here. This one wanted her to succeed.

"Sorry," she whispered. "I'll be out of here, soon."

It jerked again, clearly fighting against itself; Loxley decided it was a bad idea to speak to it.

She rushed from the kitchen into the darkened living room. Hiram's memories bled through her mind, the setting instantly familiar. He hadn't eaten in his own kitchen during his last day of life, but he'd spent plenty of time amongst his books. A thousand vertical lines, cut through with horizontal bookshelves, greeted her eyes in the moonlight. Their ordered nature brought her peace, like the rows of cotton in her long-lost photograph.

She rushed to the shelf and pulled out Hiram's copy of *Dracula*. It was an old, leather-bound edition, cracked gold leaf where someone had dog-eared the pages. The book had been well loved. Leafing through it, she found dozens of notes scribbled in the margins. Names, dates, places, quantities of money, inventory. She found comments about people, written in Hiram's surprisingly-clean hand: 'Has two children.' 'Cheating on wife.' 'Junkie.'

She saw a fragile network of people, ready to collapse, given the right push.

She closed the book, tucked it under her arm and crossed the room to the polished walnut gun cabinet. She opened it to a host of glittering pistols and rifles, all shapes and sizes, neatly lined up along every surface. Hiram's memory of shooting Quentin with a loud, nine-millimeter handgun troubled her, and her fingers fell on a small, snub-nosed revolver instead: something smaller would do.

Quentin had been completely surprised, and so genuinely frightened. A teardrop spattered Loxley's hand, and she shook it off. No time for that, now.

Her breath fogged as she wiped her face. The ghost's presence could be felt along her spine like static electricity pulling at her hair. It couldn't have been more than inches away. Loxley froze, awaiting the agony of its touch. She held her breath, and its horrid aura shrank from her. When she turned to see where it had gone, she saw the open door to the cellar: a jet-black rectangle broken only by a sallow face lurking, almost frightened, within.

Best hurry on, Lox. Her mother would say it every day when Loxley tried to put on her socks, and her toes would splay so the socks didn't fit. *Come on now, Lox. You gonna tempt the Devil.*

"Sorry," Loxley said to the ghost.

She checked the load in the revolver – empty. She found six bullets in a box, snapped the weapon shut and crept back outside with her stolen copy of *Dracula*.

The Duchy

HER FLIGHT ACROSS the lawn felt infinite. The shadows of the night obscured all, save for the lights of Bellebrook, and she could still see the two guards smoking and laughing on the long veranda. That was where Duke had offered Nora her job. It was probably where he'd decided her fate, and without knowing it, his own. Loxley couldn't get in that way without killing the guards, and that would alert Duke to her presence.

The manor had many entrances, though, and she was easily able to sneak around to the servants' door. It was the way Hiram preferred to get in, because it was the closest entrance to his cottage. The house had been designed that way, by necessity, before it had a kitchen installed; the servants cooked in the cottage, and if they burned it down, at least the main house would be spared. Ornate flowers, carved into the cherry wood, blossomed across the servants' door surface. Loxley ran her fingers over the grain, reminded of the master craftsmanship of her violin. The poplar beauty waited for her back at the Hound's Tail, if she lived. That was unlikely, though. She'd need Hiram's help to kill Duke, and that would put her to sleep for a few hours.

She wrapped her fingers around the freezing brass knob and twisted: locked, of course. She wondered if Hiram could open the lock somehow, and she thought of calling him. If she did, and he couldn't get inside, she would pass out on the lawn.

A sudden burst of laughter from one of the guards sent shivers down her spine. She shook the crackles from her fingers and looked around for another way inside. There was a balcony with a low railing along the second story, facing the fields, and it would have a door. The problem was that she'd have to climb the side of the veranda, and she'd almost certainly be spotted.

Why hadn't she thought to take Hiram's key from his body? The memory of Quentin's feet sliding from the furnace catwalk resurfaced in response.

Annoyed, she stole down the stone path toward the front of the house. She glanced in windows as she passed, but saw no one. Large lights illuminated Bellebrook's front, and she found there were very few places to hide unless she wanted to duck into the bushes that ran its length. That might make too much noise.

She was wasting precious time; the front door would be locked, too. She found a secluded window, unobstructed by shrubbery and just out of the light. The panes were made from old wood: well-painted but clearly showing age. Hiram had to know a way to deal with this. Maybe it was time to call on him after all.

She closed her eyes and listened.

She heard nothing. Edgewood was the quietest place in the Hole, undisturbed by the throbbing humanity below. The wind gently nuzzled the empty tree branches with a sigh. The guards continued chattering. Why wouldn't they shut up? She clenched her teeth and hummed as quietly as she could. She pressed her fingers into her temples and tapped at them lightly, trying to shut out nearby sounds.

Everything in the Hole belonged to Duke. He was the city's overseer, and soon, its god. She had to kill him – for Nora and Quentin, as well as all the other forgotten dead he'd run over in his quest. She had to show him he was mortal. Maybe she should just break the window and shoot anyone she found. If she ran for Duke's bedroom at top speed, she might get a few shots at him before his guards gunned her down. Just imagining the muzzle flashes to come made her hands shake. Without Hiram, she was certainly dead.

She hadn't told Jayla goodbye. Gorgeous eyes and full lips warmed her thoughts, but Loxley centered up on one feeling: that of her partner holding her close, arms enfolding her naked body not in an expression of sex, but one of peace. The pressure of Jayla's embrace brought more comfort than any food or music; Jayla, who waited for her on the eighth ring.

Clang.

The bleak, high-pitched noise hung in the air for a moment. Loxley strained to hear the next strike. One of the men laughed again, and she curled her fingers in rage. *Calm down, pretty baby. It's okay.*

Clang.

This one was louder. She steadied her breathing and pictured Hiram.

Clang. That smile. *Clang.* That deadly, easy laugh. *Clang.* A rumpled suit jacket and a cheap cigarette. Bit by bit, Loxley disappeared into herself as her thoughts became an intoxicating mixture of malice and efficiency.

She pulled the straight razor from her pocket and flipped it open. "Time to die, you motherfucker."

She sliced away a thin strip of wood around the glass, then jammed the razor underneath to pry out the pane. Warm air rushed over her bare skin. She quickly reached inside, unlocked the window and let herself in. Stopping short, she ducked back outside and nestled the copy of *Dracula* behind a drainpipe. She'd have to fetch it before she left, but she didn't want to try to carry it around a gunfight.

There wasn't going to be a gunfight, though. She'd nip upstairs, jam a pillow over the old prick's face and *pop* – good night. Might have to do the missus, too, if she happened to be around. Only time would tell. She made for the stairs, the razor in one hand, revolver in the other.

She rounded the corner into the grand gallery to find one of the guards enjoying a glass of whiskey at a table before a roaring fire. He hadn't spotted her, transfixed as he was by the flickering light. Her grip tightened on her blade and she slid close behind him. Five paces... three paces... she could smell his drink. Everything in her body told her to slice his throat right then and there. He was part of this. He worked for Duke, and was just as culpable as everyone else.

But Nora had worked for Duke in the plastic

factory, too. Loxley rested the razor against the man's throat.

"I'll cut your vocal cords before you can scream."

He swallowed his last gulp of whiskey and froze. "Okay."

"Hello, James," she said, her cadence borrowed from Hiram. "I work for the Consortium. Do you understand why my friends and I might be here like this, given the things we know about his operations?"

"Yeah."

"We just want Duke. I want you to walk to the back, take your men, and leave. You won't see us. Don't try, just walk away. We'll contact you at a later date to purchase the names of Duke's co-conspirators. Do you like your friends?"

Sweat beaded on his brow. "Yeah."

"Good. I'm going to let you go. Don't look at me or I'll fucking murder you and everyone else in this house. Your boss is a dead man. Don't be stupid enough to join him."

She locked back the hammer on her pistol and took a long stride away. Hiram's instincts screamed for her to slice the man's throat – after all, he was a liability – but she stifled them. She'd lied with Hiram's easy tongue, and it seemed to work well enough. The guard fled. Maybe he would bring the others back, or maybe he would lead them away. It was in someone else's hands now. The first hints of exhaustion trickled into Loxley's system like ice water. She needed to conclude her business soon, or she'd be overcome.

She swept up the stairs, her eyes darting to the landing, but she saw no threats. Fifteen seconds since she'd seen James pass through the far door of the gallery. He was at least ten seconds from his friends, so she slowed her pace. Let him have a moment to speak to the others and clear them out. Hiram only remembered three men guarding the house at night, so she hoped there weren't more. There was also the chance that James hadn't bought her story, and that he'd be back any moment.

She waited for a solid minute. Hiram was better with time than she was, but her adrenaline drained away with each tick of the clock. She felt him peeling away from her, and her legs grew heavy. She peeked around the corner and saw no one in the long corridor leading into the east wing. Pistol at the ready, she slunk down the hall to the next intersection. The labyrinth of shapes and colors in Bellebrook would have bothered Loxley, but the killer's eyes were efficient and quick, never lingering in one place for long.

Duke's bedroom was just around the corner. Was his wife sleeping there tonight? Loxley hoped not. Silently, she moved down the hall toward his enormous, gilded double doors. They were gold leaf and white, with an ostentatious pair of crosses on either side.

Not going to protect you from me.

She gripped the antique crystal doorknob and began to turn it as quietly as she could. She knew the distance from the door to Duke's bed. If he was awake, she'd put one in his brainpan. If he lay there asleep, she'd use the pillow to muffle the sound. It was a shame that he wouldn't see it coming, but this job was tricky enough already.

Her train of thought was interrupted by splintering wood and ripping pains across her shoulder. Her vision flashed as the back of her head thumped the marble floor. She screamed in agony, pressing her palm to her shoulder. It came back slick with her blood. As the door swung wide to reveal Duke in his pajamas with a smoking pistol, Loxley knew she'd been shot.

Her concentration imploded, and Hiram's essence left her like a hand leaving a puppet. Then she remembered all the times she'd let Nora in, and the dreams she'd had after. Would Hiram be there waiting? Primal dread piggybacked on her exhaustion as she spiraled into unconsciousness.

An Angel

THE ROOM THAT unfolded around her looked like her apartment in Magic City Heights, but it contained nothing of hers. Unfamiliar furniture filled her home, and bookshelves lined the walls. The place reeked of whiskey blended with stale tobacco smoke, and Loxley hummed, shaking the crackles out. This was not her home, and its uncanny resemblance only frightened her more.

Cool air slithered across her bare skin, and she gasped. She couldn't let this happen. She needed to wake up. Shadows drew long in the fading sunlight. Hiram was coming.

Hiram's grin formed in the darkened corner before the rest of it, then its two twinkling eyes, then its body emerged into the light, naked and muscular. She snatched a crystal ash tray from a nearby counter and flung it, aiming for the head. The dish struck it squarely in the cheek, but elicited no reaction save for an even wider smile.

Loxley dashed to the kitchenette and whipped open drawers, searching for any bladed objects she could find. She located a large chef's knife, but it turned to silver dust in her hand. The steak knives dissolved as she touched them, even the forks disintegrated during her frantic search. She cried out as a hand took hold of her hair and yanked her backward.

Hiram picked her up by her neck and slammed her onto the table, splintering it underneath her weight. Shards of wood dug into her back and each breath emerged as a scream. The ghost's fist crashed into her nose, blinding her with pain, and she clawed and kicked at its cold flesh as she tried to crawl away. Another blow to her head made the room dim for a moment.

She rolled onto her back, and it loomed over her, just as Duke had. It'd stopped hitting her, and its naked form swam in her vision. She closed her eyes and drew her limbs in close.

The next strike never came. The air flash froze, and her skin rippled with goosebumps. She opened her eyes to find Hiram stock still, incredulously staring at two short rows of fleshy bumps in its chest the size of thimbles. It ran a hand over them, and a vertical slit opened up where its heart should have been. Loxley could see what the bumps were then – another person had shoved their hands through its pale flesh and was pulling it apart from inside.

Gone was the snarky grin, replaced by the same panic it'd shown during its own death. Its inhuman skin parted under stress like fresh dough. No blood sprayed from its wounds, but it seemed to contain layers and layers of itself, like an onion. With a deafening scream, it was ripped in two. Then, Loxley saw her savior.

It looked like Nora, but all wrong. The legs and arms were too off-kilter, too sinewy. Stringy hair draped its face, only a single white eye visible through the strands. This was the ghost that haunted Nora's apartment, not the one who'd come to warm Loxley's dreams. Loxley scuttled back along the floor until her back hit the wall, gasping for air the whole way.

Hiram groaned. Even torn asunder, it could still make noises, and its expression was far from peaceful. Nora brought a massive foot down upon the ghost's neck and seized Hiram by the head with hands far too large to be human. The sound of tearing meat filled the air alongside a scream rising in pitch. With a snap, Hiram's head came away from its body, the dead, white skin shivering and convulsing.

Nora shoved fingers into Hiram's mouth and tore away its jaw before plunging fingers into its eye sockets. Another huge pull, and the head was shredded beyond all recognition, pieces flopping to the ground with sickening thuds.

Then Nora picked up the largest chunk and began to eat.

Loxley swallowed reflexively as the ghost turned to regard her with its cold, white eye. For a fleeting second, she understood exactly what it was thinking:

Do not call me. Do not think of me. Never come here again.

Loxley only nodded. Then a stinging slap turned her head.

* * *

I.O.U.

ANOTHER SLAP, AND Loxley blinked herself back into Bellebrook. Burning pain spread over her shoulder, and she felt dizzy and nauseous. Duke's second floor office surrounded her, its posh elegance the same as when Nora had made her phone call there. The man himself stood large over her, strands of white hair plastered to his forehead with sweat. He wore an untied housecoat over his flannel pajamas, and a tuft of white chest hair poked out from his unbuttoned collar. Her eyes traveled the length of his arm to where he clutched a brass gavel in his meaty fist.

"You know who gave me this?" he asked her, his voice flat, lacking the lilt he'd affected with her in every prior encounter. "The city. The mayor's office did."

Her arms felt stiff, and when she looked down, she discovered she'd been taped to a chair. She jolted at the sight, and the duct tape yanked her skin. The wound on her shoulder lit up, sucking her breath away. She tried to bring her arm across to tear the tape off – she wasn't supposed to have tape on her skin – but the other hand was firmly bound. She scratched on the wooden arms of the chair and hooted, trying to shake the crackles out, but they wouldn't go away. Ants marched over her calves and into the hollow of her knees, and when she went to stomp them off, she couldn't move her legs.

"Who do you work for?"

"Get... get..." She yanked her arms as hard as she

could – so hard it felt like her hands would come off – but the tape didn't budge. Her gunshot wound seared across her entire left side. She screamed as loud and long as she could.

Duke slapped her, a petty tap after Hiram's ghost, but it still shocked her. "Who do you work for?"

She heard the crackle of plastic under his feet and looked down. His carpet was covered with the same plastic sheeting that Nora used to make at the factory. "Don Fowler. He owns an apothecary on the third ring."

"That's a lie." He struck her again, and this one jangled her.

His face had turned red, his cheeks growing taut like the skin of a pepper. She used to grow peppers in another life. She remembered the way they made her mouth feel, like Duke slapping her tongue. She imagined thousands of little Dukes beating up her tongue as she chewed, and laughed aloud.

"You're not taking this seriously?" Duke stood up a little straighter and smoothed back his hair. "I heard you tell James you worked for the Consortium. I heard you call him by name. Where are they? Are they coming here now? How much time do I have?"

"I didn't say that."

"I have microphones in every room of this house."

She remembered him saying that to Nora. "I don't work for –" The prickle of tape on her arm interrupted her train of thought. She had tape instead of skin, and the chair did, too, so was she part of the chair? She wrenched her body back and forth, but he'd even bound her hips. Her mind grew fuzzy, and her mouth didn't want to make words anymore.

"When I used to work on the farm, we had cows, and sometimes, I'd have to slaughter one," he began, thumping the brass gavel against his palm. He said more, but between her gunshot wound and the tape he'd tied her down with, she couldn't care enough to pick out the order of his sentences. Nothing he said mattered all that much.

She relaxed her head and let the static inside her skull. Instead of being afraid of it, the sensation felt like a blanket covering her on a frigid night. It would help her to accept what was about to happen. In spite of everything she'd done, everything she'd sacrificed, Duke was still going to take that hammer and brain her.

Her heartbeat became a counterpoint to the rhythm of his speech. His words were a bass drum, barking pronouncements in another language. Was he mad? It didn't matter how he felt, not one bit. There was nothing left for him to do to her. She wondered if anyone would ever find the dog-eared copy of *Dracula* she'd hidden in the bushes.

He shook her, filling her with agony to displace the static. "This is important."

She hummed.

"Do you want to pray with me? This is your last chance to ask forgiveness."

Her mouth felt awkward, so she shook her head no.

"All right. The Lord can't save you from yourself."

He raised the hammer, and the lights flickered inside the office. He stopped and looked around. They flashed again, going brown for a moment before guttering out entirely. Blue moonlight suffused the office in the absence of electric lights.

You took something from me, came a low growl.

Loxley wasn't sure if she'd heard the voice or only thought it, but Duke spun around, startled. She swung her head from side to side, trying to gather her wits about her and pay attention. The big man smiled at her and licked his lips.

"Cute trick. Are those your Consortium friends?"

Scrabbling scratches like tree branches sounded on the window. Duke rushed to his desk and seized his pistol. He leveled it on Loxley's face and threw back the hammer.

"Don't be stupid or I'm going to shoot her," he called out.

You took something from me. The air wavered with the thunderous power of the voice, and Loxley swore she could hear the scream of a dying animal in its wake. She knew the one who spoke – Tailypo. Somehow, she'd stolen from him, and he'd come to collect, just as he had all those centuries ago with the farmer. He'd come to kill her for it, to eat her and make her into one of his cautionary tales. At least Duke wouldn't have the pleasure.

"What did I steal?" she said.

Duke smacked her with the butt of his gun, not hard enough to injure her, but enough to startle. "Shut up. What are you talking about?"

Quentin Mabry. You took him from me. Duke held his ears against the thunderclap speaking to them, and Loxley spied a wispy green vine growing out of the side of the oak desk. It popped out a few leaves, and was soon joined by shoots.

But she hadn't stolen Quentin. He'd come of his own accord, and the man who shot him was dead as well. But now Hiram's bits were inside her, so maybe Tailypo wanted them. Would the beast rip Hiram from her, or just eat her whole? She imagined Tailypo pulling off her head like Nora had with Hiram's spirit, and she swallowed. The beast was going to destroy every part of her.

You took a life from me, and I always get back what's mine, Duke Ashley Wallace.

"If you want to dance, come on out!" Duke shouted in his booming voice, but it paled in comparison to Tailypo's. A tree root snaked across the floor, barely missing Duke's foot as he jumped backward. Pale as a sheet, the big man whipped his weapon back and forth, searching for any target he could find. "Come on! I fear no evil, for the Lord is with me!"

He ain't going to save you from a deal you made for yourself.

"The Devil's lies!" Duke's voice creaked. Loxley flinched as he fired a shot into the darkness. In the muzzle flash, she saw a forest sprouting in his office. "I didn't hurt any Quentin!"

Then she remembered. "But you did. You brought this on yourself."

"Shut up!"

She looked Duke dead in his terrified eyes. "You told Hiram, 'If she has anyone with her, that person has to die, too. I don't care who it is, just take care of them.'" She remembered his words to the killer because she'd lived them.

His eyes widened. The gun shook in his hand. "How did you hear that?"

"Hiram did exactly what you asked him to. You took Quentin away. It's your fault."

He stumbled backward over a root and caught himself next to the tree that had once been his desk. "Shut up!"

"But it's your fault," she said, leaning forward, able to forget the tape for a blissful moment. "This is all your doing!"

A rippling, hairy shape formed on the vine-encrusted ceiling, drooping down like a big drop of oil over Duke. In a single graceful motion, it landed on him and removed his pistol hand with a sickening crack of bone. In the terrified screams that followed, it ravaged Duke with teeth and claws, muscle and sinew, pausing to taste his steaming entrails while he still lived.

Loxley shut her eyes until it was over.

Warm light scattered against her eyelids, and she opened them to find the office pristine as it had once been, and no sign of Duke: no blood, no meat, nothing. She looked down at her bindings; they'd been slashed open with no harm to her flesh. Her shoulder had been bound in bright white gauze, and she felt no pain. She pulled free of the chair and rubbed her bare wrists in astonishment. Listening carefully, she didn't hear a soul.

She fled Bellebrook with all speed, only stopping to collect her precious copy of *Dracula* from the bushes. She knew the agriculture manual was there, too, but it was time to let it go. It was the last piece of the life she'd once had.

Never come here again.

CHAPTER SEVENTEEN
NO HOME

THE SUN HAD already begun to illuminate the western side of Edgewood. Loxley trudged across the eighth ring, far too cold to care anymore. When she finally came upon the Hound's Tail a sign on the front doors said, 'Closed tonight.' Finding them unlocked, she pushed them open, anyway. She passed the coat check and found the entire staff seated around the stage, the smell of coffee and cigarettes thick in the air.

"You bitch. You fucking bitch," shouted Jayla. Tears streamed down her face as she rushed to Loxley and squeezed her as tightly as she could.

The bullet wound in Loxley's shoulder snarled in protest, and she squeaked, "Why are you cussing me?"

Jayla interrupted her with a hard kiss, and the fight drained from Loxley's muscles. She fell limp, suspended in her lover's arms, leaning on her strength. Jayla eased her into a chair, and Loxley felt as though she might pass out right then and there.

Her limbs came to rest, heavy under the weight of the things she'd done.

Her breathing slowed, and she heard someone tell the others to give her some room. She turned her head to look at Cap, who was the saddest she'd ever seen him. He slouched in a chair like a sack of flour, his face drawn and beaded with sweat. His kitchen uniform looked even worse than before.

"I'm sorry about your knife, Cap. I tried to steal you another," she said. "I lost yours in the guy who killed Quentin."

"It's okay," he mumbled in reply. "It's a good place to lose it."

Jayla waved the rest of the group away. "Okay, folks. She's home. Ya'all just go to bed and we'll figure out what to do later."

Wearily, everyone stood to go, except Jayla, who inspected Loxley's bandaged shoulder. It still hurt, but the passing hours had turned it from a single point of pain into a low ache that covered her entire left side.

"Your vendetta cost us a lot tonight," called Tailypo, emerging from the shadows of the stage. "I think you owe all of us for bringing this on our house."

"No," replied Loxley, prompting murmurs from the crowd.

"If it wasn't for your damn fool errand, Quentin would still be here."

"Tee," Jayla began, but Loxley silenced her.

Loxley considered channeling Nora, but then she remembered the dead, white eye and the gnashing teeth. Better to negotiate this on her own. "That isn't what you told Duke when you ate him."

"You had a part in it, too," Tailypo growled, not even bothering to deny it.

"Doesn't matter. Can't collect on the same debt twice." She smiled, surveying the wide-eyed crowd. Plenty of them didn't believe in ghosts, much less whatever Tailypo was. Jayla's gaze darted between Loxley and her boss, and she stepped between them. Perhaps she was beginning to understand a little of the world Loxley had been living in the whole time.

Quentin believed, too – believed in all the strange things she said, believed in her as a person. She was going to miss him. Maybe he'd gone up in the steam with all of the others from the Hole, or maybe he'd became snow last night, a vigil over her trek to Bellebrook.

Tailypo stared at her with his hard eyes, no trace of his desires evident in his long gaze. She'd grown used to him watching her like a meal, but this was a man considering revenge. She felt proud of herself for seeing so much in his expression. Perhaps she was simply too tired to be distracted by other things.

"Jayla, take her back to your room," he spat. "I'll call a goddamned doctor."

The doctor was pushy, and wanted to see all kinds of things that Loxley didn't want to show him. He kept asking if she'd had relations with strange men, and was unwilling to believe that a ghost had put those marks on her. Jayla stayed in the room with both of them, answering harshly whenever the doctor asked something too personal. After the inspection concluded, Tailypo arrived and paid the doctor "handsomely for both the checkup and silence." Loxley doubted the doctor ever would have connected her with the mayhem at both the steelworks and Bellebrook. The fellow seemed to think her incapable of the most basic self-care. Perhaps his prejudice served her purposes, but either way, she was glad to see the back of him. Tailypo then told them he was "sure they had some catching up to do" with a laugh and a smile that made Loxley uneasy.

After the doctor left, Jayla gingerly undressed her and brought her to bed. They didn't make love, but they lay entangled for hours, Jayla stroking Loxley's hair without a single question. Loxley wanted to tell her partner what had happened that night, but the words were slippery, and didn't want to come when she needed them. At long last, she found something she could say.

"I don't want to live here, anymore," she said, tucking her head under Jayla's arm.

"Okay. Where do you want to go, darling?"

"Somewhere good. You can cook."

Jayla laughed, her voice gentle. "Is that a fact? What a gracious invitation. And what are you going to do?"

She nuzzled into Jayla's armpit, her voice muffled. "Whatever I want to."

"I see. Maybe you could help."

"Yeah. And I can grow food and play music for you. But I want to leave the Hole."

"Where would we go?"

"Atlanta," said Loxley. She felt a prickle of nerves in her belly. She'd always wanted to leave, but she'd never thought she could. If Jayla wouldn't follow, she couldn't make it alone. She didn't want to be without the cook ever again.

"I don't know anyone in Atlanta."

"I know. I don't want to know anyone." She listened to her lover's steady breath.

"You're serious, aren't you?" Jayla's voice creaked. Her voice still hadn't recovered from screaming at her. "You really want me to come with you? We ain't been together very long, baby."

"We're together? I'm your girlfriend?"

"Why wouldn't you be?"

"Nora had a couple of boys, but I don't know how many were her boyfriend."

Her fingers caressed Loxley's shoulder. "Nah. You're my girlfriend."

Loxley's chest hurt, but wrapped up in her partner as she was, she didn't feel any crackles. What if Jayla was kidding about coming with her? "Your girlfriend has to leave the Hole. I want you... You need to come with me. If you don't –"

Jayla squeezed her hard. "Okay."

The Accounting

LOXLEY STOOD OUTSIDE a nondescript building on the fifth ring. Faded letters on its brick front read 'Robert Calhoun, Accountant.' Hiram had ruminated on this place, and with very little effort, Loxley had found it. She clutched ten torn pages in her hand, and the wind seemed to want them just as much as she did – they were the first ten entries in Hiram's copy of *Dracula*.

She pushed open the glass door to find a dour man sitting behind an extremely plain desk, its only adornment a brass lamp with green glass. The walls were a cream color with water stains in many places. The carpet was a dull brown. Some would have said it was a terrible place to work, but Loxley would have liked it even better if it had no windows.

The man looked up and smiled, a thin snaggletoothed grin.

"I like your office," said Loxley.

"Thank you," he replied with a polished, easy voice. "May I help you somehow?"

"My name is Loxley Fiddleback," she said, starting the conversation in as sensible a place as any.

"I'm glad to hear it."

She shuffled her feet nervously. "You work for the Consortium."

He shook his head slowly and folded his hands on the desk. "I'm afraid not, dear. This is a privately-held office. Now is there something you need?"

"You're lying."

"That's a very rude thing to say, madam."

"It's okay. I would lie, too," she said, handing him the pages.

She felt an immediate pang of guilt as she did so. Duke might have been a killer, but if he'd been telling the truth, he was only trying to feed everyone. The Consortium did little to take care of people and even less to save them, yet folks toiled away in its name. What if Duke had succeeded? Would the Hole have been better, even for a time? She thought of Nora and Quentin, steeling herself as she let go of the papers; no part of Duke's conspiracy deserved to survive.

He slipped a pair of glasses over his eyes and stared down his nose at the pages. "And what's this?"

"Duke Wallace was going around behind your back, planning to throw out the Con. There's the proof."

He tapped the stack with an ornate fountain pen. "Really? You should give this to the authorities. That sounds very important."

"I know you work for them. You were going to make a deal with Hiram McClintock."

His smile disappeared. He removed his hands from his desk, where she could no longer see them, and sat up straighter. He probably had a gun under there. She pointed to the pages, stopping on the first margin.

"It ought to be easy to find out if Duke has been hiding stuff from you with these," she said. "I know he has."

"Maybe I should call him and ask."

"You're never going to find him. He's dead."

He cocked his head. "Did you kill him?"

"No. Well, sort of I did."

"Why shouldn't I call for help? Have you arrested?"

Loxley nodded. "I can see why you would, but I have the names of the other conspirators in Nashville and Atlanta. I don't have a lot of demands."

"You think we're going to pay you?"

"You were going to pay Hiram nearly two million dollars. It was all he could think about until the night I killed him. Did your friends tell you he was dead?"

He reached up with one hand and straightened some papers on his desk. "That was mentioned to me, yes. They have the body."

"Can I have the knife?" she asked, her voice a little louder than she wanted.

He grimaced. "Is it yours?"

"I used it, but I was borrowing it."

"From whom?"

It would've been a great parting gift for Cap, but she could see it might be difficult to get. "Never mind."

His polite smile reappeared, though his mouth quivered at the corners. He flipped to a blank page in his ledger and picked up his pen. "How much do you want, and how do we contact you?"

She motioned to the desk. "Do you want me to write for you so you can keep your hand on your gun? I think that would be smarter of you, even though I don't want to hurt you. You saw what I did to Hiram."

"Little girl, there are three very large men in the back. Maybe I should call them and we can torture the information out of you."

His curt manner actually put her at ease. She was so used to people saying one thing and meaning another, but this man spoke as plainly as possible. His office helped shield her from distractions, and together, they made her words clean and easy.

"That would be stupid because I don't want much. Also, I don't know most of it because it's in a book."

"Two million dollars is a lot for un-validated information."

"I just want a hundred thousand, and I'm going to leave town forever. You're never going to see me again. I hate the Consortium. I hate Duke Wallace. I don't want anything to do with you anymore. I just want to get my money and leave."

"And where will you go? We're everywhere."

"I just want out of the Hole."

"I think you'll find every other city to be much the same as this one."

"No. Tailypo won't be anywhere else. Neither will Duke's men."

He adjusted his glasses. "A hundred thousand seems like a fair estimate, if Hiram's intelligence is any good."

"It's very good. Duke killed several of my friends because of it."

"Do these friends of yours have names?"

She started to answer, but thought better of it. She rubbed her palm on her shirt so she wouldn't flap it. "No."

"What about their families? Don't they deserve some compensation?"

"Duke's driver, a woman named Marie, was shot and is dead in the basement of his cottage. She has a son staying at Gardendale. He's not crazy." It was strange to say that about someone else. "Duke had his mom killed, but didn't want to hurt him."

"Okay."

"You have to get him out of there... and send him to a good school. Maybe give him a good job."

"That might be arranged. We can check him out at the very least. And how am I going to contact you?"

Loxley swallowed, searching for her center. Talking about Marie's son had made her uneasy. "In a day, you're going to come to the Hound's Tail in the eighth ring with my money. You need to bring an extra ten thousand for the owner, Tailypo. Duke gave him some trouble, too."

"And we'll do the trade then?"

"Yeah. If you're not there by midnight two days from now, I'm going to burn the pages without ever leaving the building, and we'll see if you can unravel the rest of the conspiracy by yourself. Don't think about doing something to me after you've paid, either." She paused, meeting his gaze. "You couldn't protect Duke from me, and you don't look nearly as important as him."

Then, she left as quickly as she'd come. No one bothered her all the way home, though they almost certainly followed her. As she walked into the relative safety of the Hound's Tail, she hoped they had. She pitied anyone who tried to enter Tailypo's domain without his say-so.

At Auction

LOXLEY WATCHED THE dancing dust all along Tailypo's hallway and swallowed. Jayla didn't know she was here; no one did. She never thought she'd come up to the third floor of her own free will.

It felt older somehow in the cold corridor, as though many years had passed in only a few days. The lamps with a cold starlight glow, as opposed to the warm flames that had been there before. In their brighter illumination, she saw the half-stripped and rotted boards peeking around the runner rug. Little lines of white followed the wallpaper seams where it had begun to peel, and the high ceilings bore dark stains along the crown molding.

Nausea poisoned her guts. The illusion of life had

passed from this place, leaving only a spirit. She glanced back at the stairs. There was life that way. Jayla was that way. Loxley could just go back and get her to help.

She shook her head. This wasn't Jayla's world, and Loxley never wanted it to be. She'd have to deal with this on her own. Ants crawled up her shins, and she stomped a foot.

The lamps snapped back to their dim orange, shadows surging forward to smear away the nasty details. The paisleys crawled once more, and she couldn't see the motes of dust through the gloom. He'd heard her.

She stopped at his door, raising her hand to knock, but hesitated. This was the part where he called out to her, but she only heard the flutter of gas lamps. She tapped his door with a single knuckle, and it opened.

No fire crackled inside Tailypo's office, and his forested walls had grown blue without its warmth. Loxley shivered as she entered, the dense, humid air fogging her breath.

Tailypo sat at his desk, an all-black suit cutting his form into his enormous leather chair. He scribbled a few notes into a ledger before closing it. When he met her gaze, she found his eyes hollow and red.

"I miss Quentin, too," she said.

A polite nod preceded, "Say his name again, and I'll take your fucking tongue."

She shifted from foot to foot. He was already mad. "I came to make a deal."

He stood up, resting one lanky arm against his desk and the other on his hip. "Did you now? Why would I want the likes of you?"

"It's not for me. It's for money."

"What makes you think I need that human trash?"

She pointed to his book. "I saw you writing in your ledger."

"The Devil's business isn't a cash affair."

"You're still open, even though Quentin is dead."

He bolted over the desk and bounded forward to the screams of animals before wrapping long fingers around her neck. He squeezed tightly, but not so much that she couldn't breathe. "You got a short memory, bitch. I told you not to say his name."

His breath stunk of old meat and rotted teeth, and he pulled her face close to his. She flapped her fingers and looked away, eyes watering. Electricity shot through her neck where he touched her. He was changing, becoming the dead.

"C... Come on," she croaked. "Come into my head and see what's there for you."

He snarled, his frigid drool dripping onto her exposed collarbone. "Maybe I *should* see what's inside."

"There's a –" Loxley flapped her hands harder, trying to get them back. The animals' incessant screeching threatened to overwhelm her and cut a rift between her mind and her mouth. Her tongue stuck to the back of her front teeth and she squeezed out the next words. "Za-Za-szaa... Th-There's a pretty girl that lives there. B-Bet she'd like to meet you."

"Look me in the eye, bitch."

He turned her head this way and that, but she wouldn't look into him. *It's okay to be afraid, pretty baby. Sometimes that's a good thing.* "I can hear you just fine."

"What's this fucking deal you came for?"

"Ten thousand dollars. You help me walk out of here."

He shoved her into the wall, and stars flashed in her vision. She'd told Jayla right – they had to leave the Hole. Loxley wouldn't be happy without miles and miles between her and this man.

He crouched in front of her, withdrawing a cigarette case from his suit jacket pocket. "How've you got ten grand?"

"Don't light that. I'm going to hit you if you light that."

Tailypo chuckled and licked his lips, before returning the smokes where they came from. Once he'd secured the case, she told him everything: about *Dracula*, the Consortium, her deal. She'd wanted to withhold something, but she couldn't figure an angle. The Hound's Tail was the only place she could stay, and if he sensed she was lying, he might throw her out.

"Not bad," he grunted, standing. "Not fucking bad at all." He strode to his desk and leaned against it, folding his arms and laughing. "You just walked in there and told the guy to pay up? Unbelievable."

With him further away, her heartbeat settled. "You think I'm stupid, but I'm not."

"I don't think you're stupid. I think you're chickenshit."

She cocked her head. "I did it. Do you want the money?"

"I think you could've gotten more... But yeah, I do." He walked behind his desk and hefted a case – Loxley's poplar beauty, its faux leather dinged across the front where she'd slammed the lid times beyond counting. "So then we come to your fiddle. You want your fiddle? It's not free, you know."

A jolt ran across her skin, and she stomped her feet. "You..." She smoothed out her next few words with a toneless note.

Tailypo sniffed. "Quit your humming and name a price."

"That's mine."

"I bought it – with *my* money. Let's try again."

"Quentin gave it to me."

He sat down, leaning back in his chair. "Wasn't his to give... And don't bother thinking up ways to steal it off me. Never forget that I always get back what's mine."

There was no way around it: if she wanted her treasure, she was going to have to pay. Her eyes flicked around the office, as though she'd see something that would clue her into what she should offer him. What was a voice worth?

"I'll give you a thousand dollars... plus the ten thousand," she said, and he began to laugh. She guessed again: "Two thousand?" He laughed harder until his face turned red.

"Yeah, hey listen. That's great, sweetness, but we're not doing that. Let me lay this all out for you: you got nowhere to go, no one who will broker this deal for you, and because of you, my..." He stopped and sucked his teeth, "my friend is dead."

"Hiram shot him. Duke ordered it."

He swept the taxidermied mice from his desk. "And *you* brought it into my house!"

She had to stand her ground. She couldn't back

down. She'd slapped him once, and she might have to do it again. "What do you want from me?"

"I want you gone," he growled. "Along with ninety percent of the deal. It's being brokered with my club, my men and my guns, so you ain't worth shit. I don't even want you here when the deal goes down, in case you make someone trigger-happy."

"How would that work?"

"You sell me the book right now for ten-thousand, and I put you on the midnight train out of here, anywhere you want to go."

"And my violin?"

"All yours, honey," he cooed, pushing the case forward.

"Ten won't buy me a farm." Even as she said it, she knew the dream of her own farm was dead.

He gestured to her. "Loxley, I want you to know that I care about that. I genuinely give a shit. I care because I know you can't be set with this. It won't even get you through one year. I care because this was the one chance in your miserable fucking life to see some real success, and this is *my* one chance to ruin it. When I met you, I think it's safe to say I was in love."

He rifled through his desk drawer and pulled out a stack of bills. It was thinner than she thought it'd be, but she could see the markings: one-hundred dollar notes. He then picked up the instrument case and brought them to her. "But now, I see that you ain't nothing but trouble. You hurt me, baby: when you rejected me, when you distrusted me, when you got Quentin... when he followed you. Just like them farmers from forever ago, you got to come in here and change everything so it suits you." He held up her prizes, the money and the fiddle, and smiled. "So why don't you take your shit and get the fuck out of here before I decide you're better off dead?"

It wasn't what she wanted, but it was a way forward, and she'd made do with worse. Maybe the column of steam wasn't the only way out of the Hole.

Caller

"Hello, Mister Calhoun."

"Hello, Miss Fiddleback. Is everything all right?"

"Yes. I gave your book to Tailypo. He's going to sell it to you. Same time and place."

"That wasn't the plan. Are you in distress? Say, 'I'm fine,' if you're in distress."

"No, sir. I'm leaving town."

"Where are you going?"

"Goodbye, Mister Calhoun."

"Safe travels, Miss Fiddleback. We'll find you if we need you."

The Midnight Train

CLOUDS MISTED OVERHEAD, impregnated with dust from the rising plume of ash. Drops of water clung to Loxley's cheeks like cold freckles, almost undetectable under her thick layer of makeup. Eyes, cheeks and (most specially) lips had been expertly coated in preparation for this journey. It was almost too much – almost – but she could bear it for a little while. Jayla squeezed her hand as they ascended the steps into Edgewood Station and opened the doors.

The sprawling platform before them took Loxley's breath away. Fancy restaurants, all closed up for the night, clustered near each entrance, and newsstands hawked magazines she'd never seen before. A lone liquor store buzzed with a small neon sign, and very few people occupied the rows of polished, wooden benches laid out before her. A single, bored rail agent stood watch behind a row of brass cages under the ticketing sign. Iron girders crisscrossed the ceiling in the most delightful pattern, vibrating subtly as Loxley regarded them sidelong. She comfortably slid her eyes along them, forward and back, up and down.

"Not now, baby," said Jayla, gently touching the back of Loxley's hair.

She hadn't realized she'd been shaking her head to push the lines around, but as soon as she stopped, her heart jumped. Loxley nodded, biting her lip as her eyes dropped to the ground. Jayla's fingers slid down her neck to her shoulder, and pulled her close, the deep pressure and warmth calming her aching chest.

"It's okay. I'm here, and you know that."

Hours before, though, Loxley had stood outside her bedroom door at the Hound's Tail, wondering what her lover would say. Jayla had said she'd come, but what if she'd been lying? Loxley pressed her hand to the wood, sensing its weight. She'd opened it many times before, but she almost couldn't push it then. It wasn't her room anymore, because she was leaving. She trudged through the dozen scenarios once again, searching for what she might say.

She ran her thumb over the stack of bills in her left hand, taking comfort in the toothy texture of the paper. She opened the door.

Jayla sat on the bed with two enormous suitcases and a smile. "Are we leaving yet? I saw you going up to talk to Tee and I thought –"

All of her words fled, replaced by sobs. She only shook her head and held up the money. Her lover rushed to her, enveloping her, showering her with kisses. Their embrace lasted forever, and when Jayla let go, it was as though warm blankets had been pulled away on a frigid morning.

Loxley easily hefted their luggage downstairs, and they retreated into the green room, where Jayla convinced her they should both be made up before venturing outside. She said they might fool even the Con men looking like that – didn't want to be followed. Loxley had let her, thinking of the fiddler in the mask the whole time, wild and confident.

Hours passed and night fell, but the club wouldn't open today – not with Quentin's death so close. When the time came to leave for the train, Cap appeared in the doorway. He led them down through a tunnel that lead to his woodworking shed in the back. Loxley emerged through a trapdoor, surrounded by his many wonders – beautiful, half-completed toys of every shape and size – and said nothing. Tools lined the walls, and a bright stockpile of oak wood stood vigil in the corner, awaiting a master's hand. This was Cap's garden. He was safe here.

She hadn't been jealous, but glad of a chance to

visit it. Her world had gone all into ashes, but he still had his. Somehow, it was a comfort to see a reflection of what she'd lost, even briefly, like a passing dream.

Together, they made their way into an alley, where a vehicle waited for them – a shiny, black car, almost indistinguishable from a Consortium car at a distance. Cap opened the door to let Loxley and Jayla into the back, then climbed into the driver's seat. Their vehicle quietly rolled around the corner, and the buzzing sign of the Hound's Tail came into view.

"Slowly," Jayla had told Cap, watching it pass them, its pink neon dancing over her lips and dark eyes. "See you later, Quentin," she whispered.

It slipped out of sight, becoming a coruscating haze in the darkened Hole streets, then nothing at all. Loxley wiped a tear from her partner's face and pulled her close. Jayla kept looking in the direction of her old home until it was far out of sight.

The rest of the journey was measured in breaths and heartbeats. Loxley didn't look out the window, except to occasionally check behind them to see if they were followed – no one there, except folks headed into the night shift.

She imagined the car as a carriage in a shadowy wood. She knew wolves padded about outside, but as long as the car didn't stop, it wouldn't matter. Let them keep their knives and claws. Forget about their guns and teeth. On the other side of this forest lay a warm bed, a loving hug and a home. They could track her through the trees, but only watch as she crossed from their world into hers. *Her world* – a place that, for better or worse, she would create for herself. A few days ago, she'd lain on the border between the living and the dead. Now, she would cross between the living and the truly alive.

And what was this new world going to be? As Loxley stood on the platform awaiting the midnight express, she considered the possibilities. The fact that she even had possibilities at all amazed her. The train was bound for Atlanta, but only because it was the most attractive of her three choices. The other two destinations were Jackson and Nashville. If she had to pass through one of them, it stood to reason that Atlanta was the safest. After all, Duke had wanted to send Nora there because he couldn't control it. From Atlanta, she could head up the eastern seaboard or down into Florida.

Jayla interrupted her thoughts. "Going to get our tickets, okay, baby?"

The ticket counter lay several hundred feet away. "I'll go with you."

"Don't be silly. No need to haul those suitcases all the way over and back." Jayla leaned in close and whispered. "We don't want to look scared. Let's just do this how other folks do."

Loxley nodded, and the woman strode toward the counter. Jayla's hips swayed pleasantly under her dress, reigniting a warm memory in Loxley's breast. For a time, at least, the two of them might belong to one another.

The time is now eleven forty-five. The Midnight Express to Atlanta, Georgia will be arriving in two minutes on platform three, came a voice over the loudspeaker.

"Miss Fiddleback?" Robert Calhoun stood about ten feet away from her, looking just as clean as he had in his office.

Perhaps her carriage had stopped in the woods a little too long. Maybe she'd traded Tailypo for a different wolf. "Yes?"

"I have something for you." He reached into his jacket.

She didn't bother trying to move. If he gunned her down right here, there was nothing anyone could do to stop him. The Consortium did whatever it wanted, whenever it wanted.

It was a business card.

He held it out for her. A phone number glistened in the middle in raised gloss ink. Flat, orange and black lines ran across the top and bottom; No other name or label of any kind.

"We sent some men to Bellebrook," he began, "and do you know what we found?"

"Everything I said you would."

"After a thorough questioning, Missus Wallace gave indicators of Duke's activities. His bank transactions corroborate some of your claims."

"Okay." *Don't stamp your feet.*

"We also spoke with one of his bodyguards. He told us how you frightened him off."

"I said I worked for you, and he knew to run."

Robert's smile bore more than kindness, of that much she felt certain. She wasn't sure what his face meant, but she could imagine how the Consortium might feel about a man who fled at their mention. "I know. I assure you that none of Duke's staff will trouble you anymore."

"Killed the only ones that did." *Look him in the eyes*.

He nodded.

She turned the card over in her hands. "What am I supposed to do with this?"

"I'm on my way to negotiate a deal with your employer for the book. I'd appreciate a call if you think of anything else... or if you have any services to offer."

She wrung her hands to still her fingers. "I don't fuck for money."

Robert chuckled.

"Is something funny?"

"I didn't think you did, Miss Fiddleback. You're a talented and unique individual. Maybe there are other problems you could help us with." He tipped his hat and turned to leave. "Stay in touch."

At once, the train came pouring into the station, hisses and chugs, a million screeches and clangs like the devil's own drum corps. She'd forgotten to play her poplar beauty to kill the sound. Loxley wanted to scream or flee, but resolved to keep fixed on Robert Calhoun. He kept moving away, and she jammed her hands into her pockets to stop them flapping. Her feet rose and fell, stomping wildly, and she felt her voice rush from her throat. He spun to look at her, and she forced her gaze to lock with his. Brakes squealed, reverberating throughout the station like its iron girders were twisting apart, and Loxley kept her watering eyes locked upon his. She wouldn't look away, not for anything.

Only when the train came sighing to rest did the Consortium agent nod and turn once more to leave.

Her knees shook, but she held fast, watching him disappear into the crowd.

She surveyed the great metal beast that had come to take her away. The train looked like the ones that traversed the Hoop, but bigger, perhaps its parent. Fluted steel panels covered its exterior, reminding her of the aluminum-covered walkways of Vulcan's Bazaar. Perhaps that was the skin this serpent had sloughed off in years past. Maybe that molting had caused it to outgrow the Hole, and that's why this train could leave town.

She wiped a tear from her cheek, and her hand came back with the dark streak of her eyeliner. Without thinking, she scrubbed at her face.

Her right hand caught on something, and she yanked it free. Had to get the makeup off; her skin was suffocating. Then something seized her left hand. She stumbled forward, moaning as she fell to her knees to scratch away the coating on her face.

"Loxley!" Jayla stood before her, half-panicked as her gaze darted about the station. "Are you okay?"

"I don't like the noise."

Jayla stared at her for a good long time, and Loxley knew she must look terrifying with her face smeared this way and that.

The woman helped her up, brushing off Loxley's legs before squaring up her shoulders. "So much for a low profile."

"A man from the Consortium came to talk to me."

Jayla froze. "What did he say?"

She smiled through her burning cheeks. "That I was unique and talented."

"That you are. Come on, now."

They hefted their luggage to a porter, who loaded it for them, then the pair stepped onto the train.

The sweet smell of old cigarettes washed over her like a forgotten friend. This was what the halls of Magic City Heights smelled like. The interior of the sleeper car had a carpet the color of split-pea soup and sky-blue walls with a maroon stripe running all along the cabin. The stripe sat close to head level, and if Loxley sunk down a bit, she could make it all look like a single line.

Jayla gave her a light push. "We're holding up the works, baby."

"You ever been on a train before?"

"Twice."

Loxley nodded to the other passengers, who looked askance at her, probably because of her makeup. "Go on without me. I want to look around."

"It's a long train ride, Loxley. Lots to see. Why don't you give these folks some peace for a time?"

She reluctantly agreed and followed Jayla to their cabin, where they settled in. Through the window, the station was warm and inviting with its orange lights and elegant décor. It was hard to believe that it lay at the top of such a dismal city. What would it be like when the train lurched forward? Would it scream as it did when it entered the station, or be smooth and rumbly like a car? She'd never ridden the Hoop.

Jayla leaned forward and began to dab Loxley's face with a handkerchief, cleaning up her smudged makeup. Minutes passed as she rubbed each spot, one at a time. "I've got a lot of work to do here." A tear slipped from one of her eyes.

"Are you crying?"

"A little. Do you know how long I've lived at the Hound's Tail?"

Loxley thought of her sprouts. During the cold months, she had to start them inside. Sometimes, they lived when she transplanted. Other times, they died for no reason at all. "I'm sorry."

"No, I'm sorry."

Loxley frowned. "Why?"

"I'm just..." Jayla swallowed. "Are we really going to be okay?"

With a hiss, the train began to move. Loxley's hand shot down to grip her lover's arm, and her attention went to the window. Her breath quickened at the sudden motion, and she watched as the station began to slide away from the window. With a flurry of lights, they'd passed out and into the houses of Edgewood, then through the city limits.

The train had begun to carry her away from the husk of her old world, from her flooded diving bell. Gone was the agriculture manual, the unread Bible and Cap's knife. She would never see Magic City Heights or Birdie or the old cooling towers with their tickling bubbles. Maybe someone was burying what was left of Nora that very moment, or maybe they already had, and Quentin had already been burned to nothing. She thought of Officer Crutchfield, rotting on a slab in a building somewhere, his ghost pacing anxiously as it awaited his cremation. Either way, the train would take her away from the bodies, from the Hound's Tail, from Bellebrook.

Far, far away from her hidden garden at the bottom of the world.

Then they passed the last lights of the Hole, and night fell over the fields like a cloud of ink. In that murk lay the farms and the tens of thousands of souls bound to them. Never had she been so close, but she couldn't have felt further away from what she'd dreamt. She knew the truth of it now. The farms might never be her life, though she didn't feel sure what that could mean.

Yet, in the silver comet streaming off toward Loxley's new days, she wasn't alone. She rested her head against Jayla's breast, listening to her lover's thumping heartbeat pass in and out of phase with the clatter of the train tracks. In time, the woman's pulse slowed, and Loxley drank in her scent.

No matter what else came later, for now, she wasn't alone.

She gave Jayla a light, tender kiss.

"Yeah."

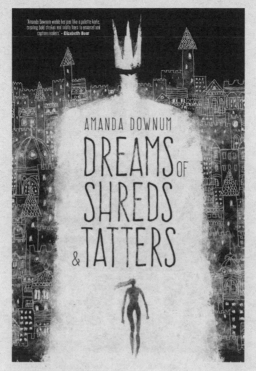

When Liz Drake's best friend vanishes, nothing can stop her nightmares. Driven by the certainty he needs her help, she crosses a continent to search for him. She finds Blake comatose in a Vancouver hospital, victim of a mysterious accident that claimed his lover's life — in her dreams he drowns.

Blake's new circle of artists and mystics draws her in, but all of them are lying or keeping dangerous secrets. Soon nightmare creatures stalk the waking city, and Liz can't fight a dream from the daylight world: to rescue Blake she must brave the darkest depths of the Dreamlands.

Even the attempt could kill her, or leave her mind trapped or broken. And if she succeeds, she must face the monstrous Yellow King, whose slave Blake is on the verge of becoming forever.

PAUL KEARNEY

THE WOLF IN THE ATTIC

'This is a wonderful, magical book, full of ancient myth and set in an England on the threshold of the modern world.'
Dave Hutchinson, bestselling author of *Europe in Autumn*

1920s Oxford: home to C.S. Lewis, J.R.R. Tolkien... and Anna Francis, a young Greek refugee looking to escape the grim reality of her new life. The night they cross paths, none suspect the fantastic world at work around them.

Anna Francis lives in a tall old house with her father and her doll Penelope. She is a refugee, a piece of flotsam washed up in England by the tides of the Great War and the chaos that trailed in its wake. Once upon a time, she had a mother and a brother, and they all lived together in the most beautiful city in the world, by the shores of Homer's wine-dark sea. But that is all gone now, and only to her doll does she ever speak of it, because her father cannot bear to hear. She sits in the shadows of the tall house and watches the rain on the windows, creating worlds for herself to fill out the loneliness. The house becomes her own little kingdom, an island full of dreams and half-forgotten memories. And then one winter day, she finds an interloper in the topmost, dustiest attic of the house. A boy named Luca with yellow eyes, who is as alone in the world as she is.

That day, she'll lose everything in her life, and find the only real friend she may ever know.

In a fractured Europe, new nations are springing up everywhere, some literally overnight.

For an intelligence officer like Jim, it's a nightmare. Every week or so a friendly power spawns a new and unknown national entity which may or may not be friendly to England's interests. It's hard to keep on top of it all. But things are about to get worse for Jim. A stabbing on a London bus pitches him into a world where his intelligence service is preparing for war with another universe, and a man has come who may hold the key to unlocking Europe's most jealously-guarded secret...

'A work of staggering genius.'
Paul Cornell